HATEFUL HEART

HATEFUL HEART

Sam Stone

The Vampire Gene Series: Book 4

Published in 2015 by Telos Publishing Ltd
5A Church Road, Shortlands, Bromley, Kent, BR2 0HP

Telos Publishing values feedback if you have any comments about this book please email feedback@telos.co.uk

ISBN: 978-1-84583-916-1

Cover Art: 2015 © Iain Robertson
Cover Design: David J Howe

British Library Cataloguing in Publication Data. A catalogue record for this book is available from the British Library.

Prologue
The Lady

1000 Years Ago

It was as if she appeared from nowhere. A lady. Heavily veiled and of obvious wealth, carrying an ornate bag. It was such an impossible occurrence that it took the two knights some time to fully register what they were seeing.

'Tell me your names?' she asked in Aramaic.

The first knight frowned. He knew the language as he had studied ancient dialect in his quest to translate the holy texts but had rarely used it as a form of speech. Now this strange lady, out alone, was talking to him directly and confidently in the idiom. What's more, he thought he glimpsed a waterfall out of the corner of his eye. When he tried to examine it directly there was nothing but empty space. Briefly he considered the idea that there was some kind of doorway, or entrance through which the strange lady had appeared but the idea was so bizarre that he dismissed it as a trick of the twilight.

'Hugues de Payens and this is my cousin Godfrey de Saint-Omer,' Hugues said politely in Aramaic. The words felt awkward but familiar on his tongue.

'Good,' said the lady. 'What year is this?'

Hugues and Godfrey exchanged glances. 'The year of our lord, one thousand, one hundred and nineteen, my lady.'

The lady nodded, 'Then I'm in the right place.'

'What can we do for you, my lady?' asked Hugues.

This strange impromptu meeting confused him. Few ladies wandered the streets alone and unprotected in this hostile land.

Much to the surprise of the knights the lady lifted her heavy veil. Her dark brown eyes met Hugues' blue gaze. Fleetingly he noticed long dark hair, pale skin, classic features. Then the lady told them she knew a great secret. Later neither knight could remember her features at all, but they had an impression of great beauty.

'I have a potent knowledge,' she said. 'Ancient. And it will bring you great wisdom and power.'

The knights were intrigued. They listened, but both considered her a mad woman, or some religious fanatic who had confused fact with reality.

'The scrolls are not meant to be taken so literally,' Godfrey explained after a while.

'That's because the scrolls lie,' said the lady. 'I have the truth here and you must protect it.'

The lady unwrapped a golden jewel taken from the bottom of her bag.

'Take this,' she said. 'One day it may help to save your lives.'

At first, Hugues refused, fearing it to be valuable and the woman to be someone whose mind had been weakened by some terrible shock.

'We must discuss this further,' said Hugues. 'We can't just take this treasure, Lady, no matter how sure you may seem that it is the right thing to do. All that you've said to us so far has been confusing and strange.'

The knights suggested she stay in their quarters near the temple mount, close to the Al Aqsa Mosque. The lady considered for a moment before accepting their kindness. She knew them to be honourable men and it would be better to explain her story in the privacy of their home.

Hugues wrapped up the jewel in the cloth and carried it against his chest as the lady walked beside him, her veil once more in place.

Back at the house the lady sat amongst their cushions. Hugues sent for his wife who joined them as chaperone, even though she did not speak Aramaic and didn't understand the revelations the lady made to the knights.

'This is a powerful weapon in the wrong hands,' the lady

said. 'If you look at another person through the jewel you can see their soul.'

Godfrey raised the jewel and looked at his cousin through the yellow glow. The view was distorted. He saw vague colours around Hugues' head, but nothing that unusual considering he was looking through a tinted yellow jewel. He didn't understand how important the piece of amber was, not then.

Hugues' wife poured the lady some wine which she sipped as she unpacked her bag, placing items before them. There was a pouch of gold coins, a change of clothing, a scroll, and some mysterious item wrapped up in a purple cloth. The cloth intrigued Hugues, and Godfrey. Even Hugues' wife, who usually showed little interest in anything that the knights were doing, actually leaned forward and examined the gold marking on the fabric. It showed an eye shape with a curved design in the centre.

'I give you the stone,' the lady said, 'in exchange for one small favour.'

'Anything,' said Godfrey rashly.

The lady smiled behind her veil.

'I give this,' she said, placing her hand on the item covered by the cloth, 'You must protect it. Keep it safe from the hands of the corrupt or it will be used for the wrong reasons.'

Then she told them of how they would be the originators of a great and powerful force. She told the knights of the Order of the Templar. Her message was so prevailing, so clear, that both men knew her story was true. Hugues and Godfrey would found a new order on its philosophy.

The lady unwrapped the cloth and inside the knights saw a box. At this point Hugues' wife began to feel ill.

'What is wrong with you?' asked the lady.

'My heart hurts,' said Hugues' wife.

The lady placed the cloth over the box and took the amber stone back from Godfrey. She placed the stone to her eye and looked at Hugues' wife.

'This is why you must protect the box and never open it,' said the lady.

Hugues looked at his wife through the jewel and saw something very unusual swirling around her. An ethereal light grew from the heart of his wife and stretched out unto infinity. He then examined his cousin and saw nothing but some vague colours shadowed around his head.

'What does this mean?' asked Godfrey.

'Danger. For her and all like her,' said the lady.

'What's in the box?' asked Hugues.

The lady told them to send Hugues' wife away.

'It isn't safe for her here,' she said. 'And you must never open this box when your wife is around.'

Once Hugues' wife had left the lady opened the lid and showed the knights what was inside.

One glimpse and the story she had told them was confirmed to be true.

'Guard this with your life,' said the lady, wrapping the box once more in the purple cloth.

The knights promised they would and as the lady left she gave them the scroll and told them one final story: the story of a beautiful immortal goddess.

'The symbol on this fabric is her sign. Use it: it will protect you and all of your kind.'

Hugues and Godfrey stared at the box long after the lady had gone. Then began to discuss their new philosophy, the new order they would found in the name of religion. They drank wine, and Godfrey made notes on a piece of parchment. They would reveal to the world the truth denied in the original scriptures. The two knights were enthused with the power of righteousness. They could and would end the war and win back Jerusalem.

'We have the proof right here,' Hugues said.

Soon the lateness of the evening and the consumption of wine took its toll on the knights and they retired to their chambers. They needed their sleep if they were to father a new faith in the morning. Neither man thought about the box as they stumbled tiredly to their beds.

The next day they returned to the room only to find the door to the street wide open. A thief had entered the house and taken the precious relic.

Hugues sank down into the cushions. He felt nauseous. It seemed that the worst sin in the world had been committed and it was not that of the thief. Hugues felt he had betrayed the lady and her trust in them had been misguided. His hand fell down beside him and it landed on the amber stone which had sunk unnoticed into the cushions. All was not lost!

'We can still tell the truth,' said Hugues.

'What would be the point? None would believe this story. The evidence of this miracle has been taken from us.' Godfrey answered.

'We have the scroll and the jewel,' Hugues said. 'Even though we can't make this public, we need to write it down cousin, so that future generations will remember this day. All must know of the night the lady visited.'

The knights did found their order. But the real story, the one which told of the relic, remained a secret among their group for over 1000 years.

PART ONE

1
Shadows of the Past

Present Day

Anxiety. The dark greeted me as I stumbled forward through the doorway. The air was filled with blood-smell – but it was rank and poisonous; uninviting even to me. A venomous rot had set in. It had the odour of age. Hands outstretched before me, I walked forward: drawn inwards by some nameless force. Under foot the ground squelched. I paused. I could see nothing, not even my hand in front of my face. Cautious, I stepped forward again. A sickening crunch echoed through the space as I stepped down and into what I knew to be gore. It felt as though I was walking through an abattoir and the remains of the dead were scattered in their vile blackness around my feet. Progress through the mess was slow, but it was important to reach the other side of the room as there lay my salvation. Something slivered over my foot and, too late, I realised that not everything was dead in the room.

Worm-like coils slithered up my ankle. I stepped back shaking myself free but something slipped around my other foot, gaining purchase as it wrapped around my leg and began to pull me down into the mess

I fell. Hands flailed. Fingers caught on a mess of rope-like vines growing from the walls. I wrapped my hands in them, trying to save myself from the thing that had me. The vines sprung to life. Like venomous snakes they struck, snapping at my wrists, circling around me until my arms were completely entangled.

The vines pulled back, stretching me taut against the other horror that had my legs. For a moment there was a tug of war. Pain screamed in my shoulders as my arms were splayed. My legs pulled straight out from under me. I fought it but couldn't free myself and there was a sense of falling into nothingness. The more I struggled, the more I became entangled. The fall, however, didn't happen. Instead I was stretched between the vine and the flesh, suspended in the air. Like a criminal on a rack. The pain in my limbs as my knees, ankles, shoulders, elbows and even my wrists all dislocate was such complete and burning agony, that I screamed.

As I opened my mouth and the first sound came out, a vile tongue licked my face and lips, forcing its way into my mouth. It grew bigger, suffocating the sound from me and I drowned in bile, vomit and the soft rotting meat of the long since dead …

I woke, shivering and shaken from the dream of *the room,* and I lay, as I did every morning, swallowing rapidly to rid myself of the feeling of that awful choking sensation. Beside me Lilly slept soundly, unaware of my angst and fear. I wasn't going to tell her about the nightmares anytime soon. They were just something I had to deal with on my own.

Gabriele moved. He slept on the other side of Lilly and the two of us curled up together like kittens around their mother. Except that is where the similarity of our complex relationship ended. There was nothing so sweet and innocent about us, although we have been called catlike in our day.

Lilly reached over and looped her arm around me, pulling me closer. It was almost as though she knew I needed her. So I curled closer, pressing my face against her hair. I smelt her scent, a natural clean and seductive aroma that was exclusive to her. I breathed her in, loving the warmth of her smell.

'Love you …' she murmured and I closed my eyes feeling safe, feeling loved.

I pushed the dream farther away. The *room* meant nothing. I was free of it, back in the real world: albeit completely changed from the one I remembered before my incarceration two hundred years ago.

'Caesare?' Gabi murmured. 'You awake?'

I opened my eyes again, looked up at the ceiling in the bedroom and turned my head to face our sleeping queen. 'Yes.'

Gabi snuggled up to Lilly, spooning her. It was my signal to leave. I really didn't want to leave her just then, but I slipped from the bed and vacated the room silently.

Closing the door, I shivered. It wasn't easy but we were getting into a routine that worked for us. Although we all slept in the same bed, we felt no urge to combine this with group sex. That's not what this was about. We loved her and she loved us and I valued my time alone with her as much as Gabi did. That's why we worked to find a routine that was acceptable to us all.

I didn't think about the two of them as I walked downstairs and into the kitchen. Modern conveniences were a marvel to me. I'd quickly grown used to using the microwave and hob when I needed to eat. Lilly refused to take on the role of housewife and so we all had to fend for ourselves.

'We're equal in this century,' she told us in the first few days of our new routine. 'Men are just as capable of cooking and cleaning and so I expect us all to do an equal share around here.'

Mostly we just ate out. I much preferred my liquid diet anyway, food was only something we had occasionally and it was more of a social thing that we adopted.

I opened the fridge and pulled out a bag of blood. Then placed it in the microwave, warming it for a few seconds. This was indeed a wonder and there was never a shortage of blood.

Lilly had contacts at the blood bank. Or rather she had a servant in there.

'It's a Renfield,' she told me. 'Humans can be useful. I have a few of them that I use for different purposes. Look at this place for example. Do you think it built itself?'

Indeed the inner sanctum of the castle, or rather Lilly's lair, was incredible. Rhuddlan, to the outside world, is just the remains of a once powerful fortress, built by a King Edward I in the thirteen century. Lilly had a group of 'Renfields' carve out the cave below. As the years passed by she installed all of the comforts of the modern world. That meant miracles like central heating which not only produced heat from the walls and floors, but also provided constant hot water for when we bathed.

I poured the blood into a mug and took it into the sitting area. Gabi and Lilly enjoyed watching television sometimes – another phenomenon – and they had a collection of DVDs that they shared with me. Mostly though, we would sit and talk and sometimes catch up on the world outside by watching the news. During these moments Lilly would curl up on the sofa between us and she and Gabi would patiently explain this world to me, answering all of my questions, no matter how bizarre they seemed.

Lilly still called me by my full name when we had our serious talks. It was Gabi who first began to call me Chez.

'You're in the twenty-first century now, Chez, and you need a name to fit.'

I didn't mind it; although at first I felt mildly irritated every time Gabi used it instead of my full name. However I can pinpoint the moment when I *did* become 'Chez'. It was the first time Lilly said it. Coming from her soft voice, with that slight Manchester accent, it suddenly seemed a fitting name. From then on, I was Chez, because Lilly named me. Strangely it was like being baptised. Lilly was our queen, our mother and our lover. She was the centre of our universe and when I was with her it was as though all the pain of the past no longer mattered.

'You're a fast learner, Chez,' Gabi had told me. 'But then with our talents adapting to any situation shouldn't be difficult.'

I reached for the remote control. I quite liked watching the news in the morning; it showed me a different view of this world from those of my companions. They had a narrow, isolated concept of reality that revolved around their needs only. They almost refused to take a real look at the world outside. They didn't want to observe the horror of human societies.

Humanity was in turmoil most of the time. There were wars, hostage situations. Why only that week a couple were released after months of incarceration by terrorists. There was *Al Qaeda*, a terrorist group. Religion, just as it had in my world, was still being used as an excuse to hurt other people.

'Don't listen to the news,' Hakim told us at the local Indian restaurant. 'I'm a Muslim and my faith believes it's wrong to kill. But in any society you'll get people who take things into their own hands.'

This world was a fascinating place and the people were so much more intelligent and informed. I think this was partly because of television. I soon realised that the information given was designed to inform people, but it also did the job of desensitizing them to the brutalities that occurred.

'Don't believe everything you see on that thing, though,' Lilly said. 'The reporters are always on the lookout for news and the bigger the scandal the better. They have an objective to create drama.'

I sipped my blood, already it was cooling a little too much. I still preferred to take it from source but Lilly was keen to avoid making others like us by accident. Only she had the ability to recognise carriers of the vampire gene. One obvious rule was to avoid blondes with green eyes as much as possible. When we did hunt, Lilly checked our food for any sign of the vampire gene before we were allowed to bite. It might have seemed like she was controlling, but I completely understood this. We didn't want just anyone joining our private club.

'I know! I'm such a snob,' Lilly laughed. 'But then, if we want a bigger family it must be planned and discussed first. Can the world feed too many vampires? That's why I think it is so rare we make others. It's almost like natural selection. Except for the fact that I can select, and so for that reason we really should take care. The skill was given to me for a reason and I believe we should use it to our advantage.'

I turned up the volume on the television and switched to one of the news channels where a bishop was being interviewed by a female presenter in her late twenties, pretty and serious, but her eyes twinkled with mischief.

'… relics are kept in the altars as common practice,' said the girl. 'It's a bit gruesome to imagine there are body parts inside our altars, isn't it?'

The camera flicked to a bishop in his mid fifties, with greying sideburns and dead eyes.

'The church has always done this,' he said. 'The so-called body parts you refer to are relics taken from saints and martyrs. They aren't inside the altar, *per se*, but are usually placed in a panel under it. Of course not all altars have them. The church dictates that it has to be verified relics.'

'What do you mean by verified?' asked the presenter.

'We have to have proof of their authenticity.'

'Why do you think there has been a sudden spate of break-ins and churches have been targeted? Why do you think they are stealing these relics?'

'We just don't know what the criminal element would want with the remains of our saints, except maybe to sell on the black market. But obviously this desecration must end...'

The door opened behind me and Lilly entered.

'Morning.' Her breath tasted of mint as she kissed me. 'What do you want to do today?'

I reached for the remote and switched off the television as she sat down beside me. Her hair was wet and she smelled of lavender body wash. It was Sunday. I glanced once more at the blank screen. 'Go to church?'

Lilly laughed, 'Yeah, right.' Then she stood and stretched like a lazy cat. She was wearing a soft robe and I could see her curves accentuated through its bulk.

'Gabi's in the shower,' she said. 'I thought maybe we could go for a walk in the mountains.'

'Okay,' I smiled. 'You look gorgeous.'

I loved to look at her beautiful wet hair, curling already in that perfectly sensuous and unruly fashion that suited her so well. When we'd first met, I'd seen her groomed and wearing the fashion of my era in the sixteenth century. It had soon become obvious that she was nothing like other women.

She curled up next to me again. 'So do you. And that blood taste in your mouth is sending me over the edge.'

'Well you know where to get your own.' I laughed, nodding in the direction of the kitchen. I drew her into my arms on an impulse, kissing her lips until the taste of blood merged between us.

After a moment she pulled away smiling and walked towards the door with that powerful, sexy walk that was totally exclusive to her.

'I'll get dressed then,' I said, standing up.

Lilly's eyes rolled down my naked body. 'I much prefer you naked,' she said. 'But I think that might draw too much attention.'

2
A Warning

Present Day

From the ramparts of the castle I watched the tourists visiting the ruins. It was my favourite place. I loved the slight lift of wind that blew in from the sea, some four miles away, and the panoramic view of the countryside around. Down below was a little hut where one or two women worked selling entrance fees and Celtic souvenirs. I'd been in there a few times when the staff had gone home and the place was locked up. I didn't take anything, but I liked to flick through the books and look at the cheap silver jewellery.

Sometimes I wandered the streets just outside the castle walls – this too was most unusual as houses had been built extremely close to the grounds, almost making it appear to be in a suburban setting. In many ways this world is no different from my world. Gifts and souvenirs were sold to travellers even in the sixteenth century and ruins, especially druid sites, drew tourists in their hundreds as they looked at the remnants of previous generations. The past is always a fascination for the occupants of the present.

From the ramparts I could feel winter approaching, even though it was still a warm day and the sky was a deep and beautiful blue. I stared down over the River Clwyd, out towards the mountains. Below Lilly and Gabi were watching a DVD, but I didn't feel any thrill for their taste in horror movies. *Hellraiser* was just a bridge too far. It reminded me too much of *the room*. As bizarre as that may seem, I am a blood sucking monster after all, but I didn't enjoy the sight of mindless violence, nor get a buzz from torture as a fetish.

'Nothing can hurt you now, Chez,' Lilly would say. 'You're stronger than ever and you have me and Gabi to back you up.'

A strange sensation tingled up my spine and I spun around on the ramparts, looking out over the water, then back towards land. Something was out there.

Cloaked, I flew down from the top, landing in the middle of the ruins. A vibration shuddered through Rhuddlan. Lilly talked of the castle as though it were a female, as though it had a heart and for the first time I really felt her. Rhuddlan was reacting violently to something.

Lilly appeared beside me, rapidly followed by Gabi.

'What is it?' I asked.

She shook her head, 'I don't know. I've never felt anything like it before.'

'It's as though, she's crying,' Gabi said.

Lilly looked at him sharply, 'Yes.'

'I feel it too,' I said. 'It's as though someone is ripping at her soul. I can't bear it.'

The three of us stood fast in the centre until the shudders ended as quickly as they began.

'Something's wrong,' Lilly whispered, her beautiful face frowning and severe in a way I'd never observed. She always appeared to be so carefree but right then her hand was crushed to her chest and she gasped in pain.

'What is it …?' said Gabi, reaching for her, but Lilly held out her hand to silence him and rejected his help despite the fact that she was almost bent double in pain.

My heart clenched in fear as I watched her. I had never seen her weakened. She pulled herself upright, staggered to the nearest wall of Rhuddlan as we looked on, following, but afraid to touch her for fear of further rejections. Her hand fell on the old wall and she steadied herself. I felt a crackle of lightning ripple in the air, looked up, and saw the sky was completely clear. It was then I realised that Lilly was using her ley power, with the support of the spirit of Rhuddlan, and she pushed back the sensation of pain that had assaulted her.

After a few moments she was standing upright again. She walked back into the square, circling the well and then expanded her circle outwards. The air shivered as she spread her arms. She raised the ley power, electrifying the atmosphere with this ancient and powerful energy. Hair stood up on the back of my neck as the force rose up from the earth. Lilly's powers had grown with every passing day. Her witchcraft was so strong that I believed her totally invincible. She could destroy the world and I was so glad that she was such a grounded person.

The air shuddered and a white hot glow shimmered above the grass as she searched and probed.

'What is it?' Gabi asked.

Lilly didn't answer. She was terrible and beautiful when the ley power swirled around her, invisible to the human eye, but obvious to us. A wind rushed up and about her legs. She was wearing a long white dress and it spread out just as her blonde curls lifted and expanded, blown out from her stunning face. Her eyes glowed a terrible, intense, green. She was as startling a vision as Medusa might have been. The power consumed her, eating at her arms and face, whipping at her torso.

A bright green light exploded from Lilly's chest, then small peaks of *Illumination* poured out in sharp shafts around her.

'Lilly!' I yelled. I was petrified that she had absorbed too much.

Just as suddenly as the wind rose, it dropped. The shafts of light disappeared. Lilly turned cold eyes towards us. Her irises were still alight with green fire.

'Something terrible has happened,' she said. 'There's this searing pain in my heart.'

Gabi and I hurried to her, surrounding her in our weaker immortal way. For how could we protect her when she was stronger than the world itself? It was a stupid male and mortal response but we loved her. So what else could we do but give comfort?

'What is it?' I asked. 'Tell us what we can do?'

'I don't know,' she said again. 'I just know it's bad.'

She wasn't weakened by channelling the power, rather she was energised, but still we found ourselves holding her between us. She let us lead her down into the lair. She was docile. Placid. Her quiet was the most frightening thing of all. I took her to our bedroom, brushed her hair, neatening her up and then she lay down on the bed her eyes open as she stared off into the distance. Her mind was elsewhere and she didn't speak.

I heard the TV switch on downstairs; Gabi was checking the satellite channels for any breaking news.

I lay beside Lilly, holding her, but her body was rigid, stone-like. Tension oozed from every pore even though she was doing her best to shield me from it.

'I love you. You're safe,' I told her, subconsciously repeating her own reassurances to me, but even as the words slipped from my lips they felt somehow irrelevant. It was as though I was making a promise I couldn't keep.

As the day passed life returned to normal. Lilly recovered from her temporary stupor. Later, the television was on and Lilly was laughing at some 'celebrities' who were eating insects in the jungle. This was indeed a peculiar pastime but at least her behaviour was more typical.

'I can't believe you watch this rubbish, Lilly,' Gabi laughed, but still he sat next to her, holding her hand.

I left the lair, not to hunt as we never did that alone, but because I wanted to feel the fresh air around me. Sometimes, I just needed solitude. So I left my companions to enjoy their programmes and went once more up onto the ramparts.

The night was cold. The smell of snow and ice lay heavy on the breeze. I flew up above the castle and out towards the sea letting the cold wind whip around me. Then I turned, following the coastline around and back inland.

I found myself in the centre of Manchester. It was such a small journey from North Wales and I swooped through the night, admiring the lights from the city and watching the people as they scurried through the still-busy streets.

Music pulsed into the air in a hurried rush as the doors to a nightclub entrance opened and a group of girls stumbled drunkenly out onto the street. As they hurried along the otherwise empty street, one of them slipped in her high heels. The girl almost fell to her knees but managed to save herself by catching hold of a concrete post. Even so, her leg splayed out and her short, tight skirt ripped up along the side of her thigh.

'For fuck's sake!' she shouted.

Her companions turned and raucous laughter filled the air as they saw her struggling to her feet.

'You okay?' one of them asked.

'Yeah, but I need to go home – skirt's knackered now.'

The other girl opened her purse and began rummaging through it. 'Come on, let's get to the next club, I'll sew you up in the loos!' she said, holding up what must have been a sewing kit.

'You're so fucking organised,' said a cute redhead.

I landed behind them as they staggered away linking arms. I sniffed the air, I could smell their cheap perfume, sweat and heat. I could taste the alcohol on their breath and the sweet smell of their blood flowing like music through their veins along with the rank under taste of something else.

They began to sing.

'Four and twenty virgins going to Inverness, by the end of Saturday night there were four and twenty less …'

It took me a moment to make sense of the words. It was a crude song.

Not for the first time I wondered about this strange society. I wasn't too sure I liked how the women in this century lacked dignity. They kept their bodies toned, were resourceful, but their minds were perverse. Women had become as men. They had fought for this, 'burnt their bras', Lilly told me. It was about equality. This meant, I supposed, that they were just as promiscuous. Women now behaved as men had always done. There were sexually transmitted diseases to be concerned about. I didn't know, however, whether there were more or less than in my time. It was a fact that these diseases were discussed more openly in the present and could be easily cured with medicines though, and this may have been partly why sex was so casual. Syphilis had been something of a deterrent once. Even though the catching of it was still unpleasant, the illness could be easily treated.

I sniffed again, and there it was. I honed in on the scent of some disease, some pox which one or more of the women was carrying. The smell was of stale semen, and a sickly mucus odour that reminded me of the kind of phlegm coughed up by the old. The girls were unclean, but I didn't believe it was something that could hurt me. AIDS, was another matter however. Gabi had warned against this deficiency in the blood that could potentially be poison to us.

'Your sister, Lucrezia, is the expert on that though,' he had said. 'She warned me years ago, when I took interest in a girl carrying the disease. I could smell something on her. It reminded me of the black death. Lucrezia said it was AIDS and it could make us sick.'

I never asked Gabi how he knew what plague smelt like, something in his eyes cautioned me from probing further. All deaths have a smell but the smell of AIDS was something I was certain I would recognise and I knew I hadn't encountered it so far.

I flew up into the air again heading back home. I'd seen enough. It only took a few small glimpses into the city in order to put my world back in place. I preferred the lair, even if at time it was somewhat claustrophobic.

3
The Fisherman

2000 Years Earlier

Kepha unfurled his sails but there was no breeze to catch the cloth. He waited for the wind to rise, but when nothing happened he wrapped them back in place and used his oars to propel his boat out into the middle of the water. Either side of him, his friends cast their nets from the back of their bigger boats, but it would be a slow process to drag the mesh across the lake and took four men to crew the fishing boats. Kepha had more important duties that night than to fish which was why he was alone, in his much smaller yacht. He couldn't trust anyone with the task he had been set. It was a duty for him alone. He had been summoned and the Princess could not be ignored, even if contact with her could lead to his death.

It was late. Night had fallen like a heady cloud over the Sea of Galilee. The day had been hot and humid, heavy with the reek of death drifting from the dungeons of the palace, but Kepha turned the boat in that direction, heading away from the other fishermen. His journey would first take him down the Jordan River.

'What took you so long?' asked the Princess as Kepha docked the boat.

'No breeze, lady,' Kepha said. 'Forgive me.'

He bowed then helped her climb aboard. As always she was heavily veiled. Some said it was because the King had defaced her in her youth. The Princess had never married, but there were rumours that rippled across the ghetto that she had birthed a child 20 years before. Now, in her mid 30's, she was too old to marry, practically middle-aged, but the gossip about her past was almost forgotten.

Kepha knew more of the real truth than most. He had been one of the disciples who followed Yohanan and his cousin, Yeshua. He had been there when the body of the Baptist was returned, defiled, to the people. He had also been present when Yeshua was crucified. The Princess had arranged the release of that body too, but she had called on Kepha for favours now and then since: it had been a condition of their martyr's return. Kepha understood from the beginning that these favours were secret and he should never discuss them, not even with his wife who would no doubt question his lack of fish on his return.

'This is no good,' said the Princess as she watched Kepha row. 'I need to reach the Dead Sea by daybreak.'

'But that is impossible,' Kepha said. 'This boat isn't big enough to carry you there in such a short space of time.'

The Princess said nothing but she placed a heavy bag down at her feet as she sat on the bench at the back of the boat. Then she reached inside and withdrew a small pouch containing herbs.

'The salt in the water will protect us, Kepha,' she said opening the bag and taking a handful of the herbs in her hand. 'And the wind will be our ally this night. Open the sails.'

Kepha did as she asked, even though he knew it was hopeless. There was no wind, and they would *never* make the sea by morning.

The Princess chanted under her breath. It was a language that Kepha had never heard and so he tried not to listen or make sense of her words. Her hand was flat when she lifted it to her mouth and blew gently. Kepha didn't expect her exhalation to have much effect but he was stunned when the breeze lifted. The herbs blew from the Princess's fingers and up above his head straight into the sails. The cloth opened out. He felt the tug, quickly took position next to the Princess and turned the rudder, catching the wind.

'It's a miracle,' he said.

The Princess remained silent but she was calm as the boat

pulled rapidly down the river at a speed Kepha would not have considered possible.

Kepha was used to her ambiguous demands and so turned the boat as instructed. She would tell him what he needed to know in due course. He was her servant and had no right to question her motives.

The Princess lapsed into sleep as the boat moved. The wind whipped around the sides, lapping water around the edges but she didn't stir not even when a rough wave splashed water onto her feet.

An hour from sunrise they entered the Dead Sea. The Princess opened her eyes looking out over the muddy liquid and, as she willed it, the air stilled. The boat glided a half mile farther and then came to a sudden halt.

Kepha cast a weighted line to hold the boat still without being told.

'Not long now,' said the Princess.

The sun came up above the water and Kepha knew the day would be cleaner and less humid than the previous. The sky had been red and bright the night previously and so the day promised to be good. He tied up the sails to stop the minor breeze from pulling at the cloth as they remained static. Then he withdrew a snack wrapped in a piece of muslin that his wife had given him before he left for the evening. It was unleavened bread and a hunk of goat's cheese. He held his meagre meal out to the Princess but she merely shook her head.

'No. But please eat,' she said.

Kepha ate. He tried to do it delicately but the bread crumbled all over his robe. The Princess said nothing. She didn't seem to notice his lack of refined manners.

When the sun was fully over the sea, the Princess stood.

Kepha stood too; he didn't know what else to do. The Princess leaned over the boat and looked out.

'There!' she pointed. 'Take me there.'

Kepha squinted into the sun but he could see nothing. Even so, he pulled the weight up, picked up his oar and began to row the boat in the direction she pointed.

'Stop,' said the Princess.

They drifted a few feet before the weighted line caught and then they came to a jerking halt.

The Princess chanted again. Above the ocean, Kepha could have sworn he saw a waterfall just a few feet away from the front of the boat. It was like a silent stream of gushing water, flowing across a doorway.

'Thank you, Kepha,' the Princess said. 'You've been a good man. You've helped me all these years when everyone else was too afraid. Now I want to reward you for your loyalty.'

The Princess opened her bag. Inside Kepha could see the corner of a wooden box. His heart lurched with an unknown fear at the sight of it. The Princess pushed the box aside and reached down withdrawing a heavy purse of coins. Then she closed her bag, holding out the small pouch to the fisherman.

'I don't understand,' he said.

'This is for you. I won't need your services again.'

Kepha could hear the thumping of his heart; it beat in his ears and poured fire through his veins.

'What's in there?' he asked stepping back.

'Nothing,' said the Princess. 'Just money.'

'No. The box. There's something in the box.'

The Princess looked down at the closed sack. 'You can feel that too?'

She opened the bag, reached inside and pulled a roughly carved wooden box free as it caught on a piece of purple cloth. It looked like a box containing jewels that any Princess might have, but somehow Kepha knew that there was no treasure inside. His heart ached as she placed it on her knee. There was a loud thumping sound penetrating through the wood. Kepha thought he saw the box pulsing with every beat.

The Princess watched Kepha closely for a few minutes. She noticed his cheeks flushing, his breathing becoming heavier. The panic in his eyes. She thought about how she had never noticed the eyes before. Kepha's weren't brown or grey or blue, they were a dark hazel, but in certain light, like this morning, they were green. When Kepha began to clutch his chest she pulled the purple cloth from the bag and wrapped it around the box. Instantly the noise ceased.

The fear lifted from Kepha's heart and lungs in a rush of expelled air as the Princess placed the box back inside the bag. Kepha thought he could make out her expression through the veil as he looked directly at her. He felt a strange empathy rush from her and was calmed.

'Forget you've seen anything,' said the Princess pressing the purse of money into his palm. 'Please. Don't tell anyone you brought me here.'

Kepha doubted he would even find 'here' again. It was just another stretch of seascape, but even without the reward he would never betray her. He bowed his head, nodded and made a whispered promise.

The Princess clutched the bag containing the box against her chest and began to climb onto the edge of the boat.

'What are you doing, Princess?' Kepha cried reaching for her, but already she had taken the plunge over the edge.

It appeared that she had climbed up on some ledge that lay under the water. It almost looked as if she was walking above the ocean but Kepha knew that to be impossible, despite the stories of Yeshua, the Nazarene. Even so, the Princess stood before the waterfall in the sky space and then, in the blink of an eye, she stepped though and the waterfall disappeared leaving nothing but open air in its wake.

Kepha rubbed his eyes. He blinked and watched the sun come up fully into the sky. He wasn't sure how long he should wait. She had said she wouldn't need him again, but he was afraid to leave in case she returned. He settled down in his boat, staring at the bag of silver she had given him. He opened it up. It was a considerable sum, one which meant he would have some independent wealth from now on.

Kepha looked back. The sky was normal. No waterfall appeared. But he waited a day. He was a loyal servant and in his own way had always loved the sweetness of her voice. It didn't matter that he had never seen her face.

4
A Stranger in the Lair

Present Day

When Lilly was in my arms the world outside didn't matter anymore. I ran my hands over her welcoming body, her skin was like silk. My lips traced patterns where my fingers touched and she groaned in my arms. We had already made love but just touching her prolonged the feeling. She was relaxed and happy; the strange occurrence of a few days ago had almost been forgotten. Gabi was out somewhere or maybe he was just watching TV – which was generally his favourite pastime. Either way, he was being discrete and I was enjoying my time alone with Lilly.

Resting on my elbow I looked into her stunning face. She wore the aspect of any woman in love, lying happily with her lover and I felt elated that I pleased her. Deep down I was carrying a vague concern that Gabi and I would be compared against each other, and that I might be found lacking. Lilly never gave any indication that this was the case and so, in her arms, I felt like I was her only lover and that she belonged exclusively to me.

I bent to kiss her just as her expression changed and a frown appeared that furrowed her brow. I ignored it, lips and tongue beginning a new exploration of her throat and working my way down to her breast. She submitted, sighing softly as my tongue found her soft and erect nipple. I suckled her and she squirmed, then gasping pushed me away.

I fell back, resting on my elbow. Lilly sat up, reached for her robe and something about the change of mood in the atmosphere made me realise she wasn't just playing some game to excite me.

'What is it?' I asked.

'Outside.'

'I don't understand.'

'There's someone here.'

No one could find our lair. No one knew we were here. So I stared at her, believing it to be impossible yet still I searched the air and found the thing that she so easily noticed without even trying. There *was* something. I stood rapidly, beginning to dress. Her instincts were never wrong. How could I have doubted her, even for a second?

Days had passed since that strange episode in the grounds of Rhuddlan and there had been no repeat of the tremor that shook our world. No reference was made on the news to earth quakes and soon we'd drifted back into our tranquil domesticity. A false security maybe?

'Stay here,' I said.

'Darling, if there is a danger, I'm the strongest and I will have to deal with it.'

My heart clenched, but I felt the truth of her words. She reached for her jeans and a sweater, pulling them on, quickly followed by a pair of knee-high boots. My male ego couldn't stand it.

'No,' I said. 'We'll deal with it together.'

Gabi was waiting at the bottom of the stairs as we descended. He didn't speak but I knew that he felt this new presence, just as I did.

'Clumsy,' I said as a ripple of the supernatural went through the air in the grounds above us again. 'Whoever it is, they aren't shielding.'

'Maybe that's because they want us to know they are there,' Gabi said. 'We could just ignore it? Maybe whatever the being is, it will go away?'

Lilly shook her head, 'No way. I'm curious if nothing else.'

We climbed the stairs quickly. One of the beautiful things about being a vampire is that we have limitless strength, never tire and we can climb a thousand steps at high speed without losing breath.

I was the first to the top, Lilly was behind me and Gabi brought up the rear. I couldn't help observing that subconsciously the two of us always rallied around her. I opened the panel that led to the doorway out into the old moat. From the outside it was operated by a keypad, a password of complicated numbers. I turned my head briefly, met Lilly's eyes and she nodded. I reached out and opened the door.

We stepped out into daylight, cloaked from any humans who might be in the castle grounds. Outside Lilly scanned the area once more.

'It's moved away, out into the forest.'

'They don't know where we are then?'

'No,' she said.

'Are they searching for us?' Gabi asked. 'Or is this merely a coincidence.'

Lilly didn't answer. I think she, like us, just wasn't sure.

'I'd rather face any potential enemy head on,' she said.

'Me too,' I agreed.

'Let's go,' Gabi nodded.

We flew up from the moat and over the castle, glancing down at the remains from an aerial view. I searched the grounds looking for anything that could be unusual. A flicker of energy flowed from the forest, I pointed but Gabi and Lilly were already heading that way. We rushed forward, ready to attack.

As we swooped down in amongst the trees, switching rapidly from flying to running, I felt the tension coming off the bodies of my companions. They were poised for attack by this unknown entity. It never occurred to me how strange this response was. We were, we believed, invincible. Yet, there we were, survival instincts tuned to maximum, expecting some kind of assault.

A faint sob, echoed through the trees.

I stopped, still cloaked, listening to the sound and feeling the atmosphere for that surge of energy that clearly wasn't human. I heard the beat of a strong, vibrant heart. Lilly and Gabi appeared by my side and we all focused in the same direction.

I glanced at Lilly for approval, she nodded and I stepped forward to investigate, knowing that she and Gabi had my back. I'm not sure what I expected to see, but it wasn't what greeted me. There was a girl in the forest. She was young; maybe sixteen or seventeen. It was hard to see what colour her hair was, she was covered in grime, but I suspected that under the dirt she was fair. I even knew what colour her eyes would be.

Tear-filled, the green orbs that met my gaze did not disappoint.

'She's one of us,' Gabi gasped beside me.

'Of course she is,' said Lilly. 'But she's newborn.'

'Who?' I asked. 'Did one of *us* screw up?'

The girl stood. She could see us even though we were cloaked and she was shaking with fear. I believe she sensed the power emanating from Lilly.

'I thought I'd never find you!' she said in English, but there was a strong accent that curved around her words with a vibrant sensuality.

'Who are you?' asked Gabi.

'Amalia,' she said. 'I'm one of you.'

'We know you're a vampire,' Lilly's cold response surprised me and I glanced at her to find her body still defensive. 'What are you doing here?'

'You're her. You're Lilly,' Amalia said. She stepped forward, her confidence returning. 'He told me to find you. He said you'd help.'

'Where have you come from?' Gabi asked.

'Harry. Harry made me.'

'For fuck's sake,' said Lilly losing her warrior stance. 'I told him to be careful.'

'I wasn't an accident,' Amalia said. 'He loved me.'

Lilly blinked, 'Where is he? I'll kill that little shit for this.'

Amalia burst into tears.

'Harry's dead.'

5
Death of a Vampire King

Present Day

'It's not possible,' Lilly said. 'We can't die. You all know that.'

We huddled on the sofa, talking softly. Amalia was sleeping like a frightened orphan in the spare bedroom. Soon after we'd brought her into the lair, giving her the comfort of a shower and some of Lilly's clothing, the girl collapsed with exhaustion. It would have been cruel to try to interrogate her further at that point and so we let her sleep.

'She's just a child,' I said. 'What was Harry thinking?'

'He's always gone for the young ones,' Lilly said dismissively. 'He can't be dead. Can he?'

Gabi stroked her arm. 'We all felt something strange. You said yourself there was something wrong, something missing from the world. Could it have been Harry?'

'I don't know. None of us have ever died before. Except you of course Caesare; at the hands of Lucrezia.'

'Yes. But even then he wasn't really dead,' Gabi pointed out, 'from what you've told me, because his soul wasn't in the body at the time, trapped as it was behind that time portal, then he couldn't really die.'

I sighed as Gabi went into that strange mode of his, of discussing me with Lilly as though I wasn't present. Lilly took my hand and we all fell into silence.

'Let's not digress,' she said eventually. 'The issue here is – can we trust Amalia? Is she telling the truth?'

'Why would she lie?' I said.

Lilly sighed. 'I hate the thought that Harry is dead. He was a thorn in my side for years, but then we became companions. Part of me hopes she is lying or … mistaken somehow.'

Gabi stiffened beside me. He was still finding it hard to shake his incessant jealousy, but I understood friendship was all that lay between Lilly and Harry and so I felt nothing. It isn't my way to worry about every little thing that might have occurred in a past I didn't share with Lilly. Harry, however, once tried to kill me. I had been almost looking forward to meeting him again at some point. It may not have been a pleasant meeting for Harry, or then again I may not have even cared in the end. Angst was a waste of energy.

The door opened and I turned to see Amalia standing in the doorway. Her eyes were haunted and scared.

'I can't sleep anymore,' she said.

'Please sit down,' I said. 'Can I get you anything?'

'I'm weakened. I need to hunt,' she answered.

Gabi stood, 'I'll get her something.'

Lilly scrutinised Amalia's face carefully.

'We need to know what happened. I'm sure that Harry told you, we are very, very difficult to destroy.'

Lilly's words felt more like a warning than a statement of fact but her expression was giving nothing away. Even so, I sensed a latent hostility towards Amalia that was out of character.

Amalia nodded, 'He said we were indestructible. He said this couldn't happen.'

Amalia cried softly then and I pulled a starched handkerchief from my pocket which she accepted with a silent nod of gratitude. Lilly remained inscrutable. She is the matriarch of us all. I had never known her to be anything but loving and warm and yet she did not welcome this child: even though she clearly needed us. For this reason I held back also. I would be kind, but I was suspicious. After all, Lilly's instincts were the basis for our survival and I trusted her implicitly. If she wasn't welcoming Amalia with open arms then there was probably a good reason.

Gabi returned with a mug of warmed blood. He held it out to Amalia and, surprised, she took it in her hands, holding the mug as though it contained cocoa. She gazed down at the contents, sniffed, then sipped cautiously. It occurred to me that maybe Amalia didn't quite trust us either. But as soon as she tasted the blood her pupils dilated. Her fangs, although unneeded, pushed down and out of her gums, protruding seductively over her full lips. She was a beautiful waif, even more so when in full blood lust.

I glanced at Gabi. He half smiled in that conspiratorial way we men have. He felt that slight pull of sexual attraction too. I gave Lilly a sideways glance. Her face remained passive, but her body was tense and so I kept my face still, giving nothing of my thoughts away, but it was clear now what Harry had seen in the girl. Her innocent persona almost hid a decadent splendour. Though I was unsure whether this was just because of the change or if she had shown signs of it as a human. Whatever it was, it didn't really matter now. Amalia was a beautiful monster, but her vulnerability was her real attraction.

Amalia put down the mug and stared wide-eyed at Gabi.

'Need a bit more?' he asked

Amalia licked her lips, the fangs retracted and once again she looked like nothing more sinister than a sweet and normal teenager.

'I think I'm good for now,' she said. 'But thank you.'

'Then talk,' said Lilly rudely. 'I want to know what happened and when.'

Amalia sat back in her chair. The shudders had left her fragile-looking body. She was calm and the blood flowed in and around her skin, bringing a natural colour back to her pallid cheeks. I traced the flow through her paper fine skin with more than a little fascination.

'Harry met me in Stockholm. We've been dating since you left,' she said.

'Dating?' Lilly sneered, 'Now I know you're lying. Harry doesn't date. Harry rapes and pillages. He's a Viking and will always be a blood thirsty murderer.'

Amalia's eyes filled with water again. 'He loved me!' she insisted.

'Just tell us what happened,' I said firmly, the histrionics were actually starting to grate on me and I felt that we really needed information fast.

'He came to me the night you left to return to this one,' she said nodding towards Gabi. 'I'd seen him around many times. He was always nice to me. Bought me drinks sometimes. But he wasn't like the usual creeps that frequent the bar where I work.'

'You work in a bar? You don't look old enough,' Gabi said.

'I'm twenty-three.'

I was as surprised as my companions to learn this news, she really didn't look older than seventeen.

'Okay. So you met at the bar … And?' prompted Lilly.

'We started dating, like I said.' Amalia was firm and definite. She cast a glance around her as though she expected to be challenged on this again, but the three of us remained quiet and so she continued. 'Then one day he revealed to me what he was and told me he wanted me to be with him.'

'Just like that?' Lilly asked. 'It all seems a little sudden. Also, how would he know that you're eligible? Are you sure you weren't … No offense … an accident?'

'No,' Amalia said firmly. 'He asked me. He said if I didn't want to he'd walk away and we'd never meet again. Of course I was scared. But by then I was in love with him and I didn't want to lose him.'

'What happened then?' I asked.

'One night I just got up the courage and went to his castle. I told him I'd thought it through and he turned me.'

Amalia relayed the usual story of her turning, her first kill, how she felt once she became a vampire and finally how happy she and Harry had been. It all sounded romantic and … well … strange. It was more like a prince-meeting-peasant-and-marrying-her tale. Even I thought it sounded out of character for Harry, but I suppose stranger things have happened.

'Unfortunately our happiness has only lasted a few weeks,' she said.

'Let's cut to the chase shall we?' interrupted Lilly. 'I don't need to hear the love story, just what the fuck happened to Harry, okay?'

Amalia paused. Her lip trembled and she twisted her hands in her lap. She was naturally afraid of Lilly, but her lips pursed and I could also tell she was more than a little annoyed by the aggression and lack of belief my lover was showing.

I placed my hand on Lilly's arm, forcing a pulse to pass into her skin that told her to be calm as I tried to smooth things over between them.

'How did you get to Wales, Amalia?' I prompted gently and she turned and smiled at me. It was a lovely grateful and charming smile. Yes. I really could see what Harry saw in her.

'Harry was bringing me to meet you. He said … you'd be annoyed with him but ultimately you'd understand that he deserved a companion too. After all, you have two …' Amalia swallowed. 'Then, about a week ago he said he wanted to show me new things. I've never been out of Stockholm and I'd always wanted to see Europe. We left on a short tour. Harry said there was no rush to get to you and so this was a nice little holiday on the way to England.

'We went to several religious sites as we made our way across France. We even stopped at Lourdes but I was afraid to touch the water. After all its holy isn't it? It might kill us.'

'You don't really believe that do you?' asked Gabi. 'Religion and its trappings can't hurt us at all. No crosses or relics. But we've all been there as far as fear is concerned.'

'I believe in God,' said Amalia, 'and the afterlife. I always have, so although I don't doubt what you say, I'd still have some misgivings about drinking from a holy well. Even so, part of me wanted to dispel the myths by travelling to the religious sites with Harry. He was so strong and unafraid. I wanted to fully embrace my vampire nature and I felt I could only do that if I was certain that God wasn't going to strike me dead if I set foot on holy ground.

'We heard about this old church from our tour guide. He said there was rumoured to be an old and powerful relic still under the altar. Harry was fascinated with this and I wanted to go and see ... Well I know it was weird, but I wanted to see if I could sense this power. Harry told me about some of your abilities,' Amalia glanced at Lilly. 'I wanted to see if I had any also.'

'Go on,' Lilly said.

'We went to the church. It was just as we'd expected really. There was almost nothing left of the original interior. It was all just ruins. So we walked around for a while, picking up old rocks and touching the walls, but I felt nothing unusual at all and Harry was a little annoyed because he thought the guide had given us false information. He said, "I'll go and rip his lying throat out." That was when it happened.

'There was this light,' Amalia continued. 'Bright and hot and it appeared from nowhere. Right in the middle of the church ruins! I barely had time to see it before Harry yelled for me to run away and hide. "Get the hell out of here!" he said, and he pushed me hard out of the way. This light appeared just in front of the altar. I fell back, crawling around the back of the stone and hid as he told me to. At that moment a figure passed through and the light looked like a ... waterfall.'

Lilly took in a gasp of air.

'Who?' I asked sitting forward.

'I thought it was God,' Amalia said and her face shone in the way that religious fanatics did when they thought the second coming was about to happen. 'That he had come to strike us down for being sinners. But then I realised that couldn't be true. The man was dressed in weird clothes. He looked like a medieval knight.

'By that time I was hiding behind the altar. I couldn't see clearly what it was. But, I was behind the waterfall ... and I could see through it. I was looking into another world, another place. It seemed to be some kind of doorway, if that makes sense at all.'

Lilly gripped my hand as Amalia's story unfolded.

'Then he said, "I've come for you – most evil and vile creature. I will eradicate your kind from the Earth." I think I screamed and Harry yelled at me to get away again. After that, an argument started between them. I don't even remember what they said to each other. It was all so fast and insane. Harry ran at him. They fought, but the knight was not overcome by his strength at all. It was as though he had his own supernatural power. As Harry drew near him he became weakened. Then the knight withdrew something from a sack tied to his waist. The light from the portal flashed brighter again. It hurt so much that I was forced to close my eyes to block the painful brightness. Then I heard it: an ear piercing scream.

'I forced my eyes open and watched as Harry crumpled to the ground. His body burst into flames so hot that the heat exploded up and around the altar. The temperature forced me back and there was this awful pain, deep in my chest. That's when my hair caught on fire.

'I threw myself to the ground, rolling in the dirt to staunch the flames and as I rolled I felt the light growing brighter and stronger until suddenly it blinked out.

'I think I blacked out for a while,' Amalia continued. 'When I opened my eyes, the knight was gone and Harry was still burning on the ground. I rushed towards him but the heat was so intense I couldn't touch him. I pulled off my coat and threw it over his body. The flames died and I knelt beside him. As I pulled back the coat to see the damage Harry's body began to disintegrate and decay. His hand was crushed to his chest, fingers clenched so tightly, it reminded me …'

'Of what?' I asked.

'My dad,' Amalia said. 'He had a major heart attack. His face and expression, the clenched fist, he looked like that … It was definitely something to do with his heart.'

'It's not possible,' Lilly interrupted. 'We're self-regenerating. Even if Harry was burnt, he'd renew.'

'No,' Amalia said. 'He was dead. And as I watched and cried over his body the whole of his torso fell apart. He crumbled to dust. There was nothing left to salvage. If there had been I'd have buried him.'

'It occurs to me,' I said. 'That we should be very concerned by the fact that this knight not only knew what Harry was, but also knew where to find him.'

Lilly looked up sharply. 'You're right. This is indeed a serious problem.'

'Amalia,' Gabi said. 'Are you sure you've never seen this creature before?'

'I'm certain. But then … he was wearing this helmet. There was a slit where his eyes would be. I have no way of knowing who was in there. It could have been anyone.'

The girl looked troubled, as though the thought of *knowing* the culprit hadn't occurred to her until now.

'Why?' she asked. 'Why would anyone want to kill Harry?'

'Oh, I can think of a few people he's pissed off,' said Lilly. 'But none with the ability to destroy us. That's what really concerns me.'

6
The Thief

1000 Years Ago

The thief was called Ali and he ran through the streets of Jerusalem, the box and cloth held tightly in his emaciated arms. He was a child, little more than ten when he discovered that the door to the Knight's home had been left open. He knew this was a good find, and it meant that this night at least he would have a reprieve from the abuse of his uncle. This night at least he would not have to lie down and please the men that passed through the hovel.

Ali ran through the darkened streets, heart racing with excitement. He had treasure and the treasure would feed them for years to come. He couldn't wait to show his mother. Their newfound wealth would enable them to leave their uncle. He couldn't hurt him or his mother anymore. His mind raced with the scenario of their new home. It would be beautiful, clean, and always food on the table.

As he reached his uncle's house a sixth sense made him pause. He stopped beside the window and glanced in. The man, the one that always hurt him the most, was waiting inside talking to his uncle. Ali's heart beat hard against his chest. He didn't want to go inside while the man was still there so he hid, hunkering down below the window.

'Where is that boy?' his uncle said. 'I sent him on an errand an hour ago.'

'I pay you good money,' said the man. 'I expect the boy to be here when I need him.'

'Yes, of course, *Sayyidi*,' said his uncle. 'The boy will be here soon, or he'll suffer for it.'

Ali slipped around the house and to his mother's window at the back. As usual she was lying in the dark, trying to keep cool.

'*Omi*,' whispered Ali. 'I found a treasure. We don't have to stay here anymore. *Omi?*'

Ali's mother's usually warm skin felt cold to the touch. She lay still and unresponsive. There was little light coming in the room from outside and Ali knew if he lit the lamp his uncle would see it next door. He pressed his ear to his mother's mouth, there was a thick dampness on her lips. Ali listened. He shut out the sound of his uncle and the man in the other room and placed his hand on his mother's heart, but all he could feel was his own terrified pulse beating through his fingers. He couldn't feel her breath on his cheek and so he rested his head on her breast.

Ali fell asleep. He dreamed his mother's heart was beating a strong rhythm and it would save him from further pain. The dream was full of happiness. It showed Ali and his mother living in their own home with food, wine and treasure all around them. His mother looked like a princess. She even wore a purple veil.

A silent screaming panic woke him and he found the cloth had slipped away from the box he had stolen.

Ali jumped away from his mother's body. Light was filtering through the window. Ali could see the bruises on his mother's face now, the blood seeping from her lips and the white film covering her eyes. His mother was dead and Ali knew his uncle had done this. He didn't know why, his uncle used his mother in much the same way that he allowed those men to use Ali.

Ali picked up the box. The treasure didn't seem so important now that he had nothing left to live for. His mother had afforded him little protection, but still she had comforted him, bathed his wounds when he was really hurt. He wrapped the cloth around the box, then stood and peeked into the room next door through a gap in the door frame. His uncle was sleeping, a wine jug, probably empty, stood by his side. His feelings went from fear to rage to grief and he didn't know what to do. Returning to his mother's bed, he looked down at her body. The heat was already beginning to turn her and it would get far worse before the day was out.

He looked at the box, removed the cloth and stroked the roughly carved wood. There was a symbol burnt into the top. It looked like a fish swimming upwards and Ali remembered seeing it somewhere, once, in the days when he had been allowed to attend the mosque to learn to read. He was sure it was in one of the history scrolls but couldn't remember what it meant. He ran his finger over the sign, traced it gently and once again he heard the thumping pulse, the recurring beat of what he thought was his own heart. It drummed over and over again like hypnotic music. He fell into a waking sleep.

In the other room, Ali heard his uncle cough. Ali jerked awake. It seemed as though hours had passed. He looked around the room for a place to hide. Maybe his uncle didn't know his mother was dead, in which case, he might come in at any time to wake her. He didn't want his uncle to find his treasure and so he wrapped it once more in cloth and took a sheet from his mother's bed, making a makeshift sack which he knotted together. He placed the box and cloth inside.

Ali stood up and crept once more to the window. He scrambled over the frame, pulling the bag with him. He had just dropped down when he heard his uncle open the bedroom door.

He sat below the window, listening, too scared to move for fear of being seen.

'In here,' said his uncle.

'I'll need three pieces of silver to rid you of this,' said a voice that Ali recognised as the undertaker. 'That is if you don't want the authorities to question you about your sister-in-law's bruises?'

'Here,' said his uncle. 'She wasn't worth it. Lazy and faithless. My dead brother would turn in his grave to learn that his wife and brat turned out to be such a burden to me.'

The undertaker said nothing, but Ali heard the jingle of

money as it exchanged hands.

'Where is the boy?' asked the undertaker. 'Am I taking him away too?'

Ali's heart lurched in his mouth.

'No,' said his uncle. 'I can still make some use of him around here.'

The undertaker chuckled. He *knew* that his uncle sold him! Ali felt sick. Anger and embarrassment coloured his cheeks. He wanted revenge. He wanted to kill his uncle and everyone who had hurt him. All those men he brought back to the house. Those men that made him do things to them. For them.

The box moved against him. It grew warm. Ali looked down at his hands and untied the knot as he heard the undertaker and another man removing his mother's body. He peeked over the sill, saw the back of his uncle and then found himself unwrapping the box. He felt an overwhelming urge to show his uncle the treasure and then to run away, fast through the streets with it. Suddenly it was free of the sheet and free of the purple cloth it came with.

'*Ammu!*' Ali said standing up. 'I found treasure and I'm leaving here. I will never come back. You murdered my mother.'

His uncle turned around slowly, 'You lying little thief. Where have you been?'

'I'm not lying,' said Ali. 'I do have treasure and it will keep me free of you and those men.'

Ali held up the box, lifting the lid. He was so sure that treasure was inside that he didn't even look before he held it proudly aloft.

'What is that? You sick little bastard!' said his uncle, but his face contorted with pain and Ali felt the blood in his own veins begin to boil.

He looked down into the box, saw the awful monstrosity inside and he knew it was hurting him. He looked at his uncle as the man fell forward, a black stain grew on his tunic and Ali felt his own heart burning as his uncle's exploded from his chest.

A sharp pain penetrated Ali's ribs. He looked up into the eyes of the undertaker.

'I'll take your treasure,' he said pulling back the knife. It grated on the boy's ribs and Ali felt a wet warmth gush over his fingers as he instinctively touched the wound.

Ali dropped the box. He slid back down against the building; a smear of red streaked the wall as he fell. His eyes stared blankly ahead, as the undertaker bent and picked up the now closed box, wrapping it back up in the purple cloth, the golden eye carved on the top like the watchful gaze of a goddess.

7
The Time Portals

Present Day

'This doesn't really fit you,' Lilly said after giving Amalia some more clothing to wear.

The clothes hung from the girl's waif-like figure. She didn't have the same natural curves of Lilly and I found myself wondering just how much of the vampire gene had filled her veins before she was turned. Lilly had explained to me that there were different levels of DNA in the gene pool. Some were watered down with other blood lines. Gabi, Lucrezia, Harry and myself were all very closely related. Lilly had been the last to turn, but she had been a direct descendent of Gabi's own daughter. A series of inter-marriages amongst cousins meant that Lilly's blood line was enhanced, not decreased by the years of lineage. Amalia may have only had a small connection to the family. She was like us, but not quite one of us, in a way that I couldn't explain or understand.

'I'll take her to get something more suitable,' Gabi offered as Lilly considered altering the clothing.

'Good idea,' Lilly said to Gabi and, within minutes he had ushered Amalia out of the lair.

'She's like a very, very distant relative,' Lilly said, once we were alone.

'I know.' I said. 'I've been thinking about that. She's a watered down version of you. Only not as tall.'

Lilly smiled and then her face dropped as she considered the consequences of Harry's actions once more.

'It's all a little too convenient. If Harry's body was so totally destroyed we can't disprove what Amalia says,' Lilly said.

'But if she's telling the truth then we have a real problem,' I said. 'She described the time portal.'

'Yes. I thought we'd seen the last of them.'

'Me too. Do you think it is connected to the Allucians?' I asked,

'I really don't know what to think. I'm still in denial. Yet, I felt something and there was that unexplainable pain in my chest. That all happened a few days before Amalia appeared. It coincides with the timeline of Harry's death that she described. I mean, if she was lying it would be quite some coincidence.'

I nodded. It would indeed have been too much of a coincidence.

'When you travelled through the portals did you ever see this knight that she described?' I asked.

'No.'

I stroked her hand.

'And I'm pretty certain the Allucians never wore armour. The thing is though, Chez, I also *know*, deep down, that it is nothing to do with them. They wanted to use our power, not destroy it.'

'I don't think it's their style either,' I said.

'Harry's dead,' she said. 'I know that's the truth. I feel it.'

'We're alone for a while now,' I pointed out and she smiled at me. 'What do you want to do?'

'I need to experiment with summoning a portal. Perhaps then I can try to make sense of this.'

We set up a circle of protection on a remote beach that lay between Talacre and Gronant. The area was inaccessible to humans, covered as it was on either side by rocks and a steep ridge of sand dunes that looked out over a sheer drop. Therefore it afforded us the privacy we needed.

Lilly sent Gabi a text to let him know our plans but she didn't tell him where we were.

Wait. I want to do this with you, Gabi replied but Lilly insisted that he kept Amalia 'busy'. She didn't want to leave her alone in our lair for some reason and I thought it wise until we really knew what was going on. Ultimately we had to prove that the girl could be trusted.

'I don't trust her,' Lilly said. 'I don't know why, but there's just something wrong about all of this. And until I'm totally sure that I'm mistaken, that she can be trusted, I don't want her to overhear any of our plans.'

This is insane!, Gabi's next text said. *Really, the girl is no threat to us. Where are you?*

'Switch this off and put it in your pocket, Chez,' Lilly said holding out the phone and I did as she instructed, cutting off the arrival of yet another anxious text from Gabi.

Lilly ran her hands over a patch of sand, smoothing it down as best as she could. The sand was wet and compacted which made the task a little easier. Then she spread a large black cloth over the area. Her symbol was painted on it in white. I recognise the Triskele, surrounded by two circles and a third, oval-shaped line that surrounded the whole thing like a huge eye. I helped her neaten the corners until the cloth was completely flat against the ground, and then placed a few rocks around the edges to ensure that the wind didn't disturb the overall effect.

Lilly was carrying a large canvas bag and from it she retrieved a plastic container of salt, which she poured around the edge of the cloth, encasing the icon in a perfect white circle. There was a strong breeze washing in with the sea as it ebbed and flowed over the damp sand a hundred yards or so back from where we stood. As soon as Lilly completed the salt circle the breeze stopped, flowing away from the salt, as though it knew not to disturb the pattern.

Lilly's phone buzzed in my pocket. I took it out, realising I hadn't switched it off properly. It was Gabi. *Don't pass through any doors. Promise me!*

He really didn't want to lose her again to the passage of time and his anxiety was understandable. I wouldn't have liked to be the one left out right now either.

'We're not passing through any doors?' I asked.

'No. I'm just going to feel for them. That's why I've built the circle of protection. We'll be safe inside and we won't be compelled to enter.'

'Okay.' I passed the phone back to Lilly and she quickly replied. I was still not up on this technology and my fingers just didn't seem to hit the right keys whenever I tried to text. Once she sent the message, she dropped the phone into the bag and placed it down inside the circle.

'Ready. Get in,' Lilly said, and she reached once more into her bag.

I stepped over the salt and stood inside next to her, then gazed down into the bag as she rummaged through the contents. It was full of tiny containers of herbs and spices, none of which I recognised.

'What is in there?'

'The basic tools of a Herb-wife. I have everything here that I might require in order to close the portal – if the need arises. Usually they close themselves when you aren't meant to pass through. But then, I'm only guessing. I've really not experimented enough with them. I was hoping I never had to cross one again.'

She was clearly enjoying using her witchcraft, but there was something else, an underlying current that felt like fear. I was intrigued. I'd never known her to be afraid of anything, but at that moment a strange energy crackled in and around all of the pleasure she was deriving from using her magic. If she had been human I'd have called it nervous energy. However I think in her case it was more a kind of anticipation of the unknown.

Lilly raised her arms then turned and faced east. She began a complicated ritual that involved devotion to all points of the compass and to the elements: Earth, Wind, Fire and Water. A silence descended until the hush became infinite: I could no longer hear the outside world. I glanced around the beach as the sound of the sea and wind receded. The sea was wild and the wind picked up around us, but within the circle of protection I couldn't hear or feel anything.

When water crashed brutally against the rocks, a spray of moisture splashed towards us and then ran down the barrier as though it had fallen onto a sheet of glass. I glanced behind us at the bank of sand dunes. The long grass swayed violently from side to side, while above our heads a seagull swooped down, swerving sharply to avoid the circle then flew rapidly away back in the direction it came from. Even the birds could feel the power emanating from the ring and they were repelled by it.

This was Lilly's power. Invisible to the eye but all of nature bent around it.

Lilly completed her prayers and she turned to face the sea once more.

'I'm going to search for the nearest door.'

'How do you know there will be one?'

'I don't. When I was lost in time and trying to get home, my search was refined for that specific purpose. I only looked for doors that were meant for me to pass through. But I've always wondered if there were just random portals dotted around. Now is the time to test that theory.'

She raised her arms and I felt the power of the ley pull up through the earth beneath us until a huge pressure built up inside the circle. After a few moments Lilly turned the power around and it looked as simple as the gesture she made to accompany it. It was a quick, almost casual twist of her wrists and then light burst from her palms. I'd never seen her do this before. Normally her witchery only showed in her eyes. Or that magnetic wind that whipped around her, lifting her hair and setting my teeth on edge. I didn't know what to do, I wanted to touch her, hold her, while the power coursed through her body, but I was afraid this would break the spell.

Even so, I found myself standing as close to her as possible. Her body exuded energy. The energy flowed around me and through me and suddenly she turned and pulled me into her arms. The surge of life-force pulsed and intensified.

'What's happening?' I gasped.

'I don't know,' Lilly said. 'I'm making this up as I go along.'

She was as surprised as I that our physical contact intensified the magic. I tightened my grip on her, slipping my arms around her small waist until she was pressed against me. I felt like I needed to protect her, but the urge was futile. She was so much stronger than I and she was controlling the power. So surely she was as safe at that moment as she could ever be.

I closed my eyes and rode the force of her magic. It grew, expanding like a balloon that's being filled with helium, and I let it sweep me along. Lilly held me close. I felt, rather than saw, that she too had closed her eyes and was enjoying the feeling. I felt safe, even though the intensity was infinite. There was, I knew, nothing to fear. Lilly was completely in control.

Just as suddenly as it began, the power rush stopped. I opened my eyes.

'What just happened?' Lilly said and her words surprised me as I had thought she was completely in control.

Over her shoulder I looked out to sea.

'I think you've found your doors …' I answered.

Lilly was silent as she stared, wide-eyed, at something behind me. I let go of her and turned. The doors were all around us. Millions of openings, like panes of running water, a multitude of suspended waterfalls hung in the air, or stood on the land. Out to sea portals danced above the water. I knew what they were of course. They were gateways leading into places of the past, present and possibly the future. For the first time since we stepped into the circle I experienced a pang of anxiety. The doors crowded around the circle, almost as though they are trying to get in.

'Time is infinite,' Lilly said. 'I always knew that, but I thought there would be some law, some rule that made it difficult to traverse.'

'There must be a rule. And an … inventor … controller … of all this, Lilly.'

'What do you mean?'

'Why do they have a *shape*?' I asked. 'They look like doorways but they are also waterfalls.'

'I don't know. I guess I never really thought about it. But I think maybe they resemble what our subconscious would expect them to. We travel from one place to another, often passing through this door and that to get to our destination. Somehow, it kind of makes sense.'

Lilly had travelled through the doors before, working her way through time, when she, like me, was trapped by the Allucians. The Allucians were, *are*, an unusual race of pigmy people. Small in stature but perfectly formed, like miniature humans. They were controlling the power of the time portals and did indeed have their own corridor of doors that stretched into infinity. The Allucian leader was a creature called Adonai. We'd never learnt his motives, but for a while he had forced Lilly to travel through time. It was an arduous and lonely journey. The purpose she derived from it was that she had to reach certain points in history, to find selected carriers of the vampire gene, in order to ensure that each of us was changed. Otherwise her very existence was in jeopardy.

But there was a darker side to Adonai and his people. They used Lilly for their own amusement. Meanwhile they had trapped me in a hell dimension that I was never meant to escape from. The room was like a living organism. A vile parody of life and death merged in one place. It ate and digested your soul, then spat it out again, only to begin the process once more. The door had drawn me, I was meant to be in there and I think it was because of all the wicked things I'd done in my life. If hell really did exist, it was that room, tucked away in the corridor of the Allucians and it waited for corrupt and vile souls.

'The doors were only open to me when I was supposed to pass through them,' Lilly said as though reading my mind. 'But that may have been because Adonai had blocked some of them. I'm not sure though. I still believe in destiny and everything did happen for a reason. Adonai was happy to take credit for it all but part of me wonders if he really did have any control or whether he came along for the ride. It was some kind of freaky game to him.'

'Maybe some of it was because of destiny,' I said, my mind's eye flashed the horror of the hell room into the back of my brain but I squashed the fear it held for me. 'Adonai had his own agenda. If he was able to appear to you in whatever timeline you were in then that would suggest he knew how to control the portals. If he could control them, maybe you can too.'

Lilly looked unsure for a moment.

'I could check a few … see if they are open,' she suggested.

'Not physically?'

'No. You and Gabi would never forgive me if I disappeared again.'

Lilly had no intention of leaving the safety of her circle. She called up a small thread of ley power and directed it towards the nearest doorway which was only a foot away. The air rippled inside the circle and then the energy field parted just enough to allow the strand to feed through. As it searched the door, the water changed colour from green to blue then red.

'What do you feel?' I asked.

'It's open. I know I could pass through it if I wanted to.'

I found myself stepping closer to the edge of the salt. I was intrigued by the doors but I was unsure what we could learn that would tell us the truth about Harry's death. Or, indeed, what was to be gained by opening portals at all. But I didn't voice my thoughts. I merely waited for Lilly to draw her own conclusions. She was so strong, that sometimes I was afraid to advise, yet I knew deep down that she would never reject anything I suggested without first considering the benefits.

'The thing I'm wondering,' Lilly said finally, 'is what this all means? What is the purpose of being able to explore the portals? I don't really want to start flying through time again.'

I nodded, 'There would seem little point.'

'What is fascinating though, is the idea of experimenting with how much control I have over the doors.'

This alarmed me. I feared that Lilly would become obsessed with her power. So far she had proved to be grounded, but Gabi and I had observed how the power was growing and expanding. It was always in the back of my mind that one day she might find it all too seductive.

'It's just as well that Lilly, and not one of us, has this strength,' Gabi had said. 'Either of us might get a little too excited and use it for all the wrong reasons.'

At the time I had agreed with him but as I stood within the circle on that cold beach in December, I was afraid that maybe the magic was getting to Lilly. I couldn't help but wonder if it were possible to receive an overload of power.

'Don't worry,' she said, reading the expression on my face. 'It is more of a vague curiosity. I don't plan to test the theory anytime soon.'

'Lilly, you and I both know that if you really wished to summon a door for a specific time and purpose, you could do it.'

She had done it before after all.

'All it takes is focus,' she nodded. 'I'm even starting to be able to read the time signature on these things. This door for example, leads back to two weeks ago and it is in New York.'

'That is fairly random,' I frowned.

Lilly looked at me for a moment, then smiled at my use of one of her favourite terms. Then she explained it all in layman's terms for my less modern brain. 'There are doors for every point in time. As every second passes there is a portal created to represent it.'

'If what you're saying is true, then there are doors occupying every space in the world,' I said.

Lilly nodded.

'Are there doors into the future?' I asked.

'Time is infinite. What's happened is often still occurring, what's going to happen already has.'

'I'm not sure I understand,' I said.

'Anything that's occurred in our past can't be changed. The moment has gone. But if it has happened in the past, and we're involved in it but it has yet to transpire in our present timeline, then there's a possibility it can be changed but it is highly unlikely.'

My head hurt thinking about it but I tried to make sense of it. 'What you are saying,' I said slowly, 'is that if we travel to a different point in time, in the past – it is still our present?'

'Of course. Any time we occupy is *our* present.'

I was silent as I waited for Lilly to send the doors away. When they had gone, we stepped across the circle. Lilly nudged the salt and the bubble of protection burst. A rush of sound assaulted my ears. The cold wind hurried in and around us. It was only then that I realised how very strong she was. She could even keep nature back – for as long as she wished.

'If time is infinite,' I said. 'Everything in the future has already happened, which means destiny is set.'

'Theoretically. But I actually don't believe in destiny. I think some things, yet to happen in our future, can be changed. But not things that are in our past.'

'That means …'

'There would be no way we could go back and save Harry … Because if there was a way, he wouldn't have died at all.'

Still confused, I wondered about the logic behind her words. I knew she believed them, felt they were right. It hadn't been in my mind to ever 'save' Harry, but clearly Lilly had been considering this as one of the possibilities. Even so, part of me couldn't accept that Harry couldn't be saved. After all, none of us were present at his death.

'But it still happened during our timeline,' Lilly pointed out, reading my thoughts again. 'We felt his death. And that means, there really is *nothing* we can do.'

8
Feeding Time

Present Day

Like a fashion model on a catwalk, Amalia paraded around the lounge in the clothing that Gabi had picked for her. The girl – I still couldn't think of her as a woman for she did so resemble a teenager to me – looked really pretty and sweet in her skinny jeans and tee-shirt. Her hair had been trimmed also.

'We went to a local salon,' Amalia giggled.

Her hair was cut into a neat bob because the singed ends couldn't be salvaged and hadn't repaired themselves for some reason.

'You've had a productive day,' Lilly observed. 'How are you feeling, Amalia?'

A cloud fell over Amalia's face, removing the *Illumination* and fun she had experienced trying on and parading all the clothes in front of us.

'Gabi has been very kind,' she said. 'I miss Harry.'

The mood plummeted as both Lilly and Amalia recalled Harry. It was difficult for me to take. Harry had irritated me and although I didn't wish him dead, I also couldn't be hypocritical enough to feel sad about it. The man did try to murder me, after all. I glanced at Gabi for help but he was lost in his own thoughts. He sprawled across the sofa, flicking through channels on the TV. He seemed to have an addiction to the sometimes useless entertainment it gave. 'Couch potato,' Lilly had called him on more than one occasion.

'Let's hunt,' I suggested as the urge to escape the closed

nature of our lair pulled at me. I wanted the wind whipping through my hair, tugging at my clothing as I flew across the sky. 'We need to show Amalia our methods anyway, don't we?'

I expected an objection from Lilly. We had more than enough stock of blood in the fridge but Lilly surprised me, however, and stood eagerly.

'Yes,' she said. 'I need to hunt tonight. But let's all stick to the rules. Please. We don't need any new surprises just now.'

Amalia was so young that she had yet to gain the power of flight.

'I can carry you if we need to fly though,' Gabi told her.

Gabi was keen to help Amalia all he could and I looked at Lilly to see if she had noticed. Our eyes met briefly. There was a slight flicker of something that passed behind her expression. It could have been jealousy but it was more likely to be a mild annoyance. She turned away, breaking the contact as she reached for her coat which was thrown casually over a chair.

I was confused at Gabi's interest in Amalia though. She was not as shapely as Lilly, instead she was rather thin and flat-chested, which was part of the reason she appeared so young. Lilly was wearing a long flowing dress of black velvet. Her blonde hair was loose around her shoulders and fell in thick, soft waves. She looked a little like the archetypal witch when she was dressed this way, but no one could ever say she was anything but unique. She was beautiful, exciting and intensely powerful. She was a perfect rose in full bloom and Amalia, by comparison, was a pallid little weed. But then maybe I saw all of Lilly's beauty and we had experienced so much together that Gabi hadn't been part of.

Not for the first time I wondered about our confusing *ménage à trois* and where it would all lead. So far it had worked out for us but only because we all pretended it wasn't happening. We were discrete about our private moments with Lilly. Gabi found it the most difficult of course. Within a week of his time Lilly had lived through a thousand years, travelled through time and met and fallen in love with another man. For Gabi nothing had changed, except that Lilly had, and it took some time to begin to lapse into a semi-comfortable companionship. It was still early days though, and that was why I was so concerned and intrigued by his attitude to Amalia. Although a relationship between them would be a perfect solution for me. I loved Lilly and the truth was, I didn't want to share her, no matter how open-minded I tried to be.

'Ready?' Gabi asked, pulling me from my thoughts.

I nodded but a flush of guilt coloured my cheeks. I am by nature, loyal. But God help me. I wanted Gabi to fall for Amalia and leave my lover exclusively to me.

Outside the air was brisk and cold. A glow of light frost covered the hills. We headed farther up the coast to Llandudno. It was a cute seaside town, with what Lilly explained were 'Victorian' seaside houses. Gabi picked up Amalia and we flew over land towards our destination. Lilly and I went ahead and I couldn't resist holding her hand as we glided through the air like two giant black birds. The wind rushed through our hair. I'd left mine loose and it had grown longer, past my shoulders, unlike Gabi who kept his trimmed to a certain length below his ears. Lilly called it his 'Jesus cut'. The similarity to religious icons was not lost on me. I liked my hair longer though. I glanced back at Gabi carrying Amalia and they looked perfect together. But then maybe I was just reading into things too much.

'Oh my God!' cried Amalia as we landed on the promenade at Llandudno. 'That was amazing! When will I be able to do it?'

'It's different for us all,' Lilly explained. 'I flew after only a few months, but Gabi took years.'

'Didn't Harry ever fly with you?' I asked.

'No. We always travelled by conventional means: cars, trains, that sort of thing. I didn't know he could do that. He never said.'

Gabi was smiling, a little idiotically, if I'm honest.

'I'm glad I was able to show you something new,' he said.

'Thank you!' Amalia kissed him on the cheek and then took

his hand. She pulled him along in girlish excitement.

'Quite the little charmer isn't she?' Lilly said.

'Yes. She doesn't seem too cut up about Harry any more either.'

We looked out to sea as Gabi and Amalia ran farther away.

'I'm still very suspicious,' Lilly pointed out.

'I know. It's not like you to be so reserved. Are you jealous also?'

Lilly turned her beaming smile in my direction. 'I don't have any right to be.'

'Nor any need.' I pulled her into my arms and we kissed. I wanted to show her that she would always have me. I could never be attracted to the pale insignificant light that Amalia gave, not after bathing in the fierce beacon of Lilly.

Lilly leaned into me for a moment, enjoying my arms around her and my lips and tongue explored her willing mouth. Excitement grew in my loins as I crushed her to me. We devoured each other. Then just as suddenly she was gone; running rapidly away and down the promenade.

'Come on. We need to show the newbie how to hunt safely, because I'm certain that Harry didn't do a proper job on that. He always was a careless boy.'

Lilly continued to run and I found myself chasing her. She was agile and fast and soon she had caught up with Amalia and Gabi as they plunged into a crowd queuing for entrance to a club. These places made excellent hunting grounds as Lilly could get close enough to our potential food in order to check it for us.

Inside, some hideous music was blaring and bodies gyrated in animalistic jerks on the dance floor. The sophistication was gone from social gatherings as far as I could tell and I mourned it. Men and women didn't dance together any more, the excitement of permitted touching once enhanced the experience. A potential lover's hand on your arm ignited a flame within you, and then it was gone, leaving a sense of palpable loss. Instead these humans mauled one another in something that looked like public foreplay. It was primal and regressive to me but Lilly and Gabi accepted it as the norm.

I saw my prey immediately. She was a pretty girl but her eyes were hard in the way that some women are in this century. She cast looks around the room. Her expression challenging, arrogant. I picked her because I wanted to knock her down, shake away that overconfidence. I detested hard, aggressive women, the sort who thought the world owed them a living. The predator in me awoke. For too long we had been eating from plastic disposable bottles. I craved the natural warmth of blood at body temperature. I stalked the girl at a distance until I was sure then I gave Lilly the signal. She moved in on the girl to check if my meal was safe. I would have hated to make this hard-faced female one of us. She was totally unsuitable and undeserving. What Lilly would refer to as 'a total bitch'.

'Oops. 'Scuse me!' Lilly said as she feigned tripping and fell against the girl, almost knocking her drink from her hand.

'Oi! Watch it you clumsy cow!' the girl barked and she rudely pushed Lilly back and away.

The contact was enough. As the girl brushed her hand down her white jeans, flicking away the cheap white wine – and thank goodness it was white or she might well have screamed her head off, or, more likely tried to sue Lilly for an entire wardrobe of clothes – Lilly looked at me and winked. I moved in.

'Hey,' I said, coming up behind her.

The girl didn't look up at me, '… fucking cow got wine on my jeans,' she muttered before sighing. 'What d'you want?' she said in a voice that sounded as though she had stepped in some excrement.

'You really are "a total bitch" aren't you?' I said, rolling my eyes, but her complete attitude amused me more than annoyed me.

'What the fuck …?' The girl looked up into my face. Her eyes caught mine. It was all it took. I could feel her will crumble the moment I caught her. So much for attitude. Her face softened as I burrowed a little deeper.

'Come,' I ordered.

I took her hand and led her through the crowd and out the back to the yard where the smokers congregate. The area was only small, little more than a balcony attached to the club. It was cold outside but there were heaters positioned in the wooden canopy that covered the area. Several people sat smoking and drinking at the benches. A group of four girls huddled underneath one of the heaters. They were shivering as they inhaled smoke and not surprisingly as they were wearing little more than strappy dresses and summer sandals. I met the eye of a man as he lit up. Instantly he extinguished the flame and returned to the interior of the club. After a few minutes I'd rid the area of all of the smokers.

'Sit,' I told the girl and she dropped automatically down at one of the benches. She shivered with the cold but at least what she was wearing was a little more sensible than the other girls I'd seen.

Gabi and Amalia joined us with their two victims. I looked at their choices, there was rarely any sexual attraction involved in our selection. This was a meal and nothing else. Amalia, however, was excited. She had picked a young boy, barely legal, and she ran her hands over his chest and between his legs.

'He's got a hard-on,' she said. 'I love that. Don't you just love it when they come as you bite them?'

Gabi smiled, 'I guess it is kind of sexy.'

His response surprised me. I always understood him to be matter-of-fact about the food, but then I really know so little about him or his origins other than the fact that my sister Lucrezia turned him a few hundred years ago. And that he, in his turn, bit Lilly.

Lilly was the last to join us. She had chosen a girl also. She sat her victim beside my miserable companion and looked around at us.

'I didn't expect you to wait for me before you started your meal,' she laughed and it was absurd that we had held back as though we were sitting around a dinner table.

Amalia needed no further prompting. She pulled the boy to her by the lapels of his black leather jacket and she plunged her fangs deep into his throat. I felt compelled to watch her eat in some form of strange voyeurism. She was vicious, ripping and tearing, spilling blood in her carelessness. Eventually she pulled away and her victim slumped against the table.

'Look at that!' Amalia pointed to a damp patch that leaked through his trousers. 'Bet he's never had such a good time in his life.'

She was slurring, as though drunk on the rush of blood. Appalled, I met Lilly's gaze but her expression told me nothing. I was wondering how to break the news to Amalia that Harry's method of brutality and perversion was not our way. Her crudity was a major turn-off.

'Is he dead?' Lilly asked.

'No,' said Amalia. 'Harry says we try not to kill them or you wouldn't like it.'

'Good. Then lick the wound.'

'Why?'

'Because your saliva will make him heal. And although *we'd* see the scar and recognise it immediately for what it is, the human eye won't detect it.'

Amalia bent over the boy, licking and lapping at his throat, cleaning off the spillage of blood. Her eyes were on Gabi as she sat back.

Gabi ate next. He was as conscientious as always and the girl in his arms barely moved as he fed from her without spilling a drop. He was a model of how it should be done. Lilly and I had not yet touched our meals. I wasn't sure I wanted to feed in front of Amalia. I'd watched how her cold eyes narrowed as she studied Gabi's methods. Lilly eventually took the initiative and while Amalia watched her, I quickly fed from the girl beside me.

As my fangs penetrated her skin, I forgot everything around me. The blaring music receded, my companions disappeared from my thoughts and there was only me and the girl. Her blood sang her name to me. *Rhian.* Her thoughts, dull and selfish just as I suspected, poured into me as I swallowed her down. Rhian jerked in my arms, wildly aroused beyond anything she had ever experienced. She imagined me plunging into her in an alley behind the club. Casual sex was the only kind she had ever known. And even though she never felt anything from it she couldn't stop herself. Rhian liked drugs, specifically E. It loosened her up, made her friendlier, but the next day she always felt this vague pang of sickness and regret. I pulled her in deeper, felt and saw the many faces of different men, her back pounding against the wall until she was bruised and scraped. Then there was the gang bang and one of them actually videoed it. The video was shared among many who knew her. Since then, Rhian couldn't get a 'proper' boyfriend. All she was fit for, in this small, sad and insular little town, was a quickie in an alleyway.

Rhian groaned against me. I brought her to a climax and released her, closing the wound with a quick flick of my tongue. Her ugly life flitted behind my eyes, rattled through the blood in my veins and I fought the urge to bring up all her blood in an attempt to remove her horrible thoughts from my head.

Lilly's hand clasped mine. Slowly, I steadied and returned to the present, shaking my head as the last of the girl's memories slipped away.

'We're a little out of practice. Maybe we should try to get out more often and then the impact wouldn't be so great on all of us,' Lilly said.

Gabi's eyes were dilated and his mind was elsewhere. He said nothing but his demeanour told me that his experience had been similar to mine.

'Straight from the source is potent stuff,' I said. 'It is easy to forget that.'

'Yes,' Amalia agreed. 'Those little bags of blood don't give you thoughts and sex. It's a real kick.'

Lilly's expression remained inscrutable as we took flight from the balcony, leaving our prey to sleep off the blood loss. They would all have one hell of a headache the next day, but of course the hangover would be attributed to booze and drugs.

We flew across the promenade, pointing out the sights to Amalia. The girl was excited, energised and above all looking less and less like the grieving widow she had purported to be.

9
The Undertaker

1000 Years Ago

The Undertaker's body was found by the river, his throat cut. There were conflicting rumours that thieves had set upon him and that he had robbed the wrong family in their grief. The undertaker, Al Tufayl, was known in the ghetto as being a problem solver. Some said that he must have known the secrets of all the wealthy families in Jerusalem. It was believed he worked for the debt collector and took personal care of some of those who hadn't paid.

Al Tufayl's apprentice, Fadil, had seen him return with a mysterious bundle and the body of a dead women. This was not so unusual and Fadil helped Al Tufayl throw the corpse in the pauper's pit at the back of the house. He was used to the dealings of the undertaker but despite the bruises he recognised the woman and knew she was Ali's mother.

Later, the undertaker went out. Fadil knew all of Al Tufayl's habits and was aware that he was unlikely to return until late. So, Fadil went to find Ali. They'd been friends before Fadil's mother had apprenticed him to Al Tufayl, long before Ali's father had died, but since Ali had gone to live with his uncle his friend had become distant. Fadil was worried about him. He had heard rumours and the gossip hadn't been pleasant. He had been meaning to visit for some time, but life and work had kept him too busy.

It was midday when he walked through the ghetto. Fadil first called on his mother and asked if she had seen Ali.

'No,' she said. 'And you must stay away from that boy. He's trouble.'

'What do you mean?' asked Fadil but his mother shook her head and refused to answer.

Fadil knew what she had heard though so he didn't question her further. His mother fussed over him and gave him some food and drink. Fadil soon excused himself, saying Al Tufayl needed him to return, but as he left his mother's house he turned in the opposite direction, heading deeper into the ghetto and towards Ali's uncle's house.

That afternoon Fadil waited for the undertaker to return. He swept up the sawdust, and tided the workshop. Then he lay down on his pallet and pretended to sleep. Sometime later, Al Tufayl returned. The undertaker smelt of wine and through slitted eyes, Fadil noticed the new money pouch at his side. The undertaker had completed yet another successful job.

Al Tufayl lit a lamp and made his way to the back of the workshop, lifting the top from the empty casket at the back. Fadil didn't move: he had already guessed this was where the undertaker kept his money but had always been too afraid to search.

Fadil was loyal and trustworthy. He was a reliable apprentice and he worked hard. But things had changed when he found Ali at the back of his uncle's house. Flies buzzing around him, not quite dead but so nearly there. Fadil had fed his friend small sips of water. Then Ali had told him something important: something about a treasure.

'Who did this?' asked Fadil.

'Undertaker …' Ali hissed as the final breath left his body.

Fadil had never seen anyone die before. He was sure that in those moments he really could see Ali leaving his murdered carcase behind as he went onto a new and happy afterlife in *Jannah*. Even so, he felt an overwhelming sadness. Ali had been a good boy and Al Tufayl had killed him in cold blood. Fadil remembered his teachings and the holy scrolls from the Quran said that murder was a sin. It was not a sin to kill for justice however.

Fadil knew that no authority would impose this justice without proof of Al Tufayl's guilt. Even though Ali had told him who his murderer was, Fadil was duty bound to the undertaker, and as his apprentice he could not speak against him. He had a dilemma. A crime would go unpunished, and although Fadil suspected Al Tufayl was guilty of many such crimes, Ali had been his friend and it was his death he felt most strongly about.

Fadil waited until the undertaker settled for the night, then he got up and took a look at the stash hidden in the coffin. Inside was a pouch of silver coins. Fadil also looked for the package that Al Tufayl had returned with, but he couldn't see it. He removed the coins and closed the casket. Then he stood over Al Tufayl as he slept soundly in his drunken sleep. The undertaker wouldn't wake tonight, not unless Allah shook the earth and Fadil knew that was unlikely.

Fadil slipped out of the workshop and down the street. He knew what to do, had been watching Al Tufayl carefully. As a good apprentice he had learnt quickly and now felt like an avenging angel, meeting out justice.

At the tavern he met the man. Fadil had arranged it earlier with the promise of money.

'You know that my master has to keep his secrets,' said Fadil. 'The undertaker knows too much and I've been told to give you this to make sure he doesn't talk.'

Fadil gave the man the bag of silver and watched as he counted it.

'When? Where?' asked the man running a long, dirty nail over the scar on his face. He had got it years ago for owing money. It had been Al Tufayl who'd scarred him and the wound still itched. The man was more than willing to get his revenge.

'By the river,' Fadil said. 'Soon.'

Fadil returned to the workshop, he found Al Tufayl still sleeping and so, he removed the lid from the casket, took away all the money the undertaker had and hid it.

'Master! Master!' he said, shaking Al Tufayl roughly.

'What is it?' said the undertaker jerking awake.

'I was sleeping and woke to find the casket moved. Are the dead coming back to haunt us?' said Fadil.

'What are you talking about boy?' asked Al Tufayl and then he turned to see where Fadil was pointing. 'Thieves!' he roared, jumping from his bed.

Fadil watched as Al Tufayl ran to the casket, pulling it out from the wall. Fadil saw a small box, lying on the floor behind the casket. He recognised the purple cloth and remembered what Ali had told him of its contents.

Al Tufayl searched for his money, but couldn't find it. 'This,' he said, gesturing to the object. 'It's evil. It's cursed. This led the thieves to me.'

'What is it master?' asked Fadil.

Al Tufayl shook his head. 'I must get rid of it.'

'If it's evil, master,' said Fadil. 'Wouldn't it be better to cast it in the river?'

'Yes. Yes!' said Al Tufayl.

Al Tufayl left the workshop, heading off to the river and Fadil followed silently behind. True to his word, the assassin waited and as the undertaker approached the river bank, holding up the box, the man descended on him, rapidly doing what he had been paid to do.

The box fell from the undertaker's hands as the first knife was buried in his back. The assassin turned Al Tufayl to face him, meeting the undertaker's surprised gaze, then ran his dagger over his throat. Al Tufayl fell. The man walked away. So efficiently had he killed the undertaker, there was no blood on either his hands or his clothing.

But, in the tussle the box was kicked and it skittered away, tumbling down a precipice, landing in the back of a small boat laden with goods. The boatman continued on his journey, never noticing the new edition to his wares as he traversed the river. The box sank down among bolts of luxurious fabrics, and the purple cloth remained wrapped around it as though some powerful magic kept it in place.

From there it made an incredible journey that took over 600 years to complete. It wended its way across to Europe, wreaking havoc and death on anyone who had the audacity to steal it. Then, finally, it found a resting place, where it lay undetected for another 400 years.

10
The Church in Lourdes

Present Day

'It's unusual,' Lilly said when we were alone discussing Amalia's obvious differences. 'I was very strong when Gabi turned me.'

We all recalled our turning and agreed that Amalia's supernatural strength, powers of hypnosis and even her running speed were far below average.

'Maybe her heritage is very distant.' I suggested. 'It's crossed my mind many times that she doesn't resemble the family as closely as the rest of us.'

'She's more like my cousin, Francesca,' Gabi commented. 'She was very petite, almost boyish in shape.'

Lilly nodded. 'There could be different strains. We haven't experimented at all with our DNA. Perhaps the stronger the connection, the more vampiric the turn becomes, and the more power we have.'

'Of course, the obvious person to ask would be Lucrezia,' muttered Gabi.

We all fell silent.

I wasn't ready to see Lucrezia again. She had tried to destroy me on at least two occasions. The first when she tricked me into going to the city of the Allucians under the pretext of finding a vampire king. I'd gone along with it, hoping that this king would know where Lilly was, and I'd been so desperate to find her after we'd been separated. I didn't know at that time that the Allucian leader, Adonai, was responsible for that separation, nor that they lay in wait to use me in some way to help them power their city and people. When the Allucian city began to crumble, Lucrezia pushed me into a door that led to the hell dimension. I was trapped there for an eternity until Lilly found me again.

'If I see that bitch anytime soon I'm not sure what I'll do to her,' Lilly said. 'Gabi, when will you learn she can't be trusted? She always has her own agenda and destroying us might be part of it. Who's to say she isn't involved in this latest misdemeanour? Harry's dead, killed by some strange knight who can manipulate the portals. According to Amalia, he was also carrying something which could be the equivalent of … I dunno … Kryptonite to us.'

'What are we going to do?' asked Amalia coming into the room. 'You've had your private little talk now. We *have* to find and kill Harry's murderer.'

'You want revenge,' said Lilly. 'We all want that. But I have to consider all that you've said very carefully.'

'You don't believe me?'

Lilly ignored Amalia's insecure question.

'By the way you described Harry's death. Something his killer was holding drained him of his strength. Is that right?'

Amalia nodded. 'It seemed so.'

'We don't know what we're dealing with here. This has never happened to us,' I explained. 'We have to consider all of the evidence. I mean where do we …?'

'That's the point really,' Lilly cut in. 'We need a starting place. Perhaps if you take us to this church in France? I could feel for the portal. It might tell us something.'

'You mean go *back* there?' Amalia cried, and the fear in her eyes was very real.

'It's our only lead at the moment,' Gabi said. 'If you want to find Harry's killer, then we need to go back to the point of his death.'

I wasn't at all sure it was a good idea either, but I went along with the majority vote, keeping my wits sharp and alert.

We flew through the night, across the ocean and over to

France following the directions given by Amalia to the little church in Lourdes. Gabi and Lilly led the way and this time I carried Amalia. She was light and petite, a fragile flower caught in a blizzard. I held her carefully around her small waist, almost fearful that my strength might break her, even though I knew this was impossible. She may be weaker than us but she was still immortal.

'There!' Amalia pointed. 'Just ahead. I can see the church yard.'

It was almost dawn when we landed a few feet away from the ruins. I let go of Amalia and she dropped back behind me. Lilly landed ahead of us, right on the threshold of what once would have been the entrance way.

'Tell me again why you came here?' Lilly said.

'Treasure.'

Lilly looked over her shoulder at Amalia, 'What treasure?'

'We were told of a relic, that it was valuable.'

'Who told you?'

'Just some guide. I don't remember his name.'

Lilly frowned. She was unsatisfied by the answer and still very suspicious.

'I find this whole scenario very strange. Harry has never shown the slightest interest in relics of any sort.'

Amalia said nothing. She trembled as she hid behind me.

I walked forward leaving the girl. She was not my concern; my loyalty was always to Lilly alone. As I reached the threshold I felt the vacuum within the church.

'That's … wrong. There isn't even a roof and yet …'

'I know,' Lilly said. 'There is, or has been, tremendous power here. I'm surprised Harry even crossed the threshold. It's making my hair stand on edge just from here.'

Lilly looked into my eyes and for the first time I heard her thoughts. This was not a skill she had ever demonstrated before.

This was a trap and Harry walked right into it. I nodded, acknowledging receipt of her private message.

There was a spell woven over the threshold.

'What is that?' Gabi said moving closer. 'It feels …'

Amalia slid in beside me, 'What?' she asked. 'What do you feel? It all seems perfectly normal to me now.'

I glanced at her, but there appeared to be no lie or trick lurking in the girl's eyes. She really couldn't feel the power.

Lilly stepped back from the threshold and we responded, spreading out, giving her room. I already knew what she was going to do before she held out her hands, palms upwards. I felt the ley line at the same time as she did.

'There ...' I murmured.

Lilly glanced back at me, a fleeting query crossing her face as she marvelled that I too felt the ley. The air crackled, and the light show began. A swirl of invisible energy rose from the earth up and around her. For a moment I wished she was wearing the white flowing gown again: she looked so beautiful and powerful and ethereal dressed like a real witch. Instead, and for the practicality of flying she had opted to wear black jeans, a black sweater and a long leather coat. The wind picked up the edges of the coat and her hair stood out on end.

'Wow. It's like the X-Men,' Amalia gasped. 'I didn't know she could do that!'

Gabi laughed, 'Yeah – she's Storm!'

The reference was totally lost on me and so I concentrated on the light as it occurred again in Lilly's palms. Beside me, Gabi tensed. This was something I'd seen and he hadn't.

'She does that now,' I said. 'The energy's building inside her and she's going to throw it forward to break the trap.'

'How do you know?' Gabi asked.

'I can feel it. Can't you?'

Gabi looked confused, I felt him focus his strength to scan the air around us. I knew then that more had changed on the beach than I'd at first realised. My moment in the circle, embracing Lilly as the power surged through her, had given me a new and unique connection to her power.

Amalia sidled up to Gabi. Her face was a mixture of awe and fear and something else that I couldn't quite understand, but it looked like intense curiosity. It made me slightly nervous to see this feline expression on the girl's face.

I returned my attention back to Lilly: the energy was blaring and my ears began to hurt with the pressure that was building up. Just being close to her created a tingling in my skin, setting my teeth on edge: it was like a million ants were crawling all over me. I began to shake with the effort of forcing myself not to scratch my skin until it bled.

Just as the pressure reached screaming point Lilly turned her hands, and the tension switched. The relief was instant. Gabi's arm steadied me as I almost fell forward over the threshold.

'What the hell is happening?' Amalia cried. Her hands were over her ears and bloody tears rolled down her cheeks.

'Not long now!' I yelled over the howling wind.

At that moment, Lilly jerked her hands and an explosion hit the ruins. I saw the whole building rupture. Brick by brick, in slow motion, the structure unmade itself as the remains of the church fell apart before us. The bricks floated outwards, I threw my arm over my face to protect it from the blast. Then, in a flash of energy the process reversed and the world restored to its rightful perspective.

I blinked. I could have sworn the church was destroyed, but it appeared just as it had been only moments before. Every stone and pebble was returned to the position they started from. The only thing that was destroyed was the malevolent force that had been hiding inside the brickwork.

'It's done,' Lilly said. 'A trap *was* set.'

'What kind of trap?' Gabi asked.

'It was the equivalent of a shop doorbell ringing as a customer enters.'

'That doesn't sound particularly scary,' Amalia said.

'No. But what it would have done, if we'd crossed the threshold, is brought back whoever or whatever it was that killed Harry.'

'Good!' shouted Amalia. 'And then you'd kill the bastard.'

'That's the plan … eventually,' Lilly said. 'But not until I understand more of what I'm dealing with.'

'Is it safe to cross now?' Gabi asked.

Lilly nodded.

'That was powerful magic for what seems to be so little of a spell …' I pointed out.

Lilly's eyes clouded over for a moment as she searched the power, analysing the process. 'It had a long way to travel.'

Gabi and I stared at her. We were at a loss for words, but I thought I understood the implication. Someone, somewhere in time, had placed this curse on the church to warn them of our presence.

'How? When?' I asked.

'When the foundations were laid.'

I stared at the ruins. The church was centuries old, perhaps even older than a millennium. The wonder of it failed my mind. I am not a scientist, was not born in this era and sometimes I had no basic knowledge to ground the theories we explored. The mystery of the doors had always intrigued me and the science of my time was always interesting, but power that could be sent through time lay in a mystery beyond me. I shook my head to clear it. It felt like a huge cloud floated over my brain because this knowledge was something remote and alien to me.

'I haven't a clue how this works,' Gabi said, surprising me with his admission of mutual confusion.

'What the hell?' Amalia shrugged.

'The implication,' Lilly explained. 'Is that someone, somewhere in our distant past, *knew* Harry would cross the threshold and when that time came, they arrived, via one of the time portals, and killed him.'

'If that's the case, then they know all about *us* also.' I said.

'That's impossible,' Gabi murmured.

Lilly said nothing but she stepped forward and crossed the threshold. I followed immediately with Gabi but Amalia hung back. She stood at the entrance, squeezing her hands to her chest. She looked like a terrified bird, ready to take flight at the slightest sound.

Inside the walls of the ruin there was no sign of the spell, Lilly's power had extinguished it and we were safe. I didn't expect a portal to open, unless Lilly deliberately searched for and opened one.

'Look!' Lilly pointed to the blackened and scorched altar. The condition of the stone confirmed Amalia's story. 'Where did the portal appear?'

Amalia walked tentatively towards the threshold, 'I …'

'I won't let anything happen to you,' Lilly said. 'You're safe.'

Amalia crossed the doorway, casting her eyes left and right as though she expected the walls to crash down on her at any moment. She hurried forward her hand outstretched to a point before the altar. Lilly stared at this seemingly harmless spot. There was nothing outstanding or peculiar, but then I think that was the point. On the beach I'd realised that the doors could be anywhere. Humans and immortals alike could walk through them haphazardly; however the portals are as ghosts until they are activated so the likelihood of accidentally falling through into another time was rare. Or indeed, as Lilly pointed out, impossible. Only those who had the skill could use them, which raised a great many questions about our mysterious Knight.

Lilly scanned the area, her fingers exploring the air around the spot. A tiny ripple appeared in the middle as the atmosphere dimpled with the slight pressure of her fingers.

Amalia scurried back, hiding once more behind Gabi.

Lilly probed further, 'I won't open it. I'm trying to access its date and location.'

'Since when has she been able to do that?' Gabi asked, casting a look in my direction.

I shrugged, said nothing, but as Lilly explored the portal, my fingers tingled. There was the sensation that I was touching the time portal instead of her and I rubbed my palm on my jeans in a subconscious gesture to rid myself of the experience.

'Mmmm. Old. Very old.' Lilly said, and then withdrew her hand much to my relief. 'What's that?'

We turned in unison to look at the thing she was indicating. Protruding from behind the altar was a charred hand.

Amalia burst into tears, 'It's Harry!'

11
Harry's Remains

Present Day

We circled the body, staring down at the burnt remains of Lilly's one time companion and the first vampire she had made. Her thoughts flowed around me like a piece of velvet wrapping up a much treasured relic. She recalled her accidental turning of him, during the raid made by his men. Harry, once King Harald of Sweden, was no more. He was definitely dead and his body had been left exposed to nature.

His corpse was intact but burnt down to the blackened bones. His skull, jaw open in a silent scream, reflected the torture of his painful death. My eyes fell on the outstretched hand. Veins charred and protruding, he appeared to be pointing at someone or something and his burnt out sockets stared blackly into the empty space. The direction corresponded with the position of the portal, so I dismissed it as being unimportant.

'You said there were no remains,' Lilly said to Amalia.

'I saw him die!' the girl insisted. 'There was *nothing* left.'

'Maybe his body did try to regenerate,' Gabi suggested as his arm went around Amalia and the girl fell against him, shivering but not crying.

Lilly was silent as she knelt before the carcase. Her aura lapped against it and a blue light glowed over Harry's limbs as she scanned the remains for signs of life. Eventually she turned the corpse over and I could see a blackened hole in his chest. It was as though someone had thrown a viscous substance, an acid, into his heart. What remained was only an abyss in his torso where this vital organ should have been.

My hand flew to my chest in an involuntary gesture. I knew that my body was destroyed this way once but my soul wasn't present and so Lilly was able to save me by healing my body and restoring my spirit. I didn't remember the pain of that death, but I could imagine that Harry, in full awareness would have suffered the most excruciating agony.

Eventually Lilly stood, walked away and stared once more at the hollowness that had been the portal.

Amalia threw herself beside Harry, weeping uncontrollably, 'Harry. Oh God! I never would have left if I'd known! Maybe I could have helped you.'

I placed my arm around Lilly as Gabi comforted Amalia: he had fallen so easily into the role of her protector.

'Can he be revived?' I asked.

Lilly shook her head, a silent tear slipped down her cheek. 'He's dead. There's nothing left of him inside that broken shell.'

'I'm sorry.' I didn't know what else to say and my words were little comfort to her.

I let Lilly cry her secret tears until the slight tremor left her body and she pulled on that core of steel, which made her such a strong personality, to steady herself. Behind us, Amalia, sobbing in Gabi's arms, was inconsolable. I wondered if some of it was guilt, but wasn't about to cast any blame as I felt she had suffered enough.

'Come,' said Lilly eventually. 'We need to go.'

'Should we bury him?' I asked.

'Not here. We'll take him home. He deserves a funeral on his home soil. It's what he would have wanted.'

We took to the air as the dawn filled out into morning. Gabi carried Amalia, as I held the remains of Harry's body. We were silent, swooping through the blue sky. As always we were cloaked from humans, and even as we passed a large jet, I stared in briefly at the passengers as they travelled through the air, totally unaware that they had passed a family of vampires carrying their dead. I toyed with the idea of scaring a few by revealing myself and the body of Harry, but it was only a fantasy and by then the plane, flying much faster than us, had long since passed.

We reached Stockholm by midday. It was a cold, frosty day but the sun was out and the air deliciously crisp. Lilly guided us across the city and slightly inland until we found the small converted castle that she once shared with Harry.

Halfway there, Amalia's sobbing dried up and she snuggled into Gabi's arms like a sleeping baby. It was a brief respite for us all. Her constant snivelling was falling on less than sympathetic ears where I was concerned and by the tenseness in Lilly's shoulders, I suspected it was irritating her a great deal.

As we landed in the courtyard, Amalia woke, looking around her in a bemused and very human way.

'The castle,' she said.

Gabi patted her as though she were some kind of pet that needed to be consoled. I was the last to land, but as my feet touched the ground, I was immediately following Lilly who entered the building via the kitchen. She had a key secreted somewhere outside and so we entered without having to break in.

'All the best advice recommends not leaving keys under your doorstep,' Gabi said.

'Do you really think anyone would be stupid enough to break in here?' Lilly said over her shoulder.

Inside, Lilly quickly retrieved a key from a drawer and before I had time to look around – I admit, I was curious about this place as I had never been here – she scurried towards a door just off the main larder.

'This way,' she said, quickly opening the door and hurrying down the dark steps before I had an opportunity to question her.

Behind me, Gabi and Amalia followed in silence. I wondered if Amalia knew where we were going and considered turning to ask but Lilly was rushing so far ahead that I feared she may leave us behind.

There were no lights in the basement, not a problem for us as we, like cats, can see perfectly well in the dark. I traversed a narrow staircase that led directly down into a wine cellar. Once there, I found Lilly waiting and as we joined her she pulled a lever beside a rack of dusty and expensive wines and a door, made of solid brick, scraped backwards to allow us access.

I found myself in a labyrinth of corridors, which I suspected infiltrated the foundations of the castle. Lilly walked ahead, twisting left, then immediately right. She knew the route well, but seemed unwilling to discuss where we were going. I had an excellent sense of direction, but I became confused and disorientated. The deeper we went, the less sure I was that I could find my way back. I could see how this would have been a good defence for the castle's occupants. Humans who didn't know their way, in this utter darkness, would probably experience an intense claustrophobia.

'Where are we?' breathed Amalia, directly behind me. 'I don't like this.'

'Lilly knows where we are,' I explained.

We burrowed deeper and the corridors became so narrow that I had to alter the way I was carrying the corpse. I threw his chest and head over my shoulder and Amalia, face to face once more with Harry's shrivelled gaze, began to weep loudly again. By this time her wails were really starting to irritate me.

'Shut up!' ordered Lilly a few feet ahead and Amalia fell silent immediately. 'We're almost there.'

'There' turned out to be a huge crypt, hidden in the heart of the foundations of the castle.

'Harry's predecessors stopped burning their dead and buried them here for a time. Sometimes he would come here to reflect.'

There was a glass vase, small and slender: the type a lover may give with a single red rose inside. Lilly reached out and took a long reed from it. I had thought it the remains of a rotted stalk or a branch but soon realised, when she stuck it against the wall, that it was a long match. Flame flared from its tip and she applied it to one of the torches placed around the outer wall of the space. Orange fire illuminated the room.

'Morbid,' Gabi said stepping into the cavern.

I looked around the room as Lilly lit the other torches; it was about fifty feet high. There were alcoves built into the walls and inside each one lay the remains of some relative of Harry. In the middle of the room, were several large stone sarcophagi. Dusty and cobwebbed, the place was the stuff of nightmares, but there was a calm silence and centre to the space that made me almost want to lie down there too.

'You feel that?' asked Lilly and I nodded. 'Harry would want me to put him here, I think. I can't bring myself to bury him, and definitely not burn him. I think his body has suffered enough. Also, and I know this is insane, supposing his body does suddenly regenerate? If I leave him here, safe from further harm, one day if he wakes he'll know exactly where he is.'

It made sense. It was still so difficult to comprehend that one of us was dead. I understood her desire to plan for a possible revival. I placed Harry's body on top of the nearest sarcophagus and took off my long leather coat, draping it over him.

'Thank you,' Lilly said.

'Y … you, think he might wake up?' asked Amalia. Her voice trembled.

'It's possible but I doubt it. He feels dead to me.' Lilly answered. 'Even so, the dead have been known to rise among us.'

She didn't explain further and for this I was glad. For some reason I didn't want Amalia to know anything of my past.

We stood around Harry paying our silent respects and watched his body sleeping in that final grotesque moment of his death. The torch flames flickered over our faces and over his remains and I wondered if I would ever be able to forget his rictus grin. It appeared to be a reflection of an end that was almost mine. Not for the first time since Amalia appeared in our lives, a shiver of apprehension passed through my limbs as though warning me that the end was still waiting just around the corner and no matter how I tried, my fate, so briefly escaped, would somehow come full circle to find me.

12
Stockholm by Night

Present Day

Lilly enjoyed showing us her old haunts and our first evening in Stockholm became a walk down memory lane for both her and Amalia.

'This is where I first met Harry,' Amalia told us as we entered a bar positioned on the waterfront. 'I was dancing with some of my college friends over there.'

Amalia led us to a booth and the four of us slid in.

'What I don't understand is how he knew you could be turned,' Lilly said. 'It was a bit of a risk considering he loved you. You could have died.'

Amalia turned sheepish eyes towards Lilly, 'You checked me for him. The first time he saw me. And you told him "no".'

Lilly looked around the club, then shrugged. 'I've checked a lot of girls that took Harry's fancy in this place. I don't remember any of them.'

The waitress came to take our order. She had long dark hair that came to her waist.

'Nice,' said Gabi as he watched her walk away, hips swaying, and Lilly burst out laughing.

'She's just your type. You should chat her up.'

I glanced at Amalia. She blinked, her cheeks flushed and she looked both embarrassed sand confused by Lilly's laughter.

'Don't you get … jealous, when he does that?'

'Why should I?' Lilly shrugged. 'He can do what he wants.'

'Harry said you didn't like promiscuity.'

Lilly sat back in the booth, she was relaxed and happy that evening, despite how trying the day had been. She smiled kindly at Amalia. I think she realised that the girl's perspective of us all had only come from the very narrow observations of Harry and in some ways Amalia could not be blamed for her ignorance.

'No. I didn't like how Harry used women. That's what I had a problem with. Besides, recent events have made me get over myself a little on that score.' Lilly cast a salacious glance in my direction and then quickly rolled her eyes over Gabi. She was sat between us and I slid my arm around her waist pulling her into my embrace for a slow kiss.

Amalia fell silent as did Gabi. A quick glimpse in his direction told me he was feeling less than happy that Lilly and I were kissing again. But I ignored him, as he did me when he took the initiative first.

'Would you like to dance, Amalia?' Gabi said, and they left the booth.

I pulled Lilly closer, 'I want you so much.'

'Mutual,' Lilly replied. 'Wish we could get out of here and be alone.'

Not much chance of that though, her thoughts fell into my mind as my tongue explored her mouth.

We should stop this, I projected back. *It's not fair on Gabi, he senses our new connection.*

Lilly sat back, 'We should probably share what happened on the beach.'

I didn't reply and at that moment Gabi and Amalia returned.

'My turn,' I said, jumping up and taking Amalia's hand.

I pulled her back onto the dance floor and left Gabi alone with Lilly so that he could redress the balance and kiss and hold our girl in privacy. I mimicked the movements of the dancers, and let's be honest, I may think the dancing to be grotesque in this century, but I'm an excellent chameleon and so fitting in came naturally to me. Amalia didn't notice my surreptitious glance in the direction of my lover. Nor the flush of resentment that coloured my cheeks as Gabi crushed her to him, his tongue raping her mouth. If our lives were to retain balance I'd have to learn to quell this new found jealousy. I couldn't help feeling that things had changed since that moment on the beach. Lilly was exclusively mine but she and Gabi just hadn't realised it yet.

I smiled at Amalia, 'So, what do you think of Gabi?' I was rewarded with a slight flush on her pale cheeks.

'He's nice,' she murmured flicking her eyes in his direction.

Gabi and Lilly were talking intensely now, only stopping as the waitress brought the drinks and placed them down on the table before them. This time Gabi didn't check out the girl as she walked away, he was too engrossed in Lilly. The music ended and Amalia and I walked back slowly. I slipped into the booth beside Lilly, as Amalia sat down once more at Gabi's side.

Under the table, Lilly's hand gripped my fingers. I massaged her palm with my index finger but she didn't look at me. Instead she picked up her drink with the other hand.

Oh my God, I love you! Her thoughts slipped easily into my mind, and I think it was because I was waiting for them, hoping she would talk to me and share these private things.

'… Lilly?' Amalia was saying and both of us jolted as though we'd been burnt.

Gabi was staring at us, wide-eyed. 'You two were miles away,' he said. 'Perhaps you need to … get a room?'

I smiled at Gabi's raised eyebrow, but guilt clenched my chest.

'I think that, perhaps, is a very good idea,' Lilly said. 'Gabi, do you mind entertaining Amalia?'

'No. The sooner you get some down time, the better we might all feel. The air is tense right now,' he said.

'I know. Sorry.' Lilly leaned over and kissed Gabi, then took my hand and led me away.

'What's going on?' I heard Amalia say as we left.

'Nothing. They just have something to take care of. Want to find a restaurant? Why not take me to your favourite place?' Gabi suggested.

Lilly and I left the bar and ran hand in hand through the

streets, like two children who'd been allowed outside after weeks of isolation.

'I so needed to be alone with you,' I said.

'Come.'

We flew up into the air and back over Stockholm. The city lights were beautifully bright in the winter night and I enjoyed the flight over them as we headed back to Harry's castle. I couldn't stop touching her, every bone in my body, every particle of flesh on my bones, wanted her.

We didn't land in the courtyard this time; Lilly led me straight to a balcony on the first floor and pushed open the French windows. After we'd interred Harry's body, we hadn't bothered to explore the castle. Instead we'd flown out and away back to Stockholm. Even so, I knew instantly that this was Lilly's room. It smelt of her.

Looking around I saw the cosmetics she used, even though she had no need for them, and a bottle of her favourite perfume stood on the dressing table. The room was predominantly white and purple, both colours I knew she favoured and in the centre, the most important item, the bed, a huge four-poster, was draped in purple velvet and white voile. She had turned down the covers, or someone had, but I didn't think about this as we fell together onto the soft cushioned mattress.

My lips showered her with kisses as I began to strip her clothing from her perfect body. I had never needed or desired her more. Every kiss drew a small sound of pleasure from her lips and she rolled with me on the bed, fighting to remove both her and my clothing simultaneously.

When she lay in nothing more than her underwear, I fought the urge to just pounce on her and take her. We'd spent so much time being discrete that it felt wonderful to have the whole castle to ourselves and have no fear of being overheard.

I pulled away the bra, suckled her nipples and Lilly cried out.

'Oh Chez, oh please …'

'You want me?'

'You know I do …'

She pushed me back and away and for a moment I thought she had suddenly changed her mind. She was on all fours on the bed; her fangs were out in her excitement. They were always a symbol of her true desire and I felt reassured that she did want me. I lay back, waiting for her to move and she crawled to me, every beautiful sinew rippling with power. She was, and I know its clichéd, like a beautiful, powerful cat stalking its prey.

Her fingers found me first, gripping my cock until I ached. She stroked its length while the nails of the other hand slowly ran over my balls. I groaned under her touch. She knew exactly what I enjoyed. Her tongue lapped me, and I loved how it pushed long and slim and pointed between her fangs. I lay and let her suck me, groaning with pleasure, and then she rolled her body up and over me.

'You're so beautiful,' I whispered.

'You are so … big.' she said and laughed.

'It is that obvious that I want you then?' I smiled.

She straddled me. I wanted to push up and into her, but Lilly was ever the tease and of course her underwear, a lace thong, was still in the way. She wasn't going to give me what I wanted so quickly or so easily so I rolled her over and lay above her half expecting a fight. She laughed, melting under me, wrapping her legs around me. Sex with her was always fun as well as passionate.

I ran my nails over her breasts lightly, looked down at the faint red welts that appeared and then faded as my tongue licked over them.

Now, she ordered and it took me a moment to realise she hadn't spoken but had sent me the thought.

As you command. I reached down, pushing aside the thong and then, in one swift movement I entered her. I felt that slight resistance of her tightness and she gasped as I began to fill her. She opened to me, rocking gently against me until I was buried all the way inside her. Her body pulsed around me as I began to move, and my excitement was enhanced by a new revelation. I could feel what she felt, merging with my own sensations. I was inside her mind and she in mine. I tried to withdraw my thoughts, but Lilly pulled me deeper, and I couldn't resist: I lost myself in her. Her mind, her body, it was all the same. I melted into her skin, merged with her soul. My flesh became hers, hers mine as our hearts touched. Somewhere, deep in my subconscious, I knew we weren't really merging, the imagery was metaphorical, but the actuality was spiritual.

I'm not a man of flowery words. These descriptions are difficult for me. But when I say I belonged to her, mind body and spirit. That is perhaps the closest description of this moment I can give.

The orgasm, when it came some time later, was inconsequential by comparison, but it was double in its intensity. I felt Lilly's pleasure, just as surely as I felt my own. We had come a long way since the day on the beach when her power had channelled through me as she searched for the doors. At that moment I realised that *our* power was a conduit to each other. It was a startling revelation, but I rolled with it like a surfer riding a powerful wave. Always there was that sense of danger, but the thrill and excitement outweighed the fear of losing yourself in the sea.

Later, we lay together in silence, waiting for Gabi and Amalia to return.

'I don't want to share you anymore,' I said.

Lilly stretched beside me. 'I know,' she said.

I searched for her mind, but for the first time in days she was closed to me. I had no right to make demands, but I needed her to belong to me and me alone.

'I know I have no right to say this,' I said.

She didn't answer, but she curled up silently beside me, her arm over my chest and around my neck. Her lips pressed against my skin in a silent kiss.

'Gabi and Amalia are back,' she said as sleep slipped over me.

13
The Architect

Six Months Ago

An otherwise peaceful landscape was roused by the constant vibration of the jackhammer as it tore into the concrete, ripping up the old flooring of the church. John Noble glanced inside the shell of the building as Carl Shaw, ears protected, head covered in a bright yellow hardhat, tore away at the ground like some crazed über dentist fighting the war on tooth decay. The drill whirred and yelled as Carl pressed it down harder, his body shaking with the effort as the bit rebounded from a particularly solid piece of rock in the ground beneath.

The air was thick with dust. Noble was feeling unusually stressed. There was a tension vibrating through the swirling atmosphere that had little to do with the din created by the machine. He backed away, his head pounding in rhythm with the drill.

Outside the church he lifted his helmet and scratched his head of thinning mousey hair. His eyes itched from the dust, and his ears were ringing with a tinnitus caused by the noise. Then, the sudden silence as the drill switched off caused Noble's heart to beat with a new anxiety. He turned back to the doorway. Uncertainty made his hand tremble as it rested on the hollow frame.

Inside, Carl pulled off his protectors, gazed down into the hole he had drilled, then glanced over at Noble.

'Boss. Look at this,' Carl said.

Carl was kneeling by the hole as he approached.

'What is it?' Noble asked.

Carl didn't answer. He just stared down into the crevice. Dust still hung thick in the air, settling in slow-motion around the opening like a low level earth-stained fog. The air cleared slowly as Noble knelt before the gap. The goggles he was wearing kept the bulk of the grit from his eyes, but the atmosphere was redolent with the smell of wet soil. He breathed it in. The smell reminded him of the old damp cellar in his childhood home. He had always loved the earthy smell but this, here, just didn't feel right.

A dark black bulk lay under a fine layer of soil and concrete dust.

'The drill wouldn't cut through …' said Carl.

Noble reached down, his hands found damp, dirty fabric that should have rotted long ago carefully wrapped around something else. He pulled the object up and out of the ground and set it beside him. Then he pushed aside the cloth to find a roughly carved wooden box. He turned the box around in his fingers. The wood felt warm to the touch. *Curious.* A faint marking was engraved on both the top and the bottom, Noble recognised the symbol as the *crux ansata*, a sort of cross with a looped handle at the top. He ran his thumb over the wood, and winced as a splinter pierced his flesh. He pulled his thumb away and sucked it..

Noble wrapped the box back up in the soiled cloth, tucking it under his arm as he stood.

'I'll have to check this out,' he told Carl. 'I'd appreciate it if you didn't say anything to anyone else until I find out if it's important.'

Carl rolled his eyes, 'I know the score.'

Noble had bought the church as an excavation project. He was an architect and he had converted churches before, turning them into luxury homes for the wealthy. It was becoming something of a fashion among the elite to live with a graveyard as their back garden. Usually there were stipulations on the purchase. The outer structure was not to be changed, the graves must remain intact and the altar, if relics were known to be underneath, must be incorporated into the general design of the house, or in some cases had to be removed by a dignitary of the church. Strangely this latter stipulation had been missing in this case so Noble had quickly removed this cumbersome and often annoying feature.

His design detailed that the old flagstones be replaced by modern underfloor heating. Old church buildings were often excessively cold, but modern homes had to be welcome and warm.

Noble lost money every time the project was delayed. Since buying the church there had been a series of problems. Stupid things like equipment breaking down; deliveries not arriving on site in time to begin the work and then one of his men was injured and almost died when a digger took on a life of its own. Finally, when work began on the church, Noble's crew had been surprised to find a layer of concrete under the flags which delayed the project still further.

Noble left Carl working on the remainder of the flooring and took the box back to the onsite office, a caravan in the field beyond the graveyard. Once inside he unwrapped the box, scrutinising the symbol. The *Crux Ansata*, also known as the Ankh, had been used as a symbolic sign of life throughout Egyptian history. Noble knew there was mention of it in several hieroglyphic translations, and had noticed it in images of the Goddess Sekhmet. Sekhmet, the lioness, a powerful warrior that was seen to be the protector of Pharaohs, always held the Ankh in her hand. So why would it be featured on a box, buried right underneath a church altar? The only explanation was that the box contained some kind of ancient and valuable relic.

At that moment Noble's phone began to ring in his pocket.

'Hello?'

'Mr Noble?'

'Yes?'

'It's the diocese estate agents here. I just had a weird phone call from Rome. Did you place a call there today?'

'Me? Er … no. Why would I do that?'

'Something about a relic. Did you find a relic under the altar of the church we sold you?'

'No. Must be some kind of mistake.' Noble didn't understand why he found himself lying. He didn't like the fact that one of his crew, probably Carl, had betrayed him like this. 'The diocese is funny about these things Mr Noble. If you have found something then please can you hand it in to your nearest church? I could send someone round for it.'

'No.'

'I can't send someone round?'

'I didn't find anything. I don't know what you're talking about.'

The estate agent sounded unconvinced, 'Well if you're sure. It's just a bit odd. You see you're the only person who's bought an old ruin in Scotland recently …'

'I told you,' Noble said. 'I don't know anything. Maybe someone is winding you guys up.'

'Winding us up?'

'It could be a prank …' Noble suggested.

As he hung up, Noble wondered at the speed with which this had happened. It all seemed a bit mafia and he felt even more concerned than he should have been. The church couldn't do anything legally. They'd sold the property. There'd been no stipulations. It was their own fault. So what, he had found something. *Finders keepers.*

He stared at the casket. There was something important about this. Something *wrong*. He could just *feel* it. He wondered what was inside. He ran his hands over the wood, feeling for a catch or lock, but he couldn't even find hinges. The lid of the box was fixed snugly and wax was used to seal the rim.

Smash it open, he thought, but no sooner had the idea entered his mind than the fear of what he would find inside gripped him. He wanted to know what it was, but damned if *he* was going to open it. Besides it could be precious and by destroying the box he might affect the value of its contents. That was probably why the church wanted it so much.

Noble looked out of the window and back at the site. Carl was drilling again and Noble was certain that the sound hadn't stopped at all since he left the area. No time for him to call and who would be able to have a conversation with that racket going on.

He stroked the lip of the box again, then ran a nail around the rim in a subconscious gesture. The lid pulsed against his fingers as the box jerked.

Noble backed away, staring with paranoid phobia. Surely he hadn't imagined the movement?

Afraid to touch the wood again, Noble threw the dirty cloth back over the box. Immediately a stillness settled over the container. He wrapped it up. First in the cloth, then in bubble-wrap and packed it into a small wooden crate full of straw. There was only one person who'd know what to do with this and he would need all of the information there was to hand.

Half an hour later the courier arrived. He was a small stocky man with a broad Glaswegian accent. Noble examined the delivery address carefully. There wasn't room for error. The address read, Professor Björn Adelman, University of Stockholm, Department of Archaeology.

Satisfied, Noble signed the collection note and watched as the courier carefully loaded the box into the back of his van. He didn't start to feel better until the van drove away from his office, down the road, and turned the next corner. After that it was out of sight, out of mind.

Noble got back to work, reviewing the church plans, making some small modifications. He didn't look up at the street again. He didn't see the black sedan pull up outside his office, nor did he notice the two priests who got out of the car and headed his way.

14
A Lull

Present Day

Gabi slept in another room that night. It was as though he knew our little *ménage à trois* was coming to an end. As I drifted to sleep I heard him and Amalia return, but chose to ignore them. Instead I spooned Lilly, listening to the steady thump of her immortal heart as it beat through her back and I pressed my chest against her skin until it felt as though we were merging again.

Lilly wasn't asleep but she didn't respond to the pressure of my cock against her buttocks. I didn't mind. It was more about love than lust at that moment but touching her always drew this response from me. I adored loving her and the intimacy we'd achieved was glorious.

A few hours later I woke to find the bed empty and for a moment disappointment engulfed me. I believed she had slipped away to join Gabi, but then I smelt the cold outside air as it drifted in through the open balcony windows. I left the bed and walked unclothed to the windows and looked out to see Lilly standing in the moonlight. She was naked and glowing in the cold: a beautiful and terrifying phantom. She was the stuff of fantasies as well as nightmares.

I admired Lilly's bare shape, the curve of her hips, the prominent bottom that was pert and smooth, and the gorgeous path of her spine. She was leaning on her arms, looking out towards the snow-covered mountains. The air was so cold that my breath froze on my lips. I felt the frost touch my skin, but we can bear any extremes of temperature with little discomfort.

'You seem far away …' I said.

She didn't turn but her neck bent towards me and her head fell down closer to her chest.

That night, that moment, reminded me of the time we'd parted all those years ago and Lilly had returned to her quest of travelling through time to save the vampire gene heritage. I felt a strange sense of *déjà vu*.

'You're planning something,' I said.

'Not planning precisely. But mulling over the possibilities.'

I came up behind her, put my arms around her and pulled her round into my embrace.

'You won't leave without me.'

'No,' she said.

'Promise?'

She nodded and my lips pressed against her cold cheek.

'Then don't shut me out. I need to know what you're thinking.'

'And you will,' she answered. 'When my thoughts are clear and my direction is decided.'

I pulled her back into the room, closing the balcony windows and shutting out the cold, night air. Then I wrapped my arms around her possessively in the bed, and kissed her cheeks, hair, neck and shoulders over and over until warmth slipped back into our skin.

I made love to her once more, and then we both slept. I was so incredibly happy and loved. Somehow, though, I could sense that something was coming. These shared moments were just the lull before the storm.

15
Harry's Legacy

Present Day

'Are we staying here for a while?' Amalia asked.

We were in the breakfast room. Lilly had telephoned the housekeeper to let her know that the castle was once again occupied and the staff had returned to remove the dust sheets and provide food for us. It was strange being looked after like this, after the months of living in the lair, barely seeing anyone unless we ventured out. I quite liked it. It made me feel as though we could almost live as part of the human world and forget that we were anything but one of them.

'For now,' Lilly said. 'I need to tidy Harry's affairs, which is going to be very difficult indeed since we never expected this to happen.'

Amalia looked down at her full plate, then pushed away the breakfast in a dramatic gesture that signified to us all she was recalling her dead lover. I held back a deep sigh. Her dramas blew hot and cold on an hourly basis.

'I thought maybe you'd want to go back to England,' Amalia said. 'I could see to Harry's affairs.'

I found myself staring with interest at Amalia. Had she hoped to inherit the castle? Harry's wealth? *Curious.*

'There isn't a will,' Lilly said softly. 'He never expected to die. You understand that don't you?'

'Y ... yes. But ...' Amalia stuttered. 'There is a will ...'

'What?' Gabi said. 'Why would he ...?'

'Amalia,' Lilly said. 'I own the castle. There is only money that Harry would leave in various accounts, some of which I'm joint signatory on. Even without a will, we can get access to all of his assets if need be. Why, therefore, would he make a will?'

'I don't know. It was strange, but before we left for our trip to see you, he made a will. He said he "had a bad feeling" about something.'

Lilly shook her head, and I sensed that she was feeling as baffled by this revelation as I was. She stood up and walked away from the long mahogany table and turned to gaze out of the window, looking outside at the mountains.

'I assume you are the beneficiary,' she said.

Amalia sat back in her chair and burst into tears. 'I don't know! But he said he was taking care of things. He said he was afraid for me.'

I looked around the room and met Gabi's eye. For the first time he was showing no sympathy for Amalia. That nagging suspicion that was always with Lilly and I seemed to be permeating into our companion's brain at last.

'We're like a squabbling family after the death of a rich relative,' Lilly said, turning back to face us. 'To be honest a will is pointless. Harry would have to be proven dead for any legal notice to be taken. I doubt that any of us are willing to hand his body over for examination?'

I was horrified at the thought. It would surely mean our discovery?

'Really none of it means anything to us.' Lilly continued. 'Money is only a means to help us keep our secret. And our secret must be kept at all costs. So you see Amalia, your tears are wasted. We don't want Harry's wealth, you can have whatever you need or want. I'm surprised at you bringing this up actually. I assumed, at least until his murderer was found, that you would want to remain with us.'

'Oh I do! I'm afraid to be alone!' Amalia cried. 'But I didn't know if you wanted me to be with you. You seemed happy enough as you were.'

'We are happy,' Gabi said a little too quickly. 'But that doesn't mean there isn't room for you in our lives.'

Amalia smiled at him and I glanced at Lilly, but she kept her back turned to us. I searched for her mind and found again a closed door and I knew she was deliberately keeping me out.

'What's important is that we find out what happened and who the killer is,' I said. *And how to destroy him before he destroys us,* Lilly thought and I forced myself not to answer aloud.

'If you want some security, Amalia,' Lilly said, not letting it go, 'we can arrange for you to have your own bank account, your own wealth. Although, truthfully you only have to ask and anything you want is yours.'

Amalia didn't answer but her cheeks burned with embarrassment. She probably wished she had never mentioned anything at all about Harry's wealth. It was, after all, a very mercenary attitude in view of Harry's murder. It also gave a new aspect to her personality, one that hadn't been so obvious at first. Amalia, despite her appearances, was definitely a survivor and she would look out for herself despite our help.

We fell into silence, each of us nursing our private thoughts, and the vacuum of sound left created a heaviness in the atmosphere that was hard to dispel.

'There's only one way to learn the truth,' Lilly said, finally breaking the silence. 'We have to travel the portals once more.'

'No!' Gabi said, knocking his chair over as he stood up. 'You can't disappear again.'

'I have no intention of disappearing, Gabi,' Lilly said. 'This time we're going together. This time I will control which doors we traverse.'

Gabi's mouth opened then closed as he searched for the right response to this revelation.

'You can do that?' he asked finally.

'Yes. She can.' I said.

Amalia and Gabi sat quietly as Lilly and I explained what had happened on the beach. We didn't, however, say anything about the way she had channelled both of our energies.

'I know I can control the doors,' Lilly said.

'But what if you're wrong?' Gabi asked. 'What if this is all a trap? We really don't know what we're dealing with.'

'That's precisely why we need to go back to the time when the trap was set in the foundations of that church. Someone in the eleventh century knew that Harry would walk through those doors and they were waiting for him.'

'You've clearly been thinking this through,' I said. 'But I have to agree with Gabi that this may be a trap.'

'We should wait,' Amalia said. 'Maybe it won't ever happen again. It could have been a fluke.'

Lilly sighed, sinking into a chair at the table. A weary determination furrowed her brow and I knew she was struggling to explain herself.

'I'm not given to paranoia but I really believe that something is out to get us. Maybe it is waiting at different points in time, ready to pick us off one by one just at the moment we become complacent. I'm not prepared to risk any of your lives on waiting. We attack before we are ambushed. That's the only way we can deal with this.'

'I agree,' I said. 'But there's more that we need to consider here.'

I let my companions wait while I ordered my thoughts around my explanation. They stared at me patiently as though they too were already thinking the same thing that was in my mind. If this powerful force could plan eleven centuries in advance, then what was to stop them from knowing exactly when and where we would travel through time to search for them?

'Somehow, I think this is the right thing to do,' Lilly said. 'But I want you all to be safe, so maybe I should go alone. We can't risk all of our lives.'

'No,' I said. 'Wherever you go, I'm going with you.'

'You better not even dream of disappearing on me again,' said Gabi.

I turned to Amalia and saw the confusion and fear on her face, 'You don't have to come,' I said.

'You're joking right? Miss an opportunity to travel through time. Fuck! I'm so with you.' Amalia's cheeks flushed and I wasn't sure whether it was from fear or excitement but my misgivings about her were temporarily eased. I couldn't help noticing the expression on Gabi's face as he looked at the girl: pure lust. I glanced at Lilly, concerned she had seen this too, but she had turned away once more to look out at the mountains. Her green eyes, glowing with anticipation, withheld secrets of her innermost thoughts and her mind was once again clamped shut.

16
The Two Priests

Six Months Ago

John Noble was in his office, his back to the door, when the priests came in.

They stood and watched him quietly for a moment before some sixth sense made him turn around. The two men just stood there watching him. Noble's eyes flicked from one to the other, assessing them. There was a roughness about them. It was as though they had seen darker things than a priest should have. They were almost identical in height, one, a dark-haired man, had an expression of quiet fortitude around his mouth. Noble noticed it because it reminded him of his father. The set of his jaw, tight with determination, was usually the first sign that John was in trouble. It made him feel weird to see this look on the face of a man of the cloth. The other man was blond. He had softer eyes that were a bright and intense green. Both men were dressed in black suits, white collars around their necks. Noble was unnerved, but he tried not to show it.

'Can I help you gentlemen?' he asked.

'Mr Noble,' said the blond priest. 'We've come about the relic.'

'What relic?' Noble replied almost too quickly. 'I keep being asked about this and like I said to the diocese estate agents, I don't know about any relic.'

'We just want the box. Mr Noble. It's the one you've found under the altar. No one is going to make a fuss and make you change your plans. We just need the box.'

Noble considered his position. There was no way they could know for certain what had been found. This had to be just coincidence. He turned and leaned back against his desk. One hand folded across his chest, the other curved up under his chin. He knew that right now his instincts about the box were right. There was something important about it. He had been right to send it away. No way was he going to be bullied, and certainly not by a couple of priests, even if they looked as though they had escaped from the Matrix.

'Who are you exactly?' he asked. 'By what authority have you come here?'

'I'm Father Anthony,' said the blond one. 'This is Father Declan.' He indicated his colleague.

Noble looked from one to the other. 'Father Anthony and Father Declan?' Noble sighed. 'It kind of figures.'

He had been brought up a Catholic, and had always had the utmost respect for the clergy. It was partly why he had started restoring churches. Although the main motivation was the money he made from selling them afterwards, the justification of bringing the exterior back to its natural and original beauty and grandeur was something that Noble prided himself on.

Father Declan stepped forward, 'Please Mr Noble. You don't know how important it is that we get this relic back.'

'*If* there was a relic,' Noble said. 'I'd give it back immediately. It's no concern of mine. Why would I hold onto it?'

Both priests exchanged a look.

'That's what we don't understand,' said Father Anthony. 'You've dealt very fairly with the church and we've dealt fairly with you. Why you are holding out like this is something we can't conceive.'

Noble pushed himself off his desk and stepped towards the priests. His confidence growing.

'Look guys. There's obviously been some mistake. Someone has called in a hoax. It's beyond me who would do it, but maybe it was one of my men having a laugh. You can speak to them if you like.'

'No,' said Father Declan. 'That won't be necessary.' Holding Noble's eyes with his own, Father Declan's hand slid smoothly inside his suit. *He's going for a gun!* thought Noble with a momentary panic, but the priest's hand emerged with nothing more sinister than an oblong of white card. 'Here's my card, just in case you do find something, okay?'

Noble realised he had been watching too many films. He stared at Father Declan's hand for a moment before he took the card. He remained silent and thoughtful as the priests turned and opened the door to the office.

'Just a minute,' Noble said. 'If there was a relic – and I've told you there isn't so this is purely hypothetical – then why does the Church want this particular one back so much?'

'What do you mean?' asked Father Anthony, pausing on the threshold.

'Well the phone calls and your visit … you all seem pretty desperate.'

'Mr Noble, we have a duty to our saints and martyrs to ensure that any relic used from them is given the utmost care. We can't have them falling into any hands. I'm sure you understand.'

'Oh right,' Noble replied, but the answer confused him even more as he just didn't believe it was the only motivation.

Noble had always prided himself on being a good judge of character. He had always been able to tell if someone was lying to him. Father Anthony's words just didn't ring true.

'Are you sure you don't know where the casket has gone?' asked Father Declan.

'Positive. Sorry. I can't help.'

The priests left and this time Noble closed and locked his office door behind them. He was surprised to see the slight nervous tremor on the hand that turned the lock.

Through the window he watched as the priests got into the sedan. He quickly jotted down the licence plate as they drove away. He didn't know why it was important to do this but his suspicions were aroused and his bullshit meter had kicked in as soon as the priests arrived. For a start, he didn't think for one minute that 'Ant and Dec' were real priests. After all would a real Catholic priest be wearing a wedding ring or indeed any jewellery at all? Yet the fact remained, as Declan gave Noble his card, he had indeed been wearing a ring and on his wedding finger. He wasn't sure, but he could've sworn that as the light hit the gold there was a faint, almost indistinguishable symbol engraved there. It looked like an eye.

17
Carduth

Present Day

We stood in the wasteland outside of the ruins at Lourdes. Lilly, her arms outstretched, scanned once more for any anomaly. She looked both beautiful and terrifying as her hair blew out within the whirlwind of power she raised from the nearest ley line. She was dressed once more as a warrior. Tight jeans, sensible boots, a sweater and long leather coat covering the scabbard holding the broadsword that was secured around her tiny waist with a strong leather belt.

'I never travel through time without this,' she had said as she fastened it around her waist. 'Even though I know it's quite ironic.'

I thought her attachment to the sword a little peculiar. After all, we had the ultimate weapons in our mouths, ready whenever they were needed. Plus our superior strength made hand to hand combat effortless. Since my turning I had never feared anyone in battle and I knew that Lilly was far more powerful than any of us. Lilly's love for using this sword, however, made me wonder if wielding it were merely symbolic to her. It epitomised the Amazonian female that she was.

'Wow! She's like Zena,' Amalia said. 'Except with blonde hair.'

Gabi laughed. I didn't understand the reference but I did get the sentiment. Lilly's aura, especially whilst holding the sword, glowed with immense and vibrant power. She was a Goddess and we mere feeble mortals by comparison.

Amalia squealed in fear as the wind raised and whipped around her. She pressed herself closer to Gabi and he, being ever the sucker for the fragile female, wrapped his arms around her protectively. I frowned at them. The girl was growing evermore annoying with each passing moment.

Why do we have to bring her? I thought and Lilly laughed out loud. She looked terrible, insane; drunk on power and her laughter drew another whimper from Amalia.

I don't want to leave her alone, Lilly responded. *You've heard the saying, 'Keep your friends close and your enemies even closer?'*

I met Lilly's gaze. *Which category does Amalia fall into?* I asked.

When I find out, you'll be the first to know.

Her mind slammed shut, closing me off suddenly as a new sensation rippled through the air. The hairs stood up on the back of my neck. Vibrant energy rippled in the wind around Lilly. Her aura changed colour, becoming a deep purple and the significance to this was not lost on me. She was displaying the colour of the third eye and her psychic powers were reaching a pivotal moment.

'I feel one!' Lilly yelled over the wind.

'Where does it originate?' I asked.

Gabi and Amalia stepped back as a tiny wrinkle appeared in the air before the door of the church.

'This one reaches back to before the foundations were laid. We should arrive in time to see the witch or warlock who set the original trap. And then maybe we'll get some answers to learn who is behind this,' said Lilly.

'What do you mean by this one?' asked Gabi.

'There are several others, but I'm dismissing them before they open,' Lilly said.

Gabi glanced at me, his frown an open question, but I looked away unable to explain. Lilly's powers were growing with each passing day. I didn't have any answers. I didn't know where this was all going to lead.

The portal took shape. A tall, angular fountain shaped in the space of a doorway. The wind dropped as suddenly as it raised and Lilly lowered her arms, walking towards the anomaly. She skimmed it with her hand, then licked her palm in a symbolic gesture of tasting. She tasted people, so why not time?

'The dates are correct. I'm going through.' She withdrew her sword from the scabbard.

'Wait!' Gabi said. 'We're doing this together, as we all agreed.'

Lilly looked at him, 'I don't know what I'm going to find on the other side.'

'That's precisely why you're not going alone,' I said. I stepped up beside her. 'Perhaps Amalia shouldn't come though. She's weaker than us. She may even become a liability.'

'I won't!' said Amalia appearing at my side. 'I need to see this. I'm not afraid of what's through there … I'm only scared of …'

Her eyes fell on Lilly.

'You have nothing to fear from Lilly,' Gabi said.

Lilly remained silent and I knew that Amalia's instincts were right. She should fear Lilly. Lilly would kill her in an instant if she suspected any form of deceit.

'We'll all go through,' Lilly said as she plunged forward.

I waited to bring up the rear as Gabi and Amalia slid through the time portal, both tentative with their hands outstretched. At the last moment Amalia froze but Gabi caught hold of her around the waist and dived forward, throwing them both through the door. Once they were through, heart pounding, I pitched forward into the cold embrace of water that wasn't wet and crossed time and space in one small step.

The last time I'd crossed a time portal I had been thrown into a hell dimension, lost for centuries until Lilly found me again. I couldn't help comparing this moment with the previous one, recalling briefly how my sister Lucrezia tricked me. As I fell forward into this new era I almost imagined Lucrezia's hands reaching forward, this time not to push, but to pull me back and away from the woman I loved.

I was still on my feet as I stepped into the new time. For a moment I experienced an intense disorientation and then I found Lilly holding my hand and Amalia and Gabi gazing wide-eyed around them. They looked dazed and confused.

We were indeed still in the same spot of land, but the landscape was very different. It was full dark. Gone were the ruins of the old church. Instead, around us lay a cluster of tiny houses. One of which, the nearest to the church land, had a smallish pen around the structure with a few farm animals clustered inside. Even in the dark I could see the houses were constructed of straw and mud, covered with some kind of whitish paint and held together by black beams. Shuttered windows stared out, like black bottomless eyes, onto a muddy square surrounded by the buildings. A well lay in the centre. Above it was a winch wound with rope and a wooden bucket dangled over the abyss below.

Behind me the portal made a barely perceptible thrum, but it was enough noise to spook the animals. A chicken squawked. Frightened, the bird jumped up into the air, wings flapping uselessly until it fell back down inside the pen. This set off a chain of reaction from the other animals and for a few moments, all of them stirred. A horse began to pace the pen, snorting and sniffing the air, while the only cow lowed mournfully.

I glanced at the portal: all was well, but it lay open behind us glowing on the otherwise opaque landscape.

'It's only visible to us,' Lilly said observing my interest in the doorway.

It was as though the village were under the influence of some spell. Despite the panicked chicken and noise made by the other animals, it remained quiet, all occupants apparently in bed.

Lilly walked onto the barren land that would soon house the church from our future. 'What era is this?' I asked.

'Oh. Didn't I say earlier? No, of course I didn't. It's exactly three am on Friday, the twenty-ninth of October. Ten fifty-two AD,' Lilly answered.

'The Middle-Ages,' Amalia said. 'This is so exciting.'

'Impressive,' said Gabi. 'You even know the time.'

Ignoring Amalia and Gabi I joined Lilly as she paced the area where the church foundations had already been laid.

'Can you see anything?' asked Gabi.

'It's the first stage,' Lilly said. 'Although they've laid the foundations, there's no spell attached to them.'

'Look!' Amalia whispered.

We turned to see a figure wrapped in a thick black cloak heading our way.

'Hide!' Lilly gasped.

My companions and I sank back into the shadows, blending with the dark covering of the nearest building. The figure, who I assumed was male because of his height, build and clothing, moved into the area marked out by the foundations of the church then stopped. Fortunately for us he had kept his head down, allowing us time to 'disappear'. From my vantage point I observed the man as he entered the space. He walked around, slowly. It was almost ceremonial, as though he were marking out a ring of power in the centre of the foundations. Suddenly, he threw back the hood of his cape and glanced warily back towards the tiny village.

The moon was full but even if it hadn't been I'd still have been able to see him clearly. He looked like a monk of some sort. There was a bald, shaved area on top of his head and straggles of greasy-looking hair over his ears. The hood that had covered him was attached to a brown cowl, both of which were smothered in dirt and the odour of unwashed flesh filled the air.

The monk stretched, yawned and gave a massive fart. A girly titter rippled into the air, quickly hushed by Gabi as he clamped his hand over Amalia's mouth. The monk's arms dropped, he looked around, peering into the shadows, but I knew he couldn't see us.

'Who's there?' he asked but his words were hushed and it was then that I realised that he too did not wish to be discovered out that night. His movements were nothing to do with the village and his presence clandestine.

Amalia remained silent, suitably chastised and after a few moments the monk, satisfied that he was imagining noises, returned to his task of walking the foundations. This time he reached into the deep pocket of his robe, pulling out a pouch. He hesitated in his stride, then began to pour a thin whitish powder down into the ground.

Beside me, Lilly hissed under her breathe. *Ground bone,* she thought.

I smelt the air, wondering how she knew this as I couldn't tell at all what the powder was.

What does it mean? I asked.

Black magic.

Gabi's eyes scrutinised my face as Lilly and I conversed and guilt at his exclusion pulled at my insides. As she felt my remorse, Lilly's mind closed like a flower shrinking back as the sun's rays disappeared into nightfall. She looked deep into Gabi's eyes. I felt that call of power, something changed in the wind, and suddenly I knew she was talking to him too. I wondered how long they had been conversing this way, and if this skill was new to me only. I quelled the stupid jealousy that surged into my heart and returned my focus to our situation. Of course, if she could talk to me privately, then surely she could talk to him. Why hadn't I realised that possibility before?

The monk completed his circuit and a shower of ground bone was slowly sinking into the foundations. Once more he reached into his long pockets and pulled out a short, but sharp knife, and another pouch. When he opened the bag, a subtle herb smell drifted into the air and Lilly fidgeted beside me.

Powerful stuff! A combination of herbs, bones and dried and ground human organs.

I didn't reply. The monk scooped out fistfuls of the powder which, in the dark, had a reddish tinge, and scattered the stuff around him, turning in a circle with his arms outstretched.

He's creating an inner circle. A protection for himself from the magic he's using. It's likely he's going to raise some kind of demon, Lilly thought.

But, surely there is no such thing? I answered.

Lilly shrugged but didn't answer. Her eyes glowed with excitement and curiosity.

'What's he doing?' whispered Amalia, only to be silenced once again by Gabi.

On such a still night even the quietest sound carries and the monk looked around. His cold gaze fell in our direction; his eyes squinting as though this made him able to see through our shields. We were all cloaked, invisible. It was the first trick I'd learnt and even Amalia had mastered it with great success. At that moment, I looked at this mysterious monk, who was clearly human, and I wondered if somehow he could see through our barriers.

'It is as you said, Master,' the monk said under his breath in Latin. 'Strangers travel our lands. Thanatos, Lord of Death. Hear my plea. Help me protect the relics of today from the evils of the future.'

From somewhere within his robe, the monk extracted a small box, he knelt down within the smaller circle and using the knife he began to dig a hole. A wind picked up around the foundations, spinning motes of dust up into a small whirlwind. Miraculously the bone fragments remained on the earth but they lit up, luminous. Just as Lilly had said, the bone was the source of the power.

'He's calling on a spirit that will control the souls of all the dead who inhabit those fragments. Powerful juju,' Lilly whispered.

The circle closed in a whoosh of sound. Silence descended once more on the village, but within the foundations the monk was working his magic.

'Carduth, Lord of Time. I call you. Empower this circle; infuse these foundations with your power. Thanatos, Lord of Death. I beseech you; help me protect the earth from the undead evil.'

'We can talk now,' Lilly said. 'But still in quiet tones. The circle keeps all sound out as well as any interference from other elements.'

'Why do all these fanatics all sound the same?' I whispered. 'So much ridiculous ritual in the name of one religion or another ...'

'This is peculiar,' Lilly said. 'He's calling on Thanatos. In Greek mythology he's basically known as ...'

'Death,' interrupted Amalia. 'Or the person in charge of the dead ...'

Our eyes turned to the girl and for the first time I felt an intense curiosity about her origins.

'Yes,' Lilly agreed. 'He's very little known though. Rarely made an impact in Greek history as he was completely overshadowed by the tales of Hades … I'm surprised you've heard of him.'

Amalia shrugged.

Gabi and I remained silent but I was aware that something had changed in our little circle. We had now become aware that Amalia was not quite as simple as she at first appeared.

'Who the hell is Carduth, then?' asked Gabi.

'He is being hailed as "Lord of all Time",' I pointed out.

'That's right,' Amalia said. 'But I've never heard of him and I studied mythology … it was kind of a hobby.'

'Yes and I doubt this guy has ever heard of *Doctor Who*,' muttered Gabi.

The monk was now on his knees praying.

Lilly was silent and I wondered if she was thinking, like I was, that Amalia's sudden explanation was a little too convenient. It was almost as if she had anticipated any questions we might ask at a later date.

'You must tell us more about your hobby, sometime, Amalia' I said. 'You might have some useful information.'

Amalia shrugged again, 'It's silly really …'

At that moment a bright, sharp light grew immediately before the inner circle in which the monk stood.

We could hear nothing. As Lilly had pointed out the circle retained all sound.

Below our feet the ground rumbled. A tiny shudder shook the foundations of the church, but the cluster of houses remained still and silent. I thought again that a spell *had* been cast on the village and it kept the occupants asleep and unaware of the monk's practices. It wasn't too far a leap, considering the power the man was raising now. It wouldn't have been too difficult to administer some form of potion to the villagers.

I can lip read: a skill that has developed over the years, but was one that I had first honed in my days spent in the Vatican.

Therefore I watched the monk talk. He was chanting a psalm that was probably a spell. I quickly relayed it to my companions.

'Carduth, Lord of all Time. I empower you in this moment. Bring forth your sword of flame. Reveal the power of the saint.'

The light in the circle grew and within the glow appeared a shadowed figure.

Amalia gasped and shrank back in terror. 'It's him!'

He arrived, as we had, exiting from a time portal. Just as Amalia had described, the figure was wearing medieval armour. A shaped helmet covered his head and most of his face, cut out just above the lips. It revealed a cruel and cynical mouth, a squarish chin. A narrow opening ran across the helmet allowing its wearer to gaze out. I could just see his eyes: they blazed with inhuman zest. His entire body was covered in chainmail. Over his chest hung a highly polished breast plate and a white mantle baring a familiar symbol: an Ankh.

I felt a surge of rage emanate from Lilly seconds before she drew her sword.

'Murdering bastard! I'll kill him,' Lilly said through gritted teeth.

Sword arm raised, she ran headlong at the circle. It was completely irrational, and out of character for her to react so suddenly. But these were strange times and I hadn't taken into account the depth of feeling she had had for Harry. Lilly struck the energy field with her sword. Immediately the metal dented the air around the circle, a ripple echoed and jarred around the foundations. Lilly was powerful, the strongest of us all, and for one long moment I believed she would penetrate the monk's magic and kill the entity within. Then the force-field bounced back. The sword in Lilly's hand shattered like glass and she was thrown backwards, away from the circle. I caught her as she staggered then I looked on with horror as the monstrosity, which was Carduth, turned towards us.

Our shields were still in place but I was certain that both Carduth and the monk could see us now.

I stared through the slit into Carduth's eyes and hell came crashing down.

I found myself back in my hell dimension prison. This time I was fully aware of the horror around me. I could taste the stench of blood as it leaked out of the walls, dripped from the ceiling and seeped up from the floor in a pool of stink around my feet. The blood was black, vile; a foul smelling, poisonous ichor. I knew that under no circumstances must it touch my skin or I'd be lost here forever and Lilly might never again be able to retrieve me. The fluid began to expand, entrails and limbs – worse than any butcher's shop floor – took on a life of their own as they reached for me. I stepped back. Blood soaked fingers ripped at my hair, pulled me backwards …

I struggled like a mad man in her arms before I realised that Lilly was pulling me away from the circle. As I broke eye contact with Carduth the world righted itself and I found I was still in the eleventh century before the foundations. I met Lilly's eyes. They were wide and scared for the first time in all the years I'd known her.

The monk's circle was holding fast and he stood wide-mouthed within the safe confines of his inner circle of power. As Carduth approached the edge of the outer circle the spell ignited and he was thrown backwards onto the soil before the monk. The monk stared at him, their eyes met and a silent scream of terror punctuated the monk's open mouth. Carduth was up and on his feet instantly, moving towards us once more. But he stopped short of the circle this time and slowly began to withdraw something from a leather pouch that was tied to his waist.

'Through the portal! Now!' Lilly yelled.

Gabi and Amalia ran quickly towards the waiting doorway. I was still dazed as I let Lilly pull me along. A sharp pain began to clutch at my chest. My heart burned. The breath expelled from my lungs and I stumbled against Lilly. She staggered, gasped, but continued to drag us both closer to the portal.

A surge of energy exuded from the doorway and the strange waterfall began to slow and appeared to be freezing over.

'It's closing!' Gabi shouted.

'Like hell it is,' Lilly said and pushing Gabi and Amalia

through the portal ahead of us, she dived forward, taking my confused and trembling body along with her.

We fell, rather than walked, back through into our own time. Lilly and I rolled as we tumbled over the ruins of the church. My head smashed into the hard stone of the door frame, bringing my tumbling body to a halt. I was battered and bruised, stunned briefly from the fall and from the gallop through time but I quickly staggered to my feet to find Lilly poised before the doorway.

The portal closed as a wave of ice rippled over the surface like a flash-freeze and the door disappeared. Lilly fell to her knees and stared at the spot, her chest heaving up and down as her lungs gasped in ragged breaths.

My ears were ringing, but as my body rapidly healed I became aware once more of the sounds around us. The noises I had taken for granted prior to crossing the portal. A plane was flying overhead. It was the sound of the twenty-first century.

I looked up at the sky.

Amalia was crying again. This time I understood her tears. Carduth was a terrifying adversary.

'Chez,' said Lilly as she came out of her daze. 'What's happened to your shirt?'

I looked down and saw the scorch marks and briefly felt again the searing pain that had warmed my chest prior to returning to our time.

'He has a weapon. I told you!' Amalia cried.

I glanced at Lilly, Gabi and Amalia in turn. Everyone of us had the stain, directly in the place where our hearts were.

'Did anyone actually see what it was?' I asked.

Lilly didn't answer. Gabi and Amalia shook their heads.

'We were too busy running,' Gabi said. 'But I felt …'

'Like your heart was being burnt out of your chest?' Lilly whispered.

'Yes,' I answered. 'What *was* it?'

'I don't know,' Lilly said. 'But I'm going to find out.'

18
A Change in Dynamics

Present Day

'Who or what is Carduth?' Gabi asked again as we closed the door of the lair behind us.

Back in Rhuddlan it felt as though we had put some distance between us and this mysterious creature. It was strange how we had bolted home without discussion, leaving behind the ruins at Lourdes and the Castle in Stockholm.

'Research is our friend,' said Lilly firing up her laptop.

'I've never heard of him,' Amalia said. 'And as I said, I studied mythology. He doesn't exist.'

Nevertheless Lilly searched the internet but as Amalia had commented, no such person showed up in any mythology.

'There isn't even a name that fits or is close, that's assuming we have the spelling right of course.' Lilly said.

She tried various spelling options, but still came up with nothing. I felt useless. Technology was still something that eluded me and I had no concept of what it meant to use the internet. I knew that it contained infinite amounts of information but the whole idea of it felt like a big black hole. I couldn't get past the feeling of unreality when I attempted to use this kind of gadget.

'It's because you're totally attached to the real world,' Lilly said. 'And actually this is all virtual reality. It will take some time but one day you'll figure it all out if you're interested enough.'

I wasn't convinced I ever would be.

Amalia went to her room and I found myself alone for the first time in several days with my two companions. I sat down beside Lilly as she scrolled through 'pages' on 'sites' trying to take in exactly what she was doing.

Gabi sat down in the armchair across from us. He watched us silently but as I glanced up at him, he appeared on the brink of asking a question.

'This is hopeless,' said Lilly putting the machine down on the coffee table. 'I can't find anything and I feel like it's all a complete waste of time.'

'I don't do angst,' Gabi said suddenly. 'And so, I'm going to bow out gracefully.'

'What are you talking about?' Lilly asked, but I already knew the answer to that, had felt it all along.

'You two belong together. You've had experiences that have given you a bond beyond the one you have with me ...' Gabi answered.

'What are you saying?' Lilly said.

'I love you, and you love me. That's never going to change.'

'Of course it isn't!' Lilly said.

'The thing is, you're not *in love* with me now.'

I said nothing. Gabi spoke the truth, even if Lilly hadn't realised it. Besides, I was selfish, I wanted her to myself – hadn't I already declared that?

'No,' she denied. 'Gabi –'

'Please darling. Let's make this easy on us all.'

'We can't do this now. We have an unknown enemy that's out to get us!' Lilly said. 'We need to be together.'

'Brushing this under the carpet won't help us be strong, Lilly.'

I left the room, allowing them time to talk things through as I felt I had no place being there, eavesdropping on the end of their relationship as lovers.

I went upstairs, deliberately tuning out from them as they talked.

'It's all going well ...'

I stopped. Amalia was talking to someone in her room. I

moved to the door to see who she had allowed to enter, and then stopped as it occurred to me I wasn't hearing a response to her one-sided conversation. She was on a mobile phone in her room and I could hear snatches of a very guarded conversation.

'No. I mean it … trust me now … Gabi and I …'

A rustle of movement made me aware that she was coming to the door of her room. Surely she sensed I was there? I backed away silently, dropping over the balcony down to the bottom of the stairs.

In the kitchen I began to clatter around loudly. Then I tuned back into Amalia.

'I have to go … think someone …'

It was difficult to zone out the muted sounds of Gabi and Lilly talking in the other room and so I heard no more of this strange exchange. I decided I would watch Amalia closely from then on. Deep down, like Lilly, I hadn't trusted her. It was peculiar how none of us even thought to ask if she had a mobile phone. We had taken her at face value and during those strange times it appeared to have been a mistake.

I thought of going in to the lounge and interrupting Gabi and Lilly, of taking them upstairs so we could confront the girl but that would have been melodramatic and certainly not productive. Whatever her agenda or motive for being with us, Amalia wasn't going to just admit it. No. The best solution would be to wait and watch.

Lilly came into the kitchen and I poured some freshly warmed blood into a cup for her. She sipped it, leaning against one of the cupboards. I began to tidy up, moving used pots into the dishwasher.

'It's weird how we continue to do mundane, normal things,' Lilly said. 'I mean, shouldn't we be living in dust-filled crypts in rags? Yet here we are. In luxury. Washing the dishes.'

'We may be immortal but we aren't monsters,' I said.

'Yes we are. But we're not revenants and we have highly developed intellect.'

'Well, some of us do,' I smiled looking up to the ceiling.

Lilly smiled back but her eyes were sad.

'Everything okay?' I asked.

She nodded. Her thoughts floated into my mind as she took another sip of blood. *Gabi and I are through. You got what you wanted. I'm all yours.*

You don't seem too happy about that, I thought.

I am, Darling. It's just ... She struggled to form her thoughts, tiredness emanated from her mind.

The end of an era ... ? I suggested.

'Yes,' she answered and her shields dropped down, closing me off from her thoughts and emotions.

As Amalia entered the kitchen Lilly began to bustle around like a mother hen, offering the girl blood, and even warming it for her in the microwave. I said nothing. Normally Lilly had little to do with the girl, but suddenly she wanted to make her welcome.

Putting down my cup I left the room and went out into the hallway. It wasn't the right time to tell Lilly about Amalia's secret phone conversation and anyway I wasn't sure what good that would do until I had more information. I resolved to watch the girl, perhaps even try to get my hands on her mobile phone. *Although, that could be pointless since I can't use one of those damn things!*

Upstairs Gabi was moving his stuff from the bedroom.

'What are you doing?' I asked.

'Didn't Lilly tell you? I'm moving in with Amalia.'

'Oh! Does Amalia know?'

'Yes. While you two were "getting a room" in Stockholm. Amalia and I got to know each other a little better too ...'

'Ah. I'm really not very observant ...' I said. 'Listen. Gabi. I ...'

'Don't say it.'

'What?'

'That you're sorry, because I know you're not. Nothing is really going to change around here. But this small adjustment will make us all a little less tense, maybe ease up some of our jealousies.'

'I am sorry,' I said. 'I don't want to cause you pain.'

I left him as he silently continued to move into the other

room. There really wasn't any more we could say. But we are grownups: a few hundred years on the Earth teaches you that angst really is a pointless pastime.

As I entered the kitchen I met Amalia's eyes across the room, they gave nothing away except that she was happy and relaxed. I smiled at her and she smiled back. The conversation could have been innocent and until I was sure of anything else I wasn't going to upset this new domestic arrangement. It suited me far too well. Lilly was mine. We were safe in Rhuddlan. What could possibly go wrong?

19
The Archaeologist

Five and a half months ago

Björn Adelman was working towards a deadline as he sat at his desk writing his latest research paper. He had given the office strict instructions not to disturb him, that's why he was a little annoyed when Anja, his undergraduate researcher, burst into the room with the packing note for a parcel that had arrived from Scotland.

'Anja!' Björn said, 'I said I wasn't to be disturbed.'

'I know, Björn, but this arrived and I knew you'd want to see it as soon as possible.'

Anja waved the documents with a small, slender hand. She was an attractive girl, with long mousy hair, blue eyes and a warm smile. She was incredibly smart too: in line for a first in her degree. Björn had spent many hours working with her; her research diligence had been unsurpassed by any students he had worked with before which was why he had given her the opportunity to work so closely with him.

They'd first met while camping out at a dig. Sex among the researchers was casual. It meant nothing more than a momentary satisfaction and was always fun. Anja had been very accommodating and Björn had soon learnt that she was a good worker as well as being very good in bed. Anja never over-stepped the mark in daily business either, so Björn carried on their relationship beyond that initial one-night stand. That's why he knew she wouldn't disturb him on a whim.

'Okay. What is it?' he asked, pushing aside his keyboard.

Anja placed the document on the desk with an unopened letter. 'From your friend in Scotland.'

Björn looked down at the delivery note and the envelope. 'That's peculiar. Noble normally phones me before he sends anything for me to look at.'

'So you weren't expecting anything?' Anja said, a slight frown creasing her brow as she stepped back from Björn's desk. 'Sorry. I thought it might be urgent.'

Björn rubbed his short beard as he picked up the delivery note and examined it.

John Noble had been sending artefacts to him for years. Usually he would find a gold chalice, or candelabra or the occasional cross covered in precious jewels. Björn would find him the best price and the Church would never know. Björn had a group of private collectors of religious items who never asked questions, but paid the best price without quibble. This arrangement had worked well for them over the last few years.

Björn opened the envelope, looked down at the letter and frowned. This *was* unusual. Noble's normal careful writing was hurried and frantic as he explained the origins of the relic.

'Well?' asked Anja.

'Oh. It's nothing.' Björn said quickly. 'But you were right to bring it to my attention.'

'Should I unpack it and begin an initial examination for you?'

'No!' Björn said, and he knew by her expression that he had responded a little too quickly. 'This is a private matter,' he explained. 'A favour for a friend. I can't justify using University resources on it. It's something I'll do in my spare time.'

Anja left but not before Björn gave her an instruction to bring the box straight into his office.

When the door finally closed behind her, and the box sat on the desk before him, Björn began to worry what he would find. He was unsure whether any of his collectors would be interested in a relic of this nature. He had never had requests for these things, but then he had never had them to offer before. Even so, the instruction he received from Noble was to 'examine' the contents and feed back on his findings, not to find a buyer.

He opened the crate and rummaged inside, his research papers and deadline long since forgotten in the excitement of examining this new discovery. Pushing aside straw, he found the bubble-wrapped item but he didn't withdraw it from the box. As Björn stripped away the packaging his fingers brushed against wood and an extraordinary, warm, tingle leaked up into his hand. He looked down into the crate. There he was greeted by the sight of the dirty purple cloth. In his excitement he pushed the fabric aside and stared down at a symbol of the Ankh.

'How peculiar,' he murmured.

He reached inside, carefully extracting the box and began his examination. Externally it was in good order, well preserved, though roughly carved. This was surprising considering that it had been found, according to Noble's letter, merely protected by the old velvet cloth in which it had been wrapped. Björn ran his hands over the engraving, it was old and faded but still very visible and considering where the box was found, Björn knew that the symbol was completely inappropriate.

He opened his top drawer, took out his camera and snapped a digital photograph of the engraving. Then, connecting his camera to his computer, he began to download the picture straight into his database. Once on the database, Björn set the computer a task to search for anything in the archives that showed this inscription. While the computer compiled a file of possible connections, Björn returned to the box. His hand rested on the top as he carefully drew a line in the wax seal with his envelope opener. The box grew warm once more under his fingers and he had the distinct impression that something throbbed and pulsed inside it. It was a disquieting feeling.

The seal broke easily, but Björn paused. He was overwhelmed by the certainty that there was something alive inside. He lifted it to his ear and listened.

Silence.

I'm going crazy, he thought, once more placing the container down on his desk. *What did I expect to hear?*

Carefully, he began to prise off the lid. It was stiff and required a lot of force, but as the lid began to loosen the impression of warmth rushed into his hands once more. Björn stopped. Perplexed he stared down at the symbol, then back at the screen of his computer.

A list of over a hundred possible meanings were downloading into the file. Mostly, Björn saw that the connection was all to do with the Egyptian Goddess Sekhmet, and there was some information about how early Christian's used this sign as the symbol of their religion. He knew he would be wading through lots of irrelevant material before he could possibly find the right correlation.

Something nagged in the back of his brain. Perhaps he had come across a similar symbol years ago, but had long since forgotten? Björn returned to his computer, flicking through files of mysteries unsolved but nothing jumped out at him immediately. Sitting back in his chair his gaze fell once more on the relic box and the crate behind it.

He stood, lifted the crate from his desk and placed it on the floor beside his chair, then glanced down into the straw. He had forgotten about the piece of blackened fabric in his excitement to view the box. Björn reached back into the crate and pulled the soiled material out. He held it out before him. The first side was completely blank and so he flicked the cloth over and here Björn found something very strange indeed. It was faint and faded, almost gone but this was a symbol he did recognise. An eye-shaped emblem, with a Celtic triskele inside. He had come across this pattern many times, at various points and places in history, but had never quite found any reference to its significance. Except once …

Björn sat back down and after a moment's thought as to where it was to be found, pulled up the file. The triskele appeared on the screen. It was a photograph of a hieroglyphic tablet found in Egypt and this particular one had been dated 2000 BC. There was a corrupted drawing of a female figure beside it. Only this female, unlike all others drawn at that time, had yellow hair, not black, and it was long and flowing down to her waist. Half of the image was missing, but Björn could discern a belt strapped around her waist – with what could be a scabbard hanging down at her side. It was an unusual image, but one that he had thought related to some fictional Goddess that never took off in Egyptian history. Björn remembered this artefact well as there had been many discussions regarding its authenticity. One idea was that somehow the picture was a hoax but it had never been proven.

Björn stared at the information on the tablet. He had always dismissed this one as superstition but today with the strange box on his desk, he began to wonder. The tablet told of a powerful creature that drank blood and described the only way it could be destroyed. The vampires, for that was definitely what this referred to and there was no point in denying it, had their own symbol of power. Björn glanced down at the cloth, now spread out over the box before him, and back at the screen. There was no doubt in his mind that this was indeed the same symbol.

Björn looked once more at the letter sent by Noble. *The church was built in 1455. That would be when the relic was placed there.* Two symbols, thousands of years apart. One found in Egypt, one Scotland. The distance and the time scales were too great for there to be any real connection. But then Björn had seen this emblem in other places, in other parts of the world: he just needed to remember where.

He pulled the cloth away from the box, his curiosity as to its contents increased by the new information. He found his gaze held by the Ankh. It felt like a warning, yet the Ankh had always been used for positive things. It meant safety.

Björn picked up the box again. The lid was loose now, all he had to do was lift the top and look inside, but something about the whole situation made him cautious. He wasn't a religious man by nature, his choice of career had dispelled any myths of the supernatural, and he didn't believe in magic. But something from his childhood made him think twice about disturbing the relic. After all relics were supposed to be the body parts of saints.

'What's in there?' asked Anja as she placed a cup of coffee on the desk beside him.

Björn looked up, surprised to find her in his office.

'A relic,' he said without thinking. 'I didn't hear you come in.'

'You've been in here hours. I thought you'd need this.'

'Thank you.'

Björn took the coffee and sipped at it, glancing briefly at his computer: the screen was on power save, that only usually happened after an hour of inactivity. Björn blinked, looked at his watch. Three hours had passed since Anja first brought in the box and he couldn't remember most of that time.

'So, what kind of relic is it?' Anja asked.

'I don't know …' Björn answered. He felt sluggish, confused as though he had fallen asleep. He could hear the regular strike of a drum, like a beating heart, thumping steadily over and over again. It was mesmerising.

'You haven't opened it yet?'

'No.'

'Probably not much point anyway,' Anja said. 'It'll just be a shrivelled finger or something.'

'Yes. Probably.' Björn answered. He sipped the coffee again hoping it would revive him.

'I'll just take this away,' said Anja. 'It won't be important. You can forget all about it now.'

'I will forget about it,' Björn repeated.

Anja bent over the relic box – Björn noticed she was wearing thick black leather gloves – then she picked up the cloth, turning it around so that the emblem was facing downwards. She wrapped the fabric over and around the box. Only then did the beating seem to stop.

As Anja took the box away, Björn fell asleep. He dreamed of opening an unusual box and seeing what it contained …

20
A Plan

Present Day

As before the portals emerged around us, but this time Lilly was perfectly in control. The four of us were standing inside a circle she had drawn in the sand. As each door arrived Lilly scrutinised it, sending out that subtle beam of energy that set my teeth on edge and made the hairs stand up all over my body. As she waded through them, closing all the ones that she didn't require, Gabi, Amalia and myself remained quiet. It was as though we were all afraid to disturb her for fear that this disruption to her concentration would cause some major problem.

'This one,' Lilly said. 'It goes back to 1314.'

'We'll stick out like sore thumbs,' Gabi said. 'We're hardly dressed for the middle ages.'

'That's why we need to cloak ourselves as soon as we arrive.'

I didn't ask where we were going, I already knew and my mind went back to the moment when this plan was first formulated. Now we were executing it and, for better or worse, the four of us were going to step across the threshold of yet another portal in time.

'I found this on the internet,' Lilly handed out a printed picture to each of us. 'We need to have a plan.'

I looked down at the paper in my hand and saw the image of a knight. The armour was the same as our mysterious Carduth, with the exception of the symbol on the knight's white mantle. This one was of a bright red cross.

'Knights Templar …' Amalia said and I saw a slight flush appear in her cheeks as she caught herself. A wave of confusion emanated from her. She didn't like to display her knowledge. As the days passed I observed these minor lapses and became convinced that she knew a lot more than she was letting on.

'The outfit is just the same,' Lilly explained. 'With the exception of the Ankh on our guy instead of the cross.'

'You think they are connected?' asked Gabi.

Lilly had been doing her research and she had discovered the origins of the Knights and the time of their supposed downfall.

'To give you a quick rundown. They were first established in 1129. Rapidly built a reputation as skilled fighters in the crusades, but also accumulated a huge financial empire. They grew in size and wealth for almost two centuries. Then a jealous king, who owed them a lot of money, accused them of being witches and had them all tortured and burnt. Modern day rumours say the Knights' organisation still exists, that a few of them escaped and survived. Factually, much of the property and wealth owned by the Templars was never recovered. There had been rumours they grew into the *Illuminati*. Equally, the Masons are also supposed to be connected. All of this is of course just conjecture.'

'What's this got to do with us?' asked Amalia.

'Don't you see? The *Illuminati* is purported to be one of the most powerful conglomerates in the world. They are supposed to have fingers in political pies as well as corporations.'

'I still don't get it.'

'Amalia's right,' Gabi said. 'It's only a very vague connection we have here. I can't see why they'd be involved at all. How would they even know about us? And if they did, why not attack years ago?'

Lilly wouldn't be put off; she was convinced that the Knights were connected with Carduth but she couldn't understand the suddenness of the attack either.

'Let's forget the *Illuminati* then … They feed into conspiracy theories worldwide, but there may not be any connection with our guys. However, the Knights Templar is the closest thing we have to this.'

I could see the familiarity but didn't know what it meant to us – or what we could do.

'How do we find out more?' I asked. 'Like you said, they aren't supposed to exist anymore …'

'True. But we could go back to the time when they *did.*'

It took a moment for her words to sink in, and for us to realise the significance of her suggestion.

'Time-travel? Again?' asked Gabi. 'Isn't that a little risky?'

'It might be, but it's the only thing we have to our advantage. Something is out there. I, for one, don't want to wait for it to catch us up. I want to attack first, ask questions later.'

'How?' I asked.

'We call a door and we find out what really happened to the Templars.'

The door was positioned about five miles away from where we stood and out to sea. Lilly closed down all of the open portals and then dropped the protective circle.

'How do we get there? Swim?' asked Amalia.

Gabi picked her up, 'Like this,' he said, taking off and heading out towards the door. Lilly took my hand and we followed.

We hovered before it, until Gabi took the initiative and flew through, still holding Amalia. I followed and Lilly came through last.

The portal opened up on the river Seine in Paris, France. This time I wasn't disorientated at all and was alert enough to quickly cloak myself, floating to the bank little more than an inch above the water. Ahead of Lilly and I, Gabi still held Amalia in his arms and as he landed beside me I noticed we were directly behind Notre Dame Cathedral.

Lilly landed and began to walk rapidly around the church. She had briefed us thoroughly before we left and so I recognised that the soldiers surrounding the place were those of Philip IV of France. Just as we expected, a scaffold had been raised at the front of the church. It was March 19, 1314. We had come to see two men, Jacques de Molay and Geoffroi de Charney, sentenced and we wanted to hear and see all that occurred as the events played out.

A crowd had gathered around the site. People in this century were even more grotesque than in my own time where public executions were fewer but Machiavellian murders were common behind closed doors. King Philip IV had ordered the execution of these once-powerful men as a way of erasing his debt to the Templars. Over the last few years many Templars had died at the hands of his soldiers and this was supposed to be a key moment in time.

This was the day of sentencing, and as the Archbishop of Sens came out onto the platform the crowd began to cheer. He was wearing a long robe and white mantel, dressed in fact as though he were about to give Mass to the crowd. Several cardinals followed, standing around in a sycophantic bundle. Then a ragged group of men were brought forward, chained, filthy and flea-ridden.

A soldier stood below the scaffold, holding a large parchment before him.

'Jacques de Molay, Templar Grand Master, Geoffroi de Charney, Master of Normandy, Hugues de Peraud, Visitor of France, and Godefroi de Gonneville, Master of Aquitaine. Step forward and receive your sentence from the King, the Church and from God.'

They were chained together by wrist and ankle and so they staggered up the steps like rhythmless puppets. At the top of the staircase a soldier grabbed the arm of the first man, dragged him to the front of the scaffold which caused the others behind to stumble along rapidly, almost falling over each other.

'Jacques de Molay. You were the Templar Grand Master,' the Archbishop began. 'You have confessed your heresy. This day you will be sentenced and begin your punishment for your crimes against God, the Pope and the King.'

Molay drew up his chains, forcing his bowed back straight. He looked out into the crowd. Fierce blue eyes, ignited with anger and pride and the crowd took an involuntary step back. Until that moment maybe some of the crowd hadn't believed that the Knights were witches and magicians but there was something in Molay's eyes that told them it was probably true.

'People of Paris,' he called out over the square, 'I have been imprisoned for seven years now, awaiting the sentence today. I have been called heretic. Witch. Accused of having relationships with Satan himself. I spent my life an honourable man. The code of the Templars, to protect the weak and fight heresy, means nothing now. The confession I gave was tortured from me. I am no heretic. I have loved and honoured my country. But I *am* a traitor!'

The crowd jeered. They still expected his full admission.

'I'm a traitor to my order!' Molay continued. 'I have betrayed my faithful followers and for that I deserve no less than to die. I will not admit to your allegations. I did nothing wrong. But I did give in under torture. I lied to save myself further pain and now I truly regret my cowardice.'

At that moment the man chained next to him came forward.

'I confess!' he yelled. 'I'm Geoffroi de Charney, Master of Normandy. I confess to having betrayed my order under torture. I am no heretic. Confessions were forced from us under duress.'

Although Charney lacked the eloquence of Molay, his speech was no less well received; the crowd yelled and cheered in excitement. They had expected a routine sentencing.

The Archbishop and the cardinals stood open-mouthed and in shock. They didn't react as the two men began to tell the crowd the story of their torture.

'I refuse to accept this sentence,' Molay continued. 'These men are your enemies. Hypocrites and murderers. The Templars have fought for you, for Christianity! Yet this is how we are repaid ...'

At a sign from the Archbishop a soldier appeared and, with clenched hands, he hit Molay in the face. Molay fell in a heap at his feet, pulling down the other three men on the chain link. Blood burst from his nose and mouth but he made no attempt to cover his face. The crowd fell silent as they watched the beating until Charney kicked out at the soldier, in defence of his friend, whipping the brute's feet from under him, so that he fell forward, pitching over the edge of the scaffold. He fell into the throng with a grunt, then pushed and shoved his way through the laughing crowd, running back up the steps to renew his assault, this time on Charney.

'Stop!' yelled the Archbishop immediately. 'Take them away.'

Lilly told us what would be coming next. The cardinals and Archbishop would convene to discuss their public humiliation. But the King would take matters rapidly into his own hands.

'This is our moment of opportunity,' Lilly said. 'We need to get into the gaol before the men are sentenced to immediate execution.'

'Why?' asked Gabi.

'We have to talk to them and discover the truth about Carduth.'

Still cloaked I leapt into the air, landing silently before the scaffold stairs. Lilly was directly behind me. We left Amalia and Gabi outside to watch for any change in atmosphere or the appearance of Carduth.

We followed the ragged band, as they were beaten and battered, dragged unceremoniously from the scaffold. They were thrown into a cart, then wheeled rapidly away from Notre Dame and back to the Bastille.

We reached the prison seconds after the main door was closed.

'Damn it!' said Lilly. 'The Bastille is notoriously difficult to break in or out of. The front entrance would have been the easiest way.'

At that moment a small boy ran past. He picked up a large stone from the ground and hurled it at the door to the prison's main entrance. The boy ran as fast as his small legs could carry him, diving down behind a wall. Within seconds the door flew open and a large man, with greasy black hair, lurched out of the doorway. He glanced out in the street.

'Damn you! One of these days you'll be in here and then we'll see who's doing the knocking!' he yelled. 'Little bastard.'

As he leaned on the door, his beady eyes darting around the street, the urchin sneaked away in the opposite direction. The door-keeper soon grew tired of looking around and began to withdraw just as a young woman walked up, carrying a basket of strong-smelling cheese.

'Fresh cheese, *Monsieur*?' asked the girl and the door-keeper leered at her. Leaving his post he stepped forward.

A few moments of bartering later and the door-keeper returned with a wedge of cheese and closed the entrance door behind him. By then, still cloaked, we'd easily slipped inside. It was a convenient window of opportunity and it made me nervous that we had entered so very easily.

'Arrogance,' Lilly said. 'They believe this place invulnerable, but they didn't count on a two invisible immortals just walking in.'

Once we'd passed through the main reception, there was just one more gate to traverse and we were through into the prison itself. We made our way through the narrow corridors, following the sound of the chains. Rats scurried in and out of the cells. The place was foul. It smelt overwhelmingly of shit and piss. Luckily for us Molay and Charney were deposited in a holding cell on the ground floor which meant we didn't have to go down into the bowels of the place, but the stench from below permeated the floors, drifting upwards to assault my sensitive nostrils.

'These two are for the fire for sure,' a soldier said as he threw the two men into a rat-infested cell. 'No point in taking you farther down, you'll be back on the scaffold before the day's done. Burning like the witches you are.'

Molay said nothing, he sat down on the dirty floor as though he had entered a salon full of aristocracy.

'Scum,' Charney muttered as he sat beside Molay. 'God punishes sinners. I don't believe we deserve to die, Jacques, old friend, but if this is our day then at least we have told the truth and our souls will be cleansed.'

Molay nodded. 'It was the honourable thing to do.'

Lilly appeared beside me, holding a key in her hand. I looked around and saw the two soldiers sleeping off her bite. She smiled at me wickedly. A small smudge of blood was on her lips. I kissed her, licking away the traces and then we turned towards the cell and uncloaked for the first time since arriving in this century.

Molay and Charney didn't look up as the key turned in the lock. They were on their knees praying. I suppose they expected more blows from the soldiers. Or perhaps they hoped for a merciful death. Either way, both men remained in prayer, heads bowed.

'Come with me if you want to live,' said Lilly.

At the sound of a female voice, Molay and Charney's heads snapped up.

'All we want is some answers,' I said. 'Then you can escape here.'

I could almost see the doubt and suspicion creeping in behind their eyes. Molay scanned our clothing, recognising it immediately as alien to their world. Lilly's gorgeous long curls were tied back into a ponytail, she was wearing black leather trousers, a black sweater and her sword belt, though empty since her sword had been destroyed, was slung over her hips, but there was no mistaking her female shape.

'Who are you?' asked Charney. His eyes were round and confused but he stood immediately, pulling Molay up with him.

'Let's rid you of those first,' Lilly said. She stepped forward, touched the locks lightly and the chains fell off to the floor.

Lightened of their burden the men could move more rapidly and they did so. Backing away in terror to the rear of the cell.

'I mean you no harm,' Lilly said. 'Look. The soldiers will be returning within an hour to take you to be burned on the express orders of the King. If you want to live you need to come with us. Time is running out.'

Molay was the bravest and the first to step forward. He took Lilly's hand and she swept him up, turning rapidly and running with supernatural speed. I scooped up Charney before he could protest, silencing him with a quick stare into his eyes.

Retracing our steps through the corridors we found the gatekeeper sleeping on a pallet by the door. He barely stirred as Lilly opened the door and we were outside again.

I gulped in the fresh air, surprised to find I'd been mostly holding my breath inside the prison. The escape had been too easy though and I still felt a little concerned.

This could all still be a trap! I thought and Lilly nodded to me, taking flight with the terrified Molay still clasped in her arms.

About a mile outside the city I flew down into a shallow forest and deposited Charney by a slow running river.

'The Scarlet Pimpernel would be proud,' Lilly said landing beside me.

Lilly closed her eyes and I felt a flutter of her power cross my mind as she sent Gabi a message telling him where to find us. This was the first time she had used the telepathic power at any distance, but it was effortless to her.

The two men fell to their knees before the water, scooping it up into their dirty hands.

'I hope that water's safe,' Lilly said.

I shrugged, 'They've been living in a filthy prison, and I don't think it will matter much if it isn't.'

'How are you?' Lilly asked them as the men recovered and turned trembling towards us.

'What are you?' Charney asked.

'You wouldn't believe me if I told you,' Lilly said. 'But I hope you do believe that we don't intend to harm you.'

'You saved us …' Molay said. 'But why?'

'You may know something that could help us with a problem we have,' I answered.

'I'll cut to the chase,' Lilly said. 'Do you know of anyone who goes by the name of Carduth?'

Molay and Charney shook their heads.

'Never heard that name before,' Molay said. 'Are you a witch?'

Lilly folded her arms across her chest, the movement was defensive, but she looked relaxed. I knew she felt sympathy for the men, just as I did. They were pawns in a bigger game of chess the king was playing.

'Yes. I guess I am a witch – of sorts,' Lilly confirmed. 'But witchcraft isn't anything to do with Satan. I don't even know if there is a God, never mind a devil.'

'You confirm all of our own thoughts,' Molay said. 'So much evil has been done in God's name.'

'The thing is, there's some evil being done to us, in our world,' said Lilly. 'And we don't know by whom. But we recognised the armour as being similar to the Templars. However, instead of the cross, they have this sign.'

Lilly picked up a stick and drew the symbol of the Ankh on the ground.

Molay stepped back surprised.

'I know this sign. But …' he turned to glance at Charney.

Charney looked down. 'Yes,' he nodded. 'The Archbishop had something like that. It was on a necklace. He wears it under his cassock.'

'How do you know?' Lilly asked.

'He's a lover of boys,' Charney shrugged. 'I caught him with one of the *castrati*.'

Charney explained how he had threatened to expose the bishop if he discovered he had abused any of the other boys in the choir.

'I was arrested soon after that,' Molay said. 'I knew he had the King's ear, but was surprised at how powerful he had become.'

'We heard that the King had you arrested because he owed a lot of money to the Templars,' I said.

'He did,' Molay said. 'But we were never going to ask for it back. He's the King.'

'I suspect,' Lilly said. 'That the Archbishop implied you were. If he wanted you out of the way, it was the best thing to do. If you were accused of heresy, no one would believe any accusations you could throw at the church.'

Charney nodded, 'Precisely.'

21
Carduth's Army

1314

The four of us wandered through the streets of Paris like phantoms haunting the city. After obtaining food and clothing and horses for Molay and Charney we'd seen them ride away.

'We'll be fine,' Molay said.

The Templars did have hidden wealth and the two of them knew how to retrieve enough money to get them out of the country. They would begin a new life. The order, once powerful world-wide would have to remain an underground society from then on.

'How can we let them go?' asked Amalia. 'It could change the course of history. They are supposed to die today.'

'I just can't return them to the prison,' Lilly said. 'I don't know why but it *feels* like the right thing to do.'

'But if they do rebuild their order, maybe it is them who control Carduth.' Gabi suggested.

'I doubt it,' said Lilly. 'If anything they'll be on our side from now on.'

Back at Notre Dame a fire was lit and two hooded figures burned. History, it seemed had not changed at all. We stood invisible in the crowd. I could smell death in the air, long before the flames lapped up the legs of each of the victims.

'Some more poor stooges …' Lilly said.

The crowd believed that it was Charney and Molay who died in the flames however and we did nothing to change that view. History was safe and I believed, like Lilly, that our intervention had changed nothing. It all came back to Lilly's philosophy about time and time travel. She always believed that nothing we could do in the present would affect anything that had officially happened in the past. Although I admit I never understood it.

'Why do you think that is?' Gabi had asked once.

Lilly shrugged, 'Maybe history always has a way of righting itself. When I was thrown back in time and had no control over the doors, I was worried about all of my actions, all of the time, in the event that I did something to change the future. But my reasoning was bizarre. After all I took victims, and thought nothing of their deaths. If you think about it rationally, to us "history" has already occurred. Therefore our actions, in the here and now to us, actually have already occurred in our historical past. I doubt we can do anything that isn't meant to happen.'

'So, what are we going to do next?' I asked.

'I'm going to see the Archbishop,' Lilly said. 'And this time I'm going to use glamour rather than stealth to get in there.'

I watched Lilly turn herself into a boy. She appeared to be wearing clothing of the day but in Italian style. A doublet and hose, a short cape slung over narrow shoulders. The curves of her body smoothed out to androgynous lines. Her hair became wispier, less curly and turned black. As for her eyes, the green I was always used to turned dark brown.

'The benefits of being a witch,' Lilly smiled, but it wasn't Lilly's smile I could see. Instead it was the arrogant sneer of a teenage Italian boy.

We found clothing for the rest of us so that we could avoid draining our strength. Using the cold invisibility so much brought on the hunger so much quicker. Already we had to feed and so we went out, Lilly leading the way as she always did, and found sustenance in a soldier's barracks. We fed from the men as they slept but didn't kill.

'It's really not much fun doing it this way,' complained Amalia.

'We need to be unobserved,' Lilly said. 'No suspicion or

superstition to rear its head while we are here.'

We learnt that the Archbishop held audiences twice a week. His first, soon after the execution, however, had been cancelled without explanation. So we had to wait, enjoy the city and its delights for several days before we could see him.

'We could just call a door and jump to the day,' suggested Amalia.

'No. Every time we do, we risk some warning going to Carduth. And until we know all that he is capable of, or where he is, I'd rather be subtle.' Lilly said.

'But there aren't any bathrooms here,' Amalia whined. 'I feel so dirty.'

'We could go skinny dipping in a lake outside the city,' Gabi suggested smiling, but Amalia sulked on and Lilly pointedly ignored it.

It was stressful having the girl along. I constantly had to watch everything she did. It was particularly challenging preventing her from talking loudly in English in the town when we were visible.

'Amalia,' Gabi said softly. 'We need to remain unnoticed. Don't you understand what we're doing here is dangerous?'

'These are mortals. They can't hurt us,' Amalia said. 'I could crush them with my bare hands.'

'Maybe so, but this is a suspicious era. They fear the supernatural and we must avoid being seen. Please. Do this for me. Discretion at all times.' Gabi smiled at her but the smile didn't reach his eyes. He was rapidly becoming as disenchanted as the rest of us.

'I'm hungry,' Amalia murmured. 'Get me someone to eat, Gabi. Please. Then I'll feel less grumpy.'

A few minutes later, Lilly returned with a young peasant boy and casually handed him over to Amalia.

'Eat. Then shut whining. But he's your kill, so you dispose of the body.'

I smiled. Remembering how that was always a rule with her.

A few days later the audience was arranged with the Archbishop. I would take Lilly, pretending to be her older brother, and request that he be seen as possible *castrati* for the choir. It wasn't really the Archbishop's job to interview the boys, but he had made it his personal mission.

'Singing to God is a holy practice,' he said as Lilly and I stood before him. 'Only the truly devout should be permitted to join the choir at Notre Dame.'

The Archbishop was a thin, cruel looking man. Dressed in his formal robes, they added bulk to an otherwise lacklustre frame.

'I'm willing to allow you to test my brother,' I said. 'A private audience maybe?'

The Archbishop smiled, 'Precisely what I was going to suggest.'

Every one of the Archbishop's entourage was dismissed and I bowed out with them. Then I waited outside to hear from Lilly. I wasn't afraid for her, I knew she could kill the man if he gave her the slightest amount of trouble.

A few moments later I heard Lilly's thoughts floating to me.
I've opened a window for you.

I found the window in question and slipped through, cloaked as always, so that the Archbishop wouldn't see me.

'Come boy, don't be shy. I have to prove that you are a *castrati*. We cannot just take anyone into the choir. It would never do if your voice suddenly broke.'

Lilly was making a show of slowly removing the clothes. In reality her leather trousers and sweater all remained intact below the surface of the glamour she was projecting. I'd learned that if I squinted I could see through the magic, and see the woman I loved instead of the image she was hiding behind.

'But I have a letter, your reverence,' Lilly said. 'From the church in Rome.'

'Yes. Yes. But these things have been known to be forged.'

Lilly projected the naked body of a pubescent boy to the Archbishop. The bare chest was hairless, and down below lay a shrivelled and useless penis as the image of the boy had no testicles.

'Perfect!' said the Archbishop then he embraced her.

By this time the supposedly holy man had removed most of his clothing, revealing a body that was thin and wiry. Lilly's expression, as she observed the man, never moved from the cynical sneer of a boy.

The Archbishop took her hand, leading her around a screen and out into a room at the back. A make-shift bed lay in the corner and I knew this was used all the time for the Archbishop's exploits.

'Just a minute,' I said. 'What are you doing to my little brother?'

The Archbishop balked as I blinked into visibility. Lilly dropped her boy visage, and stood every bit the powerful, warrior woman she is, taller, stronger and fuller figured, dressed in twenty-first century clothing.

'What is the meaning of this?' stuttered the man.

'Witchcraft is what you'd call it I guess,' said Lilly. 'But this is the real deal, not some jumped up charge you've created as a way to rid yourself of an enemy.'

The Archbishop opened his mouth to yell.

'No,' Lilly said, waving her hand across his mouth and his jaw clamped closed. 'You won't shout. You won't talk. Not unless I tell you to. I want answers and you're going to give me them. I'm not above torturing a holy man, but then with your perversity, I don't believe you are "holy".'

Once again I was taken aback by this new display of power. Lilly was showing all the signs of being able to control her skills just by thought.

A long chain containing the Ankh dangled down the emaciated chest of the Archbishop. Lilly ran her fingers over the necklace as the man squirmed unable to move.

'Tell me about this?'

'A cross, used by early Christians,' the Archbishop stammered through suddenly freed lips.

'What does it mean to you?'

'N … n … nothing.'

'You're lying. Who gave it to you?'

'No … It's just a …'

Lilly slapped him hard across the face. 'Don't lie to me you perverted little bastard or I'll make you a *castrati* right now.'

'I ... I ... Rome. I received it in R ... Rome.'

'Who gave it you?'

The Archbishop shook his head. He fought the power that held his lips in check, made his limbs paralysed.

'I can't. He'll kill me.'

Lilly looked over at me and smiled. Then she slapped the Archbishop so hard he fell across the bed. She bent over him. Her nails grew into demon-like talons and her hand hovered over the man's belly before gliding lower.

I said and did nothing. You might think I'd be appalled by this display, but you have to remember we are monsters and we weren't pretending to be anything else. Lilly was doing what came naturally and I could tell she was enjoying herself for the first time in days. She raked her nails into his chest, drawing blood as an example of what she would do elsewhere.

The Archbishop tried to scream but nothing would come from his mouth but a choking gargle. He emptied his bladder. The stench of urine stung the air.

I folded my arms, leaning back against the door frame.

I found the Archbishop's eyes on me, pleading for help, but I had no empathy for his sort. I'd seen too many of them walking the halls of the Vatican in my father's papal service.

'I'd tell her what she wants unless you really have a yearning to become *castrati.*'

Lilly's nails worked lower, she raked his testicles, but not in the slow sensuous way she had mine. Her nails dug in, drew blood immediately, and she cupped one of them, squeezing until I heard a disgusting pop.

Tears streamed from the Archbishop's eyes and his body wrenched in pain. But still the scream couldn't escape his frozen throat. Vomit spewed over his lips and onto his chest and body. Lilly paused, wiping her blood-soaked hand over the sheets. The smell of sickness and urine blended into a sickening odour.

'A new order ...' the Archbishop gasped. 'We have a new order.'

'Run by whom?' I asked.

'Carduth!' he gasped. 'He's a magician and he says he can control time.'

'Where can we find him?' asked Lilly.

'I can't …' gasped the Archbishop but as Lilly moved back in towards his scrotum the answer poured from his lips amidst tears and more sickness. 'Rome. He's in Rome. He's the right hand of the Pope …'

'Thank you,' said Lilly. 'You see how much easier it is to just tell me the truth.'

'He will kill me for this …' cried the Archbishop his voice cracking with every sob.

'I'll save him the trouble,' I answered, reaching down and embracing his head in my arms.

I snapped his neck and the sound of breaking bone echoed dully in the small room.

'Good,' said Lilly, licking her fingers. 'We're starting to get somewhere. At last someone who knows about Carduth. Now we have a clear direction.'

We ransacked the room. Taking money and jewels to make it look as though the Archbishop had been murdered during a robbery. It would make Carduth less suspicious if word got back to the Vatican before we arrived.

'Maybe I shouldn't have killed him …' I said but without regret.

'We had to. He'd have told Carduth we were coming, and I like maintaining the element of surprise,' said Lilly.

22
The Empath

Five and a half months ago

As Anja tidied away the crate, repacking and labelling it, she failed to notice the letter that had fallen underneath Björn's desk. She carried the crate to the larger office, closing the door on the sleeping man. He wouldn't remember anything and her source would pay well for this rare little treasure.

She had taken things from Björn before. It was easy to deny receiving the items from whoever sent them. It didn't matter, because things went missing all the time through courier services and there was no way of tracing it back to her. Anja had a nice arrangement with the delivery guy, Hans: he was a friend of hers from way back. They'd grown up together, shared a campfire as their parents worked. Hans had it sorted, he would return to the depot, pretend to check the crate back in saying there was no one there to receive it. When the order to try again came, the crate wouldn't be found. No one would know where it had gone and the warehouse would be searched. It would be one of those mysteries.

Of course this only worked when the piece was something illegal. Anja had known for some time that John Noble sent Björn artefacts to dispose of for him and they'd split the profit. She doubted that Noble had placed any insurance on this one, or even described truthfully what the crate contained. Therefore she knew Noble couldn't make much of a fuss when he learned it had gone missing.

Her source had phoned to warn her that a box might arrive.

He always seemed to know when something important was coming.

'I'll pay handsomely for this one, Anja. As always, I'll expect your discretion.'

'Don't worry, Björn won't even remember it arriving. I've never let you down before, have I?' Anja said.

'You're a very talented girl, Anja,' her contact said.

He was a complete mystery to her. She neither knew his name, nor direct contact details. He always contacted her. Anja thought it incredible that he always knew when something was heading her way. He must have insider knowledge, which was why she was extra careful to reveal nothing at the university.

'It helps that Björn is so very susceptible,' Anja said. 'Another situation might not be so easy.'

'You're very modest,' said her contact. 'I like that about you. Someone will be there to collect from you shortly.'

Anja stared into space for a while before realising that the contact had hung up on her. She put her mobile away in her purse and returned to the crate, making sure the box was packed securely. Then she placed the top back on but didn't bother to tack the lid down. It wouldn't matter to her contact; she knew he must be local. After all, the collections were always quickly arranged. She tried not to analyse this too much though, or think too deeply about her source. Something told her he would know if she began to build any real information about him.

Anja went back in the office to check on Björn. He would sleep a little longer yet and when he woke, he would be refreshed believing all of the suggestions she had planted.

The first time she touched his mind had been on the dig. There had been a great find, some rare coins in mint condition. Fortunately, only she and Björn had been present. She kissed him, feigning excitement and while her hand was on his head, Anja sent the first charge into his brain. After that he was open to her.

Anja was an empath, which meant she could feel the emotion of others. Usually when she touched anyone, she felt a long rush of their feelings. She had spent the first few years of her life growing up in the circus where her mother and father performed.

Her father was a hypnotist, her mother an acrobat. From an early age she exercised both her body and her mind until they were honed and strong.

Her father taught her everything he knew about hypnosis, but what Anja had learnt on her own one day, quite by accident, was that when she was connected to someone, using her empathy, she could in fact, reverse the flow of energy. Using hypnotic techniques, she could persuade her victim to believe anything.

At first she used this to make people feel better about themselves. She hated the despondent feelings that poured into her from the minds around her. Generally she avoided physical contact. It made it easier to shut out the thoughts of others. What she had learnt from this contact was that most people were very unhappy. As an empath, she took that feeling on and they felt better, but she had to swallow the poison of their sadness. It was depressing and miserable. She really despised the after-taste of touching another mind but there was little she could do about it until she discovered her other talent. Anja came from a long line of empaths and, like her aunt before her, would have eventually drowned in other people's sorrow. It was not a future she wanted for herself.

Despite her control, she still avoided contact with people but touching Björn was easy. He wasn't miserable, he was so focused on his work that this was all he cared about. The rush of thoughts she received from him reassured her that long term contact would be beneficial and not harmful to her. His ambition was palatable and she didn't mind sharing that drive to find rare artefacts. It enhanced her personal pursuit of wealth and helped her contact gain access to all of those priceless items he desired.

After finding the coins, Anja had taken Björn back to her tent and, after removing the memory of the coins, she replaced it with the imagery of their love making. She couldn't resist making him believe she was the best lay he had ever had, but in actual fact, the only contact they'd really had was Anja raping his brain.

It was ironic when she considered all the passes she had rejected. To think she would fuck this boring, middle-aged man. Aside from anything, he barely washed and his beard was always caked in food. There was no way Anja would ever let someone like him near her but she had used his subjectivity to her own advantage. She would gain a first in her degree and Björn would feel that she was talented, would recommend her to other posts next year when she finished the course. This way she was guaranteed access to more of the artefacts her contact needed.

At that moment the outer office door opened and the collector arrived. It was evening but he was wearing dark glasses. Anja knew better than to try to make conversation with him. Her words would be greeted with silent distain. It was the usual man, 'Boris' she liked to call him in her mind. He was over six feet tall and reminded her of the archetypal German. Not that she knew what nationality Boris was as he never spoke.

'Here it is,' she said and Boris removed a thick envelope from his pocket and passed it to her. As always he was wearing thick leather gloves to ensure that his skin didn't come in contact with hers.

Anja took the envelope but waited until Boris had gone before opening it. True to his word, her contact had paid her triple the usual finder's fee. Pleased, Anja placed the envelope in her purse, and then went to wake Björn. As Björn opened his eyes, he found Anja fastening her skirt; her underwear was in her hand. He glanced down at his trouser, finding them around his ankles. For a moment he was disorientated and then the rush of memories returned. He had bent Anja over the desk, lifted her skirt and pulled away her panties. Then he had fucked her, hard, until she was screaming his name over and over again. Afterwards, she had finished him off with a blowjob.

Anja kissed him and then helped him pull up and zip his trousers.

'You were amazing,' he said.

She smiled at him kindly.

'Can I buy you dinner?' she suggested. It was the least she could do. Fucking with his mind like this was starting to make him very forgetful.

23
The Sword

Present Day

'The next part of this journey is going to be extremely dangerous,' Lilly explained. 'That's why I think it best if I send you two home.'

Gabi and Amalia stood before the Seine, gazing out at the re-opened door.

'I understand the need to protect Amalia,' Gabi said. 'But I should stay with you and Chez.'

'Gabi. I know how you feel,' I said. 'I'd be hurt if it was me, but Amalia may need protection in our time. We just don't know what's going to happen.'

'And,' Lilly continued. 'If anything happens to me you might all be stuck here.'

'You're pushing me away. You two just want to be alone now,' Gabi said.

'No,' Lilly took his face in her hands. 'No. I'm afraid for you all. I know I need back up which is why I'm allowing Chez to stay. Besides, Amalia and you ...'

Gabi shook his head. Amalia was a rebound. I knew that and so did he. I felt for him. Guilt lodged in my chest as I gazed into his sad eyes. He hadn't asked for this, but then neither had we. Even so, I always knew our *ménage à trois* was on borrowed time.

It took a little more persuasion before Lilly managed to convince Gabi it was for the best. Wearily he entered the portal with Amalia and as Lilly closed the door behind them, leaving us still in 1314, I wondered if this was the last time we would see either of them.

'I feel bare without my sword,' she said. 'I need to buy one.'

The local blacksmith had a range of readymade weapons. Lilly lifted and swung several swords until she narrowed the choice down to two or three that fitted into her scabbard and which suited her hand.

She was using glamour once more and was appearing as a young male aristocrat.

'What of this one, Monsieur?' said the smith as he produced a fine looking sword. It was shiny and immaculate, new off the anvil. 'I made this only yesterday.'

In the centre of a round pommel was a thick piece of amber. The grip was longer than the Viking sword Lilly was used to, the fuller less deep. Lilly lifted the sword, swung it, weighed it in her hand, then slid it carefully into her scabbard. It was a perfect fit which meant, that despite the different sized hilt, the sword itself was virtually the same length as her previous one.

'How much?' she asked.

'It's yours,' said the smith. 'Take it.'

'What do you mean?'

'I'm not a superstitious man,' he answered. 'However a few days ago, a priest came to see me. He told me you'd be coming and that I was to make the best sword I could for you. He gave me the size, weight. He also gave me the amber which he said must be placed in the centre of the pommel. He told me to tell you that if you look through the centre the truth will always become clear to you. Then he paid me handsomely.'

Lilly looked at me. I shrugged.

'He said to tell you "thank you". He told me you saved his master's life and this was repayment. I took his money, thinking he was insane. I mean, how could he know that a stranger would come this way and you look just as he described? When he left though, I had the strangest compulsion. I had to make you this sword. And now, here you are. Just as he said.'

'Thank you,' said Lilly, because she really didn't know what else to say at that point. 'Can you tell me anything else about the sword.'

'Just one thing. The priest told me that the amber was given to his ancestors by a very brave lady. It had been passed down from mother to child and, he said, it had magical properties.' The smith looked around, 'I didn't tell you this of course, and I'll deny making the sword if word gets out.'

'You have nothing to fear from us,' said Lilly.

The smith nodded, 'It's superstitious times. Just the other day they executed men that had done the country proud in the crusades … I'm not political, don't really understand these things, but it seemed to me they weren't witches.'

I chose a sword for myself and we paid the man for that. He never commented on the church stamp, clearly visible on the pouch full of coins. Fortunately for us the authorities had kept the death of the Archbishop quiet. Underneath her clothing, Lilly was wearing the necklace taken from the man's cooling body and the Ankh swung provocatively between her breasts.

On the street, Lilly withdrew her new sword from the scabbard. She gazed at the pommel for a long time, then raised the hilt before her, looking through the centre. She moved in a circle while keeping her eyes focused through the yellow stone. As her eyes passed over me she gasped. Then she looked over the pommel at me.

'What is it?' I asked.

She held out the sword.

'Look around. What do you see?'

I saw Paris in a golden glow. The buildings and people were hazy as I expected they would be. I turned full circle and caught Lilly's image in the glass. The glamour was still in place, but through the amber I saw the true and real countenance of Lilly. I glanced up from the stone, saw a boy before me and then back down through the glass. Lilly was illuminated, a glowing goddess. Her aura was made of gold and purple.

'Wow.'

'He was right. It has magic properties. When I looked

through the amber and saw you I could see your aura glowing vividly,' Lilly said.

I explained what I saw. 'The world looks dull, even the people – all except us.'

Lilly nodded. 'This may indeed be a valuable weapon although I'm uncertain how. I've learnt to respect magic in any form. And destiny. Things always happen for a reason, even when I fight against it, it's all meant to happen.'

We took to the air, heading towards Rome. Neither of us spoke of the blacksmith and his strange visitor again. Midflight I glanced at Lilly's waist and saw the pommel shining in the sunlight as the sword swung lightly at her hip. It looked comfortable, as though it had always belonged at her side. Whatever the reason, whoever the priest was, the sword was meant for Lilly, of that I was certain, and one day she would use it for something important.

24
Vertigo

1314

The streets of fourteenth-century Rome were bustling with pilgrims from all over Europe. It was a strange and alien place to me, even though technically it was the place of my birth. But I found this century to be savage in comparison to my birth time which was some 400 years later. I felt out of step.

'What's wrong?' Lilly asked as we looked for any sign of open portals in the streets.

'It feels strange. I feel like I don't belong here.'

'We don't. That feeling will continue until we get back to the present.'

'You experienced this disorientation?' I asked.

She nodded. 'You get used to it eventually. It becomes absorbed into everything else you're feeling.'

My skin prickled and burnt in the sun. It was the kind of sensation I'd experienced when I first turned, but never since. I felt nauseous and a strange vertigo threatened to pull me down onto the filthy streets. I stumbled, eyes blurring, staggering like a blind man. Lilly grabbed my hand. The world righted itself and I leaned against her gasping for air.

'Better?' she asked after a while.

I nodded.

'Sorry. It hit you hard then. I had forgotten that it can take a few days before the symptoms occur. Because you all seemed okay, I thought it was only me that had felt the time switch fever.'

'It was like a fever. Your touch has sent it scurrying away though.'

'Good. Can you walk?'

'Yes.'

We continued on into the city until Lilly found a tavern that she deemed not *too* flea-infested for our patronage.

'Sleep is the best cure,' Lilly said laying me down on the bed as the Innkeeper closed the door behind him.

'No. I'm fine,' I said but despite my protestations I soon fell into that deep dark dreamless sleep of the exhausted.

A few hours later I woke to find Lilly sitting by the window, gazing out at the night. It was full dark and the night sky was clear. The air, though tainted with human waste, smelt cleaner and less polluted than the air of the twenty first century. The sky was filled with a million stars. It was a beautiful, pure sight.

I watched Lilly silently from the bed, she appeared miles away, and I could see that she didn't belong in this world but was good at adapting. She had learnt this incredible patience after long years of being away from her time.

I glanced around the room; it was basic but warm and the bed was comfortable.

'How are you feeling?' she asked.

'Like I've been hit with something very heavy and very solid.'

Lilly smiled, 'Yep. Time-travel can do that to a guy.'

'Strange. I never felt like this in your time.'

'I've just been thinking about that. I think moving forward in time is different from moving backwards. It's like we are less welcome in the past. Maybe it has something to do with paradoxes.'

I sat up cautiously. The room spun pushing the confusing thought of time-travel away from my mind. I placed my feet on the ground. The feeling of disorientation receded and my heart began to pump my vampire blood rapidly around my body as though fighting the effects of some deadly virus. I pulled myself to my feet. Lilly sat forward but didn't rush immediately to my aid.

The ground stayed firm as I crossed the wooden floor to the window.

'I do seem to be fighting it now.'

I put my hand on her shoulder, looked down into the ocean of green that gazed up at me with concern, then relief.

'Good. Because I really didn't want to have to send you home.'

My heart jolted at her words. The thought of leaving her, possibly losing her again was something I couldn't bear to consider.

She stood, kissing me lightly on the corner of my mouth and I turned my head to meet her lips fully. We held each other for a while, and the world became as right as it could be. I loved her more at that moment than I had at anytime previously. Her touch gave me strength, her breath poured life into my lungs, and as always the blood in my veins – the vampire gene blood – beat with the same rhythm and time as hers did. I felt that flow of energy again, that joining of thoughts and minds that had become unique to us.

Time stood still as we flowed in that haven of love and unity. Her thoughts floated behind my eyes, I felt her fears and anxieties.

I kissed her eyes, showered her face with more.

We may not survive this … she thought.

'I know,' I said. 'But we will go down fighting.'

'I'm hungry,' she said, reluctantly withdrawing from my embrace.

We left the tavern by the window. Hunger screamed in my gut as we flew across the city which was barely constructed to the level and size I'd once been used to, and nowhere near the capacity it achieved in the future. The buildings looked like shacks to me, little more than hovels in some areas. Except for those that always had the wealth and privilege.

We flew over *Palazzo Laterano.*

'This is the main residence of the Pope in this era,' I told Lilly.

She nodded, 'I wondered where it was. After all, the Vatican wasn't the official residence until the late fourteenth century, was it? I should have remembered you would know.'

'Indeed. The history of Rome, and that of the Papal lineage, was part of my childhood education ...'

On the outskirts of the *Palazzo* was extreme paucity. Poverty called us in the shape of a lowly whore staggering drunkenly through the streets away from a tavern. We landed before her and the soft thud made her look in our direction. I let her see me, but Lilly cloaked herself in shadows.

'Hello there! What's a fine gentleman like you doing out here at this time of night?' asked the whore. She grinned. Her two front teeth were missing. She stepped closer to me, hand outstretched.

'Feeling a little lonely tonight then?'

I said nothing. The breeze brought her odour to me, and I could see the grime filling the creases in her hand. She stroked my coat.

'You are indeed a very fine gentleman,' she whispered. 'You could afford a little company, couldn't you?'

'We don't want sex with you,' Lilly said appearing at my side. 'We need something else.'

My hand grasped the whore's throat choking off the salacious cackle before it could bubble from her lips. Her eyes bulged with fear and lack of oxygen. I gazed into them, soaking up her terror, feeling aroused by it in a way that her dirty, used body would never affect me. I lifted her off her feet, twisting her head sideways and waiting for Lilly to test her. The whore was paralysed with fear, but her feet twitched like a body dying at the end of a hangman's noose.

'Must I?' Lilly sighed. 'She really smells.'

Despite her protestation, Lilly licked the woman's skin and quickly nodded. She was safe. No sign of our gene code there. I pulled her closer, bending her neck still farther over until the whore's pain radiated through her flesh. Then I bit, deep and unforgiving, lapping up the alcohol-laced blood.

A few minutes later Lilly held the woman close, drinking from her until her heart stopped.

'God. What was she drinking?' Lilly said, pushing the body aside.

'I'm guessing but I think it was *Grappa*.'

'It tasted like … shit.'

I laughed. 'At the moment I don't think we can afford to be too fussy my darling.'

I felt better, stronger, despite the weakened quality of the woman's blood. My body used it anyway, and my limbs no longer felt fragile, the world we occupied no longer suffocated me.

'Right. We need to find Carduth and I'm guessing he's in this *Palazzo Laterano*.'

I took her hand. All sense of fun left the atmosphere around us. We'd fed. We were strong. We would find this bastard and kill him. Lilly's fingers trembled.

We're invincible together! For once I felt that I was the strong one of the two of us. She pressed herself to me, arms slipping around my waist. The pommel of her sword pushed against my leg.

'I love you,' Lilly said. 'Now let's go and kill this bastard.'

I held her a moment longer, breathing in her scent and sending my energy into her cold limbs.

I love you! I thought, then released her. There was no point delaying any more. As long as Carduth lived, all of us were in danger. He had thrown down the gauntlet and now it was time for the duel.

25
The Missing Parcel

Five Months Earlier

John Noble stared into space as he listened to Björn's voice on the other end of the phone.

'I don't know what has happened, my friend. I have chased the courier company, but they say they tried to deliver and no one was here to receive it. Then, somehow, the parcel was mislaid in the depot. I'm still hoping that it will suddenly be delivered.'

Noble sighed. Björn's voice sounded tired and stressed. He had always dealt fairly with him before and Noble had no reason to disbelieve the professor. It was strange though, that this parcel, among all the valuable ones he had previously sent, was the only one to suddenly disappear.

'I put a note inside, explaining its origins. It was a relic I found under a church altar,' Noble explained.

Björn took a breath. 'A relic? You've never sent me anything like that before.'

'I wanted your opinion. Björn, there's been some strange things happening since I found it.'

'You should have returned it immediately to the church …'

'It wasn't in the usual place in the altar, Björn. It was buried *beneath*. Like a talisman, or, dare I say it, like a dirty secret.'

Björn went quiet for a moment. 'You sound tired. Perhaps you should tell me what's been going on?'

Noble explained about the visit he had received from the two mysterious priests and about his phone call to Rome.

'At first I was worried they'd pull rank on me and shut the

project down. That's why I avoided telling anyone. But then, when there seemed to be so much interest, I became suspicious.'

As Noble found himself relaying all his fears and phobias to Björn, he suddenly realised how absurd they were. So what if two priests came to visit? What were they going to do? Ban him from entering the pearly gates? Getting things off his chest made the whole situation suddenly ludicrous and somewhat less frightening.

'Strange,' said Björn. 'The church is very much a rule unto itself. They sound like mafia ...' Then Björn laughed and the tension left the conversation.

Noble found himself smiling for the first time in the last few days.

'Yes. It's a bit ridiculous,' he laughed. 'I need to get out more.'

'We all get tense and paranoid sometimes, my friend,' Björn said. 'I'll let you know as soon as the parcel turns up. But that part of it is worrying. There have been a lot of parcels not arriving when, and how, they should, recently. I think the courier company may have a thief working there. I'm going to ring their complaints department and voice my concerns.'

'Okay. Keep me posted,' said Noble.

When the call ended, Noble stared out into the street from the public callbox. His paranoia was a massive lump of anxiety right in the middle of his chest. He was glad he hadn't had this conversation on either his landline or his mobile. Somehow he knew it could be traced. He had made a special effort, driven almost 60 miles away from his office and into Glasgow to make the call. The journey had taken almost an hour and a half, and he was not looking forward to the return trip in the rush hour traffic, but he still felt it was worth it.

Through the glass Noble noticed a brightly-lit coffee shop that looked warm and welcoming. Outside the wind was howling and rain had begun to patter against the phone box. He headed over to the shop but was soaked before he even reached the door.

Inside, Noble found only one vacant table and so he sat there, eyes scanning the other customers. He picked up the menu and tried to concentrate on it, but his mind was elsewhere and kept jumping away from the printed letters until they made no sense at all. He was hungry, but the thought of eating made his stomach churn.

'Are you ready to order?'

Noble looked up to find the waitress standing beside him, pad and pen ready. She was a short, cute girl in her mid-twenties with black hair, cut into an urchin style. Noble observed how it suited her slightly impish face. She had startling green eyes.

'Erm … coffee, please.'

After clarifying whether he wanted milk or not the waitress left and Noble found himself staring after her. He felt confused, but didn't know why. He tried to focus, once again on his conversation with Björn, but it all felt so distant and far away.

'Hey! Breathe there, fella!'

He came to with his head between his knees.

'What … happened?'

'You fainted,' said the waitress. 'Just as I brought you the coffee. Lucky for you this priest knows first aid …'

Noble lifted his head and gazed into the eyes of Father Anthony. The priest nodded at the waitress and she walked away to serve her other customers.

'We have to talk Mr Noble,' said the priest.

'I have nothing to say,' Noble said, sitting up. 'What are you doing here? Did you follow me?'

He leaned back in his seat, head spinning. Blackness lurked once again around his eyes. Nausea mixed up his insides.

'Did you open the box?' Father Anthony asked.

'What?'

'You have to tell me if you opened the box, Mr Noble. Your life and the lives of many others are at risk. Don't you understand that?'

Noble noticed how kind Father Anthony's eyes were. They were green, not dissimilar to his own. He hadn't observed that on their first meeting. He looked deeper into them and felt himself slipping away again. He closed his eyes, shook his head in a vain attempt to clear it.

'I … don't know anything about a box,' Noble said.

'Of course you do. You sent it to your friend in Stockholm. We always knew that.'

'You. *Knew?*' Noble said.

'Yes,' Father Anthony answered.

'Then it was you who took it from the couriers!' Noble said.

'Good heavens, no! We're not thieves, Mr Noble.' Father Anthony sat down in the chair next to Noble. 'How are you feeling now?'

Noble glanced up, looked around and noticed that the cafe had slowly emptied. The waitress was behind the counter taking money from an elderly couple. As his eyes moved over the room the dizziness returned along with a sickly vertigo. Noble closed his eyes and rubbed his hand over his forehead.

'Dizzy, sick,' he mumbled in explanation.

'Yes. Not surprising really. You came in contact with a very powerful relic,' Father Anthony said. 'And with your heritage it was bound to have an impact on you.'

'I didn't open it,' Noble whispered suddenly. 'I started to, and then, I *felt* something.'

Father Anthony patted Noble's arm.

'How far did you go before you stopped?' Father Anthony asked.

Noble opened his eyes and once again met the priest's kind gaze. Anthony stared deep into his eyes. For a moment Noble felt a strange sensation, it was as if someone had reached into his mind and was carefully wading through the reams of information held there. It was a gentle pressure, almost reassuring.

'Oh no,' Father Anthony murmured under his breath. 'You partially broke the seal …'

'What's happening? *Who are you?*' Noble gasped.

'That's a long story, and I'm not sure you're ready to hear it,' Father Anthony said.

'Tell me anyway. I deserve to know what's going on.'

'There's something out there, something that can kill a whole lot of innocent people. And I think you've let it out.'

26
Palazzo Laterano

1314

It was around two in the morning when we landed on the roof of *Palazzo Laterano*. Lilly knelt, listening to the movements in the building. I stood, looking out over the courtyard, searching for any sign of soldiers who might be guarding the *Palazzo*. It was still dark as I scrutinised the grounds and at first there was no movement at all. Then the door of the barracks swung open and a group of men marched out, fully clothed and carrying swords. As they advanced noisily towards the courtyard and out of the dark, several soldiers revealed their positions as the new shift took over from them, before we even had an opportunity to look for them.

Lilly was by my side. *Convenient. Now we know exactly where they all are.*

It was *too* convenient and I heard the irony in her thoughts and nodded my agreement. We cloaked ourselves, then flew down, hovering over windows.

'Raymond … why don't you come back to bed? You've been working for hours,' said a female voice. 'I feel lonely.'

'Katerina, I need to send this letter. It is important.'

'What is more important than me? You said you loved me …' whined the woman, but as I listened more carefully I noticed a slight edge to her voice. This was more like a game she was playing. Something she pretended to feel perhaps to please her lover.

'The Dulcinians,' the man murmured. 'But I'm finished now,

and will come and give you the attention you crave, Katerina.'

The curtains of the room were closed, but there was a slight gap through which I could make out the figure of a man as he moved across the room. With a jolt I realised I knew who he was. I had seen his portrait hanging on the walls of the Vatican along with all the other Popes before my father's reign. It was Pope Clement V.

A cynical sneer moved my lips as I heard the sounds of their lovemaking. This Pope, like so many others, had a mistress to warm his bed. I wasn't surprised, merely amused.

What is it? Lilly asked and I poured my memories of Clement into her mind.

He was reluctantly involved with the destruction of the Templars, but obviously benefitted financially, just as the King had, I explain.

'The Pope isn't our concern,' Lilly whispered. 'Only Carduth.'

'I know. But how do we know who Carduth is, Lilly? We haven't even seen his face.'

A few minutes later we slipped inside the palace through an open window.

The hallway was dark and quiet. Most of the household was sleeping. We moved through the rooms, listening to snatches of conversation wherever there was any.

'The Pope can't be disturbed right now ...'

'I'm so tired ...'

'... need to snuff all candles in the corridors ...'

'Carduth said ...'

I stopped outside the door that led down into the kitchen. Lilly reached for the handle but I placed my hand on hers, shaking my head. *Let's listen first ...*

'The Cardinal is the biggest hypocrite of all,' slurred a male voice. 'He talks of destroying Satan and the enemies of his people ... He behaves like he's Pope ...'

'Shush!' whispered a female. 'You know he has spies in every corner ...'

'Yes ... murdering bastard,' replied the man. 'Here's to Antonio ... may his soul rest in peace.'

Glasses clinked together as the couple saluted what appeared to be a dead friend.

'I hate him,' slurred the man.

'I know. Now let's get you off to bed. You're meant to be back on duty in the morning.'

'Carduth is the Devil ...' he murmured.

'He's definitely known here then,' whispered Lilly. 'But where is the bastard?'

We searched the rest of the palace until we found what appeared to be a cardinal's chamber but the bed hadn't been slept in. Carduth was nowhere to be seen.

'This is ridiculous.' Lilly said. 'I feel like we're on a wild goose chase. We've learnt absolutely nothing at all about Carduth.'

'We could search the mind of the man servant, at least extract Carduth's image from his mind ...' I suggested.

'Okay. You do that and I'll search this room for any clues as to where he might be.'

It wasn't hard to find the male servant; his loud snoring echoed through the walls of the lower floor. I remained invisible as I slipped down the staircase and into the kitchen which was huge and full of fresh produce that I presumed was waiting for the cook to prepare for the household the next day.

Behind the kitchen was a row of rooms, or rather an annexe that had been tagged on to the main house to accommodate the kitchen and waiting staff. The man I wanted was in the third one along. I entered his room silently and stared at the sleeping form, feeling the steady beat of his heart as his chest moved up and down. He slept alone. The room was small, windowless, and only held a single cot with a straw-filled mattress. Beside his bed was a basic, roughly carved table bearing a jug of ale and a tankard. In fact the room was little more than a cupboard. I wondered if the soldiers in the barracks had better facilities than the household servants. It was as basic as it could be.

I leaned over the man. The smell of stale ale drifted from his breath as he slept open-mouthed. I sat down on the side of his bed, stroked his forehead and he murmured incoherently in his sleep. His hair was greasy and lice-infested, but I had no fear of grime and parasites as both had a natural aversion to vampires: dirt couldn't cling to my skin and insects scurried away from me, their fragile fangs couldn't pierce my tough flesh.

'Open your eyes,' I suggested and as his eyes drifted open I plunged into his mind.

He grunted with the first intrusion but fell quiet soon after. All snoring stopped, his breathing became silent as his mouth closed and I probed his mind for Carduth. Alberto was his name and his thoughts were confusing and bland. I merged my mind with his; helped him shape those inner anxieties into images and words …

… scares me. Alien. Wrong. He's a man of God and yet I can imagine him doing the most unspeakable evil. Cardinal Carduth … scares me and the others. He knows our thoughts, knows our sins, before we've even committed them. He has some link or direct connection with God. Once I heard him speaking to someone, but there was no one else in the room. It was strange how he paused as though he were receiving instructions, or indeed was involved in a two-way conversation.

Scares me … Mustn't look at him. The girl went missing when she disobeyed him …

'What girl?' I asked.

'Delfina … scullery maid. He looked into her eyes and she followed him. We never saw her again …'

I stood and released Alberto back into a safe dream. He wouldn't remember me or my invasion of his mind. It was unfortunate that his thoughts were so vague. I'd pulled some images of Carduth, but in Alberto's mind the focus was on the Cardinal's robes. Dissatisfied with the thoughts I'd found, I tried once more to focus on Carduth's face in Alberto's memories. There was mousy hair, brown eyes that swirled with a thousand snakes. Terror struck Alberto's mind as he squirmed in his bed, the nice dream I placed was being swallowed up by a black and terrible phobia.

I left the room with only a vague impression of Carduth but it was still more than we had before. On the way back to the kitchen I listened in at the various doors and on the spur of the moment slipped into the room of the maid servant who helped Alberto to bed. The door was locked but I forced it and it gave easily.

The woman was in her forties and looked worn by hard work. She too was lying in her bed drifting to sleep with the exhaustion of the day hanging on her limbs like a weighted cloak. I startled her as I sat beside her on the bed but grabbed her before she could call out, gazed into her eyes and made her mine.

… wife's tales. All of it. That girl, Delfina, was a slut. Most of the footmen had her at one time or other. Carduth just dismissed her … why would he need to do more?

Eyes. Eyes like black writhing snakes … don't look at him unless you have to. Glow around him, like black light … don't look into his eyes.

Carduth's image floated behind my eyes. I had trouble putting this demon figure together with the knight I had seen at the foundations of the church in Lourdes. Curious, I left the woman's room and dipped in and out of all of the kitchen servant's rooms exploring each of their minds for more information on Carduth but came away with little more.

Lilly was looking in the chest at the bottom of the bed when I re-entered Carduth's room.

'Look what I found,' she said, holding up a mantel that bore the mark of the Ankh.

'This is definitely our man,' I said, and then I sent her the images I had gathered from the servants. 'They all see the same thing and actually have no clear image of what Carduth really looks like.'

'No,' Lilly answered. 'Maybe they are really seeing him as he is.'

'Meaning?'

'I don't know about everything that goes on in this world, but if we are possible then anything else is. Maybe he's some kind of demon with an axe to grind.'

I thought about the possibility and my mind slipped back into the recesses of my deepest darkest horrors. I had to agree with her. If there were portals that could take you into different times and a hell dimension disguised as an ordinary door on a long corridor, then yes, there certainly could be demons.

'What now?' I asked.

'I want to kill this bastard. You know that. But I think we're wasting time searching for him. If he's as smart as he seems, he'll always be one-step ahead of us. That's why I think we need to go home. There's nowhere in the world safer than Rhuddlan. I think we're going to wait for Carduth to come after us and we're going to fight him where we're strongest.'

'I like that plan. A lot. Let's get out of here.'

Lilly opened the door and Carduth was waiting for us on the other side.

27
The Letter

Five Months Earlier

Once he drew a blank with the courier, Björn gave up on his search for the missing box.

'It'll turn up, Björn,' Anja had said. 'No point in getting worked up about it. Come back here.'

He didn't remember going back to bed or what happened between them when he got there. In fact Björn found that he was getting more and more forgetful as the days wore on. Anja had moved into his apartment with him. He wasn't quite sure when and how this had happened, but having her there was a tremendous help. He found he could concentrate more on work now that she was organising his life. Their sex-life was good, although afterwards he always felt drained and confused and needed to sleep a lot. *It is probably because she is young and so insatiable*, he thought.

'I'm getting old,' Björn murmured as he worked through the papers on his desk.

The cleaner had been in that morning and had tidied his office and his desk at the university. It was a little annoying that she had moved so many things around and now he couldn't find the notes he had made for his latest report. Björn flicked through a stack of hand-written notes, and then began to wade through the pile of files and reports that the blasted woman had chosen to straighten.

'Damn it! I knew where everything was yesterday.'

'Are you complaining about the cleaning woman again?' Anja

said from the other office. 'You know your desk was chaos.'

'Yes, but it was my chaos – and I had a method to the piles. Now they are all jumbled up.'

Anja came in and placed a cup of coffee down on a battered coaster beside his computer monitor. Then she kissed him on the head. Björn felt it was vaguely parental and wondered, not for the first time, how their relationship had suddenly changed. He felt like he had no authority where she was concerned. She was acting more and more like his wife – or worse his mother – every day. That wasn't how things were supposed to play out and it annoyed him in a way he couldn't understand. It was a deep rooted resentment and it was irrational but he couldn't help feeling it.

'I can help if you like?'

Björn felt a vague surge of irritation at her offer. 'No. One female organising my room is quite enough for one day.'

Anja laughed, 'Just as well. I have my interview today.'

'Interview?'

'Björn! Don't tell me you've forgotten that too!'

Björn looked up from his desk. Anja looked stunning in a black fitted trouser suit, with a dark red shirt.

'You look nice,' he said.

'Well. I have that job interview. With Caradien Industries.'

'The oil company?'

'Björn!' Anja said again. 'Are you joking now, because this really isn't funny?'

Björn sat back in his chair, admiring her. Her mousey blonde hair was tied back today. She was the epitome of sophistication and professionalism.

'I wrote a reference for you,' he said.

'Yes. The job is for an artefact expert, remember? They need someone to assess any historical objects they find on their oil sites.'

'I remember,' Björn said. 'Did I give you a good reference?'

Anja sighed. 'Yes. The best.'

'That was silly of me. Especially if you're going to be working somewhere else in the world.'

'We talked about that, don't you remember? Mostly I'm still going to be based in Stockholm. Anyway, I must get out of here or I'll be late.'

Anja left the room and Björn returned his attention to the pile of papers on his desk and, in a fit of mischief, pushed over the first mound his eyes fell on. The papers tumbled over the centre, filling the area that the cleaner had cleared in order to give him some room to work. Immediately his desk felt normal, but a pang of guilt made him begin to re-tidy the folders and he stuffed the loose papers back inside haphazardly until one in particular caught his eye. Björn recognised Noble's handwriting immediately. He held the piece of paper, a scrap really, almost as though it had been torn from a notebook. It was unusually hurried, but distinct and decisive. It was a letter he hadn't seen before, but somehow appeared to be very familiar.

Björn, my dear friend,

   Enclosed is a very unusual find that I felt compelled to send you. I've found a most peculiar relic and it was buried – not in the altar – but underneath!

As Björn read down the letter he soon realised that this was the note Noble had described sending with the box he had found. Björn felt confused. He had been very forgetful lately, he knew that, but surely he hadn't totally mislaid the package from Scotland? He read the letter again, taking in all the details and this time he knew, was totally certain, that he had read this before.

Of course Anja would remember if he had received the parcel. He looked at his office door and opened his mouth to call her back in. But something made him hold back. He rubbed his eyes. The image of a box covered in a blackened dark purple cloth came into his mind and he remembered seeing a symbol. A *crux ansata*. He glanced at his computer. His head began to hurt, but he pushed through it until a burst of memory rushed back into his brain.

He had been doing a search, looking up the origins on the

symbol and *there had been another sign*. He remembered!

He stood up in reflex, hurried to the door and looked out into the other office where Anja worked. She was shutting down her computer, picking up her handbag and coat when she noticed him watching her from the door.

'Björn?' she said.

Anja had been there! He *remembered*!

'Anja … I … was just trying to get a glimpse of your lovely bottom before you left …'

Anja laughed, 'Wish me luck?'

'Of course!'

Anja opened the outer door. She glanced back, a small frown on her brow but as she saw Björn smiling, she waved and quickly exited into the main campus.

As Björn stared at the closed door a rush of memories came back. His head hurt so much that for a moment he thought he would pass out. Fragments of moments burst behind his synapses. Anja entering the office bringing him a parcel. Anja looking into his eyes. Anja touching his arm. A strange feeling of well-being. Words. Whispers. Orders.

His head throbbed. Eyes ached and genuine pain stabbed at his heart as the memories slowly returned and began to form into cohesive moments.

He stayed in his office, sat at his desk. Pain wracking his head. Maybe he was having some kind of seizure? But the thoughts and feelings poured in. The recollection of genuine times. Even so, Björn did not want to believe what he knew was the truth: that the last twelve months of his life had been a lie, the memories of their closeness, fake. Anja was not at all what she appeared.

In her absence he allowed the torment to colour his face. Sickness pulled at his insides as he recalled every detail of her betrayal. He thought back to all of the passionate moments, the intimacy, the kisses and the exchanges of words of love. Deep down he knew these memories weren't real. Somehow – maybe she had drugged him – she had managed to place false ideas and recollections into his mind. Surely that was impossible?

Björn's mind went back to the first dig. A flashback of pain as he saw the gold doubloons; Anja's hand touching his forehead. The stabbing sharp shock that pulsed into his brain through her fingers. He had been her stooge since then. All that time!

He closed his office door, sat down at his desk once more and looked again at the letter. He felt tired rather than angry. He was such an old fool. Why on earth did he imagine that someone as beautiful and vibrant as Anja would want him?

He didn't know how he was going to play this. Maybe he would just let her go to the new job, forget he even knew her. He wasn't sure. After all, theft was a serious crime, and there had been rather a lot of parcels disappearing over the last few months. Could he in all conscience let her go onto another company, perhaps to do the same? More importantly, could he let her get away with making a fool of him?

He contemplated calling the police. His mind toyed with his story. It would be an interesting interview. He could almost see them laughing at him as they locked him up in a psychiatric ward. *You say she hypnotised you, Professor? Then stole expensive artefacts? Oh and she planted fake memories inside your head? Well they'd have to be false wouldn't they? Can you imagine this lovely girl giving you a blow-job? Just wait here while we bring a Doctor to see you …*

Björn dropped his head into his hands. He loved her damn it! He had believed everything! Even though deep down he knew, on some subliminal level, that no way would someone like her ever have anything to do with him. Björn had wanted the dream even more than he wanted his career, which, until he met Anja, had always been his main interest and obsession.

No. He wouldn't say anything. Aside from the obvious, that he would be a laughing stock, his main concern would be his own slightly illegal dealings with Noble. The artefacts he had received, although legally obtained, should really have been declared to the Scottish Heritage Trust. History belonged to everyone, but Björn and Noble had made money from it. No matter how unimportant this may have been at the time, what they'd done was every bit as illegal as Anja's behaviour.

Björn looked at his monitor. He opened his desktop and

searched for the picture he had taken of the box. He knew enough about computers to realise that even if Anja had deleted the evidence, he would still be able to retrieve it. But Anja hadn't deleted it.

'Sloppy,' he murmured.

Anja had become over-confident. She trusted her skills. It hadn't occurred to her that something might jog those hidden memories back into Björn's mind.

Björn saved the files onto a memory stick, and also uploaded them onto a backup storage website he used from time to time. Then he carefully deleted them from his PC. Once this was done, he rubbed his forehead. A flash of false memory floated behind his eyes, Anja on all fours on the bed in his apartment. The thought occurred to him that he had never seen her apartment, or even knew where she lived before she moved in with him full time. He waded into the student records and within moments he had the address.

Jotting it down on a piece of paper he stood, reached for his coat, and went into the outer office. He searched her desk. Opening the drawers, he rifled through trying to find anything that could give him some answers. In the first two drawers he found nothing that wasn't university related. In the bottom drawer however he found a few personal items. A lipstick and mirror, a library card, a small purse, and, inside the purse, there was a key. Björn stared at the key for a few moments. It looked like a house key and he knew Anja would be interviewing all day long. He put the key in his pocket next to the piece of paper with her old address. It wasn't far from the university and it wouldn't hurt to swing by there.

He filed Noble's letter in the bottom drawer of his desk and locked it. He would have to be careful from now on. He was going to do a little investigation of his own. Find out who and what she was. Memory pulsed once more behind his eyes, Anja gasping in his arms as she orgasmed. He didn't want her messing with his head anymore, but the truth was he wanted a real taste of what she had been pretending to give him. And he had every intention of getting it.

28
Cardinal Carduth

1314

Carduth wasn't surprised to find himself face to face with his enemy. He was dressed as a cardinal, not an avenging knight this time. I stared into his face, seeing only an ordinary man, not some crazed and avenging angel. Nor some creature with snakes in his eyes either.

'Guards!' he yelled. 'The Bishop's murderers are here!'

In an instant a stream of soldiers poured up the stairs, out of rooms and along the corridor towards the Cardinal's room as though they had been lurking, waiting to pounce. Lilly reacted by slamming and locking the door. But we knew it would only hold against the onslaught for a short time.

'The window!' I said, throwing back the curtains only to find that the window was bricked up.

'This was a trap all along!' Lilly gasped. 'But why? What does he want? How the fuck did he know we were here?'

The door creaked under the pressure.

'It doesn't matter. We can fight our way out of this,' I said, drawing my sword.

Lilly pulled her sword out of the scabbard and we faced the door. The hinges groaned and then the door crashed open.

Carduth's men stumbled and fell over each other. Some of them tumbled to the floor and were trampled as others poured in ready to cut us down.

'Stop!' Carduth said. 'I want to interrogate them.'

The Cardinal entered holding aloft a thick wooden box. A

faint engraving adorned the lid. It was an Ankh.

'And we want to talk to you also,' said Lilly. 'She held her sword high and her stance showed her battle experience throughout her years of exile lost in time. She was a terrifying image and the soldiers nearest the front of the row took an involuntary step backwards at the sight of her.

'Silence!' Carduth ordered.

'You've seriously got to be kidding me,' Lilly answered. 'You don't call all the shots here, Carduth. You murdered my friend and for that I want an explanation at the very least.'

'Leave us,' the Cardinal ordered, and the soldiers obediently filed out without questions. They were like an army of sleep-walkers, completely under his control. Outside they stood silently, waiting for further orders.

Carduth had a regal bearing. He walked forward holding the box aloft as though it were some kind of weapon. His manner revealed a man who was used to getting his own way. I met his gaze, turning on my vampire hypnosis. I watched his eyes go blank, saw him lower the box and then a viper shot from his eyes and from its open mouth squirted poison right into mine. It bit into the air while I back-pedalled, falling against the bed.

Lilly yelled. Her sword spun through the air and cut the flying snakes in half. They disintegrated in mid air, turning to a black, powdery dust.

'I'll kill you if you try that again,' Lilly warned.

'Then tell your friend not to try to force his will on me,' Carduth answered.

I opened my eyes to find I could still see, but the poison had blurred the vision in my left eye and it stung. It felt inflamed.

'The effects don't last,' Carduth said. 'Not on one of your kind, at least. If you had been human you would have been permanently blinded.'

'So you're some kind of warlock?' Lilly said. *Are you alright?* she thought, and I nodded.

'No. I'm nothing as mundane as that,' Carduth answered.

'Then what?' Lilly asked.

'I'm a time-traveller. As you are. I've just learnt a few tricks along the way.'

'How do you know about time-travel?' I said.

Carduth smiled and it was terrible. 'I'm not ready to reveal my nature, nor my secrets to you. But I will say this, I'm sworn to destroy you.'

'Then stop talking and let's do this ...' Lilly said. 'If you really believe you *can* kill us that is?'

Carduth smiled. 'Anja was right. Your arrogance is your weakness.'

'I don't know an Anja,' Lilly replied. 'So maybe you're mixing us up with someone else, or maybe you're just confusing us with people that really give a shit about your opinion. Either way you are mistaken.'

By now we had backed away to the furthest wall, Carduth was slowly drawing closer.

'That may be true, if indeed you were *people*,' Carduth hissed.

A faint drumbeat began from somewhere in the room. The sound grew with every step that Carduth took. My ears hurt, my eyes began to sting and burn and my heart beat faster as the intensity of the noise grew. I glanced at Lilly, she was clutching her chest, tears of blood streamed down her face.

'You think you are the strongest, yet you are the most vulnerable one of them all because you are the source aren't you?' Carduth said, and his hand fell on the box.

Lilly fell to her knees still gripping her sword. *Run, Chez! Save yourself!* She held the amber pommel aloft and as Carduth raised the lid of the box, Lilly swung the sword weakly in his direction. All this time I was paralysed by the drums, but there was little pain, as whatever was in the box was being directed at Lilly.

The lid suddenly slammed down and Carduth backed away. 'Where did you get *that*?' he cried, raising a hand to point at the hilt of the sword.

The amber stone in Lilly's sword glowed in the candlelight, casting a faint yellow shadow on Carduth.

Suddenly my limbs were released and I hurled myself at Lilly, scooped her up in my arms and barged past Carduth and through the men blocking the door. Without direction from Carduth they tumbled like wooden soldiers. Carduth had fallen back also, shielding his face, but from what I just couldn't understand. I ran down the stairs, bulldozed through a group of men guarding the main door and, still clutching Lilly, I ran full pelt out into the night. Within minutes I was soaring through the air holding Lilly close to my racing heart.

A few miles away from Rome we landed. Lilly was dazed, but slowly recovering. Her eyes were raw and burnt, and there were criss-cross scars of bright red highlighting the veins and arteries in her arms and face. It was as though her blood was burning from the inside.

'What was that?' she asked. 'I couldn't move, couldn't fight.'

'Neither could I, but it only paralysed me, whereas you …'

'My heart hurts.' She pressed her hand against her chest and only then did I notice the sword still clutched in her hand.

'You need to feed,' I said. 'It's the only way you'll heal.'

'Yes. But Chez. Why did he stop?'

I stared at the sword. The amber stone was still glowing faintly. I remembered our brief observation that the stone showed the world in a different way, revealed auras, and I wondered what we would see if we scrutinised Carduth through it.

'You need to hold onto that, Lilly. I think it just saved our lives.'

Lilly stared down at the hand that gripped the sword. She opened her fingers and the skin peeled away from her hand, clinging to the sword. She grimaced but we vampires don't generally feel pain over minor grazes and cuts. There was an imprint burnt into her hand where the sword, or her flesh, had grown so hot it appeared like a brand.

'I don't think the sword would have let me release it,' Lilly said. 'Even though I could barely lift it before me, my grip never failed. What the hell is going on Chez?'

I looked out into the quiet Italian countryside.

'I don't know. But we have to get out of here. I feel you're more at risk than everyone else now.'

'No. I'm the strongest of us.'

'Under normal circumstances I'd say that was true. But whatever Carduth has in that little box of his, it is completely toxic to you. Like he says – you're the source.'

Lilly sheathed her sword; she was looking stronger and healing with every passing moment.

'I'm suddenly very worried about Gabi. I don't know why, but we need to get back home right away. Maybe it was stupid coming here in the first place. I'm not sure we've learnt anything more at all.'

I didn't agree, but I kept silent. I think we'd learned many things but it would all need to be assimilated. Carduth was some sort of a warlock, despite his protestations. He had a powerful weapon: although since this first began we'd always known that he wielded some power. He could control the time portals too. But what was most intriguing of all was that Carduth knew so much about us. He knew Lilly's strengths and weaknesses and that made him a very formidable enemy. At least now, we also knew we possessed something that could not only weaken him, but perhaps negate his power. The only question was, why?

29
Anja's Place

Five Months Ago

Björn's investigation led him to an apartment, a few streets away from the University. It was within walking distance but he still took his car, parking across the street so that he could study the building first. It was a five-story block, built in the 1930's, having those square lines that had been popular for a time. It wasn't at all the type of place in which I would have expected Anja to live. There was something vaguely decadent and old about the building and he always imagined she would live somewhere modern, like his apartment. Perhaps that was why she had made herself so at home there.

The main reception entrance was open and unmanned. Björn walked in and headed straight to the lift. Nervous guilt brought a slight film of sweat to his cheeks and under his arms. As the doors of the lift opened Björn came face to face with an old woman, carrying a basket with a cat inside. He nodded politely, stepping back to allow her to exit into the reception. Then feeling conspicuous he quickly entered the lift and pressed the button.

Anja's apartment was on the second floor. The lift jolted, doors opened. Björn noted how the lift wasn't quite aligned with the level of the floor and was careful as he stepped down slightly into the corridor. He looked both ways. The apartment block was incredibly quiet, fortunate if you were planning to enter someone else's property without their permission. He glanced at the numbers on the nearest doors, assessing which direction he needed to go to find Anja's, and then turned right as the lift doors closed behind him.

He heard the lift descending back down to the reception area, and hurried along the corridor looking for number 219. He wanted to be inside before anyone else came onto the floor. Not that what he was doing was that illegal. He had the key after all and wouldn't be breaking in as such.

He found the apartment and fumbled in his pocket for the key. *It's not there!* Panic surged into his face. The key was gone! He had lost it! He felt around his pocket, discovering a hole in the lining. He patted his jacket, the key had fallen inside and so he pushed his fingers through the rip, whilst holding the key from the outside of his jacket, guiding it back through the hole and into his hand.

The lift clattered to a halt again behind him, having returned from reception as he pressed the key into the lock. Björn glanced down the corridor once more, then rapidly turned the key. He threw himself into the apartment, closing the door behind him gently, as he heard the lift doors open. He rested with his back on the door, listening to see if hurried feet were running his way, but there was no sound at all from outside. His guilt was making him paranoid but, other than his dealings with Noble, Björn had always been generally honest and spying like this was breaking his inner code.

As his breath steadied, Björn began to look around the small hallway noticing a pile of letters on the floor at his feet. He picked them up, looked at the name and address printed on each. Then he placed them on the table beside the door.

He shuffled down the short corridor and entered the first room he came to. A large lounge with a very high ceiling, opened up before him. This was a surprise as the hall ceiling had been low. Around the room were several cabinets displaying vases and artefacts of varying quality.

'You have been busy, Anja,' Björn murmured.

It seemed that Anja retained some of the things she had stolen. So, might the box still be there? Björn hurried through the apartment.

In Anja's bedroom he found a handful of the doubloons she had stolen from the first dig. He scooped them up, examining the coins, then realised they were fake from some modern *mardi gras* in the United States. He put them down in disgust. Then he turned to the bed. It was made up, and ready for her return. Anja had no intention of letting this place go it seemed. If nothing else she was keeping her 'treasures' here.

He opened the drawer at the side of the bed. Inside he found her passport and a few photographs. A young circus performer, a girl of about twelve, smiled back at the camera. She was heavily made up but her young, pre-pubescent shape belied the adult make-up. The next picture was of a circus family. A father, mother and daughter. The father was dressed as a magician or … He looked again at the young girl. The pale, slightly dirty-looking blonde hair. Björn turned over the print, and on the back, written in very small writing was a date and a sentence. Björn reached into his inside pocket and pulled out his reading glasses.

The Great Shlome and his family. Hypnotist to the Stars.

The date indicated that the picture was ten years old but the colours of the print were bright and vibrant, as though it had only been printed recently. A few more pictures showed the family, but none of them had anything written on the back. Björn returned them to the drawer and closed it. Then he continued his search of the apartment, rifling through drawers and cupboards until he was satisfied that he knew enough about Anja to justify his actions.

He found expensive artefacts among fakes. It was almost as if Anja took and sold some things, but kept others, maybe even had some of them reproduced for her own amusement.

By the time he had finished his search Björn knew more about Anja than he had ever known, but still she remained an enigma. He found letters from her parents. They were still performing, touring Sweden and Europe with a huge American Circus. None of what he found was particularly helpful, except the information that Anja's father was a hypnotist. It explained a lot, but not everything. Hypnotists were not supposed to be able to make you *really* forget things, nor were they reported to have the ability to plant fake and detailed memories long term. At least not to this degree. He had always thought those kind of performers were fake anyway, sure that the volunteers they pulled from the audience were planted there. They had to be for the health and safety laws that now governed Circus performances.

Using his mobile phone Björn took pictures of the artefacts he recognised. Some of them he recalled receiving and then 'forgetting' about. He had been remembering more and more as the hours had passed since the first jolt of memory.

He glanced at his watch. Two-thirty. He had been there for hours and he knew that Anja would be finishing the day-long interview by 4pm.

Björn tidied up the evidence of his intrusion, returning the pile of letters to the floor in the hallway. He left the apartment feeling less guilty knowing now that Anja was a thief. But he wasn't sure what he was going to do about it. A vague plan formed in his mind. He could lay a trap for her perhaps? Or maybe just give an anonymous tip off to the police about this place? It occurred to him that his fingerprints would be found all over the place. Björn shrugged. He could come back another day and rectify that.

In the lift he returned the key back into his jacket pocket then pressed the button to take him back to the ground floor reception. First, he would go and get the key copied. Then he would return to the University, replace it in Anja's purse. By the time she returned from her interview he would be behind his desk, working hard again.

The doors opened to reception. Björn stepped out as a priest passed him. He didn't glance back but it occurred to him once more that this was indeed a weird apartment block. A smile peppered his lips, amusement bubbling up into his throat. He stifled the hysterical laughter as he saw the old woman with the basket hanging around on the door step.

'You be a good girl now, Elsa,' the old woman said. She was walking her cat on a lead. 'You have to learn to do this outside now ...'

A crazy cat lady, a priest and Anja – circus child and hypnotist. What a weird mix. Wonder who else lives here?

Björn walked away down the street chuckling to himself. His mood was surprisingly light considering all he had learnt. It was such a relief to realise that he wasn't losing his mind after all. As he reached his car a thought occurred to him. He would play along with her, find out what she was up to and then he would pass her onto the authorities. But first, he had have his own little bit of revenge.

30
Suspicion

Present Day

'What happened?' asked Gabi as we stepped back through the portal, arriving at exactly the same moment that he and Amalia did. 'I thought you were staying behind.'

We were in the grounds of Rhuddlan and I felt the warming embrace of magic, mingled with the winter sunshine, vibrating through my feet and into my body as we walked towards the entrance to the lair.

'Let's get inside,' Lilly said.

'It's a long story, but a lot has happened since we last saw you,' I said, then explained about our meeting with Carduth as we closed the door behind us and began our descent down the long staircase.

'Oh my God!' cried Amalia. 'He's going to kill us all. We're doomed!'

I had to resist glaring at her. Her reaction was typically overdramatic and totally annoying. Gabi hugged Amalia absently but his eyes were on Lilly and I could sense the fear he had for her. I'd persuaded Lilly to feed before our return and so she looked healed and as strong as ever but I could still see a fine trace of the burn scars on the veins on her throat.

As soon as she reached the lair proper, Lilly sat cross-legged in the lounge and meditated. I could feel her accessing the ley power that sustained the nature of Rhuddlan. The vibrations around us increased.

'I'm raising a ward of protection,' she explained. 'No one

will get in here. Not without us knowing about it.'

'What if … ?' Gabi began.

Lilly opened her eyes and met his gaze with steady green eyes.

'What if Carduth opens a portal that leads in here?'

'The intent behind the magic is what makes it work,' Lilly said. 'Carduth obviously has some advanced knowledge of using magic, but I don't know if he can manipulate ley lines. But on the basis that he might be able to do that, or actually have enough control to arrive wherever he pleases by using the portals, I've focused the power to repel all use of portals within the domain. Not even I could summon one here.'

'I thought you said the portals were everywhere,' Amalia said.

'They are. But right now, any that did or could open within our lair are now effectively blocked. It's as though I've taken hammer, wood and nails and boarded up all entrances … except it's a hell of a lot stronger than that obviously.'

Amalia went into the kitchen and warmed some blood, bringing in a mug for each of us. I took my mug, sniffed the contents, then drank the blood straight down. Gabi nursed his mug and stared at the blank television screen. He didn't reach for the remote control to switch it on, his mind was miles away.

Lilly never touched her drink, but continued to meditate. I could feel her searching and probing the area around Rhuddlan, looking for any sign of invasion.

Amalia drank, then took her mug back into the kitchen. I heard the water running as she cleaned up. Then my mind's eye followed her as she went upstairs to hers and Gabi's room. I waited a reasonable time then I stood and left the room. I wanted to know what she was up to.

Outside her room I listened to the tapping of her fingers as she sent a text. Her fingers were moving rapidly over the keys. I heard a faint ping as she sent the message. Then, as I had before, I jumped over the rail and landed silently below just as she came out of her room. I began to climb the stairs.

'Hey. Are you okay?' I asked smiling at her.

She nodded but her eyes didn't meet mine.

'Gabi was looking for you …' I said. 'I need to just get something for Lilly from our room, then I'll be in. We need to talk more about our game plan.'

Amalia went back to the lounge dutifully and in those few moments I hurried at supernatural speed up to her room and searched for the phone she had been using. I was determined to discover who she had sent the text too.

Downstairs I could hear the faint murmur of my friends talking. I couldn't be gone too long and so I looked in what I thought might be good hiding places. I quickly searched Amalia's bags, including her make-up vanity case, but after looking in drawers, cupboards, and a quick rifle through her underwear drawer, I couldn't find anything suspicious.

Maybe she's carrying it on her person. That would stand to reason. If I had a guilty secret I probably wouldn't let it out of my sight.

I heard movement downstairs and paused. Someone was in the kitchen, maybe Amalia again. I looked around the room, making sure there was no evidence of my search. I knew Amalia was up to something. I just didn't know what and if it was important.

I returned downstairs and back into the lounge. Lilly hadn't moved and Amalia and Gabi were sat together on the sofa quietly drinking more blood.

'Chez,' said Gabi, 'I'm concerned that this means that Rhuddlan has become our prison. We'll all go stir crazy if we have to hide down here all the time.'

'If and when we go out we must just remain alert,' I said. 'Carduth seems to have knowledge of where we'll be. He knew we were in his room at the *Palazzo*. I have no clue how as we didn't even know where we would end up. The thing is, unless we find out how he gets this knowledge, we are at risk anywhere but here.'

'Rhuddlan is our safe haven, just as it has always been,' Lilly said. 'At least here we know we are relatively secure from attack.'

Amalia met my eyes, then blinked and looked away. It would seem she had a guilty conscience, but then maybe I was imagining it? *Perhaps I should tell Lilly of my suspicions and we could search the girl, find that phone and see exactly what she was up to?* I thought. But did I want to play my trump card so soon? Or was it better to wait and catch her when she believed she was beyond reproach? I weighed up the situation against the possible outcomes of waiting. One or more of us could be killed at any time.

Lilly, I thought, finally making a decision. *Amalia has a mobile phone. She was talking on it the other day to someone and just now I heard her texting. I think we need to see who she is communicating with.*

Lilly's eyes didn't open. She made no move at all and I thought perhaps she was too far away in her meditation to hear my thoughts.

A silence fell over the room. It was as though we had all entered a different time zone, similar to the dense atmosphere I felt whenever we crossed a portal.

'I want your mobile phone please, Amalia,' Lilly said.

Amalia sat upright on the sofa. 'What?'

'She doesn't have ...' Gabi began then stopped as he met Lilly's gaze. Her eyes were balls of green fire.

'Oh yes she does,' Lilly said. 'It's in her pocket.'

'I ... what's this all about? You all have phones ... except Chez, as he doesn't seem to know how to use one ...' Amalia said lightly. 'Why can't I ... ?'

Lilly was in front of her in seconds. 'The phone?'

Amalia reached inside her pocket, withdrew a phone and handed it to Lilly.

The phone was switched off and there was a pin number that had to be entered.

'The pin?' asked Lilly.

Amalia shook her head; blotches of colour were fouling her cheeks. 'It's *my* phone. Occasionally I text my family. My parents don't know that I'm ...'

'The pin?' Lilly asked again.

'This is an invasion of my privacy!' Amalia said.

'If you have nothing to hide, then there's no reason why we shouldn't see the contents of your mailbox.'

Amalia stared at Lilly, fear and apprehension danced behind her eyes and I was reminded once more how she was such a watered down version of us.

'Gabi?' Amalia said.

'The pin,' Gabi answered. I was glad to see that there was no way he would side with Amalia against Lilly despite the change in dynamics.

Amalia took the phone back, entered her pin and handed it back to Lilly.

Immediately Lilly looked through her texts. The air was tense as Lilly read each one, then she held out the phone to Gabi.

'They were in Carduth's room at the palace ...' Gabi read aloud. 'There's a date, time. The same as you described to us.'

Amalia sank into her cushions.

'Who is Konstantin?' asked Gabi. 'He's the person you sent this too.'

Amalia said nothing.

'Who is Konstantin?' Lilly asked again.

'He's ... a friend. Just a friend.'

Gabi struck Amalia firmly across the face. The impact sent her hurtling across the room into the television. The flat screen shattered as she hit it. Black glass burst over the beige carpet in a shower of sparks and the frosted glass unit that held it crumbled to the floor as Amalia landed on it.

Lilly had the girl by the throat and up against the wall before she could shake off Gabi's stunning blow.

'Don't lie to me. I want to know. I want to know everything.'

I felt the power rise. The air became electrified as Lilly pulled energy up from the ground below.

Amalia choked out a scream. I stood beside Lilly waiting to rip the girl's throat out if she failed to come clean. The air crackled, both Amalia and Lilly's hair lifted up with static energy.

'He's my boss …' Amalia blurted.

'What?' asked Gabi.

'I work for him. He hired me to examine artefacts. I'm an archaeologist …'

'What bullshit is this?' Lilly said.

'He lied to me …' Amalia cried. 'Once I signed the contracts he *owned* me. I had to do everything he said.'

'Amalia,' I said calmly. 'You're a vampire. Any ties to your old life should have been severed. What can a mortal man do to you? What you are saying just doesn't make sense.'

Lilly dropped the girl and Amalia fell in a heap at her feet. 'Talk.'

'You don't understand. If he finds out … he might kill me.'

'If you don't talk,' said Gabi, 'we definitely will.'

Tears flooded from the girl's eyes as a jumbled story poured like an uncontrolled waterfall from her lips. Lilly and Gabi sank down onto the sofa as the story unfolded, but I didn't move. I didn't trust her, even though I could tell that every word she said was true.

PART TWO

Anja's Story

1
Björn's Revenge

Five Months Ago

Preventing Anja from using her hypnosis on him was far more difficult than he could have anticipated. Björn returned to his apartment, waited for her to come back and then avoided physical contact with her as much as possible.

He knew that she would have won the job. If not for her skills, charisma and references then she would have employed her unusual talent to persuade the interviewer. So, when she arrived home, he had the champagne chilled and instead of attempting to hug her he placed the glass in her hand.

She was excited, glowing and didn't notice his physical avoidance. Maybe it was a relief for her that he didn't try to touch her that evening.

'The job is everything I ever wanted, Björn. There will be travel, but you needn't worry, I won't be away all that much.'

'You mustn't be concerned about me, Anja,' Björn said. 'You have to follow your dream. This is what *you* want isn't it?'

'Yes. Of course. Thank you for understanding so much.'

'Let's go out to dinner,' Björn suggested. 'I booked a table.'

'You had that much confidence in me getting the job?'

'Naturally. You were the best candidate.'

Björn knew all the right things to say to keep her suspicions at bay and she was so enthused that it never occurred to her to doubt her power over him. They ate out, a juicy steak and some fine red wine. Anja drank a lot more than she usually did and when she went to the bathroom at the restaurant, leaving her half filled glass on the table Björn used this opportunity to pour a specially procured clear liquid into her drink.

By the time they got home, she was reeling. She felt spaced out and confused.

'I feel sick,' she said, running to the toilet.

Björn held her hair back as she emptied her stomach of all the rich foods they'd enjoyed. Then, helping her stand as she brushed her teeth, he slipped off her dress and led her to the bed. She did this meekly in a dazed and drunken way.

'I drank ssuue mush,' she slurred, but of course Björn knew that really it was the Rohypnol he had placed in her drink.

As she collapsed unconscious on the bed, Björn got to work, first tying her wrists tightly to the bedposts, then, her ankles, legs wide open.

He left her there, covers thrown over her naked body, and went back into the lounge. He lay on the sofa, draping a duvet over his legs and slept.

The next morning Björn woke to Anja's startled yell from the bedroom.

He wandered into the room, stared at her terrified face as she pulled on the ropes. Then he drew back the covers and looked down at her naked body. There was a small scar on the right side of her abdomen. Björn knew it was from an appendix operation. In his fake memories, Anja's body had always been perfect and unscarred. His vision of her was different in other ways too. She was much thinner in reality than her hypnosis had led him to believe. He had thought her curvier, with fuller breasts. The truth was, she had the body of an athlete. Leaner, more wiry, and her breasts were tiny, almost pre-pubescent.

'What are you doing? Let me free!' Anja said with an edge to her voice.

Björn ignored her, but he felt a small prickle at the back of his neck and realised she was using something in her voice to return him to his usual catatonic state.

'Björn? Björn. You know you must listen to me …'

'Shut up,' he said. 'Be quiet or I'll gag you.'

'Darling … is this some kind of joke?'

On her thigh, Björn saw another scar. This one was long, thin and white. It was an old scar.

'Where did you get that one?' he asked. 'Some accident in the circus?'

Panic flooded Anja's face but still she tried to lie to him, 'I don't … I … haven't. I don't know what you're talking about … *There is no scar.*'

Björn rubbed the back of his neck and focused on the mark on her leg. Slowly it began to fade and disappear, and he realised that Anja was starting to get to him. She had spent months planting triggers in his brain, why hadn't he realised that it would be so easy for her to control him again. He shook his head.

'There is a scar,' he insisted. His finger traced it and he watched in amazement as it reappeared before his eyes. 'You lying bitch. I told you keep quiet.'

Anja fell silent. Her mind was all over the place and she could feel the fury drifting through Björn as he touched her skin. She needed to save her moment, wait until his guard went down. It would eventually; it was human nature after all that he would finally believe he was in charge and not she. That would be her moment.

Björn's touch burned her skin, Anja hated it. She had always despised the feel of someone else's flesh and so had never allowed it. Now she felt his lust rising, his eyes were all over her nakedness, seeing it all for real for the first time. His thoughts pushed into her. Her girly, less womanly, figure was turning him on in a way her fantasy shape hadn't.

I thought I was so clever moving in here with him. Believing he was firmly under my influence. Panic began to rise higher in her chest. What was he going to do?

'You've been playing me,' he said.

'No!'

'Shut up!'

His slap was firm but not bruising, just enough to show her he meant what he said.

'Playing me. All this time. Pretending you loved me.'

Anja considered lying, but her cheek was stinging and she was afraid to talk again in case Björn kept his promise of gagging her. She would have no chance at all to work on him if she was silenced. She hadn't come all this way, worked this hard, just to fail now. She let him paw her. His fingers flicked over her small nipples. Sickness rose in the back of her throat but she resisted the urge to squirm, instead she pretended to respond to him.

'You see, I have all these memories in my head. Things that happened between us that I thought were real. But now I know it was all false, Anja. You never even really seduced me. You just played with my mind. You don't even look the same. You're like a teenage girl in shape, not womanly at all.'

Anja opened her mouth to speak once more but the look in Björn's eyes terrified her to silence.

'I'm going to have some of what you pretended to give. Then. I want you out of here and out of my life.'

'No!' Anja gasped. 'Björn … you can't … *Rape* me?'

'How can it be rape, Anja? We've been living together. Everyone knows that. There won't be a court that believes you …'

'*No!*' she said again. 'I can't … I don't …'

'You don't what? You can only play the whore in my mind?'

Björn began to strip. Anja closed her eyes, her head shaking denial from side to side. She couldn't bear intimacy; the pain of his emotions would drive her insane. That's what *they'd* told her. Physical contact had to be kept to a minimum.

He was on top of her now. His nakedness touching hers and it was torture. The violence of his anger burst into her body, screamed through her head and she couldn't deflect it. His lust was fuelled by his violence. Anja tugged at her bonds again, but Björn was used to tying knots, hadn't she seen him secure the crates after a dig?

'Please …' she whispered.

His breath was hot and foul on her face. She tried to twist away from his bearded kiss. She could smell the food still lurking in there, the unwashed odour of his body. It was too vile, too grotesque. A scream bubbled up in her throat as he positioned himself between her legs. His hand reached down and brushed her pubis sending a surge of his desire through her. It was monstrous how her weakness excited him.

He opened her up as no one had. The pain was more than she could bear. Her eyes rolled up in the back of her head as he pushed a little harder.

'Oh yes,' gasped Björn. 'You're every bit as tight as I thought you'd be.'

He pulled back, pushing hard and this time buried himself deep. Anja didn't react as his hate and lust poured into her mind. He grunted above her, she was open now, mentally and physically and he was brutalising all of her. Spittle dribbled from her mouth as she lay comatose but still so aware.

He wasn't in any hurry and so it went on for a while. When he came some part of Anja returned as he withdrew. His cruelty was gone, she had survived it. He would let her go now. She would stagger out of here, back to her safe haven across the town. But, he didn't release her, just threw a blanket over her once more and went to sleep at her side. She lay awake, stunned as blood and semen seeped out between her legs. She had never known such pain.

Hours later, he woke and the torment started again, by then Anja was too afraid to speak or object. She lay silent and still as he grunted above her gasping her name as though they really were lovers. She had spent months assaulting his mind, feeding him false memories, telling him he loved her and she loved him. As she lay beneath him the reality of her situation dawned on her. She had built this. She had created the monster that was now Björn – didn't she then deserve all he gave her?

Hours, then days, passed. Her contract arrived for her new job with instructions for her start date. Björn opened her mail, read her the instructions.

'Looks like your first assignment is next week,' he said.

Anja said nothing. She hadn't spoken a word in over two days.

Björn threw the letter down on the bed then bent down and untied the ropes. His eyes avoided her gaze.

'I want you out of here,' he said.

She could barely stand as she struggled off the edge of the bed. Björn watched her, but didn't touch her as she staggered, limbs stiff and sore; muscles cramping after the unnatural position they'd been forced into. Inside the bathroom, Anja locked the door, collapsing on the floor. She sobbed as she rubbed her chafed wrists and cramping calves.

He had fed her water, but refused her toilet breaks. Her body stank of piss but worst of all as she sat, back to the door, knees bent, she could smell Björn's semen. It was all over her legs, smearing her thighs mingled with the blood from her broken hymen. His lust hadn't physically hurt the second and subsequent times, but her mind was brutalised. She felt fragmented, scared and weak. All of the things she had never been.

Anja crawled to the edge of the bath, pulled herself up and began running the water. She would get clean, swill away Björn's stench, then pack and get out of here. She sat on the toilet as she watched the bath fill. She didn't feel in control. Her body was undermined by lack of mobility and food.

As the bath filled she stood on legs that felt fragile, as though any step might break her bones. Then she tested the water, switching off the taps. She climbed in carefully but the water stung her in places she never knew could be sore. Her vagina felt ripped. She glanced down as the blood and secretions discoloured the water. Her fingers probed downwards. She hurt, so much, but it was probably just bruising. She lay back letting the water soak her, then she reached for the body wash and began to scrub until her skin hurt. But no matter how hard she washed, she couldn't seem to remove the stench of Björn's sex. She knew she would never feel clean again.

2
Suicide Attempt

Five Months Ago

Anja awoke. Her eyes felt blurred and her arms and wrists stiff. She tried to lift her arm but found it attached to something. A scream bubbled up in her throat. *Björn! He's tied me down again …* Her terrified eyes flew open to a bright room, different from Björn's apartment. Where had he taken her? What was going on?

'You're awake. Good.'

A face appeared in the light, leaning towards her. A man wearing a white coat. He smiled at her kindly. Then flashed a brighter light into her eyes. She gasped. Blinked.

'Good. Reflexes seem sound. How do you feel?'

She opened her mouth but the first attempt brought no sound.

'Dry throat?'

He held a glass of water to her cracked lips. She sipped. The lubrication helped.

'Where am I?' she croaked.

'My dear, you are in hospital. You tried to kill yourself.'

'No,' Anja shook her head. 'I would never …'

Memories flooded back into her mind. Björn's rape. The terror of those days tied down and left to stew in her own body fluids. She felt so dirty. Especially inside. In her head. In her blood.

Anja lifted her hand and saw a bandage on her wrist. Her other arm was attached to a drip.

'We had to give you three transfusions. You are incredibly lucky to be alive.'

'I slit my wrists?' she said.

'Indeed you did. Good job your boyfriend found you. Although he did leave it rather late. It was touch and go for a while.'

She closed her eyes. Memories flooding her brain as she flashed back again to the bathroom. The razor. The release of blood. The first cut had hurt, but nowhere near as much as Björn had hurt her. Letting the blood leak from her veins had brought something of a release.

'Where is he?' she asked.

'Who?'

'Björn?'

Her eyes were more focused as she opened them again. Seeing the surprise on the doctor's face, Anja paused before asking her next question.

'Where is Björn? You said he found me?'

'No. I did.'

Anja turned her head. She found herself staring at Konstantin Caradien. For a moment she couldn't remember how she knew him. Then the memories crashed in. He owned Caradien Industries and was her new boss. But the interview for Caradien Industries seemed a lifetime ago.

'Please leave us,' Konstantin said and the doctor nodded, leaving the room quickly and discretely. The door closed silently behind him.

'You're in one of our hospitals.' Konstantin said.

'What happened?'

'I began to feel concerned when I rang your mobile many times and there was no answer. We tried several avenues to contact you. I knew about your relationship with Adelman, I always check up on my potential employees, Anja. In fact I knew all about your parents and … your special gift. It's why I hired you.'

Konstantin Caradien was wearing gloves when he shook her hand. *How odd*, Anja thought as disappointment coloured her face briefly. She had hoped for physical contact. It would have helped her assess what the Caradien Industries' Chairman was looking for.

'Please sit down, Anja,' Konstantin said.

His voice was warm and friendly, full of sexuality. Anja scrutinised him with interest. He was attractive, mid to late thirties, she guessed. He had dark blond hair and intense blue eyes that danced with mischief as he smiled at her. Anja found herself responding to his charm; his baby-faced good looks. He even had dimples that she found quite endearing.

'Your reference from Professor Adelman is excellent,' Konstantin said. 'It seems your qualifications are well deserved.'

'I worked hard,' Anja said. 'I'm dedicated to archaeology.'

'Mmmm,' Konstantin smiled. 'How do you think your experience will aid Caradien Industries?'

The question was one she had been expecting and she had her answer ready but Anja hesitated to use it. Something about Konstantin made her question herself. He was a closed book. Despite his friendly aspect there were none of his emotions floating in the air for her to explore. For the first time she felt blind. Anja realised with a jolt that she had gone through most of her life relying on her empathy. How she behaved was a reflection of other people's thoughts and feelings. In this situation she had planned her answer, but would have tested Konstantin on smaller comments, feeling her way to his needs by judging his reactions. But it was impossible to tell at all what he was thinking.

'The truth is …' Anja began. 'I would … the company would …'

'Yes?'

'I love relics. I respect history, but we would have to come to arrangements that suited all parties … wouldn't we?' Anja felt insecure.

Konstantin said nothing. His face retained a vague, kind smile.

'I mean … Caradien would be paying me … so …'

'That is *exactly* the right answer. Obviously, Caradien Industries strives to be as environmentally friendly as possible.

We will always weigh the needs of the company against the needs of our country. History is also important to us, otherwise we wouldn't have this very imperative role for you.'

Anja nodded and breathed at the same time. The movement was awkward and made her more aware of how tense she had been feeling.

'The job is yours. If you still want it?'

'Yes. I do,' she said a little too quickly.

'Good. I hoped you would say that. I have the contract drawn up for you to look at.' He held out a thick wad of paper. 'Please take your time. You *must* read all the codicils before you decide to sign.'

Konstantin closed the door behind him, leaving Anja to her thoughts. She stared down at the paper in her hands; the first page held the details of her salary. She blinked, re-read the page then gasped. Her days of stealing relics to subsidise her family were gone. 11,000,000 Krona a year would go a long way. If she were careful, she could stockpile money. Money meant freedom, she had always understood that. Saving money was something she had always been good at: why buy luxuries when you could just as easily steal them? Anja picked up the pen lying casually on the desk before her and she flicked to the last page. There was no reason to read on. All she needed to know was here, on the front page. She quickly signed her name and, as if he knew she was ready, Konstantin returned.

She handed the papers to him.

'I'll get my secretary to copy this,' he said. 'And in the meantime, let me show you your office.'

It was just a few short feet down the hallway from Konstantin's office and it was no less large or impressive than the Chairman of Caradien Industries' had been. There was no through door to the boardroom; instead there was a large bathroom that led discretely off from the sitting area.

Inside Anja found a large Jacuzzi, a full sized shower, a toilet and a bidet. The room was decorated in black and white classical tiles. It had a Greek feel to it. It was absolutely stunning.

'Oh!' she said in surprise. 'Very nice.' *I don't think I'll ever really use it though,* she thought. *What a waste ...*

'You signed a contract with me,' Konstantin said.

Anja's mind returned to the hospital room. Her head was fuzzy and her wrists ached. She lifted up her arm again, squinting at the drip that fed into her arm.

'What is this?' she asked.

'Morphine. We don't want you to feel any pain.'

'I'm fine. Can you tell the doctor to remove it? It's making me feel weird. I don't even know what you were saying.'

'I said. We take care of our own. You signed a contract with me.'

'I'm sorry. I must be a major disappointment to you right now. I haven't even started my job and already it looks as though I'm completely unstable.'

Konstantin sat down in the seat beside her bed. 'You haven't disappointed me Anja. I need to know what happened though.'

Anja closed her eyes. Her mind was confused. A flash of memory brought back Björn's rape.

'Björn's dead,' said Konstantin as though reading her thoughts.

Anja's eyes snapped open. 'How?'

'He shouldn't have done what he did to you,' Konstantin continued.

'I guess I deserved it. I was foolish.'

'You are under contract to me. I can't allow you to be ... damaged.'

Anja closed her eyes again. Her cheeks flushed. She felt confused and embarrassed by the conversation. She was sure it was just the medication but she could have sworn that the words Konstantin used implied she *belonged* to him somehow.

'I'm fine,' she said. 'Björn's really dead?'

'Yes.'

Anja shook her head. A prickle of guilt fluttered over her scalp. Björn was dead. Somehow she knew it was her fault.

'He deserved it,' Konstantin said. 'He was a rapist. Maybe he was the one who cut your wrists too. Possibly he became afraid you'd go to the police.'

'No. He knew I couldn't.'

'I can't have anyone damage my property,' Konstantin said. 'You see I have a very important job for you …'

'I know. Relics …'

'That's not what I mean Anja. Do you know anything about your heritage?'

The morphine filtered farther into her blood stream, tiredness overwhelmed her. Anja's mind slowly drifted away as Konstantin talked. She had a strange dream. Crazy. One where he told her all about the existence of vampires and time travel. She knew it was a dream. None of those things could possibly exist.

'Now all I need from you is the relic …' Konstantin said.

Anja drifted awake again, 'Relic …?'

'Yes. The one you stole from Björn. Who did you give it to?'

Sleep crashed down and darkness smothered her mind. She drifted on a sea of her treasures. Relics, artefacts, jewels and coins: all hers and she loved them. But there was a box, somewhere distant. She tried to reach for it but it floated away.

'I don't know …' she murmured.

3
Konstantin Caradien

Four and a half months earlier

Anja knew she was in love with Konstantin long before he took her out of the facility and back to his home. She would have done anything for him. He came every day to see her and during those visits she learnt a lot about the world she thought she once knew. He gave her proof: showed her pictures of the monsters. Sometimes, they had even been caught in the middle of the act of killing. Anja knew that Konstantin was right when he called them an 'abomination'.

He placed her bag in the spare bedroom.

'You'll be safe here. Safe from the authorities, who, by the way, are still looking for Björn's murderer … But here no one can touch you, Anja.'

'Konstantin? Why me? How can I help you?'

'You do not realise how important you are my dear. Meet me downstairs when you are settled in and we'll talk.'

Konstantin left her alone and only then did Anja look around the room. It was large and beautiful. A four-poster bed occupied the centre of the room and was covered in pink lace. Furniture of a quality that she would probably never dare to use – a stunning, ornate dressing table painted in white and gold, matched the doors of the fitted wardrobe. Anja opened the doors and found it was a walk-in. Filled with beautiful clothing. She ran her fingers over silks, velvet, laces. All the clothes were her size. Konstantin had prepared this place, this room, just for *her*. No one had ever been so kind and thoughtful to her.

After closing the wardrobe she noticed another door. Beyond she found her own bathroom. It reminded her of the one at the Caradien office building only this one was even more luxurious, with classic beige tiles. It was perfect. It was ultimate opulence. She loved it.

Anja unpacked her toiletries into the ensuite bathroom, then left the room to join Konstantin down in the drawing room. As she walked back down the expansive staircase she admired the paintings on the walls. They were old portraits, some of the faces reminded Anja of Konstantin and so she reasoned they must be ancestors of her benefactor.

'My dear. Please sit down.'

His manners were impeccable. Old fashioned but not in a negative way. Anja had learnt that Konstantin was always respectful, no matter what the situation. She wondered if he adhered to tradition as some form of OCD. He never took his gloves off and the touch of his skin somehow gave her no insight to him.

Anja sat down on a beautiful, regency sofa. It was surprisingly comfortable.

At that moment a butler appeared carrying a tray bearing two glasses of champagne. He held out the tray to Anja and she glanced at Konstantin uncertainly.

'We are celebrating. Please take the glass. I'm sure you'll enjoy it. It's my favourite, Cristal.'

Anja took the glass and the butler moved on to offer the other to Konstantin. Anja was impressed that the man's eyes never once strayed to the bandages that still covered her small wrists.

'What are we celebrating?' Anja asked.

'Your return to health and also to a successful working relationship.'

Anja sipped the champagne. It was nothing like the cheap plonk she'd had before. It was delicious, a bone dry wine, and she immediately enjoyed the rush it gave her.

'It's gorgeous,' she gasped.

'I know. I can't help but indulge myself.'

The butler returned with canapés. He served them, then placed the remainder on the coffee table between them.

'You like your antiques,' Anja said admiring the table.

Konstantin smiled. 'I am somewhat old-fashioned in my tastes.'

'I like it,' Anja said.

Later he made love to her. She was trembling, afraid of the rush of thoughts and emotions he would pass on. But Konstantin was considerate. He used a condom; she could feel the sensation of his cock fucking her, but none of his emotions. His gloves remained on the whole time and he didn't attempt to kiss her lips, even though his mouth paid attention to the rest of her body. One of the worst things about Björn's rape was that surge of his emotions, she felt his hatred with every touch.

Anja was confused that even though Konstantin's body touched hers, she still felt nothing from the man, but it was a huge relief.

She came as his tongue explored her. She had never been allowed to feel passion, nor was she able to abandon herself to lust for fear of the intimacy it would give. But even as she ran her fingers through Konstantin's hair, she felt nothing more than the natural sensation of touch. It was as though her gift had been turned off and she could finally relax.

'There's nothing to fear, Anja,' Konstantin told her later. 'I'm going to take care of you. You never have to worry again. And you'll never need to steal.'

'I don't know how I can repay you,' she said.

'I do. Who did you sell the relic to?'

Anja cast her mind back. She thought of all the little clues she had picked up over the years of dealing with her mysterious benefactor, but she couldn't put the pieces together.

'The courier was German I think. Always the same man,' she said. 'But my contact never allowed me to see him and his calls were always anonymous. He always contacted me. Strangely he knew when I'd have something coming in that would be of interest.'

Konstantin lay beside her quietly. He didn't touch or hold

her. There were no displays of love or affection but Anja didn't know how lovers should behave and so she only briefly observed this.

'Looking back now, I just don't know how it was possible.'

'Anything is possible in a world where real monsters live. You need to accept that. Sometimes we can't explain why or how things occur and yet they still do. We need to set a trap for your mysterious friend. Do you still have the mobile phone he calls you on?'

'Yes.'

'Good. You'll begin work on a site we found tomorrow. There are some interesting relics. I want you to behave as you would normally when you see something you're going to steal.'

'What do you mean?' Anja said.

'I mean, if you have to use your gift on my employees then do so. Treat this as a regular day for you.' Konstantin said.

'You want me to steal from you?'

'Precisely.'

'But. You said I didn't have to steal anymore …'

'That's the point really; you'll do everything you normally do, except you have my permission to do it. Technically you won't be stealing.'

Konstantin slipped out of the bed and returned to his own room to sleep. Anja slept peacefully for the first time in weeks. She felt safe and loved. She no longer had to think or plan anymore. It was a huge relief to feel no responsibility.

The next day she began work on the dig. It didn't take her long to find something she wanted. There were coins … four hundred years old. They were in excellent condition and would be very easy to shift. This was the kind of artefact that her contact usually went for. Anja didn't consider how convenient it was that the coins were there. She had always been lucky that way.

As she walked from the site, the stash in her rucksack, her phone vibrated in her pocket. Anja pulled it out and answered, but she already knew who would be on the other end of the line.

'Anja? You have something for me?'

'Yes,' she said but as always she was bewildered as to how the man knew.

'Good. My courier will meet you at your apartment in Stockholm.'

'My apartment?' Anja was surprised by this.

'The one where you keep your personal possessions. Well done on getting in with Caradien, by the way. This could become very lucrative for you …'

Anja stared at the phone long after her contact had hung up. She felt sick, insecure. How could this person know so much about her? And, if he knew all about her apartment as well, then what if he knew she was planning to set him up?

There was a limo waiting at the entrance to the dig for her. She climbed in to find Konstantin waiting for her. He was smiling.

'I noticed you received a call. It was him?'

Anja nodded, but her face was pale and fear and nausea weighed heavily in her stomach.

'He knows everything about me. He knows about us.'

'Of course he does,' Konstantin said. 'That's what's so intriguing.'

'He'll know he's being set up …'

Konstantin shook his head. 'He has no reason to suspect you. People with that kind of knowledge often believe they are invulnerable. By letting you know he has information about your life he's implying he can access your thoughts, but it doesn't mean he can.'

Anja wasn't convinced. After all, she could access other people's thoughts, albeit by physical contact mostly, and sometimes by being in close proximity. This man had neither, and yet he knew all there was to know about her life.

'I have someone based at your apartment already,' Konstantin was saying. 'They live in the block so won't be suspicious. We're going to follow the courier and find out exactly where he goes.' Anja nodded and Konstantin patted her hand with his gloved fingers. 'I told you that I will take care of you Anja, and I will. Nothing is going to harm you. It's crucial we get that relic back though …'

'Why?' she asked.

'It's a matter of life and death. I told you in the hospital. There are supernatural beings in this world. We need to cull them. The relic is the only thing that can do that …'

Anja wanted to ask what he was going to do, but was afraid to hear the answer. Konstantin, she realised, was something of a fanatic. He liked to be in control which was why she was now living under his roof.

'What … what will happen when you find this relic?' she asked finally.

'Then, my dear, you're going to play the best deceit you've ever attempted.'

'Me?'

'Yes. You're crucial to our success …'

Konstantin's limo pulled up outside her apartment. Anja hadn't been back there since the day Björn hurt her. She stared up at the building.

'I don't have my –' she started to say.

'Here,' Konstantin held out a shiny key and she knew without doubt it would open her door.

'Do the exchange as normal. When you come out, take a taxi back to my house,' he said.

Anja climbed out of the limo hefting her rucksack over onto her left shoulder. Then she entered the reception area without looking back. She heard the limo door shut and the car pull away as she pressed the call button for the lift.

4
Salome

Four Months Earlier

A vague pain clutched at Anja's heart as she stared at the box. It lay in her hands, pulsing, throbbing. She hadn't asked how Konstantin had acquired it, or if her old contact was even still alive. She just knew that he now had the box and deep down she was afraid to ask the question, just as she was too scared to ask what had really happened to Björn.

Since being in hospital, Anja's access to the media had been zero. There were no newspapers in Konstantin's house. Nor was there a television in any of the rooms she had been in. But then, she hadn't been in Konstantin's private suite. He came to her room for their liaisons and he always left soon after, preferring to sleep alone. Anja didn't mind that, it was her preference to be alone also: it was what she was used to. Being with Konstantin made her feel both safe and endangered at times: it was confusing. Physically she felt no threat. His body language was always benign, he never raised his voice and she was given everything she wanted without even needing to ask, but deep down, Anja knew it would be a serious mistake to cross her benefactor.

The box writhed in her lap, or appeared to. Anja jumped, looked down at it again and then back at Konstantin.

'Should I open it?' she asked, her eyes wide with fear and apprehension.

'Not now,' Konstantin said. Then he took the box from her and placed it in the safe behind his desk.

He took her hand and led her upstairs, stripped her trembling body, then pleasured her until she screamed.

'Why an Ankh?' Anja asked later as they lay in bed.

'It's the symbol adopted by the order,' Konstantin said.

'What order?'

'An organisation I'm involved with. We are dedicated to rid the world of all supernatural entities.'

'So the relic really belongs to your organisation?'

'Oh yes. It belongs to me.'

Konstantin explained it all again. Very carefully. This time, the third time she had heard the story, Anja began to understand it all a little more.

Their leader had been a man called Carduth. He discovered the monsters, way back in his time, which was in the fourteenth century. They were running things then, the whole of Rome had fallen to them and their kind. It had taken him a while, but Carduth had discovered their secret and it had to do with time-travel. Anja didn't really believe in monsters or time-travel, she thought humans were monstrous enough, especially some of the thoughts she had been privy to, and time-travel was the domain of television shows like *Doctor Who*. Still, she listened to Konstantin though she treated his words like a story, a fairytale, something to enjoy but not really believe in.

'How did Carduth discover their secret?' asked Anja.

'He saw one of them passing through a portal of time. He is a natural magician and he recognised the magic that the vampire used. He mimicked it. Then he travelled through time himself to set traps for them.'

Anja's head began to hurt a little. Again, she felt a tingle of lie in his words, or rather embellishment, but couldn't understand why.

'How did he know where they would be?' she asked.

Konstantin smiled. 'All in good time, Anja. All in good time.'

Then Konstantin told her the bible story.

'John the Baptist was pure. The first of our kind.' he said. 'You could say he was the founder of our order. Salome, the stepdaughter of King Herod came to him. She wanted to corrupt the holy man and he spat in her face. You see he recognised her as the whore she was. She was a spoilt girl, used to getting all of her own way. Salome couldn't take that kind of rejection. So, she pondered the problem. John was imprisoned in Herod's dungeons. She could have him tortured – could even accuse him of something. Salome knew she wouldn't be satisfied with that. That's the reason she danced for Herod.'

'The dance of the seven veils?' Anja asked.

'Yes. The dance made Herod want the girl more and she'd been playing him, stringing him along for quite some time.'

Playing me! Anja shuddered as Konstantin's words reminded her suddenly of Björn's.

'She asked Herod for John's head on a platter,' Anja said, remembering the story.

'That's the rumour … but actually, no. She asked for his heart to be cut out and given to her. Because if she couldn't make John love her, want her, then she could at least own his heart.'

'Ew. She was pretty sick,' Anja said, a shudder rippling through her.

'It was her instinct to play games, to be the centre of attention. In a way she was a victim of her own fate. John, of course, needed her to do what had been foretold by God. He was a holy man and couldn't be corrupted. Otherwise we wouldn't be here right now.'

Anja closed her eyes and Konstantin's story washed around her.

Salome was in pain as she danced in her chamber. Swirling and moving her hips to a music that only she could hear. The air was heavy with the odour of incense. It was supposed to make everything seem better, smell better and it appeased the Gods in some way that she didn't understand.

Her body ached. Ever since the monthly curse had begun, the thing that her mother said made her a woman, Salome had felt different.

Herod sent one of the eunuchs to see her soon after. The eunuch looked like a man, but was neither man nor woman. He had a high voice and feminine ways. But he showed her things, things that her body liked. Massaging oils into her skin, his hands explored her intimately. She couldn't stop his hands, even if she had wanted to and he worked her, touching that place between her legs until something happened, a release of some kind, that made her feel happy and relaxed. She wanted him to come again and see her, but he never did. Sometimes she touched herself but it didn't feel the same as when the eunuch had visited her.

Then she had been travelling with her mother, a brief visit into the market to examine the new import of silks. Herod had ordered it; he wanted her to see something of the world outside. Wanted her to appreciate all that she had in the palace.

Salome liked outside. The smells were different, not as foul as she had been led to believe and the people were interesting even if they did appear to be so alien to her that they barely seemed real.

When they passed the temple and she heard him talking, she had to stop and see who it was. 'John the Baptist', someone in the crowd informed her. 'He will save your soul.' But Salome didn't know what a soul was. Her life was about possessions and pleasure. She didn't think about any 'after life'.

Salome watched John through her veil. There was something about him, a roughness that she liked. It was far different from Herod and the only other men she came in contact with, the eunuchs. She thought about John lying with her, touching her as the eunuch had. She wanted him.

She weaved through the crowd, leaving her confused mother behind until she was a few feet from him. His speech moved her. She felt the urge to be cleansed and renewed by him, her eternal soul saved by the love of John's God. She would do it too, if he wanted her, if he would spend time with her.

John's eyes fell on Salome's veiled figure. His body stiffened. A tiny tremor rippled up his spine. He felt he was looking at death. An insane, unreasonable desire to lift the veil overcame him. He wanted to see the true face of the demon, the temptress, before him. His hand reached out. Salome was almost in his grasp and then suddenly she was surrounded by the King's guards who spirited her away. John took a step towards them, he had to follow, he had to know who and what she was for he was certain she wasn't human.

He found himself seized. The temptress screamed as she witnessed his capture. John struggled until he was knocked down and then dragged away by the soldiers. The crowd yelled in protest in a collective clamour. Herod's men couldn't take their saviour! They stormed the prison walls, shouting and yelling, demanding John's release.

Kneeling before King Herod, John felt no fear. He always knew this moment would come. He felt his impending martyrdom approaching.

'You dare defile my daughter,' Herod said.

John raised his head. His pure eyes met the spoilt and corrupt gaze of the King.

'She was a woman in the crowd,' John replied. 'I did not know who she was.'

Herod grew silent. He knew he couldn't kill John, as much as he wished to. The tales of his heresy reached the King daily but he had decided to forbear it to keep the peace among the people. For John was beyond reproach in his life. He lacked sin, and preached of goodness. Herod did not want to be the one to destroy him. He couldn't find a single reason worthy of that decision and he knew that by killing the man he would only be creating a martyr, and martyrs were even harder to kill.

'I have no difficulty with you, John who they call the Baptist', Herod said. 'You are not above the law and you speak of good, not evil. You cannot think this allows you to disrespect the person of a princess.'

John said nothing. His fate was in Herod's hands and there was little point in wasting words. He was taken away, stored in the dungeon but fed and given clean water. He wasn't beaten, or tortured. One day soon, Herod would just release him and he could continue with his prayers and baptisms.

The eunuch visited Salome again that evening. As he removed her clothing down to one discrete veil, lay her down and began his sensual massage, Salome noticed a slight movement in the ornate panel that separated her mother's chamber from hers.

For a moment she could not relax, but the eunuch was determined to bring her to pleasure and so she closed her eyes and thought about John. Her passion flooded the eunuch's fingers and as he left the room, leaving the girl swooning on her cushioned chaise, the panel opened and her step-father stood before her.

He told her he wanted her, would give her anything if she lay down and opened her legs to him. Salome was afraid, disgusted. She had never liked the King, but was always respectful to him.

'No!' she said. 'Don't touch me!'

Her mother, drawn by the commotion, entered her chamber. For a moment Herodias and Herod regarded each other. Herodias shrugged and Herod left the room.

'He's been good to us,' Herodias told Salome. 'You shouldn't anger him.'

'You want me to give myself to him?' Salome sobbed.

'He is the King ...'

The dungeon wasn't so bad; John had slept in worse places and at least he ate regularly. Then she came to see him, the temptress. Somehow John knew that this role was important. That she was important to the future.

'I'm sorry,' she said. 'I never meant you harm. I wanted to hear what you were saying. Herod wants me. But I want to be yours.'

John was silent but he stood and moved towards her, raising the veil that covered her face. Then he saw. He really saw who and what she was. John screamed. His death was near and this was a true portent.

Salome couldn't make him stop screaming. It was as though the sight of her sent the prophet mad. The guards came, beat him into silence. Salome backed away as John's screams became words.

'Whore of Satan,' he said. Then he pulled free of the guards, ran at her and spat in her face. 'Your children will be the spawn of the devil.'

Salome stumbled from the dungeon, blinded by tears she felt her way along the walls of the palace, back to her chamber. She fell down into her cushioned bed.

Herodias found her crying.

'How can you waste such tears on this peasant? ' her mother asked, 'When Herod will give you anything you desire.'

'I want his heart,' Salome cried. 'I want his heart!'

Salome was in pain. Anguish. She danced in her chamber. Swirling and moving her hips to a music that only she could hear. She could no longer bear to see her reflection in the looking glass and so a veil hung over the offending item. A distant music echoed through the palace as John's words came back to her. She was destined to be a whore. Her children would be evil. She was the spawn of Satan.

Anja opened her eyes as Konstantin finished his story. She had totally immersed herself in Salome's world. She felt her pain, understood her anguish.

'What did John see?' she asked.

'He saw her soul. He saw her future. He saw, I suspect, her gene code.'

'I don't understand.'

'All of us are born with a specific DNA. This is what makes us who we are. Salome was from a certain gene pool. She was a carrier of the vampire gene. She didn't know this and was in some respects innocent,' Konstantin explained.

'Then she wasn't a demon or devil? She couldn't help it. I feel sorry for her.'

Konstantin breathed in slowly and then exhaled. He still lay naked in the bed beside Anja. They did most of their talking after sex until Konstantin grew tired and left for his room. He stayed longer that night and even though he paused, Anja knew he had more to say.

'No, she couldn't help herself. That's certainly true. If she had been given the right guidance things would have been different. She wouldn't have spawned Herod's offspring. Everyone deserves a chance to be redeemed, Anja. Despite whom they are.'

Anja felt Konstantin's cool blue gaze scrutinising her in the dim light. She knew she was missing something that had little to do with the moral of this story. Or maybe it had everything to do with it. Not for the first time she wished she could feel Konstantin's emotions. Then he took her hand. His cotton glove felt soft and comfortable.

'John was not so innocent,' he said suddenly. 'He too bore offspring to a woman he'd met some years before. You see he was corrupted long before his days as a preacher. Of course

God is love, God forgives sins, and so John found a new path and became known as the Baptist and the cleanser of sins. He never knew that he was a father.'

'How do you know this?' Anja asked, but somewhere deep inside she knew the answer.

'I'm a direct descendent of John,' said Konstantin. 'And you ...'

'No!' Anja gasped. 'Don't say it ...'

'But I must. You need to understand. You are descended from Salome. You carry the vampire gene, albeit very faintly, in your blood. It's why you are so gifted Anja. It's why you are who you are.'

Anja's tears flowed.

'No! I don't want to be the temptress. I don't want to be a demon.'

Konstantin smiled. 'God is love. God forgives sinners,' he repeated. 'Redemption is at hand, Anja, now that we have the relic.'

Anja buried her face in her hands and sobbed. She was afraid now for her future, afraid for her eternal soul and worse of all afraid that Konstantin would no longer want her.

5
The Transfusion

Four Months Earlier

'When we rid ourselves of these demons, your blood line will be purified, Anja.'

Anja clung to his words. She wanted to be pure, redeemed. She wanted her place in heaven and Konstantin was so close to revealing how she could do that. Over the last two weeks she had begun to believe in him. He cared about her, wanted the best for her at all times.

'How can I help?' she asked. Desperation seeped from her every pore. She had to prove herself worthy.

'Another blood transfusion,' Konstantin said.

Anja was surprised. 'You will clean my blood, free me from the gene?'

'No my dear girl, we will give you a concentrated dose by giving you a transfusion from someone whose blood is full of the gene.'

'Who?'

Konstantin didn't answer. They were in the limo, heading back to the clinic where she had woken up after her suicide attempt. Anja was quiet. She gazed out of the window, her thoughts floating back and forth through the events of the last few weeks.

'I don't understand,' she said finally. 'I thought I already had the blood, why give me more?'

'It's time you earned your keep and saved your soul, Anja. You're going to join them. You're going to become one of them and then you are going to tell us when and where we can find them. After that, the relic will be used against them.'

Anja was stunned. This wasn't the role she had expected to play. She thought somehow that Konstantin's plan involved her using her gift to access information about the vampires. She felt betrayed. Her heart burned with fear and her stomach churned. The colour drained from her cheeks and she turned watery eyes to the profile of her lover.

'I thought …' she murmured. 'I thought you *cared* about me. Wanted me to be saved. But instead you want to turn me into one of them!'

Konstantin patted her hand, 'Of course I do, my dear. But I hired you to do a job. Surely you read *all* the codicils on the contract? No? How silly of you. The thing is you turned your entire life over to me. You're mine and as such I will look after you, but I expect you to help me, and the order, eradicate the evil that is corrupting this world.'

'Who are you?' she asked. 'Really. *Who* are you? And who is this *order*?'

'We are the offspring of the Knights Templar. The *remaining* offspring. The original order was destroyed many years ago, my dear. I'll tell you that story sometime. But since then the residual members of the order dedicated their lives and wealth to the destruction of the vampire gene.'

'You never loved me,' she muttered.

Konstantin was silent and as always his emotions were closed to her. A few minutes later the car pulled into the clinic, and Anja was met by Doctor Graham and what looked like a security guard. The guard took her arm and led her inside. Konstantin stayed in the car but leaned out of the door.

'You're sure this will work?' Konstantin asked.

'No,' said Graham. 'But in a few hours she'll come in contact with them. She'll either become a meal or they will pass her over as they do all other carriers of the gene. Then we'll know the transfusion is enough to fool them at least.'

'Will she turn with their bite?'

Graham shrugged, 'All tests indicate she will turn. But …'

'Yes?'

'There's a possibility she might just die.'

Konstantin closed the limo door, then rolled the window down. 'I don't want to lose this one; she's too useful in other ways,' he said. 'I've invested a lot of time in her. Make sure you do everything you can to ensure she lives. Don't fail me.'

The window rolled up and as the car drove away. Graham turned back towards the door of the clinic, a slight flush colouring his cheeks. Not for the first time he wondered what would happen if he failed. He suspected that Konstantin had other uses for the girl that had nothing to do with business, but all of that was none of his concern.

Inside, Anja was strapped to a bed, her arm already hooked up to an IV. Graham noticed she had been crying.

'What are you going to do to me?' she asked.

'A transfusion. I believe you've already been told that,' he said. 'But to be more specific, we're taking blood from you and replacing it with different blood. You'll feel a little discomfort, but no lasting ill effects.'

Anja fell silent and she allowed them to prod and examine her during the procedure without complaint. Her chest hurt and tears choked the back of her throat. She couldn't trust herself to speak for fear of losing her control and turning into a blubbering mass of self-pity. It wasn't her way to be emotional. As the transfusion was prepared, she reined in her feelings, hardened her heart. What had she expected after all? All men were duplicitous; she had always known that. How many hearts had she seen into only to reveal the selfishness, the lust? It was partly why she had always kept people at a distance. She had let Konstantin in, trusted him. After the hatred of Björn she had wanted someone to really love her, and Konstantin had fooled her with his kindness.

As the new blood pumped into her veins, Anja knew she was going to do the job she was contracted to do, no matter what. Perhaps if she did it well, Konstantin would be pleased with her. She hated the desperate feelings she had for him: she had rarely allowed herself emotions, only caring about her possessions. Even though she realised it was foolish, she couldn't stop herself or change what was happening. She needed Konstantin. His silent emotions were her drug. His sex her release. All of these things had been denied her in the past.

She lay back and allowed the blood to sing through her body.

Later, Konstantin's chauffeur came for her. He brought her new clothing, a pair of skimpy PVC shorts, a clingy cotton crop top and a pair of pixie boots: the kind of things that ordinary girls wore to go out to night clubs. Anja didn't feel 'ordinary'. She had a potent mix of blood pumping in her veins. She wasn't quite sure how she felt.

Konstantin was waiting in the car when Anja got inside, dressed in the new outfit. She noticed that the top had long sleeves to cover the bruising on her arms from the transfusion. He had thought of everything. Bile rose in the back of her throat as she considered his betrayal but she swallowed it back and pulled the old Anja out. He had a right to demand her loyalty. Hadn't he done so much for her already?

'Put some make-up on,' Konstantin said, holding out her make-up bag. 'In a few moments we'll be at the club. It's a favourite hunting ground of the vampires. There will be three other girls there, around the same age as you. You'll pretend to be friends with them. They also work for me and are expecting you.'

Anja applied some make-up using a pocket mirror. Her face was blank; she gave nothing away of her feelings. It was, after all, what she had been doing her whole life.

'Here's your ID,' Konstantin continued, placing a driver's licence beside her. 'Look at this.'

Anja put down the mirror and took the photograph that Konstantin held out to her. It was a picture of a man and woman. They were the most stunning couple she had ever seen. The woman was tall, with long blonde hair that fell in waves to her waist. The man was handsome in a throw-back Viking way.

He was not slender but stocky. His hair was also long and blond. They both had startling green eyes.

'Are they brother and sister?' she asked.

'I doubt it,' Konstantin said. 'He's your target. Do you think you will recognise him?'

Anja looked long and hard at the picture. 'Hard not to really. He's very striking.'

Konstantin nodded. 'Yes, and he has to believe that you are what he needs.'

Anja continued to look at the picture but said nothing.

'He's called Harry,' Konstantin said. 'She's Lilly. It will be her that tests you.'

'Tests me?'

'She always checks Harry's food before he eats.'

Anja shuddered. A flush filled her cheeks. Palpitations made her heart beat irregularly with fear. She put down the photograph and picked up the ID.

'Amalia Andreas,' she read.

'This is the new you. After tonight you'll be starting work in the bar and will have a new address. You're going to do everything you can to persuade Harry to turn you and then, when you've infiltrated their world, you're going to betray them to me.'

The limo pulled up outside the club. Anja looked through the window to see three girls waiting for her.

'*They* haven't arrived yet. So you have time to go in, get a drink and calm yourself before you work your magic on him.'

'What if it doesn't work? What if he's immune to me, blocked. Like you are.'

Konstantin turned to Anja and smiled, 'I have every confidence in you.'

He held out her purse. Anja opened it and slipped the driver's licence inside, and then flicked through the rest of the contents. She noticed it contained enough money for a typical evening out and more, along with a lipstick and a mobile phone.

'In case of emergencies the phone is on direct dial to me. The limo will be here when you come out after making contact.'

Anja pulled a fake fur coat from the back seat, draping it around her shoulders. She felt cold and weak. Then the chauffeur opened the door and she slipped out onto the side road. For a moment her back bowed with the weight of the burden she carried, then, with a deep breath, she straightened her spine and walked towards the girls.

The three girls surrounded her as though they were old friends.

'Amalia,' a girl with short cropped brown hair said. 'Great to see you. What's your poison? I'm dying for a Kir Royale. I'm Suzanna.'

'Julietta,' nodded the dark haired girl. 'We've got your back sister.'

'I'm Lucy,' said the redhead. 'We've got lots to talk about. The boss says I need to fill you in on Harry's sexual quirks.'

'How do you know them?' asked Anja.

'Because I've had him babe,' smiled Lucy. 'He was under strict instructions not to kill that night; otherwise I wouldn't have risked it.'

Anja drew in a sharp breath.

'Come on,' said Suzanna. 'We need to set the mood for you. You're just his type you know. He likes the girly, innocent look.'

The four girls headed inside the club and Suzanna went straight to the bar, coming back a few minutes later with a waiter in tow. He led them to a booth and the women sat down, and swooped on their drinks.

'*Skål!*' said Suzanne and the girls repeated the salutation, clinking their glasses together before taking a swig.

'And to Dutch courage,' said Lucy smiling at Anja.

'Oh!' Julietta said. 'They're here.'

All four girls continued to look at each other and Anja fell into the game they played of chatting and laughing and drinking as though they had always known each other.

'Let's dance, Amalia,' said Suzanna, and she dragged Anja up onto the dance floor.

The strong cocktail was beginning to work its magic and

Anja was feeling the beat of the music as she danced with Suzanna. Over the other girl's shoulder she recognised Lilly and Harry, as they slid into a booth on the other side of the room.

'How do I get his attention?' Anja whispered.

'Kiss me,' Suzanna said.

'What?'

'He likes girl on girl action ...'

Anja was floating in Suzanna's arms as the girl kissed her full on the lips and rocked her body in rhythm against hers. She was surprised to find Suzanna's mind closed to her. She couldn't hear her thoughts, nor feel her emotions at all. She went with the moment, pretending she was kissing Konstantin because he had never once kissed her lips and she often wondered what it would be like.

A moment later Anja opened her eyes and, glancing over Suzanna's head, she saw Harry watching them. Even across the room she could make out the intensity of his green eyes. Sexual energy burst from Suzanna and down into her skin.

'My skill,' Suzanna said against her lips. 'We all have one.'

Anja found the woman hard to resist as her whole body ignited with lust, she kissed Suzanna more passionately, stroking her hand over her breast, cupping and squeezing it.

'Ohh ...' gasped the girl. 'I like you ...'

But the lust receded a little and Anja began to think clearly again about the job in hand. She noticed that Harry was now hovering at the side of the dance floor and Lilly was nowhere to be seen.

Someone bumped against Suzanna. Anja looked up into the pure green pools that were Lilly's eyes. She felt soft fingers brush her waist and in the same fluid movement she watched Lilly walk away, her fingers pressed to her lips as she licked the sweat-covered tips. Anja knew she had been tasted and tested. She continued to gyrate sexily with Suzanna, and glanced over almost casually at Harry and Lilly, but it wouldn't have mattered if she had stared blatantly. In that one moment of contact Anja had felt Lilly's sense of self. She considered herself invulnerable and her arrogance was her weakness. Through this minor contact Anja knew she could read the vampires, and that meant she could touch their minds in other ways too.

Anja caught Harry's eye as he looked over towards her with regret. She had been found unsuitable. This meant the first part of the experiment was a success. The vampires had recognised her as a carrier. Technically Anja was safe from his bite as Harry wouldn't touch anyone who was likely to turn. Anja knew this as Konstantin had been thorough in his explanation that the vampires kept their little group exclusive.

Anja left Suzanna on the dance floor and strolled over to the bar. She bought another drink and casually looked around only to find Harry admiring her again. She was certain now that Konstantin had done his research well. She was Harry's type and it wasn't easy for him to let go of his interest.

'Tell me about his sexual preferences,' Anja said, sitting back down at the booth beside Lucy.

Lucy smiled and leaned forward, whispering into Anja's ear. 'He likes girls who look virginal. Plus, he gives it rough. I could barely walk for a week ... He'll throw you all over the place and if you're a little uncomfortable with the size of him, he gets off on it. I found he liked it best when I was screaming as he took me from behind.'

Anja nodded. She stood up and made her way over to the bathroom as she had just seen Harry heading that way, following another girl who had been approved by Lilly.

6
Becoming Amalia

Three Months Earlier

Anja held out a drink to Harry over the bar. She had been working there a few weeks, just as Konstantin told her she should do. She no longer lived in Konstantin's big house, but now resided in an apartment close to the bar. It was simple and basic, the type of home she would have if she was a barmaid. Konstantin thought of everything.

She was thought in the bar to be a student working her way through university. She barely spoke to the other bartenders, the place was always busy and Amalia, as she was now known, didn't really care to become involved with any of them. At least Suzanna was working there as well, so there was someone she could talk to.

'She's frigid,' said one male bartender to another. 'I asked her out and her face just did this blanking thing. Never seen an expression like it.'

'She's probably into women,' replied the other as he filled his tray with individual
orders.

'No. Definitely frigid. I saw a girl come onto her the first night, she blew her out completely.'

'Who cares,' said Suzanna as she put her tray down beside the boys. 'You guys make me laugh, if she's not interested in fucking you then there must be something wrong with her, right?'

The men quickly took their trays, embarrassed at being caught out.

Anja came over and began to mix her drinks order. Suzanna smiled at her. 'You're a fast learner,' she said.

'Yeah. But I seriously wouldn't want to do this for a living forever,' Amalia answered.

'Who would? But the boss does have these crazy schemes.'

'What do you usually do?' Amalia asked, still curious about her new friend.

'Anything Mr Caradien tells me.' Suzanna picked up her tray and walked back to the booth she was serving.

Anja turned to see Harry sitting in one of her booths. He had been there every night now for the last few nights.

'What can I get you?' she asked smiling at him in a way that deliberately showed her dimples.

'Amalia is your name, isn't it?' Harry said.

Anja cocked her head to the left and met Harry's gaze. 'Yes. How did you know?'

'I asked the other girl,' he pointed to Suzanna as she bustled past them, her tray full again with new orders.

'Anyway,' Anja said shyly. 'What would you like?'

She came back a few minutes later with a tall glass of beer and as she placed it before him, Harry reached out and stroked her hand. Anja reacted immediately to his touch, pulsing her will through him in exactly the same way she had with Björn.

'I need you,' Harry said.

Anja smiled, 'Yeah? You and twenty other guys a day that come through here. What makes you so special?'

Harry grinned and flashed a little fang without realising what he was doing. Anja kept her face straight, she knew he was aroused, but wasn't sure how quickly she should give into his interest and agree to a date.

A few minutes later she met up with Suzanna at the bar.

'The boss says hurry it up,' Suzanna said.

'What? I'm not serving fast enough?'

'Not the bar boss,' Suzanna laughed. 'Who gives a shit what he says? I mean Mr Caradien.'

'Oh!' Anja's cheeks flushed.

She had not had any contact with Konstantin since the

chauffeur had left her and a case full of clothes over at the new apartment. The first night in the new flat she had cried herself to sleep, but after that she realised she just had to get on with the job. Maybe then Konstantin would reward her; bring her back into his life. She couldn't help wondering if somehow she had done something wrong. It was made even worse that all of her instructions came to her now via Suzanna or one of the other girls. Konstantin, despite giving her the mobile phone to reach him, had never made any attempt to call her. Even though she desperately wanted to hear his voice Anja daren't phone him. He had said that the phone was for emergencies.

Anja pulled another glass of beer then headed back to Harry's table.

'On me,' she said.

'Does that mean you are willing to spend some time alone with me?' Harry smirked.

'I'm not the kind of girl that spends "time alone" on a first date. I expect to be wined and dined. If you're asking me out then you ought to know I like to be well treated.'

Harry laughed. Anja liked his bright green eyes. He had a sexy smile too, and if the truth be known, since Konstantin had shown her how good sex could be, she found herself missing the contact. Maybe this wouldn't be so bad after all. She even found herself wondering at his size after Lucy's comment. Could be interesting.

'I finish at 10 tonight,' Anja told Harry.

Harry glanced at his watch. It was 9.30. He smiled at Anja.

'I can wait half an hour …'

They went to a good restaurant nearby. Harry ordered steak. Anja noticed he ate it very rare, and as he bit into the barely cooked meat, his pupils dilated. It was like he had taken a hit of coke. All the signs were there that Harry was indeed everything Konstantin said, with one exception: that night he was the perfect gentleman, and he never made a move on her. Instead, he accompanied her home and, kissing her cheek, left her at the outer door of her apartment.

Anja went inside feeling a little nervous. *I wonder if the myths are true and he has to be invited in?* she thought.

As she prepared for bed she heard an unfamiliar trilling sound. It took her a moment to realise that it was the mobile phone in her purse, she opened it, looked at the 'number withheld' message, and then quickly answered.

'Anja?' said a voice.

'Yes?'

'That's mistake number one,' Konstantin said. 'You're not Anja anymore. You are Amalia.'

Anja sighed.

'How did it go tonight?' he asked

'Good. We ate a dinner. He eats his steak blue …'

'I know all that,' Konstantin said and for the first time Anja heard something akin to emotion in his voice. He sounded impatient. 'I mean, how did it go in terms of physical contact?'

'He was very gentlemanly. But he did hold my hand over the table, and, he kissed my cheek. He's susceptible. I pushed a few random ideas his way and he acted on them without any sign of wondering where the thoughts came from.'

'That's excellent news! Now, come to the door and let me in. I think you deserve a reward.'

Anja's heart was in her mouth as she ran half-dressed to the door of her apartment. Konstantin was waiting there for her. She let him in and he fell on her long before they reached the bedroom. She had never seen him this desperate but she couldn't shake the feeling that he was just marking his territory. That, even though he wanted her to sleep with Harry, he still thought of her as his.

As Konstantin left long before the morning, Anja felt light hearted. *He loves me. He really does.* She was determined to help him destroy the monsters and even though she found Harry quite charming, she would never forget that she really belonged, heart, body and soul, to Konstantin Caradien.

7
Harry's Companion

One Month Earlier

Anja lay in Harry's arms. Her whole body shook from the vigour of his lovemaking and from the exertion of using her empathy to control his natural urge to rip out her throat.

'I love you,' he said. 'I want you to join me, be one of us.'

'Are you sure that's a good idea? After what you've told me about Lilly, your maker. She'll be furious with you.'

'Perhaps. But she won't be mad for long. Lilly is quite fun deep down and she is with her lover Gabriele and also this new one, Caesare Borgia. How can she deny me companionship?'

Anja lay quiet but her hand was pressed against Harry's heart. She massaged the spot in a subconscious gesture as she sent him waves of emotion until he was almost in tears.

'I won't be without you,' he said. 'You're perfect for me.'

His lips found hers. Anja felt his fangs pressing against her mouth. She placed her hands either side of his head and forced her will back inside him. Every time Harry became aroused his teeth emerged. The first time they'd fucked Anja could only just keep up with him, and was mentally exhausted from holding him back. He wasn't like other men, normal human men. He was susceptible, just as she had told Konstantin, but he wasn't as easy to manipulate.

Earlier that day, Anja had returned to the clinic. She was having regular top-ups of the vampire gene carrier's blood.

'It's important that we are ready at all times. From the sound of things, Harry is on the verge of turning you,' Konstantin had said on the phone. 'Don't miss your appointments with Doctor Graham.'

'The bruising …' Anja said.

'You know how to deal with that. Just make him always see you as perfect, no matter what.'

Keeping an image of her perfect persona before him was the hardest thing of all. It was draining. Anja couldn't wait for Harry to fall asleep beside her, or to leave, whichever he felt like doing tonight. In fact she put the thought in his mind that he should get back to his castle.

Harry frowned. He rubbed his forehead. Anja's mind shrank back from him, relieving some of the pressure she had put there when she realised she had pushed too hard.

'I need to get back to my place tonight,' Harry said. 'I want to make some arrangements. Think over what I said. I need you with me Amalia. I really don't want to lose you and every day that you remain mortal, I'm afraid something will happen to you.'

'Being mortal isn't as scary to those of us who are,' she said. 'The chances of just randomly dying are quite slim.'

She watched him go, leaving by the window in a flamboyant gesture to remind her of the power she would obtain as a vampire.

'You'll have limitless strength,' Harry had promised, 'and such power to control the minds of humans. You can't imagine what that feels like. To actually be able to persuade someone to think what you want them to think.'

A sharp piercing apprehension squeezed inside her chest as Harry spoke. She wondered if he knew what she was doing and if this was his way of telling her she had been exposed. Ironically though, it wasn't the case. Harry really believed her to be all that she made him see.

As she closed the window her special phone rang. She hurried to her purse, pulled out the mobile and answered quickly.

'Anja?'

'No. My name is Amalia,' she replied.

'Good girl!' said Konstantin. 'Now tell me what I want to hear.'

'He's ready. He wanted to change me tonight. But I held him back because I wanted to talk to you first.'

'You've been visiting Doctor Graham as I told you? You can let him turn you any time now.'

'Konstantin. Are you *sure* this is what you want me to do?' Anja asked.

'Yes.'

'Konstantin … I need to know … I need to understand something. What will happen to me when the vampires are destroyed?'

'You'll be cleansed of their infection.'

'How?'

'Amalia, don't you trust me?' Konstantin asked.

Anja felt cold and scared in the way she had when she first woke in the hospital after Björn had raped her.

'Of course … but …'

'You belong to me,' Konstantin said. 'I'm not going to let anything happen to you.'

Anja hung up. She stared around the basic room, thought about the luxury that would be hers once she fulfilled her contract with Konstantin. Then he would love her again and she would be his. Wasn't that what he had promised? Wasn't that what she wanted?

Anja began to pack a bag. She hated the clothing she had to wear as Amalia. It was nothing like her regular wardrobe which was smart rather than flamboyant. She threw in the mobile phone and charger on top of the bag. Lifting the fake fur coat from the back of a chair, Anja slung the offensive item over her shoulders. Then, lifting the bag she headed for the door.

Tonight, her last night as a mortal, she wanted to spend it in her own flat, just outside of Stockholm. She would look once more upon her things, her beautiful relics and artefacts. Those were the objects she had retained for her own purposes and they weren't to sell to anyone. They were the things she loved the most. Old and beautiful they told her of ages long past, worlds that no longer lived, civilisations that had since disappeared.

Once in the street she hailed a taxi and told him the address. As she reached the familiar streets, Anja felt an overwhelming sense of relief. She hadn't been here since she had first met Konstantin. It would be so pleasurable to hold the few remaining real doubloons she had secreted and to sleep in her own bed.

The taxi pulled up outside of the building. Anja looked up. She knew which window of her apartment looked out onto the street. The window was a dark hole just like all of the others on that floor.

Inside the building, the reception was empty as usual. The occupants paid a hefty maintenance fee that was supposed to cover the handyman who lived on the premises and someone manning reception overnight. It was gone 4 in the morning. Anja never saw anyone at reception, day or night and so she wasn't surprised that the desk was empty now. She waited for the lift, which came quickly and as she climbed inside, pressed the number for her floor, a feeling of unreality made her feel unsteady on her feet. She gripped the rail as the lift ascended. A momentary anxiety flitted across her mind. She was going to be changed and she was afraid of what would happen. She pushed away the thought. *Not tonight. I'm home!*

The landing was empty. This was a quiet neighbourhood and Anja had never had any problems or concerns about living alone here, but the dimly lit corridor made her feel strangely afraid. She imagined eyes lurking in every corner, watching her progress as she hurried to her apartment.

As she reached the door, she pulled out the key, fitting it into the lock in one swift movement. It turned easily and she pushed her way in, knocking aside the pile of letters that were on the floor behind the door. Inside she closed the door and dropped her heavy holdall down onto the floor. Then she stooped to pick up the letters that were scattered at her feet.

She quickly looked through the mail, picking out anything important and throwing aside anything that looked like junk mail. She took the stack down the hall, switching on the light as she moved towards the lounge.

The room was completely empty.

Anja stared around her, no furniture, none of her artefacts. Everything was gone! Everything! She had been robbed!

Anja ran from the room, back down the hall and into her bedroom. There she found the same situation; all of her personal effects were gone. The only thing that remained was a cheap fairground teddy that she had brought with her when she left the circus to move to Stockholm. Anja looked at the bright yellow bear as though it were something malevolent.

Then she fell to her knees before it, grabbing this remaining piece of her childhood to her. She hugged the bear and cried.

Konstantin! She thought, *I must ring Konstantin and tell him I've been robbed. He'll know what to do.*

She rifled through her purse and then remembered that the phone was in the bag she had left in the hall. She quickly fetched it and pressed the redial button.

Konstantin answered immediately.

'My apartment has been robbed. I don't know what to do,' she blurted.

'The studio?'

'No. *My* apartment!'

'Ah. Oh my dear, I should have explained. I didn't know you would go back there.'

Something in Konstantin's voice stopped the trembling in Anja's knees.

'You *knew*? You knew my things had been stolen and you didn't tell me?'

'Not at all. Nothing has been stolen, Amalia. It's merely been packed away to be kept safely for you.'

An unreasonable rage surged up into Anja's throat, choking away the words that threatened to tumble out of her mouth.

'You. Took. My. Things.'

'Yes. For safe keeping,' Konstantin explained. 'After all, neither of us knew how long you'd be living your new identity.'

'You took my things!'

A deep sigh drifted down the phone.

'Why are you there tonight?' Konstantin asked calmly.

'I came to spend … Don't turn this on me, Konstantin. You had no right to touch my apartment. I pay for it. There was no reason for this. I've owned this place for two years now. Why did you do this?'

'Amalia. When your job is finished all of your possessions will be returned to you. If you want them.'

So that is it, Anja thought. *It's extra insurance to make sure I do the job he's paid me for. Next he'll be holding my family hostage as well.*

'When this is over,' Anja said, 'I want my things returned and I never want to see you again.'

She ended the call. A few minutes later it rang again, but this time Anja didn't answer. She turned it off, then threw it back into the bag. Picking up her house phone, Anja dialled for a taxi. A few minutes later she was leaving Stockholm, heading out towards Harry's castle.

It was time she became strong. Time she moved things permanently forward. She didn't know if she would survive the night once she allowed Harry to unleash his fangs but she was unafraid. Once, some months ago now, she had stared death in the face as she slashed her wrists. She was ready to square up to it once more. It would be a battle of wills but she was determined to come out of it alive.

No matter what Anja had to do to get her things back, they were all she had, all she worked for. She would continue playing Konstantin's game, feed him information on the vampires, after all, what did it matter to her if they died? They were nothing to her. Anja had learnt long ago that wealth was freedom. It was what drove her and she reflected on the irony that her greed had led her into this intrigue. She had willingly become Konstantin's bitch, all for 11,000,000 Krona a year.

What did I expect would happen? All men lie. Nobody pays extortionate salaries without wanting blood in exchange. I've whored myself to a devil disguised as an angel. Maybe I am like Salome. But when I'm done with you Konstantin, when I have my money and my relics, then I'm going to rip your cold heart out.

Anja lifted her bag, left the apartment and quietly closed the door behind her. As she stepped into the lift she turned and met the gaze of a priest standing in the lift beside her. The man nodded, but said nothing. Anja felt her heart speed up. She was sure the man knew she was some kind of evil thing. He was a man of God. He had to recognise that she was the spawn of the devil, just as Konstantin said.

The lift opened on the ground floor. Anja hurried out and through the reception, not stopping to see where the priest went, or even wondering why he had been there at four in the morning.

Anja didn't cry as the taxi drew away from her old existence and nearer to Harry's place. She had no tears left. Soon Harry would suck that old life from her but she would rise from the grave, stronger, faster and thirsty for revenge.

8
Betraying Harry

Lourdes – One Month Earlier

'Are you sure you want to see this church?' Harry asked. 'I didn't think this type of thing was your bag.'

'It's supposed to be haunted,' Anja said. 'I was wondering if we can see supernatural things.'

Harry laughed, 'You're a funny girl. I've been around a few centuries. Can't say I've ever seen a ghost in all that time.'

'Indulge me?' she smiled.

Harry couldn't resist her. He marvelled at how happy she made him. He had never had sex with one of his kind, Lilly had been very definite about that kind of contact with him, but it beat human sex any day. With Amalia he felt no need to hold back. If he didn't intend to kill, Harry had always been aware of his own strength. Now, he didn't need to take care. She was strong, unbreakable. Admittedly, she was not as strong as he had expected her to be, but even so she was immortal. He loved how the change had affected her eyes. They were more vibrant, greener and an intelligence lurked there that he had been only vaguely aware of while she was human. These days too, she gave him as good as she got. If he disagreed with her, she argued her point and often won. He wasn't sure why, but he liked how persuasive she was and although physically she wasn't as strong as him, mentally she was every bit his match.

'I'm strong enough,' Amalia shrugged.

'Maybe. But I'm sure you'll grow stronger with time,' Harry said, not for the first time.

Anja nodded and they climbed into the taxi with the guide who promised to show them the church.

On the journey Anja felt calm.

'This is a very special church,' Charles, their guide, said. 'It is centuries old and it is said to be built on the site of great magic.'

Harry shrugged. Anja took his hand and tried again to feel his thoughts and feelings but nothing happened. Ever since the change she had lost the art to control him. At first she was concerned that he would see all of her faults. But the vampire conversion had taken her completely by surprise. She had grown more beautiful. Her once mousey hair, was now a thick and rich blonde. Her skin had whitened to a pale, pure ivory and all scars and old injuries disappeared from her body. There was no sign of the scars on her wrists and no evidence of the months of daily transfusions she had undergone at Doctor Graham's hands. In fact it was as though all her slights and sins had been eradicated from her flesh.

The church loomed before them. Anja nodded politely as Charles talked, but didn't really listen to the historical background because she didn't care about it at all. She was merely fulfilling the role she had been paid for.

The taxi came to a halt on the rough road, some one hundred yards away from the ruins. Charles got out first then held the door open for Anja and Harry.

As they stood before the threshold, Anja felt a genuine fear. There was something in the air, a faint odour, a smell of what she suspected to be old magic.

'Do you feel that?' asked Harry.

'No,' Anja lied. 'What do you feel?'

'There is definitely something different about this place.'

Harry stepped over the threshold. Charles, the guide and employee of Caradien Industries, backed away, climbing back inside the taxi.

Anja moved closer to the threshold as Harry walked the ruins.

'It's everywhere!' he said. 'Magic. Real magic! I thought only Lilly could …'

'What do you mean?' asked Anja. 'What can Lilly do?'

'Come in!' Harry called. 'You've got to feel this, it's amazing.'

Anja stayed outside of the boundaries of the ruins.

A flash of blinding light grew from a tiny ball in the air, right beside the altar. Harry turned. Looked at the light and watched in amazement as a portal expanded into a fully established waterfall.

'Oh my God! It's … a time portal.'

'How do you know?' asked Anja.

'I've seen one before, a long time ago.'

Anja placed one foot over the threshold.

Whatever you do don't cross the threshold, Konstantin had warned.

Anja stopped herself and stepped back just as a figure emerged from the portal. He was wearing full armour. Anja recognised the style, it was much like the Knights Templar, but his mantle held a blood red Ankh emblazoned on his chest and not a cross as was traditional.

'Demon!' called the knight. 'Spawn of Satan!'

Harry laughed. 'So is this a new incarnation for you Adonai? Only Lilly warned me you might be up to your tricks again.'

Anja was compelled to move closer. The knight was carrying something. She had to see what it was. The air crackled with power. It felt like wild electricity, a spectral thunder bolt, and it rippled all around the ruins.

'Adonai? I'm not God, but an instrument of his mercy! You will die this day, monster. You and all of your kind.'

Anja caught a glimpse of what he carried. It was the relic box. Anja had last seen it as Konstantin placed it inside his safe. Somehow they had never gotten around to opening it. She had always been curious of its contents.

The knight lifted the lid.

Anja felt immediate pain. Her heart was burning in her chest. She staggered and threw herself backwards, as the knight reached in and took an object from the box.

Although her eyes were streaming in pain, Anja took an

involuntary breath as she saw he held a human heart in his hand. It steamed gently, and as she watched, took on life.

Blood dripped through the knight's fingers as the heart pulsed in his hand. A loud beating sound echoed through her mind, and she shook her head to try and clear it.

Far closer to the knight, Harry clasped his hands to his ears as the sound filled his head. He stumbled forward, one hand outstretched as though to try and stop the knight.

The knight stood his ground. Anja collapsed in pain – even at a distance, it was crippling. As she watched, Harry stopped moving forward. His face contorted in agony, and his hands went to his chest. A plume of smoke emerged from his clenching fingers as his heart burst in his chest. A fire erupted in his blood vessels sending flaming blood to every part of his body. In the same instant his brain exploded, burning pain fuelled his synapses. His eyes boiled in their sockets and melted like blood-filled marshmallows, fluid streaming down his contorted face from his eyes, ears, nose and mouth. With his mind destroyed, Harry felt no further pain as he crumpled to his knees, his body burning swiftly from the inside out. The intensity of the heart, the poisonous heart, destroyed every drop of vampire gene blood that flowed in the Viking King's veins. His remains shrivelled into a burnt and mummified shell.

Anja screamed, her whole body was alight with scorching agony.

She felt hands under her arms, and Charles pulled her back, dragging her quickly into the back of the taxi.

Anja sobbed as the taxi careered down the rough country lanes away from the site, the driver apparently unaffected by what had happened.

'That was awful! Oh my God, did you see how he died?'

Charles looked at Anja. His eyes blank. 'Mr Caradien knows what he's doing. He said he'd destroy these demons and he will.'

'But I'm one of those demons!' Anja yelled. 'Is that what he'll do to me in the end? I can't die like that …'

Charles rapped on the partition between the front and the

back seats and the driver pulled the taxi over. Anja tumbled out of the back seat, dry-heaving at the side of the road.

'We have to wait here for a few minutes, then go back to make sure he's completely dead,' said Charles, looking back at the ruined church.

'Fuck you! I'm not going back there.'

A mobile phone began to ring and Amalia recognised the standard tone of the mobiles belonging to Konstantin's people. Charles reached in his pocket and took out the handset.

'Yes?' He listened and then held it out to the hysterical girl. 'It's for you.'

Anja stared at the phone. The last thing she wanted to do was talk to Konstantin, but she felt she had no choice.

'Amalia my dear, are you alright?' Konstantin's smooth calm voice sent the waves of anxiety back into the recesses of her mind.

'Yes. But the heart – if that's what it was – almost killed me too,' she replied.

'Ah. If you saw what the relic was, then you were indeed too close. Next time stay well back.'

Anja gasped with surprise. She didn't know how to respond to this casual warning.

'I'm in Toulouse,' Konstantin said. 'Let's meet up for drinks. But perhaps you ought to eat first. Charles will oblige you. Let me talk to him a moment.'

Anja passed the phone back to Charles who listened carefully before replacing the phone in his pocket.

Charles approached Anja, took her hand and led her into the back of the taxi. She was shaken and burnt, she needed to heal.

'The boss says to feed you,' Charles said, gesturing to Anja.

Anja sat astride Charles. She felt his heart beating faster with anxiety and fear, but she knew he wouldn't fight her. Konstantin was God to his employees. He owned them and they had little choice but to obey his every command. Anja wondered what it was he had on Charles. She couldn't imagine blindly feeding a new vampire, for fear they had no control. As she stroked his hair, Charles gazed into her eyes. She *pushed* with her mind, and his eyes became blank, his heart rate slowed down and he obediently turned his head offering her a prominent vein in his neck.

Anja felt her fangs extend and she bit down gently on the proffered throat as the taxi driver pretended not to watch through his rear view mirror. She fed deeply. The blood rushed into her veins and straight to her heart, healing and cooling the burning pain there. She left Charles alive, just, and after another phone call, this time made by the driver, a car arrived to take her victim away.

'I'm to drive you to Toulouse,' said the driver.

'What about … Harry?' Anja asked.

'Someone has already been there and checked. Dead means dead, even for a vampire.'

Anja stared out at the passing scenery. She felt she had no control at all over what was happening. Konstantin was still pulling her strings but she had to see this through until she got her money and her possessions back.

I wonder if his heart will still be a closed book now that I can see it through immortal eyes, she thought.

As the taxi rattled along the eighty or so miles to Toulouse Anja closed her eyes and slept. Later when they arrived, she wasn't surprised to find that Konstantin had already gone. He left a note, more clothing and instructions that she had to go to Wales.

PART THREE

Present Day

1
Deceit

'Harry never knew? You fooled him with your empathy and mind-reading ability. That's what you're saying?' I said.

Amalia sobbed gently into her hands but her cries were falling on deaf ears. We were beyond sympathy. We were beyond anger. Lilly stood trembling with barely contained rage and Gabi was so silent and still I couldn't imagine what he was thinking. I suspected he felt betrayed. I had a dilemma to deal with and had to keep my mind clear in order to do that, so I pushed back my remaining emotions and focused on all of my control until I became as still as Gabi.

'Konstantin Caradien is somehow involved with a group that claimed they were descendents of the Knights Templar?' I confirmed.

Amalia nodded. 'Yes. And we are … all of *us* are descended from Salome.'

'It's just too fantastical to be the truth,' Lilly said. 'I just don't believe any of it.'

Amalia believes it, I thought.

Doesn't mean it's true, Lilly frowned.

Gabi dropped his face into his hands and then ran his fingers through his luscious blond hair. Dark circles had appeared around his eyes, he looked tired, wrung out. He was the one most taken in by her and had the biggest axe to grind. Yet he wasn't angry. The emotion would have been futile anyway.

'There's something else. My name's Anja. Not Amalia. I don't know why Konstantin made me change it, but he insisted I always use it and never my own.'

Lilly picked up her laptop.

'What are you doing?' Gabi asked.

'I'm going to find out everything I can about Caradien Industries.'

'I need to wash my face,' Anja said.

'I'll go with you,' Gabi said.

'I'm okay, I'd rather be alone,' she said.

'I didn't ask if you were okay,' Gabi said coldly. 'You can't be trusted and therefore will never be left alone until we deal with Caradien and Carduth.'

Anja nodded, 'I understand. You've every right to feel that way.'

'Look at this,' said Lilly as Gabi and Anja left.

I gazed over her shoulder at the screen and read the information rapidly as it scrolled down.

'Doesn't tell us much really,' I pointed out. 'Just how long the company has been trading.'

'This …' Lilly pointed to a section in the text that explained the history of the company which was first founded in Rome. 'It dates back to the fourteenth century. Around the time we were in Rome and Paris.'

'That doesn't make sense Lilly,' I said. 'You saved the last members of the Templars. Why would they turn against us?'

Lilly's eyes fell on the sword still hooked to her belt. She shook her head.

'This repelled Carduth. If the Templars did turn against us, then why send me this?'

I pulled her into my arms, but she was stiff and distracted. Even so, I stroked her hair. I needed the comfort even if she didn't. I needed to touch her.

'For the first time in my many centuries of life,' she said, dropping her head on my shoulder, 'I actually don't know what to do next.'

I held her, kissed her hair. The door opened and Anja and Gabi entered. I drew back from Lilly. My love for her still felt like a guilty secret.

'I'm sorry,' Anja said.

I stared at her. I'd expected anger, perhaps even some self-righteous indignation. She was Caradien's stooge after all.

'I've never had anyone treat me as well as you have all done,' she continued as though reading my thoughts. 'I have been in this warp, no I mean web, of deceit and I didn't know how to get out of it. I didn't know what was going to happen to Harry, but I'm guilty because I led him to his death by following Konstantin's instructions.'

'You feared Caradien more than you cared for Harry,' I said.

'That's true. But I did care for Harry. Nothing could have prepared me for the shock of his death. I never expected to *feel* it.'

Lilly said nothing and so Anja fell silent.

'Amalia … I mean Anja,' said Gabi. 'We need more information. Can you tell us exactly where this facility is in Stockholm? The one where you received the transfusions?'

'No,' she said. 'If I do you'll go there and Carduth may be waiting for you. If anyone else dies, especially you, Gabi … I don't think I could live with it on my conscience.'

Gabi said nothing. His jaw was set, face blank. I didn't know how her words affected him but I felt the truth in them again. She had grown to care for him, of that I was certain.

'There's no time for such sentiments,' Lilly said. 'It's all too little and too late, Anja. You *will* tell us everything you know. You have to because this is the only way we can all fight it. There's something else you can help me with also.'

'What?'

'I'm going to search your gene pool, really scrutinise your DNA. One thing I observed from the beginning is that you aren't like us, not really, and I want to know how distant the genetic connection is. This will help us all in the future as I've always believed just one link to the vampire gene will make a person turn.'

'Okay. What do I do?'

'I'm going to taste you,' said Lilly. 'But properly. I'm going to drink from you.'

Anja swallowed. Her eyes darted to Gabi and then to me,

but neither of us were willing help her right then.

'It won't harm you,' Lilly said.

I moved from my spot on the sofa and indicated that Anja should take my place beside Lilly. She sat down reluctantly.

Lilly stroked Anja's hair and sent a calming pulse into the girl. She relaxed against her, turning her head to expose her throat but instead Lilly lifted the girl's arm and placed her wrist to her lips. She bit as gently as she could and swallowed the hot blood that bubbled from Anja's vein in a huge spurt. Then the wound healed and Lilly sat back, eyes closed. There was a slight trace of blood still on her lips.

The vampire gene swirled in the air behind my eyes and I realised that once again I had become privy to Lilly's thoughts and emotions and I sank down on the sofa, keeping Anja firmly between us. A myriad of smoky lights sparked out of Anja then disappeared into the air like exploding fireworks, leaving just one pale red line to follow. Lilly traced the genealogy, and our collective consciousness rippled through the air until it came to a complete halt.

Lilly opened her eyes. She stared at Anja for a moment. Then she stood and drew her sword. Anja yelped and jumped up but I caught hold of her and held her. If Lilly wanted to kill the girl, I wouldn't stand in her way, even though I didn't have any understanding of what I had just seen. I glanced at Gabi, he bowed his head. He didn't like it but he wouldn't interfere. Instead of swinging the sword, Lilly held up the pommel and gazed through the amber at Anja. I tried to sink once more into her thoughts but found that wall firmly in place again. I was locked out and I really didn't like not knowing what she was seeing.

'That confirms what I already suspected. You're not a carrier,' she said. 'Caradien lied to you. I suspect they developed a method to temporarily give you the gene so that I'd be fooled if I ever tested you. All of the transfusions somehow corrupted your cells and made it possible for you to turn. I'm not a scientist and I have no real understanding of what Caradien's people did, but against the odds you're here and you are now one of us.'

Anja burst into tears again. I wasn't sure if this was from relief or fear, but this time Lilly wrapped her arms around the girl and comforted her.

'One thing you need to decide,' Lilly murmured, 'is who you trust more? Caradien wants to kill all vampires. How can you believe he won't destroy you when the job is done?'

'I can't trust him. I know that.'

'Then you have to trust us, Anja. And we have to be able to trust you. If we die, you'll have no way to protect yourself. And I'm certain Caradien will finish you off at the first opportunity.'

Anja nodded. 'I know. You can trust me. I swear it on my life.'

The truth echoed in the girl's words. She believed what she said, but could we, when it truly came down to the fight, rely on her not to switch ranks again? I really wasn't sure. As I looked up into Gabi's eyes I could tell, that neither was he.

'Well, your life is what you'll be gambling with if you switch sides again,' Gabi said.

Anja nodded, her eyes filled with unshed tears again. 'Caradien's facility is in the centre of Stockholm. It's disguised as a regular working hospital ...'

2
Doctor Graham's Office

Several men, dressed as security guards, walked the perimeter of the hospital grounds. We landed, silent and invisible, just outside of their jurisdiction.

'That's new,' Anja said. 'With the exception of the one that led me inside for the first transfusion, there weren't any guards like this before. And remember, I came here every day for almost three weeks.'

'They look like a band of hard-nosed mercenaries to me,' Lilly said.

'Caradien knows that Anja has been discovered,' I said.

Lilly nodded, 'Probably as soon as her phone was destroyed.'

After dismembering the contents and snapping the SIM card in half, Lilly had dropped Anja's phone in the middle of the Ocean on our way to Stockholm.

'It's likely that Caradien has been using it to track Anja.'

'What do we do?' Gabi asked. 'Only it looks like they are ready for us, and that might mean the relic will be there too.'

'I'm going to search for a portal that will take us directly into Caradien's facility. Let's get a look at Doctor Graham's records and find out what they've been doing to Anja.'

'But you just said it's a trap,' Anja said.

'That's right. That is why we're going back to a few weeks ago. Before your transformation and to a time when Caradien won't know we visited since we didn't know and you're no longer feeding him information. I think you need to stay here in this time period though.' Lilly explained. 'You'll feel weird when you're occupying the same time and place as yourself. I'm not sure if you'll be able to cope with it.'

'No. I want to stay with you,' Anja said.

We argued it out. I didn't want to stay behind with Anja, but she couldn't be left behind on her own.

'I always feel like I'm being sidelined,' Gabi said. 'I vote we risk it and all go together anyway.'

It was night when Lilly finally drew back from the boundaries of the hospital and sent out a search for the nearest ley line. The power was found in a surprising place, just below the hospital itself. I wondered if the facility had deliberately been built there and if Caradien knew more about ley power than we realised but the thought was soon pushed aside as Lilly found a door that would take us into the right time. Lilly's research had told us the hospital was relatively new and had only been built a few years previously. We hadn't thought to check the origins of the site before that, which might have been a serious oversight but we at least knew it was Caradien Industries that had funded the build.

'The nearest I can find fits in with Anja's last visit to the doctor a month ago. The night Harry changed her. Caradien's people won't be expecting an attack at that point, as technically their plan has only just begun and Anja is still their pawn.'

The door opened. It was a blue-tinged waterfall, taller and narrower than some of the other portals we had traversed. Anja gasped as she gazed through it.

'That's the doctor's office. I went in there that final day. You're so clever Lilly.'

The room was dark as we stepped inside. It was around 6pm in this time. Gabi led the way, followed by Anja and then me. Lilly brought up the rear and I couldn't help noticing how she glanced over her shoulder just before she entered the portal. Once inside the small office Lilly went straight to the filing cabinets but left the gateway open just in case we needed to make a quick exit.

'Locked,' she said tugging the first drawer. 'Search his desk for keys.'

The four of us searched every corner of the room and failed to find anything to open the cabinet. There was a tall fridge near the door. I pulled on the handle. Inside were several phials of blood.

'Dinner anyone?' I asked.

'Strange,' said Gabi. 'That wouldn't normally be kept in the doctor's office but rather in a laboratory.'

'No keys here,' whispered Anja from the other side of the room.

'Never mind. This is quicker.' Lilly pressed her finger to the lock and a spark of power burst into the cabinet. She pulled the first drawer and this time it opened easily. 'I haven't damaged it, so we can still eradicate all signs of being here.'

She flicked through the files. Closed the drawer and opened another only to begin the process again.

'Look,' said Gabi who was searching through the papers on the doctor's desk. 'The file is still on his desk.'

Outside we heard the approach of two female nurses. I could hear the regular thrum of the hearts of both women as they walked without hurry towards the door.

'Doctor Graham had that girl in again,' said one female voice. 'I don't know. She must be bad if they are constantly transfusing her.'

'Leukaemia?' asked the other woman.

'I think so, but I haven't seen her records as she's one of his private patients. You know you're number is up when things go that far though ...'

We remained still until the women passed by the office and carried on down the corridor.

'Anja Alesco,' I said reading the front of the file Gabi held.

'That's me,' Anja said.

'That's convenient,' said Lilly. 'Chez you're leaning on a photocopier. We'll copy the file, then get the hell out of here.'

'A what?'

'You're such a technophobe,' Gabi smiled. 'Here. Let me.'

Gabi took the folder and began to copy all of the doctor's notes. Pausing whenever we heard people passing the door.

'They would probably be able to hear the machine and a least see the light as it scans,' Lilly explained when I asked why we stopped.

There were a lot of papers in the files and it took a while to collate them. Then Lilly replaced the bulky document back inside the brown wallet and placed it back on Graham's desk. She locked the cabinets and glanced around to see if the room looked as though it had been disturbed in any obvious way.

'Let's go,' she said satisfied.

'Wait,' I said. 'This all seems … too easy.'

'I know. Our luck was in today. So, yay us,' said Lilly.

An army of security guards were waiting for us back outside the facility as we crossed the threshold of the portal. I just had time to throw Lilly aside as the bullets hit me full in the chest. I fell backwards into the portal and back into the doctor's office, crashing into his desk, but was on my feet in seconds and limping back towards the portal as several pairs of feet came running down the corridor heading my way. The portal froze as I reached it. A cold icy painting hung in the middle of the room. I could still see Lilly, Gabi and Anja. They were surrounded by the men, weapons pointed in their direction.

I hit out at the wall of ice, but my hand whipped the air as the portal completely disappeared. It took a moment to realise that there were keys jangling behind me and someone was unlocking the office door. I pressed myself back against the wall and cloaked myself, pulling shadow and light around my body to create the field of invisibility.

Blood was pouring from my wounds, down my shirt and over my jeans. I wrapped my arms over the bullet holes, holding the telltale blood loss in check as a nurse and a security guard entered the room. The nurse flicked the light switch on and the room lit up as the security guard rushed in. The desk was crooked. A coat stand was strewn across it and the papers and files that had been on the desk were now scattered on the floor.

'What happened in here?' said the female nurse.

'Coat stand,' said the guard. 'Seen that kind of thing a million times. One side too heavy, the thing will just come tumbling down. You'd think these doctors would be smart enough to figure that out wouldn't you?'

The nurse laughed. 'What? Doctor Graham? He's on another planet. Let's tidy this up though.'

As they straightened the room I felt myself slowly healing. The bullets were working their way out of my chest like a nest of worms burrowing out of the earth. I caught one, just as it pushed out of my skin preventing it from dropping onto the floor. The nurse cast a final glance around the room as though she heard my swift movement.

I felt ill. It was a relief when the nurse turned off the light and left with the guard. They locked the door behind them and moved away. My cloak fell: I couldn't hold it any longer. The bullets and blood loss made me feel weak and sick. By then I was standing in a puddle of my own blood and I was aware that I had been lucky to go undetected. Lifting the bullet I sniffed it. It was made of a metal I didn't recognise, but then so much of this modern world was completely new to me. Gabi and Lilly had tried to get me up to speed, but it was going to take time. I placed the bullet in my pocket, then staggered away from the wall, only to find my legs weakened beneath me and I fell down on all fours in the middle of the room.

My arms gave way and I fell face down on the floor. Blood began to pour from me again, another bullet was working its way out. I felt weak, hungry. I didn't even have the strength to take a victim should one even present itself to me. I forced my head up and found myself staring uncomprehendingly at the fridge. *Blood. Of course!* Leaving a trail of my own blood on the floor I dragged my ailing limbs across the room. It was a slow process, but I knew this was the only thing that would help me. I had to get to it. As I reached the other side of the room I pulled myself back up to a sitting position. If I hadn't been on the floor already the vertigo would have brought me down again. My head swam, the ground came up to meet me, and I gripped the side of the fridge until the world steadied itself again.

As some momentary strength returned I reached for the handle and tugged the heavy door open. Inside, the blood was lying in packets. I grabbed the nearest bag as my fangs extended painfully from my gums. I bit the plastic. Cold blood slopped into my mouth and down my chest. It was disgusting but I forced myself to drink it, gulping down all the contents from the first bag and moving rapidly onto the next.

I sat with my back to the wall allowing the blood to absorb through my stomach and work its way into my veins. My heart was hurting, but the first rush of blood soothed the pain and began to ease the itching in the healing bullet wounds. Several more bullets were rejected by my body as it repaired. I'd never known such pain. I gathered them up as they fell into my lap, and carefully stored them in my pocket. There had to be no evidence when I left here, otherwise Caradien would know.

This thought brought me back to the question of Caradien's knowledge. We'd been ambushed outside and I had no way of knowing how they had discovered we were there. Caradien's people had special weapons it seemed. They couldn't kill me, but they had certainly slowed me down. The bullets, I was certain, were not ordinary ammunition. I'd been injured many times before and the wounds had been nothing more than a small annoyance. These injuries burnt, not unlike a minor dose of the feeling we experienced when we came in contact with Carduth and his weapon, which would indicate that whatever Carduth used, then the bullets were somehow connected.

I felt myself healing finally, but it was a slow process. I lay on the floor waiting for the strength to pour back into my limbs and just before dawn I was able to stand again. When I heard one of the nurses passing by, I opened the door, drew her in and forced my mind into hers. I knew it was important that no evidence of me being there was left in Graham's office. I watched the nurse clean up my spilt blood and dispose of the empty plastic bags I'd drunk from. I wanted her blood, but was afraid to take it. As the dawn grew into morning I slipped away, out into Stockholm, away from Caradien's hospital and went in search of a way to get back to Lilly.

As I thought of my lover, my heart began to hurt again, only this time in a completely different way.

3
Dilemma

I was in a dilemma: out of my time, away from companions, at a date before the ambush had occurred. I was about four weeks in my own past and yet this was still my present. It was enough to make my mind skitter away in confusion. In this time, Harry wasn't dead and as I knew where his home was, I could go there and warn him of the trap set by Anja and Caradien that would eventually kill him. But Lilly had explained to me that some events in time just couldn't be changed. In my time, Harry was already dead, that meant I couldn't save him. Or could I?

I walked the streets of Stockholm as the sun came up. I needed to feed again, preferably from a living body, but to do so there, where the vampire gene was so strong, would be dangerous. As the morning wore on, my strength grew but I found I was still unable to fly. This gave me new concerns and further dilemmas. I was so unused to this weakened state and I was vulnerable. If I were to come across Caradien's men again, I'd be unfit for the fight.

A teenage boy passed me on a bicycle with a plastic box strapped on the back. Blood pounded sensually through his veins. I began to follow him, running just behind and beyond his peripheral vision. As he turned into a park I pursued. It was still very early and there were few people around that morning but even if there had been the hunger would have clouded my judgement.

I ran faster, catching him as he pedalled his bike into an underpass. He barely had time to gasp as I held him in my arms and met his eyes, silencing any thought of continuing the scream that built in his chest. His bike clattered to the ground, and the box attached to the back fell to the ground open, scattering newspapers all over the floor.

My heart was thumping in rhythm with his. I was afraid. I'd come to rely too much on Lilly vetting my kills, but I had to take the chance. I had to repair, build my strength and find a way back to help my friends. I sniffed the boy's throat. Thinking back to the process Lilly used. She tasted then, she analysed. I felt again her searching mind. I licked the boy. Lightning bursts exploded behind my eyes. Yes! This was it! I followed the lines, watched them fade, saw the final one stretch out, then chased it, down and deep searching the ancestry.

I saw faces, family connections but none were familiar. Is this how she knew? Was this what Lilly recognised? How did I know if I was reading this correctly?

I bit. Hot blood. Gulping. Devouring. I no longer cared what his gene code told me, only that I could feed. I was greedy: I took his life. And as his life force coursed through me gathering momentum it washed away the last traces of my injuries.

I came back into myself as I heard the sound of cars overhead. I dropped the body, ran with superhuman speed to the end of the tunnel and threw myself up into the air. The ability to fly came back to my limbs as though it was the most natural thing. I gathered air around me, in much the same way as I did when becoming invisible to the human eye. The atmosphere lifted me and I fell up into it.

I headed towards Harry's castle. It didn't matter to me that Anja had seemed to turn over a new leaf in my present, I should warn Harry after all. Lilly would expect me to try, even though she knew there was no love lost between the Swedish King and myself.

It was mid morning as I approached the castle but as I checked the shuttered windows, and noted the silence surrounding the building, I realised that it might already be too late.

I entered the building via the kitchen as I had with Lilly and Gabi previously, picking up her key, then returning it back to the hiding place outside. It was hard to imagine that in my current timeline, that event hadn't even happened but was a moment in the future and I was careful not to do anything that might affect it. Thinking through all this was enough to make my brain ache.

The kitchen looked bare. Unused. It was exactly the type of kitchen that a vampire nest would have. There was a thin layer of dust on the worktops. But as I opened the fridge I found bottles of wine and bags of blood. I moved into the house, hurrying through the rooms.

'Harry?' I called. 'This is Caesare Borgia – I need to speak to you urgently.'

I was greeted with silence. The house was as deserted as the kitchen. I ran upstairs, searched the building room by room. When I came to Harry's room, I found empty drawers and wardrobes. He and Anja had already left for their slow excursion across Europe on their journey to Harry's certain death.

It crossed my mind that I could follow them, meet up with Harry before he crossed the threshold of the ruins at Lourdes, but I had no idea where the first part of the journey would take them and what my interference in this time might actually mean.

'Traversing time is a complex operation,' Lilly had told me. 'We never know if our presence will affect the future, change things that we wouldn't want to change. I've often thought about the problem of paradox, but trust that because we have already lived our present that it then cannot be changed. I'm not sure though. Some things can't be changed no matter how hard you try.'

I sat down on Harry's bed, feeling the helplessness of the situation. Yes. I could follow, but what if I couldn't get back to Stockholm in time to help Lilly and Gabi as they fought Caradien's mercenaries? Surely that was my priority? But then perhaps I was giving up too easily?

The sun was high in the sky when I finally decided what to do. I needed to get back to Caradien's hospital and learn all that

I could about his operation. Any information I could gather might be useful to us later on. I stood up, looked around Harry's room once more, then closed the drawers and the wardrobe. There really was nothing I could do for him now.

4
Caradien's Laboratory

Two and a Half Weeks Ago

'I need to know all you can tell me, Doctor Graham,' I said, staring into the man's eyes.

'I know what you are,' he said turning his head away. 'Those tricks won't work on me. I'm immune.'

I laughed. 'Are you also immune to my bite?'

The doctor trembled, but said nothing. He sat behind his desk. His fingers spread before him so that I could see what he was doing at all times.

It was late in the evening of the third day. I'd been watching Graham's movements and knew his entire life better than he did.

'I don't intend to kill you, doctor,' I said. 'Not unless you refuse to help me.'

'Caradien would kill me if I did.'

'Maybe. But he won't make it last as long as I will.'

Graham blinked and before his eyes opened I was beside him, twirling his seat to face me. He gasped. His mouth opened, ready to scream.

'I wouldn't do that …' I warned.

Graham closed his mouth, swallowed. He was trembling visibly now. I looked into his eyes again and saw the fear of his death swimming there. I stepped back.

'Caradien has led you all to believe that we are monsters. I won't deny that killing comes easy to me and my kind. Mostly we take the low-lifes, you'd barely notice the absence of those we kill. Then occasionally we have to take someone innocent, like I did this morning when I ate a boy, out delivering papers. I was desperate. You know why?'

Graham shook his head, mouth half open; drool leaked unchecked from the corners of his lips.

'I had to kill this child because I was injured. Bullets, knives, falling from a great height … all of these I can survive, Graham. However, one of Caradien's men shot me and it was agony, far more than it should have been …'

'I don't see …'

Graham's eyes shifted left, avoiding my gaze. I dropped a bullet onto his table.

'Yes. You do see. Don't lie to me.'

I leaned closer, fangs exposed. Graham shrank back into his chair, pushing away from me as I closed in.

'All I need to do is taste you, doctor. Then I will know everything. Your blood will open you up to me, no matter how much you resist.'

'The bullets are coated in blood,' Graham gasped.

'Of course they are. My body rejected them.'

'Not your blood. *His.*'

'Stop playing games with me, you pathetic human. Blood can't hurt me, certainly not Caradien's,' I said. Lifting him by the throat, I pulled him to my eager fangs.

'John the Baptist! Not Caradien. John's blood.'

I held Graham in the air and waited.

'We have the heart,' he blurted. 'It's poison to you. Caradien took blood from it and it was added to the metal of the bullets when they were made. Then for good measure they were coated with it.'

Blood couldn't hurt us. All blood was food and life to me, I knew that, but Graham's words had a ring of truth to them. He could be lying, but it was also obvious that he was too afraid to lie.

'Why?' I asked.

Graham stared at me, confused and scared he wasn't sure what I was asking.

'Why is it poison to us? Is it some kind of spell?'

'No. Not a spell. More a curse. Caradien told me that Salome was given the heart of John, not his head. And as they ripped it from his body, he cursed her and her blood line. All of her offspring would carry that curse inside them. In their blood. In every cell in their bodies. They couldn't escape it as it was inherent. These days we call it DNA. It's the thing that makes us what we are. There has been research into genetic memory too which would suggest that the blood itself holds some form of intelligence.'

'Explain,' I said, placing him back down in his chair once more. 'I don't understand science too well.'

'The theory is that our cells – every particle and fibre that makes us – hold an inherent memory. The research we've been doing has been based around those you might call carriers of the vampire gene. In your case that genetic memory is sparked with the bite of a vampire, another carrier of the gene. It turns you.'

I nodded. Yes. This was what Lilly had said.

'But how do you know this? And why are you even interested in it?'

'The activation of the gene is a fascination to us because it shows the trigger. If you can be turned, or rather the cells change and regenerate into something so different from humans, stronger, faster. But you know all that … What secrets might we unlock in other gene codes?'

'So that's how this started?' I shook my head in frustration. 'I don't believe this, doctor, I think there's more to it. Why you? Why Caradien?'

'Caradien says he's descended from John the Baptist,' Graham said. 'I don't buy into that fanaticism, but it doesn't really matter. It's an easy concept to consider that the vampire gene is the "Salome" and that Caradien's family is the "John". It helps me distinguish them. What's interesting though is that "John" blood is absorbed by "Salome" blood.'

'Meaning?'

'Caradien's genetic code could be changed by the bite of the vampire, but because it's essentially different from the vampire gene he might not become a vampire, but something else,' Graham said.

'What would he become?'

Graham went quiet. I shook him.

'We've only experimented with blood cells, never a person. Caradien values his people and family. We can only speculate what might happen.'

'Then speculate,' I said.

'My guess would be something *less* than the vampire.'

'Tell me, Doctor.'

Graham sighed. 'Maybe I had better show you ...'

I stepped back as Graham stood, brushed himself down and walked calmly past me to the fridge. He reached behind it, pressed a button that looked like a light switch and the wall behind it began to move.

'What are you doing?' I asked. 'If this is some kind of trick ...'

'No trick. This is the way into the laboratory. No one on the regular hospital staff even knows it exists. Caradien loves his games of espionage. I could work in a regular lab with his people and no one would question what I was doing. We are playing with blood samples after all. It's just research.'

Behind the wall was a passageway. Graham turned on a light and led me inside, closing the wall panel behind us.

'There's no one around at this time of night,' Graham said. 'You needn't worry.'

'I'm not worried. I will just kill you if you try to fool me.'

Graham turned and walked down the passage and I followed. It turned left and then sharply right. We stood before a locked door. Graham removed his hospital badge and waved it across a glass panel. The panel lit up and the door sprang open. There was a set of steep stairs, leading downwards.

'The lab is in the basement. This isn't the only way in but it's the quickest entrance for me.'

I let Graham go first and we descended into the bowels of the hospital. The deeper we went, the more I felt a strange familiarity. It reminded me of the warm tingle I had every time I went home to Rhuddlan. Then I remembered Lilly saying that the hospital was built on a powerful ley line.

A few more doors later we were in the lab. It was a huge warehouse space, with white walls and large tables, full of equipment. I looked around blinded by the clean walls and stark false light.

'I don't think there is anything you can show me here,' I said.

'Not in this room, no. Or at least I could but perhaps you wouldn't understand it.'

Graham walked across the lab and only then did I notice another door. I caught up with him as he opened it and went inside.

The chatter and howl of animals greeted me. There were several caged monkeys jumping with excitement as they heard us enter. Graham ignored them, but I checked the cages, taking in the emaciated state of the animals.

'They are starved,' I pointed out.

'Not exactly. It's just the effects of some of the drugs we gave them. They are being used for research into cures for serious diseases. It's not them I want to show you. It's this ...'

Graham approached a cage which was on the other side of the room. It was covered with a thick cloth. Graham pulled up the front of the fabric and immediately the monkeys behind us erupted into desperate sobs and screams that could only be described as cries of fear and anguish.

'We have to keep it covered as it does stress the others to see it as you can see.'

I looked into the cage, trying to make sense of what I saw. A thin, naked, child-like creature was curled in the centre of the cage. It stirred, raised its head then began to struggle to the front of the cage. The light from the room fell on its face. I held in a gasp. The creature was neither human nor animal but seemed to be a warped and confused version of both. Half human face, half dog, or wolf, I wasn't sure which, and the face was continually changing as though it couldn't sustain a definite form.

'You said you'd only experimented with blood. That looks

like more to me and I'm no scientist.'

Graham pulled a handkerchief from his white coat and mopped his brow.

'I'm not proud of this,' Graham said. 'But, the truth is Caradien owns me. He owns all his employees. The contract states that he has right over our bodies alive or dead.'

'Then why did you sign it?' I asked.

'Greed. He gets everyone with greed. He makes you a financial offer that you can't resist.'

'What happened here,' I asked. 'Explain it simply.'

Graham stuffed his handkerchief back into his pocket. 'This was an experiment with blood. Nothing more. The subject was dying. We gave him transfusions first to begin with. When Caradien realised that the subject, who had leukaemia, was unsalvageable, he made a deal with the family. We made a big show of euthanasia and sent him to sleep. But the deal was that the hospital would keep the body for research. Caradien paid the family a lot of money, arranged a fake funeral and everyone was happy. They knew that the subject was going to die anyway.'

'It's a child, not a subject.'

'It's easier for me to think of him as a subject,' Graham said. 'As I told you, we just began with transfusions. First with blood taken from a carrier of the vampire gene, then from blood taken from Caradien's gene pool.'

The child wolf mewed through the cage. I looked into his eyes, one human, one canine.

'At first nothing happened. Then he went into some kind of fugue state. Had a seizure. We thought he was dying but instead his vitals became stronger than they had been. Over a period of a few days the physical changes began to manifest. He became a full wolf, then human again. We thought we'd stumbled on something. It was exciting times.'

'He's a werewolf then? That's what you're saying.'

'No. Nothing that simple or defined unfortunately. The genetic changing continued, his body became confused – I guess that's the only way I can describe it. The condition was so unstable that even now, it cannot settle on a form. Look. He's changing again.'

I stared at the boy. Now he was growing fangs, his face became more human. Graham dropped the cloth back over the cage.

'He reacts to his environment. The monkeys affect him too. If he's around people more, then he can return to his human form briefly. We've tested him with other influences too. He changes to reflect his environment.'

'And you call us monsters?' I said. 'When you'll experiment on a child like that?'

'We never expected this. We did the transfusions because we wanted a human host to see how the blood reacted in a natural incubator. We didn't know this would happen. It was a simple experiment, one that shouldn't have caused him any pain.'

'I'd say he's in a lot of pain,' I said. 'You'd be better off putting him out of his misery.'

'Caradien won't let me. He owns the boy now, and we'll all keep observing him until one day his body settles in a form or he dies.'

I felt sick. I might have been a killer but at least the death I brought was swift. I pulled Graham away from the cage and out of the room.

'Effectively the child is a shape-shifter but lacks the control to hold onto any form for long,' Graham said. 'This is a major scientific breakthrough but we can't share it with anyone, because what we've done is totally unethical.'

'You're vile. Humans in this time are … corrupt,' I said.

Graham nodded, 'I can't deny it. Nor my part in it. It's strange, but … I needed to show someone.'

I stared at Graham wondering what I'd see if I observed his aura through Lilly's amber stone. Would it be black and snake ridden like Carduth's? Or would it be red and stressed? I expected the latter.

'Now tell me what you did to Anja,' I said. 'Because we know she's not one of us.'

Graham sighed. 'You know who she is?'

'Yes. Caradien used her, just like he's using you. She was another experiment wasn't she? Now help me Graham and I promise I'll let you live.'

He sat down at one of the desks. 'I can't.'

'You're that loyal? To that sick bastard?'

'He *knows* things. I can't explain it. Somehow he always knows what I'm thinking, or what I'll do before I do it. I'm surprised that his men aren't here by now.'

'There's only me that knows your movements. And I suspect Caradien is pretty certain of your loyalty. Maybe in the past he's had you under observation? But what would be the point when you're at the hospital. He thinks you're working for him and has no reason to doubt you.'

Graham looked at his hands. 'Sometimes I feel that I will never be able to wash them clean.'

'Graham. Think about it carefully. Who is the real monster? I am not human; I'm a vampire and therefore a creature with different needs to you. I don't excuse my blood lust, but we can control ourselves. We don't deliberately cause mayhem or look to use the human race as some kind of food source for our abattoir. We take what we need, no more. Modern culture has their vampires and they are shown as manipulative and political. All of which is nonsense in the real world. All we want to do is exist and we rarely kill to do that. Caradien is human. What's his excuse?'

Graham buried his head in his hands. When he looked up again his expression was determined. 'I know you're right. I've always known it. And I don't buy into Caradien's religious beliefs that you're evil and need to be made extinct. There's a cartel of them. Conspiracy theorists would call them the *Illuminati*, the enlightened. But I think they are really living in the dark ages. I will help you. I'll tell you all I can. But you must leave here and promise never to contact me after that. Caradien may not be watching me now, but he may be in the future.'

I promised and I sat down beside him as he explained what we already knew, that Anja wasn't an original carrier of the vampire gene, rather she was transfused until the gene took hold of her DNA and began to change her. All it then took was Harry's bite to finish the process.

'She could have ended up like that,' I said nodding to the animal room. 'So why did this work?'

'Anja is very special. She's an empath. It made her more susceptible than others might have been. Plus we didn't give her Caradien's blood. The vampire gene is strong, especially in blood. Haven't you noticed that it doesn't matter what blood group you drink from because all blood works for you. That is, I suspect, because your blood dominates any other. That's what happened eventually with Anja.'

'Thank you,' I said.

'What for? You'd have killed me if I hadn't explained, right?'

I looked into Graham's eyes and nodded. 'Of course. But you didn't have to show me all that you have.'

'One more thing,' Graham said. 'I told you I don't believe in Caradien's fanatic views?'

'Yes. I know.'

'But I've seen the heart. It's real and it will kill you if you come in close proximity to it,' Graham said. 'And the real reason I'm helping you is not because you've threatened me. It's because of that kid in there.'

'You regret what you did. I understand that.'

'It wasn't me who did that to him. Well, not all me, although I don't deny my part in it. You see, the boy had some control at first. He was changing, but he could change back. It all looked good for him. His immune system improved. He was getting better. I thought I'd done something really important, really crucial. You understand?'

I nodded.

'One morning, I came in and found him in the mess he is in today. All the tests I did, showed it shouldn't have happened,' Graham continued. 'The vampire gene was winning.'

'Go on,' I said.

'Then it changed.'

'What do you think happened?' I asked.

'Caradien happened. I discovered that he came in on

evenings, after I'd gone. He began to do some experiments of his own.'

What Doctor Graham was saying really began to dawn on me and I didn't like what I was thinking.

'You mean … ?'

'Caradien exposed him to the heart. He said he had to be sure it would work on the vampire gene blood. He had to be sure it would kill you and all your kind,' Graham said.

'It has killed one of us. That's for certain,' I said.

'Worse than that though,' said Graham. 'When I came in, I didn't just find the subject affected. Two of my lab assistants were dead also. Their hearts were burnt out of their chests, blood boiled in their veins. In short, they had spontaneously combusted.'

'They were vampires?' I asked.

'No. They were human. But they were carriers of the vampire gene and it killed them. That heart killed them. It was then I realised how very dangerous it was. You see, we don't know how many of the population carry the gene, but I suspect it's almost a third.'

5
Templars

I laid low in Stockholm, feeding carefully and biding my time. The days drifted by too slowly and as the weeks wore on, I kept my eye on the clinic, saw no sudden changes occur, and watched Graham from a distance. I kept my promise to let him live and made no further attempt to contact him, but I used the information he gave me about Anja, and investigated her past. There had to be more to her 'empathy' than we could understand. Maybe she was a third important genetic element? Thinking about it all made my brain ache. I wasn't given to deep philosophical thinking and I barely understood the rudiments of modern science. The contemporary world still held so many mysteries and at times was more magical to me than any I had occupied. But what was worse, in all of this, was that Graham himself didn't understand how the heart remained alive, or why it was poison. He had been told, like Anja had, that it was all down to some ancient curse. We couldn't trust anything Caradien had said thus far though since Graham's and Anja's stories, both supposedly coming direct from Caradien, didn't exactly match up.

I went to Anja's place partly from boredom, partly because I hoped to find information that Graham didn't have.

'Caradien's spies are everywhere,' Graham reminded me before I left.

I was cautious about entering Anja's apartment block by any regular means. After working out which windows related to her apartment, I scaled the walls and forced my entry into what looked like a bedroom. I found a pale yellow toy on the floor but otherwise the place was empty. It hadn't been what I expected.

As I passed down the hallway and into another room I found myself face to face with a priest.

'Hello Caesare, I knew you'd find your way here eventually.'

This was obviously Caradien's spy and I was somewhat taken aback.

'No,' he answered my thought. 'I'm Father Anthony. And I don't belong to the *Illuminati*, I'm a Knights Templar. And the man behind you is John Noble. He found the relic and we're going to help you bring down Caradien and his cartel.'

I turned, annoyed that I hadn't noticed the other man until he was pointed out to me. Then I leaned back against the door frame, folding my arms across my chest and stared at them both blankly.

'I think you need to do some explaining,' I said calmly. 'I'm always willing to listen to a new story. There's been quite a few told me in the last few weeks.'

'Let me start by reinforcing that we're here to help you,' said Father Anthony. 'Caradien's corporation is the stronghold of your enemies.'

'I gathered that much on my own,' I said.

'Will you come down the corridor to my apartment?' Father Anthony asked. 'We'll be more comfortable there. I've been living in this block for several months on and off, keeping my eye on Anja. We were hoping to retrieve the heart before it could be used against any of you, but unfortunately Anja had sold it on, long before I arrived.'

I nodded, following him and Noble silently out of Anja's apartment.

I merged into invisibility before we reached the priest's rooms at the end of the hall. I still wasn't sure I believed that he was who he said he was, or that he was indeed on my side, but if Caradien's spies were everywhere, they may well have surveillance active here. If the priest was telling the truth, it would probably be best for him and his companion that they weren't seen with me.

Father Anthony held open his apartment door and I passed him, becoming visible again once inside. He led us into the lounge. It was almost identical in size and shape to Anja's apartment. Or at least how it may have appeared if she'd had furniture in there. In comparison the priest's rooms were warm and furnished. I sat down on a comfortable sofa and waited for the two men to settle opposite me in two armchairs.

'I suspect you're feeling a little confused by everything right now,' said Father Anthony.

'I know I am,' said Noble. 'It feels like everything I believed in my entire life is a complete lie. Just a few months ago I knew nothing of the *Illuminati* or the Knights Templar, except of course, the usual conspiracy rubbish you hear over the years.'

'Not such a lie,' Father Anthony commented. 'But rather gaps in general knowledge.'

Noble nodded, 'Very important information.'

'This important information … Care to enlighten me?' I said.

'Of course. Forgive me,' said Father Anthony. 'That's exactly why we are here.'

I studied the priest as he talked, looking for any sign of a lie. With my background I don't automatically believe someone just because they are a man of the cloth. My experience was that generally they proved more untrustworthy than those without a white collar.

'As I said earlier, I'm a Knights Templar. I know it's difficult to take in but we're on your side. I don't need to tell you how grateful our founders Jacques de Molay and Geoffroi de Charney were after you and Lilly saved their lives – oh yes, we know about that. We also know you killed their enemy the Archbishop in your search for Carduth.'

I nodded, 'He was a sick pervert.'

Father Anthony smiled. He had honest green eyes. 'Yes. And its men like him who have given the church such a bad name for centuries now. But I'm sure you understand that the majority of priests who take up the cloth are genuine followers of God and are only interested in doing their best for humanity.'

It was my turn to smile. 'I never judge one person by another but I'm always cautious. I think what you say is true – of this generation.'

'Your era,' said Noble, 'was particularly deceitful. Quite often in the middle ages the position of Pope was used for political or financial gain and not for the good of the faith or its followers.'

'You're a historian?' I asked.

'Not really, but since this happened I've been doing rather a lot of research. You don't look much like the paintings of you,' he said. 'But I'm glad to say you are nothing like your historical persona suggested.'

'You don't really know me,' I pointed out. 'We've just met.'

'No. But there are rather a lot of historical records about you,' said Noble. 'Forgive me for being so blunt. It does *feel* like I know you. At least a little.'

'History was not always accurate where I was concerned,' I said.

I realised how very strange this must be for both of the men. They knew who and what I was. They understood that I had lived for centuries. But did they know anything else? The time-travel element for example? Did they realise that Lilly could manipulate portals that could take us anywhere we wanted to go?

'Yes,' said Father Anthony reading my thoughts again. 'We know all about it. There are some of us that can do that also.'

'It seems it's not the only thing you are capable of,' I pointed out.

'I'm an empath. Like Anja.'

'I think you'd better start at the beginning,' I said rubbing my fingers over my forehead. 'I've had rather a lot to contend with recently and I'm not very patient when it comes to hearing fragments of a story.'

'Okay. It's simple really. Molay and Charney reformed the Templars. This time as a secret society. Among their followers they cultivated families with very special abilities. Anja's family was one such, as was mine. The problem was that Anja's parents weren't expecting their daughter to run away from the circus and go to university. Anja always aspired to more. She also had a tendency to use her gift for her own advancement. It was what brought her to Caradien's notice. Fortunately the Alescos had kept their role in the Templars a secret from her and so Caradien has never looked at them any further,' Father Anthony explained. 'As for John here, he's also from a very important gene pool. It's something the three of us have in common. We're carriers. Just like you were once.'

I frowned.

'I'm sure this is a lot to take in,' said Noble. 'When Anthony told me everything I just kept shaking my head and denying it. It seemed like some bizarre dream.'

'Who is Caradien?' I asked. 'Or rather what is he?'

'We'll come to that,' Noble interjected. 'It's important you understand all of the background first.'

'Two factions were born after the "death" of Jacques de Molay and Geoffroi de Charney,' Father Anthony continued. 'One of them was the followers of Carduth, the other became the Templars that still survive today.'

'You used a name to describe Caradien,' I said. '*Illuminati?* I've heard this name on at least three occasions now.'

'Yes. They too are a secret society and throughout history have been blamed for many conspiracies. Most of which were probably true. The biggest mistake commonly made of course is when the Templars are used as the background for the *Illuminati.* We're mortal enemies and unfortunately anyone could be one of their supporters.'

'Caradien told Anja he was a Templar,' I said.

'He lied. Everything about him is a lie. In fact the history he's told all of his followers couldn't be further from the truth,' Anthony said.

'So Anja may have believed his story, but it's unlikely to be accurate?' I asked.

'I'm sure there will be some basis in truth to make it sound plausible. Caradien is extremely good at spinning tales. We still haven't learnt why he and his staff are blocked to us also.'

'What do you mean blocked?' I asked.

'Caradien knows that a lot of Templars are empathic. Somehow he's devised a way to block his thoughts and feelings from us. This is in fact how we recognise his followers,' Father Anthony explained. 'For example the spy in this apartment block is an innocent looking old lady who lives alone with several cats. I couldn't read her and knew immediately she was one of Caradien's people. By preventing us reading the mundane thoughts of these people, for fear they'd give something about him away, he has made them stand out to us. They would be less conspicuous if they were readable.'

I sat back on the sofa, stretched out my legs and folded my arms again. Thinking through all that the priest said. My brain was on information overload. It was all too much to take in.

'From the beginning we recognised a Templar involvement, but this is surprising,' I said. 'Carduth was dressed as one of your knights when he first attacked us except the cross on his front was different.' I described the costume and the Ankh.

'It's almost a sick joke,' said Noble. 'Carduth uses the Templars' image to hang his conspiracy on. The Ankh was a symbol used for sanctuary by the early Christians and is a recognisable enough image to fool anyone into believing his motives are good. Hence the priest who helped him set the trap for you in the ruins at Lourdes. I'm sure the man was coerced into believing you were demons.'

'Is there nothing you don't know about?' I smiled but felt a little irritated.

'We're trying to help you,' Father Anthony said again. 'I assume Lilly has already used her sword against Carduth?'

'Yes. He was repelled by it.'

'Good,' said Father Anthony. 'She must keep it with her at all times.'

'Who is Carduth?' I asked again.

Father Anthony went on to explain how Carduth not only had the ear of his Pope but also the King and was responsible for the systematic destruction of the Knights Templar.

'He was human once,' Father Anthony explained. 'But then he began to dabble in the black arts and it changed him. He's more demon than human now and you can't reason with him.'

'I don't believe in demons,' I said. 'It's a word often used to identify people who are truly evil. You say "Demon" because you don't want to believe a human can do the things Carduth is capable of. He's human, I'm sure of that, but I agree he dabbles in black magic. Why us, though? Why is he doing this?'

'We're not sure. Caradien insists it is something to do with revenge. His ancestor, he says, was John the Baptist. But you know this already. Anja told you,' Father Anthony said.

'Yes. But as you say, this is all from the story that Caradien told her.'

'The truth is,' Noble interjected. 'The relic *is* John's heart. We firmly believe that. But as to why it's potent to you we just don't know. Wish we could get near it. I'd love to analyse it.'

'I saw it,' I said. 'The heart was alive. It was still beating. It recognised us. I almost felt …'

'What?' the two men said simultaneously.

'That it was a person. Had a soul. Crazy I know.'

'I almost opened the box,' Noble said. 'I felt it beating through the wood. I recognised my heritage long before I knew who I was.'

Father Anthony lapsed into thought. 'In some faiths it is believed that the heart is the soul. Modern science would tell you that a person's essence, all of their thoughts and feelings are generated from the brain. The heart is merely something that pumps blood around the body. An engine in the centre of a machine. But. There's no accounting for the emotions we all feel that have little to do with logic. Modern science knows nothing of faith.'

'Blood is the thing that sustains us,' I said. 'The heart is an important part of that.'

'The blood is the life …' Noble murmured.

'I need to get back to Lilly,' I told them. 'I was thrown back in time.'

'We know. We can help you with that.' Father Anthony explained.

'How?'

'I can manipulate ley lines and send you through a portal. You see I *do* believe in magic Caesare. Even though I feel that ley power is a fairly scientific one.'

I was stunned. 'How do you … ?'

Noble patted my arm in a casual friendly gesture. His hand was warm on my skin. 'Who do you think left Lilly the sword in the first place?' he laughed.

'This is making my head hurt,' I said.

'Time travel is always a mind-fuck,' Noble said. 'You should have seen the state of me when Anthony explained. But we're going to help you, my friend. And we're coming with you. First of all though, you need some armour.'

6
Attack

'From the precise details of what happened as you returned to the present,' Father Anthony said, 'I can pinpoint a moment in time before your return, and a little away from your portal. That way we won't be caught in the cross-fire.'

We stood once more outside Caradien's institute. Father Anthony knew of the ley power there and was preparing to raise a portal. We stood inside a circle of protection.

'Not because we need it. We're not raising demons after all!' he laughed. 'It will just make our activities invisible to anyone who might be watching.

The three of us were dressed in Templar armour.

'It's made of Kevlar,' said Noble as he had helped me into the armour. 'Modern armoury is a hell of a lot lighter than the original stuff. Plus, the bullets will have a job penetrating this. Don't ask me what the breast plate is made of though – I haven't a clue and I doubt Anthony will explain it to you. It's something in the realms of myth and magic. That's all I know.'

It felt peculiar to be wearing a mantle with a cross on my chest after all these years away from the church.

'God loves everyone,' Father Anthony commented as I'd stared suspiciously at the symbol. 'You're on this Earth because he made you. We all have our purpose.'

'You don't believe we are evil then?' I said.

'You can be. But my feeling is that Caradien is far worse.'

'You're a strange mix of religion and magic aren't you?' I said.

'Both require great faith and the power comes from only one

source,' Father Anthony said. Then he completely changed the subject. 'Lilly, Gabi and Anja were left surrounded, you said?'

'Yes.'

'Okay. Well let's get there before the firing starts. We can attack from the rear. They won't see it coming.'

Father Anthony proved to be adept at time-travel and within minutes a doorway was open and we stepped through.

We appeared a few deserted streets away from the hospital and set off on a steady jog. The armour was heavy but not cumbersome because of the modern design. Having been hit in the chest by Caradien's bullets once already I knew how much they could both hurt and incapacitate me and so I was glad of the extra protection. The helmet limited my vision as I could only see through a thin slit at the front and peripheral vision was non-existent. I had to turn my head to see either side of me.

Father Anthony and John Noble had weapons. Not swords as I had expected, but each of them carried a small gun. Noble explained that the weapons weren't deadly.

'We're not in the business of killing people. These will stun only, but it will give you enough time to get your friends away.'

'I will probably kill and at least maim a few of these bastards,' I pointed out.

'That's entirely up to you,' Father Anthony said. 'I can't say I blame you, after all, they are trying to kill you.'

I was a little surprised at Father Anthony's total acceptance of my nature.

'Surely you're not just helping us out of an inherited loyalty?' I asked just as we reached the hospital.

'I'm doing this for human carriers of the gene as well as those that have turned. If the heart is used on you, what's to stop Caradien turning it on anyone who has the gene? It's our belief that it will kill humans as well as vampires. That could mean over half of the Templars in the world are susceptible,' Father Anthony said.

I remained quiet. I wasn't sure if I wanted to share

everything I knew with Father Anthony and John Noble. At least not until I was totally certain they were on my side. So far, I was taking them at face value, but I had no way of knowing if I was walking into a trap.

'We thought carriers were rare,' I said to fill the silence.

'No. You've just been lucky not to turn more so far. Lilly's talent in that area is much appreciated.'

'Look!' said Noble and I turned to face the hospital.

Lilly was slipping through the portal as the rest of us had gone ahead. As soon as she vanished a small army of twenty or so men poured out of the hospital and surrounded the portal waiting for our imminent return.

'We won't attack until you've been shot and have fallen back inside the portal,' Father Anthony said. 'Everything must happen as it did.'

I nodded, drawing the sword at my side. I was itching to kill. I remembered the pain and the bullet scars ached with the memory of it all.

A barrage of bullets sang through the air as my companions came out of the portal. I saw myself push Lilly aside. I was hit and fell back. For a moment my feet were frozen with the shock of seeing myself, but then I was galvanised into action as the mercenaries continued to fire their crippling bullets at my friends.

Lilly leapt into the air too fast for the gunmen to follow her. She took two of them out as Gabi covered Anja, taking a bullet in his spine and one in his neck. He fell down on top of the girl. At that moment I reached the back row of men. Swinging my sword I decapitated two of them with one stroke. Noble and Father Anthony came up behind me firing at the two nearest men. Each of them fell forward on their faces.

Lilly landed on the back of one of the mercenaries. His colleagues turned, firing at her, but she used the mercenary as a shield, then heaved his body up in the air, throwing it at the gunmen. The body hit them – a dead weight – and they toppled like dominos. She was on them before they could recover, smashing both of their heads fiercely together splitting their skulls open so that each man's scrambled brains seeped out on the ground as their bodies crashed back down to the floor.

Only five men were left. They turned towards me, firing. A bullet hit my breast plate and ricocheted off, hitting a gunman full in the face. His nose exploded in a glob of blood and snot and he fell screaming through a half ruptured mouth onto the floor.

The mercenaries hadn't expected a fight. The few men remaining ran back towards the hospital, looking for shelter. I pulled off my helmet to reveal myself to a surprised Lilly and then joined Noble as he knelt over Gabi. He was unconscious and so I lifted him up, freeing Anja who was unhurt.

'Let's get out of here,' I called.

Lilly nodded and we ran back down the street, Noble and Father Anthony trailing behind unable to sustain our pace.

Back at our starting point I piled Anja and Lilly through the portal Father Anthony had created and waited for him and Noble to catch up.

They arrived, panting and out of breath, but I barged them through in front of me, and taking a final look back at the empty street to ensure we hadn't been followed, I stepped back through with Gabi.

When I arrived with the others, Anthony slammed the portal shut behind us. We were now back in Stockholm but several days before the incident that we'd just escaped from.

'I think I need some explanations,' Lilly said. 'Who the fuck are you?'

'Yes, you do,' Father Anthony agreed, removing his helmet. 'But first I need to take you all to a safe house. Your friend is badly hurt, and spinal injuries are the most dangerous to heal from.'

'We can heal anything,' Lilly said.

I put my hand on her arm, 'Trust them, they know what they are doing.'

And I realised I meant it. The Templars had proved themselves in the fight. I didn't see any reason why we shouldn't now give them the benefit of the doubt, if not our full trust.

Father Anthony withdrew a mobile phone from somewhere in his armour and within minutes a black stretch-limo pulled up beside us. We all piled in and the car sped away. I lay Gabi down on the back seat.

'He doesn't look good,' Anja said. 'He saved me.'

Noble nodded, 'If you'd taken the bullets I think it would have been all over for you. At least he has the age and survival instinct to get through this.'

I sat down next to Lilly and explained what had happened since my parting from her. She took the news well but Anja was confused and kept asking questions in an attempt to make sense of it all.

'So you got hit?'

'Yes.'

'And was stranded in that other time?'

'Yes.'

'Wow!'

'Traversing time can be very confusing,' Lilly explained. 'There's so much I don't understand but I try not to think about the toing and froing too much. It's simpler that way. Treat every time as being *your* present.'

Anja fell quiet.

'We lost the photocopies,' Lilly said suddenly. 'Gabi had them …'

There's more to tell you, but it's not for Anja's ears, I thought. Lilly listened to me as I poured the images of the last few days into her. I showed her all the information I gleaned from Doctor Graham and all that I now knew about Caradien and Carduth. She sat forward in her seat, dropped her head in her hands and assimilated the information.

You have been busy. And resourceful, she thought. *I'm so proud of you, darling.*

'Nice to meet you Father Anthony, John Noble,' Lilly said when I finished my silent explanation.

The two men exchanged looks and then each held out his hand to shake Lilly's.

'Your help is most welcome,' Lilly said.

'It's an honour to meet you,' Father Anthony said. 'I'm glad you're wearing the sword.'

Lilly looked down at her hip, the sword dangled comfortably and almost forgotten at her side.

'Yes. Tell me about the sword,' she said.

'I thought you'd never ask,' Father Anthony smiled.

7
Warlock Priest

'The amber stone is a most unusual and powerful natural crystal. It's made from a solidified tree resin,' Father Anthony explained.

'Yes. I know that,' Lilly said.

'I suspect you know all about its healing properties too ...'

'I know you've done your homework, Anthony,' Lilly answered. 'I was a herb-wife.'

Father Anthony nodded.

'What I don't know,' Lilly continued. 'Is how this particular piece of amber has the ability to repel Carduth, and how it also reads auras. Interestingly I'd like to look at yours through it if I may?'

Father Anthony sat back in his seat, shrugged, then nodded for Lilly to proceed. She withdrew the sword, holding it pommel upwards before her face. She looked at the priest, then turned the amber towards John Noble as he sat quietly watching.

'You both carry the vampire gene,' Lilly said, slipping the sword back into her scabbard. 'I thought as much.'

'The stone fell into our hands some years ago and has proved to be a useful tool in identifying carriers of the gene. We don't all have your taste buds,' Father Anthony smiled. 'Plus, licking the skin of total strangers would have been quite awkward.'

'Mmmm. I suppose that would be rather tricky,' Lilly laughed. 'But how did you even know about the gene in the first place?'

'Our heritage was passed on from parent to child, the stories of our ancestry became our mythology,' Noble said. 'Except for me. I remember my parents telling me some story, about Salome and John the Baptist. A curse. But it was just a story. When both of them died suddenly in a railway accident, I was left orphaned. They hadn't given me the proof or the knowledge that this wasn't a story but a heritage.'

'Both of your parents were carriers?' Lilly asked.

'We're an incestuous bunch,' Father Anthony answered on John's behalf. 'There are families out there that know their heritage because we keep our genetic family close deliberately. Jacques de Molay and Geoffroi de Charney were brothers in more ways than in arms. It was no coincidence that you were driven to save them.'

'That ol' devil called fate again,' Lilly said. 'Thought I'd had enough of that to last me several lifetimes.'

'Not all twists of fate are bad ones,' Father Anthony said mysteriously.

'So, back to the amber. Did you merely stumble on this stone and find it showed you secrets? A fate thing?' Lilly asked.

'Good heavens, no!' Father Anthony laughed. 'We were given it. Along with a spell that has helped us devise smaller versions for all Templars to carry.'

Father Anthony nodded to Noble and the other man lifted his mantle to reveal a perfectly oval pendant of amber.

'You're a warlock priest?' Lilly said, lifting her eyebrows.

'You could say that …'

The black panel of glass separating the driver from the passengers slowly slid down.

'We're almost there, Father,' said the driver. 'The medical team is on standby.'

The car drew up to a set of huge gothic gates. The driver pressed a button on a small box that looked something like a television remote control and the gates smoothly opened. We then drove down an avenue of trees to a huge house that looked like something you would find in the middle of a country estate.

'Fancy,' said Anja.

I looked out of the window as we drew closer, observing the gargoyles, the high turrets, the large windows that looked out over the drive that watchful eyes.

'Looks like a Victorian insane asylum,' Lilly observed and then she looked down at Gabi a frown furrowing her brow.

I hope you're right about these guys, she thought as the car pulled up in front of an impressive entrance that led up to an oak double door via a row of some ten or more steps.

Two male medics were waiting with a stretcher and I lifted Gabi onto it carefully.

'Was happ'nin',' Gabi slurred as Lilly, Anja and I all stood around him.

'All's well,' Lilly reassured him and we allowed the medics to wheel him inside, following closely on their heels. We entered a cavernous hallway and the medics turned left, wheeling Gabi quickly through a set of double doors and down a corridor. The house looked like a private clinic. We hurried passed a row of closed doors and into a prepared hospital theatre.

'You'll have to stay outside,' said one of the medics. 'The doctor is in scrubs, you're not.'

'Look,' said Lilly. 'We can't catch infections. Gabi isn't in any danger from germs. No offense but we don't know who the fuck you are. No way will we leave him alone with you.'

'Okay,' he nodded. 'On your own head.'

Lilly took the trolley from the medic and wheeled it into the room. Inside we met the doctor, an anaesthetist and a nurse. All of them were wearing blue robes and masks over their faces.

'On here,' said the doctor.

I lifted Gabi from the trolley and placed him on the operating table, this time on his stomach so that the doctor could have access to the bullets penetrating Gabi's spine.

'This is going to be touch and go,' said the doctor. 'The spinal cord is a weak spot, even for you guys.'

Lilly and I exchanged a glance, then stepped back and let the doctor begin his work. At the same time, the nurse began to place a drip in Gabi's arm, feeding a bag of blood directly into his veins.

Blood helps, I thought and Lilly nodded.

The doctor extracted five bullets from Gabi's spine and back and two from his neck dropping each of them into a metal bowl held out by the nurse.

'Take these to the lab,' the doctor said. 'I'll just stitch him … Oh!'

Gabi was already beginning to heal as the last bullet was removed and the blood being pumped in his body forced its way through his veins. A groan came from Gabi's lips and he pushed himself up, trying to sit.

'Stay,' ordered Lilly at his side. 'There's a whole lot of healing to be done yet.'

Gabi collapsed forward again. 'My legs. I can't move my legs.'

Lilly looked at the doctor, 'What's happening?'

'I told you. The spinal cord, it's your weakness. Everyone and everything has one.'

Lilly put her hand to her mouth, and tears sprung to her eyes.

The nurse led me and I wheeled Gabi back on the trolley down the hallway, then lifted him carefully into a bed in a room just off the main entrance hall.

'Do you feel any pain?' I asked.

'No,' he said. 'I don't feel anything.'

'Try and sleep,' Lilly said.

It wasn't long before exhaustion closed Gabi's eyes and he slept. Soon after I followed Lilly as she hurried away down the corridor. I'd never seen her so anxious and so scared.

'We're vulnerable. We can be hurt! Oh Caesare.'

'Yes. But he'll recover I'm sure of it.' I said.

'What if he doesn't?'

Anja was waiting at the door with Father Anthony and John Noble.

'How is he?' she asked and I could see from the lack of concern that she expected all was well, just as we had.

'He's paralysed,' I said.

'What?' Anja gasped. 'Is this some kind of joke?'

'No,' Lilly answered. 'Right now he's resting but we don't know if he will ever walk again.'

Noble and Father Anthony stared at us in surprise.

'I'm sure the doctor will do all he can,' Father Anthony said. 'We have the best facilities at our grasp. Money is no object to us.'

'I know,' said Lilly. 'I'm tired. I'm so tired.'

'Come,' said Noble taking her hand. 'We have rooms prepared for you.'

'I want to see Gabi,' Anja said.

Lilly let Noble lead her away. In all the years I'd known her, I'd never seen her so afraid. I followed after them, leaving Anja with Father Anthony.

We were in the room across from Gabi. A large double bed dominated the room and Lilly collapsed onto it as Noble left us.

I pulled her up into the centre, undressing her as she lay there. Her eyes were closed. I felt the tremor inside her even though she tried to quell it. She was afraid to open her eyes and see the world, or worse still, to look into mine and see her fears reflected there. I stood, removed the armour and climbed naked into the bed with her. I spooned her, wrapping my arms around her protectively.

'You were shot by their bullets. Yet you're fine now aren't you?'

'It took a fresh kill and I was back to full strength. I was incredibly weakened though.' I explained.

'The spine is our weakness,' Lilly said. 'All these years, I've believed myself impervious to injury or death.'

'We are pretty invulnerable.'

'I'm going to kill Caradien,' Lilly said.

'Me too.'

'And me,' said Anja opening the door.

She came inside the room and sat on the bed beside us. Her face was pale. A tightness around her mouth made her look old. She had aged a lifetime in just a few short months.

'That man betrayed me at every turn,' she said. 'He'd have let his men kill me tonight and if Gabi hadn't thrown himself over me that would be me paralysed or worse – I'd be dead. The last time I spoke to him, Caradien said he loved me. He promised we'd be together after this was over. He said his doctor had a cure for the vampirism.'

'He lied to you,' I said.

Anja nodded. 'Of course he did. His "cure" was always that he'd destroy me along with you.'

Anja fell silent. Lilly said nothing, but I felt her sigh against my chest.

'Gabi's sleeping,' Anja said eventually. 'I don't want to be alone.'

I moved up and let her slip into the bed with us.

'Can we trust *them*?' Anja asked, just as sleep curled up around us.

'We have no choice,' said Lilly.

8
Paralysis

Gabi took the paralysis with much more cheer than the rest of us. He was intravenously given daily doses of blood, taken from fresh and willing donors. He grew stronger, but the feeling didn't return to his legs. Fortunately his arms were strong and he was soon wheeling himself around the corridors in a wheelchair.

'I want to do an MRI Scan,' the doctor told us. 'It would be useful to see what and where the damage is.'

'It will also tell you more about our body structure, won't it?' said Lilly.

The doctor nodded, 'I won't deny I'm curious about you. All my research so far has been purely at a distance. I never thought I'd actually get this close to you.'

'You should be nervous,' Lilly said. 'Knowing what you do about us.'

'I'm not afraid,' he answered. 'I know that you're honourable, Lilly, and you need me to help your friend.'

'Let's be clear on this,' Lilly said. 'If you are helping us, and this isn't some kind of trick then you have nothing to fear from us. However …'

'I understand,' the doctor said.

'Okay. Let's do the scan,' Gabi interrupted. 'It might help knowing what's happening in there.'

'Right. But one of us must be with you at all times,' Lilly said.

It was decided that I would go with Gabi in the limo to a local hospital controlled by the Templars. The similarity between the Knights and the *Illuminati* controlled by Caradien was not lost on me. The Templars knew as much about us as Caradien did, and yet we, powerful immortals had known nothing of any of them until now. We had lived in our own insular world, believing in our power, our invulnerability.

'We have been so arrogant,' Lilly said. 'And so very naive to think that our activities have been unobserved.'

I had to wonder why Caradien hadn't struck sooner when he could have caught us unawares.

'Caradien enjoys the chase,' Father Anthony explained. 'He wanted you to know about him. You're the ultimate predator and he sees himself as the ultimate hunter.'

'I want to see a picture of him,' Lilly said. 'I need to see the face of my enemy.'

'We have some in the archive,' Noble said.

So Lilly stayed to learn about Caradien and I took Gabi to the hospital.

'It's so weird to be carried around like this,' Gabi said as I lifted him on the MRI table. 'I tried to fly. Couldn't. And, I don't require legs in order to fly.'

Even so he remained cheerful.

'I'm really impressed by how calm you've taken all this,' I said as I wheeled him through the hospital.

'Nothing is definite,' he said. 'Any day I might just get up and walk and until I'm certain that will never happen there's no point in panicking. Strangely I feel very safe with the Templars.'

I agreed with him. Despite everything I too felt safe. We knew so little about them, they could really be our enemies and not our allies and yet I believed everything they said.

The Templar medical team had taken over the scan unit and all other personnel were sent away. The scan was being used primarily to diagnose the damage done to Gabi's spine, but it was sure to reveal other things about us, and so anyone not in the immediate group had to be kept away from the information.

'This is our radiographer, Sister Adela,' Father Anthony said, and I noticed that he never told me more than the first name of any of the team he introduced us to. The doctor who operated on Gabi was known as Father Bartholomew. Each of the team belonged to the order of the Templars, and because of the title of Sister or Father I assumed that all of them were nuns and priests also.

Adela positioned Gabi on the table, putting a pillow under his head.

'Just relax,' she said. 'Once this starts you'll be able to hear my voice through speakers in the machine. Occasionally I'll ask you to hold your breath. It won't be longer than you can manage, but it's crucial as it will keep your body still while the scan works on certain areas. We're going to scan your spine. It will take approximately an hour.'

Gabi was fed into the machine. It was like a shallow cave.

'You okay in there?' asked Adela.

'Yes,' Gabi answered.

Adela left the room and I saw her enter a booth with a huge glass window looking into the scan room. The scanning began. Gabi listened to Adela, breathed and held his breath as instructed and when the full scan was complete, she returned. The table came back out of the bowels of the machine and I lifted Gabi back into his wheelchair.

Bartholomew came in and took an envelope from Adela.

'You've deleted everything from the system?' he asked.

'Yes. All burned to disc,' Adela said nodding to the envelope. 'Okay. On to the CT room. It's just next door.'

I pushed Gabi's chair and followed Adela into the other room. This machine looked like a giant 'O'. I lifted Gabi onto the bed once more.

'What does this machine do?' I asked.

'The MRI looks at the soft tissue in the body,' Adela explained. 'This one will be a whole look at the bones around it. I'm going to do the whole body, not just the spine this time.'

'Why?' I asked.

'Doctor's orders. He wants to check out your friend's bone structure.'

This machine worked much quicker than the previous one and within a short time Gabi was back in the wheelchair and we were returned to the Templars' safe house.

'There's a bullet still embedded in Gabi's spine,' Bartholomew explained as we sat around his desk in a large office within the safe house.

'That's unusual. Normally our antibodies would treat them as an invasion and merely expel them,' said Lilly.

'It seems that has happened in this case to an extent. Gabi's natural antibodies have grown around the bullet to defend him from the toxin that Caradien inserted in them. It's calcified. There's a hard lump, in the lumbar region. With the calcification the bullet is effectively cocooned and is now no longer registering as a threat. I think this is why it won't be pushed out like the others.'

We considered the options of operating. Bartholomew said the risks were high.

'What else did you learn from the scan? Chez told me you took another one of his bones,' Lilly asked.

Bartholomew opened his file.

'Your bones are far denser than humans.'

'How dense?' I asked.

'The equivalent of iron girders I'd say. That's why you're so incredibly strong. However they are still light, which is almost a contradiction in itself,' Bartholomew said. 'All the tests show that other than the injury, Gabi is fit and strong. What's really interesting is the production of blood taken after the operation. The vampire gene blood is overpowering.'

'In what way?' I asked.

'It's like a virus. It's no wonder that carriers are affected so strongly from the bite of one of your kind. The vampire gene blood is perpetually renewing and restructuring the blood that you absorb from your victims, changing it to your own to make it palatable. You can take any blood and digest it right?'

The four of us nodded.

'But some tastes better than others,' Gabi said. 'I'm rather partial to Rhesus Negative. It's a rare one to find.'

I found myself looking around at the others. I didn't know if I'd tasted this Rhesus blood but I did know that sometimes some victims tasted different and the experience was more pleasurable.

'What else?' asked Lilly.

'I managed to confirm in my own mind,' said Bartholomew, 'what I'd initially suspected in the beginning. Your spinal cord is an area of weakness.'

'So we can be crippled. That much is clear,' said Gabi.

'If severed completely. I suspect,' Bartholomew continued, 'that you'd die.'

'Then we can't risk the operation,' Lilly said.

'I think that's my call. I want you to operate doctor,' said Gabi. 'There's no way I want to live forever in this condition. I couldn't be a continual burden to my friends. Tell me honestly, doctor, is there any chance my body will heal itself?'

'Gabi, didn't you hear what he said? You could die?' Lilly said.

'Answer me,' said Gabi. 'Will I heal on my own?'

'It's unlikely. There's no sign of that bullet moving at all, and while it's there it's pressing on your spine, preventing your lower body from working properly.' Bartholomew answered.

'Then the only chance I have is the operation?'

'Yes ... but the risks are so great ...'

'I know. But it's my risk and I'm taking it.'

The anaesthetic took longer to work than on a human and the anaesthetist had to use triple the safe dose in order to put Gabi under. Anja, Lilly and I were in a small room inside the operating theatre watching the proceedings from behind a sheet of clear glass. From our vantage point we could hear and see everything that occurred in the operating room.

'His body is fighting the drug,' Bartholomew explained. 'We'll have to try and keep him under long enough for me to remove the bullet.'

Bartholomew cut open a wound in Gabi's back, swilling his skin with anti-coagulant agents to prevent it healing and knitting together.

'This is one of those times when our healing powers are a bad thing,' Anja observed. 'Do you think he'll be all right?'

Lilly stared silently at Bartholomew but said nothing. How could any of us know how this would go? We could only hope that the bullet was retrieved and that nothing worse happened during the surgery. It was the only chance Gabi had of walking again.

'It's going to have to be quick,' Bartholomew commented. 'He's healing around my fingers.'

He retracted, picked up the scalpel once more and cut Gabi open again. Then the nurse splashed the wound again as the doctor turned and picked up a longish instrument that looked like a thin set of pliers. Bartholomew prodded the instrument into the wound, then turned once more, cutting Gabi open as the wound healed.

'This is impossible,' Bartholomew gasped. 'I can't keep it open long enough.'

Lilly left the room and as I watched through the glass I saw her appear beside the doctor.

'Explain to me what you need to do,' Lilly said.

'I'm cutting a pathway to the bullet, then I want to retrieve it,' he explained. 'It's simple but requires a steady hand and because the wound is healing so quickly I'd have to do the removal in a way that makes the risks of mistake even higher.'

Lilly took the plier instrument, 'Cut. I'll get the bullet.'

'You … can't,' said the doctor. 'I mean it takes precision and …'

'Believe me doctor, my eyesight is far more precise than yours and my hands a hell of a lot steadier. I was a healer in my day, I know a little about surgery …'

Bartholomew nodded, then cut Gabi open once more, working down as deep to the bullet as he dared. Lilly had a grip on the offending item, almost as fast as the doctor moved his hand away. She pulled back slowly, ripping her way through repairing tissue in a way that the doctor wouldn't have dared and couldn't have risked.

The bullet, covered in a hard shell created by Gabi's body,

dropped into the metal tray.

'Now what?' asked Lilly.

'Normally I'd stitch him, but his body is doing the work for me.'

Lilly peered into the wound and for a moment I shared her mind, saw the fine tissue and skin of Gabi's spine knit neatly together. Like her I prayed that this would be enough and that now he would heal. I wanted Gabi back to full strength. We still had a fight on our hands and ultimately Caradien would either kill us all, or we would kill him. I knew we'd be stronger if Gabi was in that fight but more importantly I'd grown to care for him. He was my friend and I wanted him to survive.

9
Lineage

The library was off-centre and was built into one of the towers. It was a circular room, walls covers from floor to ceiling, dotted with unevenly placed windows, that stretched up three storeys and met with a final floor, that circled the top, just under a glass dome. From the outside you could see the dome was designed to resemble an Indian palace. Inside, the walls were lined from floor to ceiling with bookshelves. Seven narrow balconies ran in rings around the circular room. Throughout our time in the Templars' safe house we discovered a whole archive of collated information in the library. Nothing was off limits to us as the Templars were trying to ensure that we knew their motives were genuine by being as transparent as possible. Yet, Lilly remained tense. The whole experience had rocked her considerable confidence and she was, for the most part, silent as we looked through the information at our disposal.

We were looking for anything we could find on Caradien and his accomplice Carduth but so far we could only find facts about Caradien. It was as though Carduth didn't really exist in history.

'It's likely he was using a pseudonym,' Noble said.

I nodded. 'Probable.'

'Strange thought,' Noble said. 'The description you gave doesn't fit at all with the right hand man of the Pope Clement V. He wasn't an Archbishop either. But I'll just pull up all I can about those in power.'

Noble returned to his laptop.

'Will Gabi be okay?' Anja asked for the fourth or fifth time.

'I really don't know,' Lilly snapped. 'But I hope so. We just have to wait and see how he recovers now.'

'Tell us what you've learned about the heart,' I said to Noble, changing the subject.

It was important that we gathered as much information as possible about our enemy while we waited for news of our companion. We still had a fight to prepare for, with or without Gabi, and Lilly was having a hard time coming to terms with the fact that it might be the latter.

'The origins of the heart are uncertain,' Noble explained as we sat together in the library, 'though it's said to have belonged to John the Baptist, that could be a myth. Just a religious slant that's been spun to provide the mystery surrounding it. But I do believe, as I told you before, that this is true.'

'You saw the box that it was in?'

'Yes. Strangely it didn't fit in with the dates at all. The box was roughly carved, but didn't look aged. The symbol burned or engraved on it, the Ankh, was picked from the air by the *Illuminati*. They use it as their sign even today, but I doubt it has much significance. The strangest thing of all was the cloth it was wrapped in.'

Noble described the fabric that had been wrapped around the box. As he illustrated the eye-like symbol, with the triskele in the centre, Lilly drew in a sharp breath.

'That's my symbol. Or rather one of my magic signs,' she explained. 'But it's an important one to me.'

'Father Anthony practices the ancient magiks as well, which is why he can manipulate time,' Noble said. 'Maybe you'd be willing to share some of your knowledge with him?'

'Yes,' Lilly said suddenly. 'Maybe we could help each other. I've been thinking about this a lot and I need to speak to him. Do you know where he is today?'

Noble looked at her uncertainly for a moment and then he took his phone out of his pocket and sent a text to the priest.

'I'm here. Are you all right, Lilly?' Father Anthony asked calmly as he entered the library minutes later.

'Where did you learn to manipulate ley lines?' Lilly asked.

'It was passed down to me, from my parents, by their parents. I'm from a long line of empaths and witches. I was lucky in that I have abilities in both areas.'

I didn't know where this conversation was leading but I listened intently as Father Anthony explained his lineage. His family stretched back through the centuries and he explained once more how he was a carrier of the gene.

'But how did you know that?' Lilly said. 'In ancient times, DNA didn't exist. Or rather the old witches didn't know about it.'

'We've always known, Lilly,' Father Anthony said.

'How?'

'Because somewhere in the early ages of our time, someone travelled back through time and explained it. They were quite specific about the knowledge and our ancestors passed it down until such a time that it made sense. When the Templars reformed we used that knowledge. Now we have blood tests that determine who is a carrier and who isn't. But you know that already.'

'This is a total mind-fuck,' Lilly said exasperated. 'I haven't been back in time and spread the word.'

'Not yet, but somewhere in your future you may,' Father Anthony explained.

He sat down at the table with us.

'Anthony,' Lilly said. 'We need to verify the heart. We need to know what happened for certain and if this myth surrounding Salome and John the Baptist is true. Will you come with me through time and help me?'

'Wait a minute,' I said. 'What about me? You aren't going alone.'

'We need someone here to protect Gabi,' Lilly said.

'Well of course you do,' Anja said. 'I'll do it. He was hurt protecting me.'

That ended the argument, but Lilly wasn't sure that Anja was strong enough and I could see the uncertainty on her face.

'There's also me,' said Noble, 'and the other Templars. Don't think for one minute that Caradien and his gang are going to get inside here without a fight. Gabi and Anja will be safe. I promise you that.'

Lilly went to change into something more appropriate for time-travelling and she came back wearing black jeans, a black shirt and her leather jacket. Draped around her slim waist was the sword the Templars had given her. I loved looking at her small waist as it carried such a powerful weapon.

'Let's go,' she said handing me my sword.

'Okay,' said Father Anthony. 'But we need to make sure that we have as much armour as possible. I'm not happy that we might pass through a portal and straight into the line of fire from Caradien's men.'

He took us to the armoury and once more I donned the Kevlar chainmail and the breast plate of the Templars. As I strapped on the boots I turned around to see Lilly dressed in the armour. She looked like an avenging angel.

'I'll wear this stuff,' said Lilly. 'But I'm not wearing the helmet.'

Father Anthony nodded, 'We probably won't need it all. This is merely a precaution. Caradien doesn't have his insider giving him information these days.'

I saw a flicker of fear cross Lilly's face as she recalled Anja's betrayal. She was still not feeling her usual confidence and I didn't know how to boost her. Gabi's apparent fragility was a severe blow that had an impact for us all, but Lilly had taken it harder than any of us.

'You're right,' I confirmed. 'But just in case they have other sources, better to be safe than sorry.'

In the bowels of the house Father Anthony took us to his magic room. It was filled with paraphernalia I'd never seen before as Lilly didn't require specific instruments to help her perform magic. Father Anthony, however, had rituals, some of which were typical of the Catholic Church who over the years had carved their own services from those originally devised by the early faiths, particularly Paganism.

On an altar lay a dagger, a bowl, a pentagram and candles. I looked around the room and observed ceremonial robes hanging on a rail. It all looked a little archaic but Lilly said nothing and her expression was blank as she looked around us. Even so, she quickly got into the spirit of things with Father Anthony as she picked up a bowl of salt and began to draw a circle with it on the floor.

'We'll do a circle of protection,' she explained to me. 'Just to block any sign of our activities from anyone who might be searching for surges in ley power.'

I nodded. It made sense as we didn't know for certain how much Caradien knew and what he was capable of.

'How do you know where we need to go?' I asked.

Anthony and Lilly exchanged looks.

'We're all going to focus on Salome and the history. We'll see what portals come up and where they lead to,' Lilly explained.

'Perhaps,' said Father Anthony. 'We should focus on your lineage.'

'What do you mean?' I asked.

'We should go back to the origins of the vampire gene. See where this all started.'

Lilly nodded, 'We can jump as many portals as we wish. Time is on our side in that way.'

I gripped her hand in the circle and felt the power pull from the earth, into my legs and through my body. The world bent, then opened before us and I saw the multitude of doors, felt the dates and times and places as they sped past us. I concentrated hard on the search for the original spark – the first time when the vampire gene formed in this world.

A portal opened before my eyes, a rapid waterfall leading out into a huge room. It was luxuriously furnished and appeared Egyptian. This was the one! I knew it. I felt the recognition. Lilly stepped forward pulling my hand and so I went with her and Father Anthony into the room.

It was dark when we arrived. I looked around, immediately alert, as I heard laboured breathing that echoed from a pallet in the corner. A young girl, sighing and gasping was pressing her swollen belly as she lay in the corner like a dirty secret.

She's in labour, Lilly thought.

'Salome,' Father Anthony said.

The girl spoke. But it was a language I couldn't understand.

'What did she say?' asked Lilly.

'It's Aramaic,' Father Anthony said and he began to project a translation into our minds.

'Are you an angel?' the girl said, staring up at Lilly as she towered over her.

'Yes,' Lilly said automatically because this was a comment often made to us by our victims. They thought us angels, but really we were devils. 'Why isn't anyone helping you?'

The girl shook her head, then gasped in pain as another strong contraction squeezed her small body.

She's only a little girl! Lilly thought and indeed she couldn't have been more than thirteen or fourteen.

Lilly bent down beside her and she stroked her stomach, feeling the contractions.

'Not long now,' she told Salome. 'Your baby will be born and you'll feel better. I promise.'

'They are going to kill it,' said Salome.

Lilly stroked Salome's head and sent a calming pulse through the girl. This was a crucial time. Maybe Salome was the carrier and we were here to witness the delivery of her first child: a child that would go on to birth many of our kind. Lilly licked her fingers, and then looked up at me.

'She's not the carrier,' she said surprised.

At that moment Salome began to cry. The baby was coming and she didn't know what to do. Lilly got on her knees before the girl. *It's not like I haven't done this before*, she thought then shrugged as Father Anthony kneeled down and held the girl's hand.

I'm not squeamish, naturally, but I turned away. I wanted to keep an eye on the door. At any moment someone could come in, possibly looking to aid the girl. But, everywhere remained silent and despite Salome's screams no one came to help her as she pushed her child out into the world.

Lilly wrapped the baby up in a sheet she pulled from the sweat and blood stained pallet.

'It's a boy,' she said tying the cord and then biting through it with her teeth.

She handed the baby to Salome, who looked down at the infant with distain.

'There's no point in loving him,' Salome said. 'He's going to be taken …'

'Why? Because he's Herod's? He can do as he pleases. Even father an illegitimate child.'

'I didn't want to tell …' Salome said as she slumped back against the bed exhausted and in shock.

'What? What did you tell?' Father Anthony asked softly. 'We need to know.'

I bent down and grabbed the girl's hand, jerking her round to face me. Then I looked deeply into her eyes.

'My baby isn't his …' she murmured.

Lilly fell silent and at that moment I heard a creak behind us. I turned to find a panel opening in the wall. Herod squinted into the gloom.

I slipped back into the shadows, merged with them at the same time that Lilly did. I pulled Father Anthony close, overlapping him. I wasn't sure if this would hide him from the King or not but I tried anyway.

'Salome! Who were you talking to?' Herod asked.

'An angel. An angel helped me birth the baby.'

From where I stood by the door I could see that Salome was feverish and sick. She was still bleeding heavily onto the straw, but she hugged the child close and glared at the King.

'My baby is sacred,' she said. 'I know he is …'

The King stepped into the room, 'Whore. Your child was fathered by a commoner. It has no place here.'

Salome screamed as the King drew closer, holding aloft a heavy wooden stick. As Herod raised it above his head, Father Anthony stepped away from me.

'Stop! I can't allow you to kill an innocent child.'

Salome cowered and covered the baby with her arms.

Despite herself she already loved her child. Maybe it was instinct.

Herod was shocked to find Father Anthony in his armour before him; I dropped my cloak and appeared as if by magic and so did Lilly. We stood either side of the Templar priest. The three of us made a formidable sight.

'Who … ?' Herod staggered back, drawing the stick in close to his chest.

'Angels …' Salome whispered. 'John said that God would take care of me.'

'Heresy!' yelled Herod. 'Your lover was no saint but a demon. A demon with a heart that still beats on after his death!'

Salome cried and screamed as Herod called for his guards. The men poured in. Even though it would be easy to kill them all the three of us remained frozen as they surrounded us.

'Wait,' Lilly said. 'We've come in peace. You're going to kill this child, yet we wish to take it from here. And the mother.'

'Kill them!' ordered the King.

I delivered an easy blow to the first guard who rushed us and sent him toppling like a rag doll into the rest of Herod's men.

'You are demons,' Herod cried.

'The child is an innocent. You won't kill him,' Lilly said.

I bent down and lifted Salome and the child into my arms. I had no clue what Lilly was planning but I would be ready to flee as soon as she gave the word.

'You've killed John,' Father Anthony said. 'But you say his heart still beats?'

'It's my fault. It's all *my* fault,' Salome cried. 'I wanted his heart; I wanted him to love me. Herod gave me his heart. It beats because I'm cursed.'

I became aware of a distant drum, the steady roll of a marching beat. The room vibrated with the echo of the heart as it thudded in response to our presence.

'Where is it?' I asked Salome quietly.

'There!'

Salome pointed to the open panel and into the adjoining

chamber. The noise grew louder, I wanted to cover my ears, drown out the din with a heartfelt scream. My chest hurt, my throat burnt, my blood boiled in my veins. I couldn't hold the girl as I lost the strength in my limbs and she dropped from my arms and shrank back into the far corner of the room, away from the soldiers and Herod, while still holding the baby.

'I curse you, Herod,' Herodias said as she stepped into view at the entrance to the room. A wooden box was grasped in her arms. 'You used my daughter for your own means, but she made a cuckold of you with a commoner.' Herodias gave an insane laugh. 'And now I curse you and all of *your* descendents. All those bastards poured from your loins forever they will know my vengeance.'

Herodias opened the lid of the box, and immediately I sprang into action. I already knew what would be inside and I wasn't taking any chances. I grabbed Father Anthony's arm and pulled Lilly along as we ran for the portal, which had remained visible and open to us. Herodias screamed as I ran past her. Lilly held out her hand and a burst of power rushed from her towards Salome. I stared as her symbol, the triskele, was burned into the sheet wrapped around the baby. I couldn't help noticing it was a purple velvet-like fabric.

'You won't hurt him!' Lilly yelled as I pulled her with me.

We crashed back into our time, rolling over as we fell in a heap. Lilly pulled the portal closed behind us, then collapsed clutching her chest. The searing pain ceased as the portal froze and disappeared.

I rubbed and found that blood had been seeping from my eyes. Then I pulled myself onto my knees, breathing heavily.

'We're safe,' I told Anthony who was sprawled on the floor beside me.

'What did you do as we left, Lilly?' I asked.

'I gave the child a ward of protection.'

I didn't have time to question her further as a strange dread rushed through my senses. I turned to look at the priest beside me.

'Anthony?' I said.

'He's not moving,' Lilly said. Clambering to her feet she came to my side and then bent down, turning Anthony over.

Blood poured from his ears, eyes and nostrils in a steady stream.

'Burning ...' he gasped.

'He's dying,' I said, my wounded heart pounding in my ears.

'He really is a carrier of the gene ...' Lilly said and without hesitation she leaned over Father Anthony and bit deeply.

'What are you doing?' I said, but I knew the answer already: she was saving his life. He was a good man and didn't deserve to die like this.

So, I sat back and watched Lilly feed. I saw her burns heal and watched as she continued to glut on Anthony's blood until his heart stopped beating. She was such a complex creature. That day, she saved a baby and a priest and then turned one of them into a blood sucking monster. Yet her motives were good. How could they be otherwise?

10
Debrief

There had been questions, naturally, and after we'd debriefed Noble another Templar arrived to take up the role that Anthony had filled so well as our liaison.

'I'm Father Declan,' the man said.

'Were they hiding you in the wine cellar?' I asked.

'Excuse me?'

'You just appeared, as if on cue.'

Declan was dark haired, unlike Anthony. He had harder features. Anja said he looked like a 'gangster' and I suspected, by his slightly misshapen nose, he had spent some time in combat of sorts. Anthony had told us that only half of the Templars were carriers and he and Noble fitted into that category but I was certain that Declan wasn't a carrier of the gene.

I took Declan to see Anthony who lay like a corpse in his transformative sleep.

'He's dead,' said Bartholomew. 'There's no vital signs at all. I'm sorry Lilly it can't have worked this time.'

'No,' said Lilly. 'It's always like this. He'll come round and then he'll have to feed.'

'Perhaps you should have sent for the medical team first,' said Father Declan. 'You maybe didn't realise this, but the Templars have made an oath, never to seek the vampire change but to protect its lineage. If Anthony does survive, I don't know how he will feel about this change.'

'You have to understand,' I said. 'There was no time to think. Anthony was dying.'

Declan was less forgiving than Anthony had been. He expressed further concerns. 'We can't have you going around biting people. Surely you must see that?'

'I couldn't bear to lose him, Okay?' Lilly said sharply. 'I accept all responsibility for his condition. I couldn't let him die.'

I shrank back towards the door confused by her display of emotion. I searched her but she had closed down to me. These alien and uncharacteristic displays unsettled me.

'I'll stay with him until he wakes,' she said sitting down on the chair beside the bed.

'Okay,' I said.

I went with Father Declan and Noble to the library and as we sat down Declan began to fire questions at me regarding our excursion.

'How did you know where to go?' he said.

'Lilly. She just knew. Well … we searched all possibilities first. But she can read the doors and there was also quite a bit of predestination involved in it.'

Declan sneered. 'You surely don't believe in that?'

I ignored him as I thought his manner irritating in a way that Anthony and Noble weren't and now understood why they were the ones trusted to contact us in the first place. I had bigger fish to fry and my mind flew back frequently to Lilly. I could feel her in the room down the corridor, but I still couldn't hear her thoughts. It was unnerving.

'What I don't understand,' said Noble. 'Is why Anthony would risk this? To go back that far, could have changed things in the present.'

I shrugged and explained Lilly's theory on paradox. 'We can't change the past as it has already happened. Everything is meant to be as it is.'

'Then you believe in fate?' Declan said.

'I suppose so. But it's a lot less complicated than that. And it doesn't involve any religion. It's more about there's only one way things can be.'

'If there is only one way things can be, then the outcome of this is already determined,' Declan pointed out.

'No,' I said. 'That's still our *future* … look I don't know how
to tell you more but Lilly can explain it much better to you I'm
sure. Mostly this is very confusing to me.'

'Okay,' said Declan finally letting it go. 'Now, tell me what
happened after you passed through the door. Omit nothing.'

Noble took notes this time as I retold my story.

'Salome isn't our predecessor?' Declan said when I finished.
'I wonder how the story became confused?'

I thought about it for a moment and then asked a question
that had been on my mind since I had learned that both the
Templars and the *Illuminati* shared the same mythology. I asked
Declan where the story hailed from.

'Originally the Templars were one faction. It was a story told
to us that we must protect the children of Salome and Herod.
We'd always assumed that meant their joint offspring. There
has always been a mix of gene pool in the Templars.'

'Yes,' I said. 'Father Anthony explained that.'

'When Carduth betrayed Molay and Charney, their
followers were told a different story or maybe a warped version
of it. The remaining Templars were divided into two factions.
At this point I suspect that Carduth told his followers that they
were descended from John, but as we know now, John fathered
Salome's child and Herod killed him out of a fit of jealousy. It's
like Chinese whispers. The fact that Herodias was a witch was a
curve ball that none of us had ever expected.'

I left the men combing over their archives and went in search
of my other companions. We hadn't seen Gabi and Anja since
our return and I felt I needed to bring them up to speed.

I found Gabi in the grounds of the house with Anja. They
were sat in an idyllic spot beside a pond. Gabi was still in the
wheelchair but his colour was good and I noted he had more
movement than before as he bent forward to throw
breadcrumbs into the water to feed the ducks. His recovery
looked promising, but I was still concerned about how slow it
was.

'I've turned into some crazy invalid,' he said cheerfully as I
approached. 'Feeding ducks, being wheeled around the garden

and being intravenously fed blood. I even need help taking a shower. I guess this is what old age feels like.'

'You're looking much better,' I observed.

'Oh no! Not that as well …'

'What?'

'People always say that when they visit the sick,' Gabi laughed.

'He's been like this since he woke,' Anja said. 'All cheerful and happy. Don't quite understand it but he's fun to be around anyway.'

I did understand it. Gabi was glad to have woken at all. When he closed his eyes on Bartholomew's operating table he wasn't sure he would live through the operation.

'At least I know that bloody bullet isn't there now.'

'It certainly gives us hope that you'll heal,' I said.

Gabi nodded. 'I am feeling much better.'

'Good.'

I left them beside the still pond and went back inside. I was exhausted and hungry and so I went into the main fridge and fished out a bag of blood that the Templars kept in supply for us. I warmed it in the microwave and walked down to Anthony's room to see if there was any sign of him waking.

Lilly was sleeping in the chair when I entered and I sat down on the floor beside her. I watched her sleep for a while, then I rested my head on her lap and closed my eyes. As I drifted off too I wondered why I hadn't shared my new knowledge with Gabi and Anja, or why I hadn't told them that Anthony would be joining our ranks. I guess I just didn't want them to worry until we were sure that the priest would survive. I still wasn't sure of Lilly's real motives for turning him. Her outburst flickered across my memory as the black corners of sleep seeped in. Maybe she was replacing Gabi in the event that he didn't recover. After all, we'd need all the help we could get when the real fight began. Part of me was jealous though. Really, why couldn't she bear to lose Anthony? Did she feel some attraction to him?

I wrapped my arms around her waist, cuddling my head

into her stomach as she slept. She didn't move and as it had already taken her down into the darkest recesses, I let sleep roll its curtain over me, sucking me down to join my lover in its enveloping warmth.

11
Anthony Wakes

I woke as a pair of feet swung over the edge of the bed and landed firmly by my head. I was stretched out on the floor in Anthony's room, but my reflexes brought me up and on my feet in seconds. Just as Lilly said he would, Anthony awoke within the first twenty four hours of his human death.

'Anthony,' Lilly said, sitting up in the chair and stretching. 'About time you woke up, I was getting worried.'

Anthony stood, his legs appeared weak and uncertain, and I reached out a hand to steady him. As I caught his arm I knew the change had fully occurred. His eyes and hair had altered in that less-than-subtle way, both becoming brighter and more vibrant. His skin, several shades paler, no longer held human warmth. I could feel the vague, steady pulse of vampire blood moving around his veins.

I held up my mug of now-cold blood to him, but it was a congealed mess.

'I'll get some,' said Lilly hurrying from the room.

'How do you feel?' I asked as I stood awkwardly with the former priest.

'Strange. But very good actually. What the hell happened?'

Before I could speak his face changed and I watched as the memories rushed back into his mind of our excursion into the past.

'The heart,' he said. 'It almost killed me.'

Anthony sat down hard on the bed.

'Yes. If Lilly hadn't …'

At that moment Noble and Declan came in rapidly followed

by Lilly, who handed Anthony a warm mug of blood. Anthony sipped it, without thinking, then spat out the contents.

'What is this?'

We exchanged glances and then watched as Anthony's first fangs sprang forth and despite his willpower his hand moved and the mug of blood came back up to his lips. As he drank, Declan explained what had happened.

'I'm a vampire?'

'Yes,' said Lilly. 'Look I'm sorry I didn't know about your oath. But technically I broke it, not you … And actually it wasn't really broken because you didn't "seek" to become a vampire.'

Anthony held out the mug for more blood and this time Declan left to fetch it.

'This stuff is really good,' he said. 'I can taste the nutrients in it.'

I smiled. Anthony didn't seem the slightest bit unhappy about his change. I watched Lilly's face as she fussed around him as though he were a new born baby.

'I've loads to tell you and show you,' she said, eyes shining with excitement, and while she began to explain to Anthony all that he was capable of, I slipped out of the room and went in search of Gabi and Anja – this time I intended to tell them all that had happened.

It was night and my companions had long since left the garden. I found them in Gabi's room, curled up on his bed, sleeping. I didn't want to wake them, but knew that the news would be best coming from me rather than from Noble or Declan, or in the worst case scenario, Anthony himself.

'Gabi,' I said sitting down on the edge of the bed.

'I'm awake,' he said.

'Good, because I have something to tell you.'

I wheeled Gabi into Anthony's room shortly afterwards and he weighed up the new competition silently.

'We need more recruits,' Anthony was saying. 'I don't know why we shied away from this for so long.'

'Tony,' Declan said. 'You know it has nothing to do with shying away. The world can't feed an entire gene pool of vampires. That's why we've always stayed away.'

'We're at risk,' Anthony said. 'This is a war. I almost died which shows how dangerous the heart is to anyone who carries the gene, human or otherwise.'

'One thing is for sure,' Lilly said. 'We need to get it back from Caradien. From what I know of him the man is a psychopath. I can't understand how he hooked up with Carduth, but he's certainly capable of killing millions of people to feed his fanatical beliefs.'

I noticed Anja in the doorway, listening silently as everyone talked and planned.

'I think I can help …' she interjected. 'You need an insider. Caradien doesn't know how I feel about him or his betrayal of me. He may still think that I'm the stupid girl who loved him and believed all of his lies. Let me be finally useful. Let me do the right thing and go back into Caradien's hospital.'

An argument erupted among us. No one wanted to risk Anja and least of all Gabi. The last few days as she had nursed him a genuine closeness had grown between them that had nothing to do with rebound or deceit.

'I'm not really one of you,' Anja said. 'Caradien made me susceptible by his manipulation of my blood. He's used me. I'm now as vulnerable as the rest of you. I'd say he's done plenty to earn my wrath.'

'You are one of us,' said Gabi. 'How you became that doesn't matter now.'

'We've been floundering here for days, wondering what to do. Using Gabi's injury as an excuse to lie low. But the truth is we don't know what to do, or how to get near Caradien,' said Lilly.

'That's what I'm saying,' Anja said. 'I'm the only one who could possibly get near him.'

'I'm the strongest,' Lilly pointed out.

'True. But would you recognise him in a crowd?' Anja said.

'No. I doubt she would,' said Noble. 'The archive photographs we had of him are strangely all compromised.'

'What do you mean?' I asked.

'There wasn't one clear shot of his face,' Lilly explained. 'It was as though every image that's been taken of him was overexposed. Except, there are other people in the pictures and they are distinct.'

'You see!' Anja said. 'There's only me who has seen him.'

'She's got a point,' Anthony said.

'Look. I know exactly how to get to Caradien. I know where his home is, and I suspect if I go there after the ambush at the hospital, he won't be expecting to see me.'

'Why do you say that?' I asked. 'He was on full alert at the hospital. Surely he'd be even more paranoid now.'

'He'll think I'm dead,' Anja said but despite Caradien's betrayal there was no sadness in her voice, only determination.

Lilly took Anja's hand, 'Okay. Tomorrow we catch up with our regular time.' She said. 'Caradien sprang his ambush, it seems only fitting that we return the compliment.'

12
The Trap

I could hear his heart beating and smell his fear as it burst into the atmosphere in a rush of pheromones. It was seductive. Sexy.

Anja was lying across the bed as Konstantin came into his bedroom and it was clear by the shock on his face, a lose drop of the jaw, which he quickly recovered from, that she was the last person he expected to see. His eyes took in the see-through dress, her pert breasts, nipples erect from either the air conditioning or excitement. I knew it was the latter.

'Anja? What are you doing here?' he breathed. 'You look … different.'

'I thought you'd be pleased to see me,' Anja said pouting.

'Of course,' Konstantin said. 'But –'

'Konstantin,' she interrupted, sitting up.

Her languid movements reminded me of a demon seductress waiting to drain the life out of men foolish enough to fall for her wiles.

Her eyes were greener than they had ever been, even after the initial change. The vampire gene, not hers by birth, had now taken firm root in her DNA and was changing her more and more every day into his immortal enemy. Even so, he felt drawn to her.

'This is risky …' he said.

'Not really. They trust me and my phone got damaged so I couldn't contact you any other way.'

'Ah. An accident then? I thought you'd been found out.' He was going through the motions, showing an outer calm that his heart rate belied.

I loved the scutter of his heart as he watched her stretch. He was hopelessly aroused despite himself and it gave away a little of his personality to me. Did Konstantin have feelings for Anja after all?

Anja laughed, 'Of course not. I have them eating out of my hands.'

'Where were you tonight?' Konstantin asked suddenly.

'You mean during your ambush?'

Konstantin nodded.

'I was there, obviously. Foolishly Gabi threw himself over me. He's dead by the way. Tell your men: nice shooting. I don't know how they managed to miss me but Gabi's over-protectiveness must have helped a little.'

Anja found the old dumb Amalia act so easy to lapse into but I wasn't sure that Konstantin was fooled. His eyes darted around the room, looking in every corner for a shadowed menace, but I was certain that Lilly's magic, along with our silent cloaking was working at full efficiency.

'Yes … they were instructed to be careful not to … harm … you.'

Anja gave nothing away as she stretched again and I watched Konstantin's eyes devour her. There was lust tinged with fear and I could sense the disgust he was trying so hard to hide from her. But even so a primal, sexual response fought against his fear of her. 'As they ran for their escape portal I pretended to follow but then hung back long enough for it to close behind them,' Anja said. 'I thought it the right moment to make my exit. When I catch up with them again I can say it closed before I could pass through.'

Caradien's heart fluttered with anxiety even as his cock hardened at the sight of her. 'I see.'

I felt Anja's pleasure as she sensed the emotion emanating from him for the first time. Despite his fear he moved into the room and sat down on the edge of the bed trying, but not succeeding, to block her from reading him. His thoughts floated in the air around him and we picked up every one of them and gathered them into a cohesive shape..

I wasn't too surprised to learn that Caradien had hoped she *would* be killed during the attack and I felt the sting of hurt that blossomed in Anja's chest as this fact revealed to her. It ached like a festering wound. But still she smiled benignly at him. Then Anja learned that Caradien wouldn't have minded too much if she had died at any time during any of her encounters with Carduth. Here, my mind stumbled. His thoughts of Carduth were disjointed and guarded and every time the name floated through his synapses, Caradien closed his mind, rapidly thinking of something else. Anja's smile faltered and her stomach churned on all the blood she had consumed before she came.

'You are a clever, devious girl aren't you?' Caradien said.

Anja forced the smile back in place and concentrated on exacting her revenge, despite Caradien's patronising tone.

'Anyway, I'm here for new instructions,' Anja said. 'And maybe some time with the man who loves me.'

Caradien's mind screamed with disgust and his body shivered in revulsion as her hand clamped around his fingers. His penis shrivelled back, skittering away from the initial lust he had felt.

'I have new instructions for you,' he said. 'In my office.'

I picked the image of the safe from his mind remembering that Anja had told us the box containing the heart had been kept there. But surely now it was always with Carduth?

She let go of his hand, 'Can't you just tell me? I'd rather spend some time in here with you.'

Caradien stood and walked confidently towards the door, but Anja reacted, vaulting around him at a speed too fast for the human eye. She blocked his exit.

'Konstantin. I said I wanted to stay here. What's wrong? Are you afraid of *me*?'

'Of course not,' he said quickly but his voice trembled and his heartbeat increased. A small flush coloured his cheeks as he backed away from her.

'Why how strange,' Anja said. 'You are totally shaking aren't you? Anyone would think you had something to hide.'

She was a predator; strong, animal and hungry. Caradien shivered as though he had walked accidentally into the lair of a hungry lioness. He reached into his pocket, fingers stumbling blindly as he searched for something.

A blinding flash lit up the room and Anja found herself trapped in a circle of power.

'Konstantin,' she said calmly. 'Why are you so paranoid?'

'I own you, Anja,' he said. 'Your life and death is in my hands.'

'Yes. I signed a contract. But I thought I meant more to you than that.'

The air outside the circle began to change and a portal burst open before Anja.

'What are you doing?' she asked. Her voice remained calm and seductive but it lacked all emotion now.

'Fetching the weapon. I think you've outgrown your usefulness.'

'So, it isn't in the safe then? The heart is somewhere else.'

'You always were a smart girl,' Caradien said. 'Unfortunately for you, not smart enough.'

'Oh I wouldn't say that,' Lilly said behind him as we both dropped the shadows that were covering us. 'You don't honestly think she would walk into a trap without back up, do you? We look after our own, Caradien.'

Caradien spun round and met her gaze.

'I might have known,' Lilly said calmly. 'Carduth and Caradien. You're one and the same man aren't you? But which came first? The chicken? Or the egg?'

Lilly waved her hand over the circle of power and Anja was instantly free.

Caradien ran for the portal, but Lilly was there before him, knocking him back across the room. The portal door froze out and disappeared.

'I don't know how you learnt to manipulate time, or why you want to destroy us so much, but I always believed paradoxes couldn't exist. So, Carduth or do you prefer Caradien? Where are you *really* from?'

'Konstantin is my name,' he said. 'Any other is irrelevant.'

'You've set yourself up as some super power in both eras,' Lilly said. 'Why do you hate us so much Konstantin? What did we ever do to you?'

Caradien backed away as Lilly approached.

'I'm a reasonable woman,' Lilly said. 'But you've killed one of my children, my first born in fact. Harry had his faults but generally he was just like everyone else, floundering in a world of confusion, trying to be happy.'

'You're a monster,' Caradien said. 'All of you deserve to die.'

'No more than you do right now,' said Anja standing directly behind Caradien. 'You lied to me. You used me and then, you would have let me die.'

She grabbed his hair, jerked his head to one side and plunged her fangs deep into his throat. Lilly reacted quickly, grabbing Caradien she flung him aside.

Anja was wild as Caradien's blood coursed through her veins. She fought to free herself but as the weakest and youngest she had no strength to break free from Lilly.

'No! We need answers. We have to find the heart.' Lilly said.

Caradien crawled along the floor, blood poured freely from his throat: Anja had done plenty of damage even though she had been stopped as soon as she bit Caradien.

I turned in frustration, not knowing what to do – whether to help Harry's killer or just finish the job Anja started. My instincts screamed at me to kill the bastard and to hell with the consequences. Anja still struggled against Lilly even though she had no chance of escaping from her superior strength.

Another flash of energy lit up the room. It was sudden and blinding. I threw my arm up across my face as I felt a burning heat explode into the room.

'No!' Lilly screamed.

I'd taken my eye off Caradien in the confusion and as I turned back I found he had opened a new portal and was heading straight for it. I ran forward, almost grasped his jacket, but my fingers slipped off the silk fabric and Caradien tumbled through the portal.

My only option was to follow. But the door froze over before I reached it.

'Chez! For fuck's sake!' Lilly shouted in frustration. 'You let him get away!'

'What the hell did he do?' asked Anja.

'Ley power surge,' Lilly said.

I stared hopelessly at her and Anja. 'Well that went better than … expected?'

Lilly burst out laughing the tension leaving her body. She shook her head at me.

'You're a nightmare. Why do I love you so much?' she smiled. 'Well at least we have the little shit on the run now. But we've not learnt very much, except that Caradien and Carduth are one and the same.'

'That's something I suppose.'

'I'm sorry,' Anja said. 'It's my fault he escaped. I wanted to kill the bastard. Lying, treacherous son-of-a-bitch!'

I couldn't help laughing as Anja stamped around in Caradien's bedroom like a spoilt child who'd had her toys removed. She had barely displayed any genuine emotion in the short time we'd known her. As she became more comfortable with us we were starting to see the real Anja.

'What's so funny?' she said finally.

'I don't know,' I said. 'Except I feel such a relief that we're still alive and now know more about Caradien than we did.'

Anja shrugged. 'He's still alive too. That means he could be anywhere.'

The smile dropped from my face. My mood sobered.

'Let's go and check out this safe of his,' Lilly said her eyes serious. 'We might find out something more.'

13
Two Tunnels

Gabi was walking on crutches when we returned. Lilly hugged him for a long time as Anja hung back looking awkward. We were in the library at the Templars' safe house. Gabi was smiling and happy and I couldn't help but feel light-hearted when I saw him. Our failure didn't seem so bad in light of this new occurrence. He was healing rapidly. We had a lot to celebrate and the look on Lilly's face when she saw how he had recovered made me feel so happy.

'We found some interesting documents in Caradien's safe. Look at these.' I said.

Noble took the pile of papers and foreign currency we'd taken after Lilly pulled the safe door completely off its hinges. An alarm had gone off somewhere in the building and we made a quick exit, but not before we removed everything from the safe.

Caradien had holdings all over the world and being such a distrustful person he had kept all of the deeds in his own possession. He even had original deeds from his properties in France in the thirteenth century. The papers were crisp and new, because they'd been brought to the future and taken care of.

'These are the kind of documents you'd usually leave with your solicitor or in a safe deposit box,' Anthony observed. 'But he certainly kept it all close to his chest.'

'They must be worth a fortune,' Anja observed.

'I don't know,' said Noble. 'Who would believe they are original in this condition? They look too perfect.'

Gabi wasn't listening, he was smiling at Anja, pleased she had returned unharmed. Once Lilly released him Gabi opened his arms and drew Anja close. They hugged for a long time. Anja nuzzled his neck her arms wrapped tightly around his waist.

'For God sake get a room you two,' Lilly said eventually.

I laughed, patting Gabi on the back. 'Bit of role reversal it seems,' I pointed out even though it was unnecessary as Gabi remembered all too well how Lilly and I had been recently.

'You're really very human in your ways,' Anthony observed.

'*We*,' I pointed out. 'Since you are now one of the family.'

'I keep forgetting that. Other than needing to drink blood quite a lot, I'm not feeling a whole lot different. Stronger, faster of course, but my emotions haven't changed at all.'

Lilly smiled at him, 'What did you expect would happen?'

'Lose my soul perhaps,' he shrugged.

Anthony froze as Lilly hugged him impulsively; he was unused to such tactile displays of affection, but I knew that he would soon lapse into our ways when I saw his shoulders relax and watched him hug Lilly cautiously back

'I'm glad you survived. Things always happen for a reason,' she said. 'You're one of us now and we take care of each other.'

I squashed a pang of jealousy. Lilly was mine, but her feelings for Anthony were confusing to me. Perhaps she had felt we needed to replace Harry? I still wasn't sure of her motives, but having Anthony around felt right in a way I just didn't understand.

'Okay, get over the group hugs everyone,' Anja said, suddenly releasing Gabi. 'What the fuck are we going to do about Konstantin?'

Noble looked up from his scrutiny of the papers. 'I can give you a few places and times to check up on him. Any one of them could be the place he's storing the heart. That is obviously going to be dangerous for you though.'

Lilly went to him, glanced over the papers frowning.

'Oh my God. I've been so amazingly stupid,' she said. 'We don't need any of this. Why didn't I just recall the door that

Caradien went through? I could have been on him immediately.'

'I didn't know you could do that,' Anthony said. 'And as you know I have some skill in time manipulation. How I've always found the time zones is by focusing on what I wanted, and where I wanted to be. There's always been a door around somewhere that could take me close to the destination.'

'But not *exactly* in the right spot or moment?' Lilly asked.

'No.'

'I can usually read temporal space around a door when I've called it,' Lilly explained. 'Sometimes I've been able to read the time and destination of a portal just as it's closed. I don't know what I was thinking not to even try that.'

'Returning now would possibly be a waste of time then?' I said.

Lilly nodded, 'I don't think the vibration or rather distribution of the space would stay unsteady for long. It would have to be within moments of the portal closing. So in this time zone it would be pointless. We've missed our moment. Plus, the place will probably be crawling with Caradien's security.'

'Do you really think you can recall his exit point and follow him?' asked Anthony.

'There's a good chance I could have done it at the time ... but now ...' Lilly shrugged.

'What's the point of being able to manipulate time and then not even using it to your own advantage?' Anthony said.

Lilly stared at him and the rest of us waited for him to continue or for her to make sense of what he was saying.

'You're right,' she said finally. 'We can be anywhere, at any time if we want to.'

Three of us crossed through a time portal into Caradien's bedroom: Me, Lilly and Anthony. It was timed within seconds of our other selves leaving the room to go and break into the safe. We cut it so fine it was a wonder that the 'other' Lilly didn't sense our entrance portal or at least our intrusion. As we arrived I saw the back of Anja's flowing dress as she left the room.

Lilly immediately stepped forward into the space that Caradien's portal had occupied and as we heard the other Lilly pulling off the safe door, the alarm exploding into life, Lilly called up the time portal and the three of us dived through, hot on the heels of Konstantin Caradien.

We plummeted into nothingness and a black abyss expanded around and below us. I was disorientated and confused. Usually we crossed the portal in an instant and so I knew that this wasn't right. I pivoted in nothingness. It was like being consumed by tar, my limbs were heavy and unmovable.

'A trap!' I yelled, but the empty space stole the sound as surely as the hollow consumed my limbs and my cry was unheard.

If my companions were in earshot, or had called out themselves I wouldn't have heard them. The emptiness filled my ears, soaked my arms and legs. My vampire eyes could find light in the darkest of nights but yet could see nothing in this pit. I fell, casting desperate eyes around me but only finding total blackness. Despair gripped me, any moment I thought I'd hit the ground, or worse, find myself back in my own personal hell dimension, back in the Allucian city's corridor of doors: the place where my time travelling adventures really began.

Something grabbed me.

Lilly!

We fell harder, faster. I gripped and held onto her and became aware of another pair of arms, wrapped around her as well. *It must be Anthony.* The free fall continued, but we could have been falling upwards, sideways or down: I had no way of telling but at least I held her and whatever happened we'd be together in those final moments.

A silent age passed before I began to make out a pinprick of light ahead of us. Sound rushed back into my ears as my eyes began to focus again. We jerked to a halt and found ourselves before a tunnel that divided halfway down in a 'Y' shape.

'Which way?' Anthony gasped.

I glanced at him, his face was stark white, his eyes wide and frightened and he gripped Lilly so tightly that if she had have been human he would have crushed the life from her.

'I don't know,' Lilly said. 'I've never seen anything like it before.'

I glanced down both routes, 'Maybe we should split up?' I suggested.

'No. That's something that really pisses me off when I'm watching a movie. You never split up when you're searching for a bad guy. The one left alone always gets killed,' Lilly said.

Anthony laughed.

'I'm serious,' Lilly said firmly. 'We're in real danger if he has the heart, and I'm sure he's heading for it.'

'Why two passages? Why the long fall?' I asked.

'He's smarter than we give him credit for. I should have known he'd be able to block us. He travels time. A skill he learnt God knows how and, he's clearly a warlock as well. It's a neat trick – wish I'd learnt it,' Lilly shrugged. 'And it shows that he knew I was capable of following him. We really need to be careful.'

We went left. It didn't really matter which path we took after all, it would be right or wrong and the worst that could happen is we'd have to double back. Or so we thought.

The tunnel widened the deeper we went. We weren't travelling on foot as there was no floor *per se*. We were merely floating. All that I saw was a physical representation of what we expected to see. The doorway, and this, Lilly explained, was unlike any she had passed through before and it was certainly like nothing I'd seen on my travels with her.

Ahead we saw the waterfall. The other side of the portal was looming and our luck was in, we'd chosen well. But as we approached the exit, Lilly drew us to her.

'Wait.'

'What is it?' I asked.

'I don't trust this. Something's not right.'

We gazed through the portal from a safe distance.

'Time is on our side,' Lilly said. 'So let me think a moment.'

Time wasn't on our side, however. There is a natural order for time and its passage. We were in some kind of limbo between times, between worlds and the portal wanted us out. The tunnel began to shorten. Without moving we drew closer. As Anthony began to yell in confusion I realised we were being propelled forward despite ourselves.

Lilly pulled back, pushed us behind her and held out her hand.

'I'll close it!' she cried.

But time was having none of it. It coughed and hacked, throwing us forward and before Lilly could react, all three of us were catapulted through the portal, like something bad being vomited up.

The floor was hard and cold and as I tumbled I realised I was rolling over stone flags. I crashed into the wall on the other side of a square brick room and it brought me painfully to a halt.

'Where the hell are we?' asked Anthony. 'And. Ouch.'

Anthony stretched his limbs, tested his arms, but nothing was broken and even if it had been his new powers would make healing occur almost instantaneously.

Lilly was examining the room before Anthony stood up. Passing through time still had this numbing effect on my body and mind. It made me feel sluggish. I looked around the room with dull interest and found that we were in some kind of basement dungeon or cell but it was empty except for us.

I echoed Anthony's words, 'Where the hell are we?

Battered and bruised I pulled myself up against the wall and shook my head to clear the fugue that lingered. Lilly said nothing; she was already pulling on the heavy oak door, only to find it locked.

'I guess we did take the wrong tunnel,' she sighed.

She turned around, shrugged and then began to search for the time portal that had slammed shut behind us as soon as it deposited us on the ground.

'It's not there,' she said frowning. 'Or if it is it's blocked and we can't go back through it.'

'How can it be blocked?' asked Anthony. 'The portals are two-way.'

Lilly looked over at me, I deliberately kept my face blank. 'Witchcraft,' Lilly said. 'We've seen it used in a similar way before.'

'So this was a trap?' I asked.

'No. More likely it was a sideways shunt to put us off his track.'

Lilly stretched her arms out, turned in a slow circle and searched for ley power. Several doors opened in a rush of violent waterfalls in the space around us.

'Be careful,' she warned. 'I don't want anyone falling through the wrong one.'

She read the locations, closing them rapidly as she rejected them until finally she settled on one. Then she stared into the watery chasm, her hand resting on her chin.

'Where?' Anthony asked.

'It's close to one of the locations I recalled from the paperwork in Caradien's safe. It's the best option if we're going to try and catch up with him somehow. I'm just feeling a little paranoid. We really need to take care if we do pass through.'

I drew my sword in the same instant that Lilly drew hers.

'Let's be ready for action then,' I said.

Lilly stepped forward to go first.

'Wait,' said Anthony. 'Let's do this together. Like you said, we're a family.'

Lilly and I stood either side of Anthony and we each took his hand. Then, taking a deep breath, we leapt into the portal.

14
The King's Resting Place

This time the travel was instant. The other side of the waterfall brought us to a dark and gloomy tomb. Or at least it looked like a tomb. It was full of sarcophagi and relics and treasures. I was on my feet for a change, and I put this down to holding onto Anthony. I let go of his hand and stepped further into the cavern.

'A pyramid?' Anthony said.

'A smugglers den more like,' Lilly said. 'This is Caradien's stash of things he's stolen over the years. He's used the power he has to help him accumulate wealth, which does explains how he's built such a powerful empire on top of those things he stole from the Templars.'

Anthony examined the artefacts and I looked around the room. It was a huge warehouse, dressed to look like the inside of a pyramid. The ceiling design was like upside down stairs and they circled around, grown smaller and narrower to give the impression that they drew into a point around a mile upwards. Along the walls were torches hanging from ornately carved pillars. A row of enormous jars lined one wall, beautifully hand painted, all completely unique.

'Where are we?' I asked. 'What year?'

'Present day, strangely,' answered Lilly. 'This place is actually a warehouse in Putney.'

'It feels weird to be in the present,' Anthony said. 'But that's how the portals work, they reflect all times, all places.'

'This looks like a set from *Tomb Raider*,' Lilly said. 'Do you think Caradien realises that?'

Anthony laughed and for once I got the reference as I'd seen Gabi playing the game on his computer.

'Why is he keeping all this stuff?' I asked.

'Power,' Anthony said.

'Yes. Power,' Lilly agreed.

'But how does it make him powerful?'

'Magic. It's all about magic. The ancient Egyptians knew all about the power of the dead. Each of these articles contains the residue of emotions left behind by their long dead owners. And because they are effectively "new", taken directly from their time and stored here, Caradien has all of that fresh emotion to call upon. It hasn't been in a real tomb, left for years to slowly fade away. I say again, he's extremely clever.'

'How on earth did one man have time in his life to do all this?' Anthony said.

I ran my fingers over the rim of a jar and felt a slight vibration. My fingers burned and I quickly withdrew my hand. Lilly was staring down at a sarcophagus. It had the picture of what could only be described as a king. Her fascination with it made me want to look also and as I reached her side, Anthony joined us at the foot of the coffin.

'Herod,' Lilly said.

I didn't understand the implication and, not wanting to show my ignorance, I waited for either her or Anthony to speak.

'This is ... crucial,' Anthony said finally.

'Yes,' Lilly answered. 'The last we saw of King Herod, Herodias was using the heart to destroy him and place a curse on his bloodline. His death would have created powerful juju.'

'Why?' I asked.

'The dead body of a king could be used for powerful magics. But this. Well, he was murdered and cursed. That makes his body parts extremely potent. There are warlocks who'd be able to use this for some very strange things.'

'I heard once that connection to the body of a dead king could give the keeper immortality,' Anthony said.

Lilly's eyes were glowing in the gloom, 'Mystical rumour. But still, maybe we shouldn't take any chances.'

'What do you mean?' asked Anthony.

'We're going to call in the brotherhood. Clear this place out. Starting with Herod. Now what else's is here?'

I hadn't deemed it possible to open a portal and allow an entire army of Templars through, with equipment to help them move the artefacts. But that is exactly what happened. Lilly and Anthony combined their strength to open a door to another safe house, a kind of storage facility owned by the Templars, and then Anthony made all the necessary arrangements.

The Templars were galvanised into activity immediately and the excitement they exuded as they took the relics back with them vibrated through the air. Anthony organised the removals and Lilly and I helped lift where necessary, until, hours later, the place was completely cleared.

Father Declan and John Noble arrived at the facility as we crossed the portal for the final time. Lilly closed the doorway and barred it; setting an elaborate trap for Caradien should he wish to pursue us through this portal.

'Nothing's going to get through that sucker,' Lilly said when she had finished. 'Especially if we have his main power source locked away here.'

'We still don't have the heart,' Anthony said. 'But this is definitely going to get a reaction when Caradien realises we've stolen his treasures. Plus, I think our lab will want to look at Herod's body.'

I was curious about Herod and the body and so followed Anthony and Lilly as they walked alongside the sarcophagus as it was taken into the facility mortuary.

'You guys really have it going on,' said Lilly. 'It seems to me that you're always prepared.'

The mortuary was attached to a huge laboratory and the King's body was brought in and placed beside an examination table. The room was stark white and clinical.

'We need to get the lid off and have a look inside,' said a doctor wearing scrubs as he entered the room. 'I'm Father

Gallin. I'm an archaeologist as well as a Coroner. We need to be careful of air pollution which is why we'll be moving this straight in there first.' He pointed to another room. It was small with a huge metal door on it and looked like some form of large safe to me.

'It's a controlled environment,' Anthony explained.

'Why do we need that?' I asked.

'We want to preserve the remains as much as possible. Regular air contains large amounts of toxins which has a corrosive effect on relics. Burials like this are designed to preserve the body. I suspect Herod was mummified. A rapid inrush of air as we open the coffin may have a detrimental effect on the remains. It's a precaution we may not need, but one worth taking,' Father Gallin explained.

We were put into pressure suits. 'Similar to those that deep sea divers use,' Anthony explained. 'The room will become something of a vacuum during the release of the lid. Then slowly the pressure will be restored.'

Father Gallin was waiting for us, in his suit, when we entered the room. The sarcophagus was mounted on a sturdy table. We surrounded it as the door to the room closed. A loud hissing sound echoed in my ears as I looked at the coffin through a see-through panel on my helmet. Visibility was better than when I wore the knights' armour but it was still restricted to frontal vision and so I focused on the coffin as the pressure in the room changed and the hissing in my suit increased. It was, I'd been told, all about balancing the pressure inside my suit to offset the crushing lack of pressure in the room.

'Okay,' Gallin said and I heard his voice echo inside my helmet. 'Here goes.'

The lid of Herod's coffin was attached to a winch and after removing the seals around the top, Gallin pressed a button and the lid began to slowly rise. A slight hiss seeped from the coffin but it was only momentary.

'Good,' he said. 'Not much air inside.'

The lid was hoisted away to the side and out of our way and I could see the King in all his dead glory, lying in state inside his coffin. A gold mask, formed in his image, lay over his face and over the bandages he was wearing his royal finery. A long robe covered his body. It was made of the finest silk fabrics and dyed a royal blue. The fabric looked new, as though he had only just been interred.

Gallin lifted the mask from Herod's face and we found him covered with linen bandages. Gallin took a scalpel from the instrument tray at his side and carefully cut away the fabric.

I found I was holding my breath and after glancing at my companions discovered that they too were feeling the intensity of this moment. It was fascinating.

Gallin peeled away the linen and I drew in a sharp breath. Herod was perfectly preserved. He looked freshly dead.

'This coffin must be centuries old,' gasped Gallin.

I looked up and met Anthony's eyes through his mask. 'It's as we suspected,' he said. 'Caradien took him fresh from his tomb.'

'But that could have been years ago still,' said Lilly.

'Magic,' I said.

Father Gallin crossed himself awkwardly in his pressure suit.

'Repressurise,' Gallin ordered to someone outside the room and the vacuum atmosphere began to fill with air.

I felt the change in my suit as the oxygen inside, balanced with the oxygen outside and after a short time Gallin gave the instruction to remove our helmets. Anthony helped me with mine as I couldn't quite figure out how to unclip it. As I pulled it away I saw Lilly remove hers and her gorgeous hair tumbled out and around her shoulders. I admired how she made the cumbersome suit look sexy. I smiled at her slowly.

'Hey. Concentrate!' she said, then winked at me.

Gallin removed the bandages from Herod's arm.

'He isn't mummified,' said Gallin. 'How incredible.'

Then he began to take blood samples from the vein, and scraped away tissue samples from his skin. The blood flowed freely. It was as though Herod were merely sleeping and not dead at all.

'This might take a while,' he said pulling open the robe and he began to cut a line through the bandages covering his chest. 'Oh God!' he gasped as he spread the fabric. 'I've never seen anything like this.'

Herod's chest was an open, gaping, burnt out hole.

'Just like Harry,' Lilly said.

'Yes. But why is the rest of his body okay?' I asked. 'Harry was burnt up completely.'

'Who's Harry?' asked Gallin.

Lilly briefed Anthony and Gallin about our former companion and his death at Caradien's hands.

'I suspect it has more to do with the blood in Harry's case,' Lilly said. 'He was a vampire, fully changed and ancient, unlike Herod who may be the source of our ancestry but still only human.'

'I still don't think I understand,' Gallin said. 'He's a carrier, he has your blood. It should have combusted as well.'

'The vampire blood gives life to every atom in the vampire, unlike in human blood.' Anthony explained. 'The change is ... magical. I'm not sure even my department, who have done the most research on this, understand why. But the bite has a chemical reaction on any victim who is a carrier. It's like ... instant evolution.'

We left Gallin and Anthony to finish the autopsy and as I stripped my suit away in the room next door, handing it to a lab technician Lilly sighed.

'It's getting more and more complicated, Chez. And I don't have a fucking clue what's going on.'

'Whatever happens now,' I said. 'The gauntlets are off. Caradien is going to be furious when he finds his treasures gone. He's going to come after us then and we'll have to be ready.'

'Herod's body is very important to him. I just know it,' Lilly said. 'Maybe Anthony is right and he's using it in some way to offset his own mortality. But how the hell did Caradien learn how to do that? Who is he? I'm missing something crucial and I'm sure going to kick myself when I realise what it is.'

At any time, Caradien could use the heart to end us all. The vampire gene could be completely eradicated from the world and that would leave a huge gap in the Templars' defences. I'd come to realise that we were essential to the knights now, and our safety was paramount to their own survival.

'Yes,' said Anthony behind me, once again reading my thoughts easily. 'The Templars need you to live. You're our last line of defence against the *Illuminati*. Even though it's not clear why Caradien would want to destroy us so much. We've become mortal enemies.'

Anthony returned to the autopsy room and once again I was alone with Lilly. I took her hand, kissed her palm and then drew her into my arms. Every moment was important.

15
Being Ready

'You stole his relics?' laughed Anja. 'God, that's rich after that bastard did the same to me.'

We'd tried to chase down Caradien and failed. All we could do now was wait, and so we returned to the Stockholm safe house to tell Gabi and Anja what we'd learnt.

'One good turn deserves another,' Lilly smiled. 'Maybe your stuff was there too. Anthony said they are doing an inventory, so we'll show you the list and pictures when we get it.'

Anja shook her head, 'No. Don't bother. I don't care about that stuff anymore. It's only *stuff* and there are far more important things going on now.'

Gabi was walking around more easily now. Every passing hour showed new improvement. He no longer needed the crutches but he was still unable to fly. It was nothing that a good kill wouldn't cure.

'I'm tired,' Lilly said. 'And hungry.'

We'd been on the go for over twenty four hours and it was beginning to take its toll. It was one of those times when we needed more than the bags of blood the Templars provided for us.

'Probably not a good idea to hunt right now,' I pointed out. 'We need to stay within these walls until we're ready to face Caradien on terms we can win.'

I took her hand and led her back to our room. Once alone, I stripped her, lay her down and made love to her. She was more submissive than normal, allowing me total control and afterwards she curled up in my arms and slept.

During the night some part of her gave into her insecurity and made her reach down beside the bed and draw up the sword, laying it beside her. I opened my eyes as the amber lit up the room at her touch, but then, realising there was no danger, slowly drifted back to sleep.

The next morning I found a Kevlar vest waiting for me at the foot of the bed. Lilly was up and ready, dressed for battle with her vest wrapped over a tee-shirt, sword at her hip.

'What's happened?' I said, jumping out of the bed and quickly dressing.

'The other facility was attacked last night. Fortunately, Caradien's men didn't get in. But the assertion is that if they know where that one is, they will definitely know about this place. Caradien may even realise we're here. Fortunately all his attempts to get in via a portal were blocked. I didn't realise this but there are many Templars with Anthony's skill. They spent the whole night holding up a ward of protection around the place. So, for now Caradien is unable to get in here by any other means than the old fashioned way.'

'Which is?'

'Physical attack. Anthony and the Templars are expecting it to happen at any time.'

Lilly left the room and soon returned with warm blood. Gabi and Anja followed.

'Let's get as much strength as we can,' Lilly said drinking her blood in one long swallow.'

Gabi was dressed in the full Templar armour. 'I don't see why you guys get the cool ninja gear and I get this,' he complained.

'We're not taking any chances with you until you're fully recovered,' Anja said. 'So suck it up.'

The four of us left the bedroom and went in search of John Noble. The whole facility was on lockdown with full security, all dressed in Templar armour. As we passed through the entrance hall, we found Noble, his arms full of books, heading our way.

'I need to just drop these back in the library,' he explained.

'Anything happening?' Lilly asked.

'So far no, but our sources say that Caradien's mercenaries have been utilised.'

'What does that mean?' I asked.

'Basically, they are preparing for full-out war,' Noble answered, then scurried off to return his books to the library.

It was a waiting game: one which felt torturous in so many ways. I wanted to go after Caradien, a full frontal attack. He needed to die. I knew though that such a pursuit could be suicide. Caradien would be ready for us and he would undoubtedly have the heart with him by now but it felt as though we were hiding away from him and it wasn't our way.

'We're going to have to be patient and above all ready for him,' Gabi said.

'You and Anja stay back when the fight begins,' Lilly said.

'I'm fine,' Gabi said. 'There's no need to baby me. Even the scars have healed.'

'Okay,' Lilly nodded. 'But it was a close call. I don't want to lose any of you.'

We stayed at the ready. Blood boiling with rage, spoiling for revenge, and the blood lust barely satisfied by the transfusion blood bags. No one was readier for bloodshed than we four were.

Anthony returned to the facility a few hours later and he found us congregated in the library with Noble.

'Sorry it's taken me so long to get here,' he said. 'The attack was so sudden we weren't expecting it. The facility is still surrounded by Caradien's drones, they are at an impasse but I had a bad feeling and so jumped through a portal to get here.'

'What's happened with Herod's body?' Lilly asked.

Anthony explained the results from the tests on the corpse.

'To all intents and purposes,' Anthony said. 'It's like the body is still alive. The blood is flowing when the skin is pierced. Usually the dead don't bleed when the heart stops. All of the blood settles in the lowest part of the body. And, of course, Herod doesn't have a heart.'

'Where is the body now?' Lilly asked.

'I moved it. It's here with me. I wanted your help to take it somewhere else. It needs to be a place that you know, but that no one in the Templars has heard of.'

'You suspect betrayal?' I asked.

'I don't know,' Anthony answered. 'But it's possible. I can't imagine how else Caradien knew of the secure unit. I don't want to believe one of our people betrayed us though.'

'I don't understand,' said Gabi. 'How can the body still be alive?'

Lilly was thoughtful, 'I know somewhere we could hide him,' she said meeting my gaze.

I knew what she was thinking long before the thought projected to me. *My own personal hell?*

Yes. Let that bastard try pulling Herod out of that.

'Anthony I think you were right. I suspect that Caradien is using some ancient magic to sustain his own mortality. It would take the form of a psychic connection with Herod at the moment of his death,' Lilly said. 'Although I have no idea how he achieved this. We were all there at the time and we never saw Caradien.'

My brain was aching with the complexity and twists and turns of each new discovery but I barely had time to think when an explosion hit the front door of the facility. I rushed from the library and ran into the entrance hall, rapidly followed by my companions. Several of the security guards were injured and a group of mercenaries was pouring into the house. The fight was on.

I swooped on the first mercenary that had the nerve to point his poisonous bullets my way. Ripping his throat out gave me a singular pleasure. One I hadn't experienced in too long. I drank his blood, then turned his weapon on his colleagues. The bullets ripped through the face of a thick set man as he ran head long, gun raised and firing, directly at Lilly.

We were ready for them. The previous encounter had taught us much and so I saw Anja jump high into the air, spinning like some martial arts expert over the heads of two of Caradien's men. Feet upwards, head facing down towards the ground, her hands reached down as she flipped over them, snapping one man's neck while her claws dug into the eyes of the other. She gouged them smoothly from their sockets and left him collapsed and screaming on the floor, his hands clasped over the bloody holes.

'Don't drink unless the body is already dead,' Lilly said in a voice so low that only us immortals could hear it.

Lilly walked calmly towards the door and through the chaos of bodies, met the eyes of one of the men who was standing pointing his gun at her. His face looked shocked, and then he relaxed, a look of dreamy worship crossing his features. He dropped his gun, and fell at Lilly's feet, rubbing up to her like a cat. Lilly bent down, licked his neck ensuring that her willing victim was not a carrier and then gorged on his blood as he kneeled happily before her.

A new batch of men rushed forward from outside. Some were taken down by the remaining Templar security and the rest fell prey to us. Anthony screamed with blood lust as he pushed his hands through the chest of a man who turned his gun towards Lilly as she fed from his ecstatic colleague. The former priest pulled the dead man's body towards him and began to drink from the open wound. I watched his back as Gabi took off from the landing above and dived down onto another two men, smashing their skulls together so hard that blood and brains splattered the doorway. Then he grabbed another mercenary, pulling him up towards his elongated fangs.

More Templar security ran from other areas of the house and into the front entrance. The mercenaries were pushed back and Lilly dropped the body she was feeding from. 'Anthony? Where's the body?' Lilly said through blood-stained lips.

Anthony pulled away from his first proper kill. His eyes were filled with blood rage. He looked around at the carnage and wiped a hand casually across his mouth.

'This way!' he said, backing off from the battle.

Gabi, Anja, Lilly and I all followed, leaving the Templars to beat back the enemy.

Anthony took us downstairs to his magic room where the King's body lay in the middle of a circle of protection. Herod was no longer in the sarcophagus but still lay in his royal robes.

Anthony lifted his arms and pulled down the circle on one side so that we could all enter. As soon as we entered it closed and we were encased in his magic.

'Your call, Lilly,' he said. 'Take us anywhere you think Caradien won't find us.'

Lilly nodded and instantly a door opened inside the circle.

I noted that it had never been so easy or so quick for her to find the right portal.

'Are you sure?' I asked.

'I always know where this one is,' she said. 'There's never any need to search. It's as though it lies in my peripheral vision permanently.'

Anthony picked up Herod's body and we stepped through the pouring waterfall without further hesitation.

16
Return to the Corridor

Sometime in the Distant Future

A cool breeze blew through the long, dark corridor. It was deathly quiet and I expected to find the remaining Allucians lurking there in wait for us as they had before. But the place was deserted. I searched for any psychic energy, or heartbeat, but all to no avail. There was no one there except us five vampires and a heartless King who couldn't die.

'They've gone,' said Lilly. 'This is a time beyond their existence. The Allucians died out long ago.'

Lilly was ethereal in the blue light that speared out through one door that appeared to be made of glass. The corridor was infinite, as it had always been. But Lilly remained where she was. Turning slowly in the circle of phantom light.

I felt sick. The place of my torture lay behind one of these doors and I had no wish to return to it. I couldn't help but cast suspicious glances at the door closest to me.

A door burst open suddenly, dead leaves rushed from beyond it and span around my feet. I jumped back, irrationally scared.

Lilly stopped turning. 'Now the Allucians are gone, the doors of time are unguarded. Maybe that's why Caradien learnt to manipulate them.'

'It also means he could find his way here too,' said Gabi.

'I'm counting on it,' Lilly said. 'This way.'

She hurried down the corridor and the four of us, all her supernatural children in one way or another, followed her closely. Anthony was still carrying the body of Herod but managed to keep pace easily as the blood from his kill was coursing through his veins and pumping strength and life into his newly defined muscles. He was wired too, I could tell, and had Lilly not pulled him away he may well have gone on a hunting spree that would have left even more of Caradien's footmen dead.

Ahead, Lilly paused before a door on the left of the corridor. I wasn't sure if it was the hell door, or whether it was somewhere that meant something to her.

'Listen,' she said, turning to face us, eyes glowing luminous green in the dark, like a cat's eyes caught in the merest glimmer of light. 'Can you hear that?'

We stopped beside her and waited patiently to hear again what she already perceived, but there was nothing.

'The doors will call you,' Lilly warned. 'In here there will be something that wants you. You have to ignore it. This one is for me, but I have no intention of following the urge to open it. If you're smart, you'll do the same.'

Anthony drew closer to Lilly, 'How will you recognise the one you are going to open?'

'I'm not,' she said. 'Chez is.'

Her words struck terror in the deepest hollows of my soul. Somehow I'd always known that the door would call me again, but I had no intention of ever going back inside it.

'Once it's had you, it never lets go,' Gabi said showing an uncharacteristic display of insight.

Up until then he and Anja had remained quiet, but now they huddled together intimidated by the corridor. Anja gripped Gabi's hand firmly, and chewed on her fear pinched mouth.

'I'm not convinced this is such a good idea,' I said. 'How will Caradien know?'

There was another sound from behind us in the corridor. A slow creaking noise as another door slowly opened. I felt an instant pain in my heart.

'Chez, Anthony! Run!' Lilly said.

Behind us a sickening white light flooded into the corridor.

Caradien was there. He had the box, we could feel it, but it wasn't open fully.

I gripped Anthony's arm and propelled him forward, even as I knew Lilly, Gabi and Anja remained behind. We ran. I opened up my mind, searching for the door. I couldn't fail Lilly no matter what.

My blood began to warm up in my veins. The feeling was familiar, and I had no wish for it to intensify. Anthony stumbled, weakened by the pain emanating from his heart. I held him up and took his burden, throwing Herod's body roughly over my shoulder. Then I pulled Anthony faster and farther away from the source of our impending destruction.

Behind me the amber stone in Lilly's sword lit up with a bright golden light. I heard a scream but couldn't recognise who it was. I glanced over my shoulder, and could see past the silhouetted figures of my friends, Caradien, dressed in his *Illuminati* armour, holding up the box, which was half open now and aimed in our direction. But even as he raised the heart, his fingers couldn't hold onto it. The amber light was doing something to him, it weakened him.

My hands were glowing. The skin that touched Herod lit up with amber light. Whatever was happening to Caradien was also affecting the King's body and the light that shone from it hurt my eyes.

Anthony stumbled again, then regained his footing. We were far enough away that that the heart could no longer hurt us and another glance backwards showed me that Lilly had Caradien on his knees, the box closed and pulled to his chest.

I felt the draw of the door suddenly. The burning pain caused by the heart, lessened with the squeeze of fear that clutched me as I drew nearer my goal.

'Here,' I gasped.

Then Anthony was supporting me as we stumbled forward towards the door.

'Open it,' I yelled.

There was another cry from down the corridor, but I ignored it, totally focused on the job I needed to perform.

Anthony reached forward, pulled open the door and as I stepped closer, Caradien suddenly came into view, right behind Anthony.

'What the hell?'

Caradien swung his sword as Anthony turned, catching him full across the forehead. Anthony crumpled unconscious at my feet, his head split open and I stumbled backwards almost falling through the hell door. I looked at Caradien and blinked. It took me a second to realise that somehow he had escaped Lilly, only to follow another portal to arrive closer to us. His knowledge of traversing the doors was astounding and probably more extensive than Lilly's.

Caradien towered over Anthony, the box clutched in his hands and I could hear Lilly, Anja and Gabi yelling as they ran down the corridor towards us.

'Give me the body of the King,' Caradien said. 'Or I'll open the box and all of you will die here and now.'

'You open that box and, if it's the last thing I do, this body is going inside this room,' I said.

I had my back to the open door and Caradien glanced over my shoulder, then stepped back with an involuntary display of disgust. I chanced a look myself. The room was just as I had remembered it, full of moving, dismembered-yet-connected body parts, which made the whole into a complete and living organism. Washed with blood, pus, semen and other unidentifiable fluids, it waited patiently to torture my soul. I knew that if I entered it once more, I'd never be able to escape a second time. But what would happen if someone like Caradien entered?

Lilly and the others arrived, stopping a few feet away as they eyed Caradien cautiously. He held the box before him like a shield.

'Why?' asked Lilly. 'You've gone to all these lengths in order to destroy us. What did we ever do to you?'

Caradien's face filled with open rage.

'You!' he cried, 'Avenging angel. That's what my mother called you.'

'What are you talking about?' Lilly said.

'Then she gave me my father's heart, in a box.'

'Your father's … ?' I said and suddenly the puzzle was coming together. 'No! Don't you realise Lilly saved you?'

'What's going on? I don't understand what's happening here?' said Lilly.

'Konstantin is Salome's child,' I said. 'His father is John the Baptist. Isn't that right?'

'Yes,' he spat. 'You came along, helped her give birth to me.'

Anthony groaned at my feet, then pulled himself up to a sitting position against the door frame. The wound on his head was rapidly healing and was now little more than a thin red scar.

'She *saved* you,' Anthony said. 'Herod would have dashed your brains out.'

'You … were the child?' Lilly said. 'Then why? It still doesn't explain this. We never hurt you. I gave you a ward of protection.'

'You left me,' Caradien gasped. 'I was treated like a dog in that household. My mother was too scared to stand up to my grandmother, Herodias, after she killed Herod. But I watched the old witch and I learnt her trade. All the time she made me do her donkey work I was watching how she blended her potions. I even saw how she preserved Herod's body to use at some later date for her black arts.'

'All of this has nothing to do with us. We didn't hurt you,' Gabi pointed out, but by then I knew it was all pointless. Caradien was completely insane. He had suffered his own hell, just as I had suffered mine and even though Lilly had saved me, and had physically saved Caradien, I doubted that his sanity was salvageable.

'I'm sorry,' Lilly said. 'I never thought to check back on the child. I thought, once Herod was dead, that your mother and grandmother would take care of you. I'm not a mother, Konstantin. I know nothing of motherhood, you must realise, some small part of your brain must understand that your suffering had nothing to do with us?'

'My grandmother taught me well when she realised I was gifted,' Caradien said. 'I was to become her instrument of revenge. I was to wipe out all of Herod's blood line and so she gave me a piece of amber, by which I could recognise those who carried his blood.'

'She taught you how to travel through time too,' I observed.

'Yes. Time travel is as old as time. While I was taking over the Templar order in Rome, gaining the ear of the Pope and the King, my mother stole the heart away from me. I came back to find her, and the heart gone.'

'The story you told me was a lie then,' Anja said. 'Just like everything else you've ever said, Konstantin. I was a pawn in your game of revenge. You told me vampires were evil, soulless things, but I know now that's not true.'

Konstantin turned his cold blue eyes towards Anja, 'You are a treacherous whore Anja, just like my mother was. She stole what was mine,' he turned to look at Lilly. 'Until I saw you in Rome, I never knew what had happened to the amber stone my grandmother ensorcelled. My father was a *saint*; he died so that all of Herod's spawn could be destroyed.'

'I'm curious,' I said. 'You say you lost the heart? Your mother took it?'

'She wanted me to die, not to fulfil my grandmother's ambitions. She was a fool. That was when my grandmother weaved her final magic. She used Herod's body to offset the balance between life and death. I'm as immortal as you are. Only I don't have to drink the blood of innocents to survive.'

'No, you just have your people kill them for you instead,' Anja sneered. 'You sicken me. I can't have any sympathy for you. In fact I wish Lilly had let Herod bash your crazy brains into the dirt. You bastard.'

Caradien stiffened. 'Give me the body,' he said to me again. 'And I'll let you all live this day.'

'Oh I doubt that,' said Lilly. 'This has been your ambition all along hasn't it? To destroy us? There's just one thing I don't understand though … why you're so affected by the amber if indeed your grandmother bespelled it in the first place.'

Caradien didn't answer, but he backed away as Lilly held the pommel up before her face. She looked through the gem at Caradien.

'That's interesting,' she said.

I opened my mind and searched for hers, looking with her eyes through the amber and what I saw made me gasp. Caradien's aura was black. It rippled with the threads of evil intent, yellow and red worms that weaved in and out of his body like swimming vipers. Each represented a soul he had destroyed and they were eating him, digesting what remained of his sanity.

'Only a pure heart can wield the stone,' said Anthony. 'He can't touch it now, it would destroy him.'

'Your mother gave the stone to someone in the order,' Lilly said. 'It must have been a hard decision to betray her own son but she knew you were wrong.'

Caradien looked from one to other of us and smiled a thin smile. He opened the box.

The beating heart of his father, John the Baptist, still alive and pumping blood from some supernatural source, swelled and screamed as its curse poured out over us. Burning pain erupted in my veins and I almost dropped the body, but this time, I found Anthony supporting me and we held it aloft, ready to throw it to the waiting tongues, arms and limbs of the hell dimension.

'Stop!' Caradien yelled. 'Put the body down.'

He closed the box once more and this time I knew what we had to do. We couldn't stay here forever waiting for one or the other to give in.

Be ready! I thought to Lilly and she nodded, listening to my unspoken plan.

'There's only one way we can do this,' I said. 'Konstantin, you put the box down and I'll give you the body.'

'Do you think me stupid?' he said.

'Then what do you propose?' said Lilly, 'Only Chez isn't going to let go until you do.'

'Leave,' I said. 'Lilly, Anja, Gabi, Anthony. Get out of here.

This is down to me now.'

'No,' Gabi said. 'We can't leave you.'

'You have to,' I said. 'Otherwise Konstantin here is going to think we'll all rush him as soon as the box goes down. Am I right?'

Konstantin's eyes darted from one to the other of us and rested on Lilly. 'They can all go – but not her. She stays. But one of you takes her sword away also.'

Lilly nodded, reluctantly holding out her sword to Anthony. 'I want you all to leave. Anthony, you know where to lead them?'

'Yes,' Anthony said taking the sword.

'Lilly?' Gabi said. 'I can't lose you again.'

'Get the hell out of here.'

Gabi threw his arms around her

I watched Anja, Gabi and Anthony go down the corridor as Anthony read the time zones on the doors. When they finally passed through one, I looked from Lilly to Caradien and waited for the final battle to begin.

'It ends here,' Lilly said. 'We do a straight swap and I don't want to see your sorry ass anywhere near me or my family again.'

Caradien nodded, 'The body?'

'The box?' I said.

Caradien bent and placed the box at his feet but kept a wary eye on Lilly.

'Give him what he deserves Chez,' Lilly said.

I lifted Herod's body above my head, then turned and threw it as hard as I could into the hell room.

'No!' Caradien screamed. 'What have you done?'

He bent down, grabbed the box and began to open it. Lilly dived at him but then crumpled as the full force of the heart fell upon us. Caradien lifted it out of the box, dropping the minor protection it afforded onto the floor, then he ran past me towards the door. Halting at the threshold.

I forced myself to turn, even though my whole body was on fire, my finger tips were actually alight with tiny flames. I knew

I was dying but I had to see what was happening to Herod's body.

Caradien screamed silently as he stared inside the portal. The King's body was being consumed. The greedy mouth of a serial killer chewed on Herod's face, as the vagina of a whore swallowed his fingers, squirming around them like a mouth sucking candy. A bodiless hand climbed inside the empty chest and began to pick at the corpse from the inside. At the same time, intestines wrapped around the throat of the King, tightening until they cut their way through his neck, severing the head from the body.

'No!' Caradien gasped, dropping the heart. It rolled into the room as though drawn to the monstrosities there.

The second the heart crossed over into the room, the pain and pressure on Lilly and I was released.

Although we could see it in the room, it was in another dimension and its hold on us was no more. I glanced down at my chest as I felt my heart smouldering within. It would take a fresh kill to repair the damage but at least I was still alive.

Lilly lay unconscious but breathing. I turned towards her, crawling across the floor as my strength slowly returned, and that was when Caradien made his move.

'You've destroyed me,' he said. 'The body has been ripped apart in there! You did that!'

Caradien raised his sword once more, lifting it high above his head. I cowered on the floor, a vain thought that I should protect Lilly from the blow crossed my mind. And then … something hit Caradien. Something cleaved right through his skull. His head split open like an overripe melon. Blood and brains poured down his forehead and over his nose. His body pitched backwards, stumbling and falling through the doorway and into the room to join the body of Herod. 'One good swording through the brain deserves another,' Anthony said coldly holding aloft Lilly's sword.

I looked into the room and saw Caradien being held, devoured and absorbed as the vine-like intestines crawled across the space, gripping his arms and legs, stretching him out and pulling him down. It was the most hideous sight I had ever seen.

'Here,' Anthony said, throwing a bag of blood into my hands. 'Thought you might need this.'

I glanced once more through the door. 'Hard to eat with that in full sight.'

Then Anthony did what neither Lilly and I had the strength to do, he reached out and closed the door, bolted it and set a ward over the entrance so that it would never again attract me or anyone else into its blood-black realms.

Epilogue
Closing the Doors

Present Day

Anthony brought us sufficient blood to help the healing process and soon Lilly and I had recovered enough to stand and return with him to the Templar safe house.

The mercenaries had been beaten back and now that Caradien had disappeared they had no one left to co-ordinate a sustained attack. So, when we returned, the house was under repair and the Templars were rebuilding their security.

'We'll have to move of course,' said Father Declan. 'Now that two of our important safe houses have been compromised.'

'Caradien is dead,' I said.

'It doesn't matter. There were several leaders in the *Illuminati*,' Declan pointed out. 'One of them will step up to take his place, but it will take them much longer to get organised now that Caradien is gone.'

'Are they really that dangerous?' asked Lilly.

Declan nodded, 'Their forces are spread farther and wider than ours. '

Lilly stood and took my hand, 'I have work to do. Will you come with me?'

'Of course.'

We returned one final time to the corridor of doors. Lilly set a ward over the corridor.

'It's power will stretch the length and breadth, reaching into all the hidden corners. This is going to take some time,' she said. 'After all, there are a lot of doors here. Even so, they aren't infinite.'

'Will you still be able to travel through time? That is, if you wanted to.' I asked.

'Yes. The portals are somewhat different as they require the traveller to be in control of them. These on the other hand, are open to anyone with even minor skill. Even so, the wards are mine and so I can always pass through them if I need to. It will make using the portals far more difficult for anyone else though and that's the intention. We can't risk the *Illuminati* having the power to travel through time. Caradien may have shared his knowledge with others, but now at least it won't be so easy for them to use it.'

I took her hand and we walked the corridor as she worked her magic. As she said, it took some time, but that at least was something we had plenty of. We held a responsibility to all carriers of the vampire gene and I was happy to spend an eternity if necessary in order to ensure the safety of our race.

A small blue box with POLICE written on it lay on our bed at Rhuddlan Castle.

'Ha!' Lilly laughed. 'What's this then?'

Gabi poked his head round the door. He looked happy and well. It was wonderful to see him and I found myself embracing him for the first time like a long lost brother.

'It's a toy. A time machine from a television series,' he said, then reached out and hugged Lilly. 'I thought you might want to try a new way of travelling.'

They laughed and held each other tightly. My heart thudded in my chest until Anja came into the room.

'Good to see you back,' she smiled.

I shoved aside the horrors we had left behind. I didn't know what the future held for us, but the heart was gone and so was the threat of the hell room. We were a beautiful, if monstrous, family, and we had survived the worst threat we were ever likely to encounter.

I took Lilly's hand and pulled her into my arms as Gabi left the room, closing the door behind him.

About the Author

Award winning author Sam Stone began her professional writing career in 2007 when her first novel won the Silver Award for Best Novel with *ForeWord Magazine* Book of the Year Awards. Since then she has gone on to write several novels, three novellas and many short stories. She was the first woman in 31 years to win the British Fantasy Society Award for Best Novel. She also won the award for Best Short Fiction in the same year (2011).

Stone loves all genus fiction and enjoys mixing horror (her first passion) with a variety of different genres including science fiction, fantasy and Steampunk.

Her works can be found in paperback, audio and e-book.

www.sam-stone.com

Praise for Sam Stone

'A deceptively readable date with darkness – watch your step! This book is lit for the much more discerning chick (and cock) who likes to walk in the shadows. Relax with it, but be prepared for sudden jewels and little masterpieces and the rug to be pulled from under your feet.' Tanith Lee on *Killing Kiss*

'Stone has such fun reinventing the material and running it through a horror-come-steampunk grinder that it works and marvellously well ... The obvious progenitor in this field is *Pride and Prejudice and Zombies* but Stone's work is far more engaging and less forced than that one-joke outing.' Peter Tennant on *Zombies at Tiffany's*

'Sam Stone without doubt is a mistress of the grisly and the glutinous. I believe that we can look forward to seeing Sam Stone develop into a major influence in the realm of blood and shadows and things that wake you up, wide-eyed, in the middle of the night.' Graham Masterton

Zombies at Tiffany's reminds me a lot of Alan Moore's *League of Extraordinary Gentlemen* or the work of H G Wells ... this is a brilliantly authored piece of steampunk literature, and then some.' Jim Reader, *Exquisite Terror*

More Titles by Sam Stone

<u>THE VAMPIRE GENE SERIES</u>
Horror, thriller, time-travel series.
1: KILLING KISS
2: FUTILE FLAME
3: DEMON DANCE
4: HATEFUL HEART
5: SILENT SAND
6: JADED JEWEL

<u>KAT LIGHTFOOT MYSTERIES</u>
Steampunk, horror, adventure series
1: ZOMBIES AT TIFFANY'S
2: KAT ON A HOT TIN AIRSHIP
3: WHAT'S DEAD PUSSYKAT
4: KAT OF GREEN TENTACLES

<u>JINX CHRONICLES</u>
Hi–tech science fiction fantasy series
1: JINX TOWN
2: JINX MAGIC (Forthcoming)
3: JINX BOUND (Forthcoming)

THE DARKNESS WITHIN
Science Fiction Horror Short Novel

ZOMBIES IN NEW YORK AND OTHER BLOODY JOTTINGS
Thirteen stories of horror and passion, and six mythological and
erotic poems from the pen of the new Queen of Vampire fiction.